THE BOOK OF LAMPS AND BANNERS

Books by Elizabeth Hand

CASS NEARY NOVELS

Generation Loss

Available Dark

Hard Light

The Book of Lamps and Banners

Curious Toys

Wylding Hall

Chip Crockett's Christmas Carol

Errantry: Strange Stories

Radiant Days

Illyria

Saffron and Brimstone: Strange Stories

Mortal Love

Bibliomancy: Four Novellas

Black Light

Last Summer at Mars Hill and Other Stories

Glimmering

Waking the Moon

Icarus Descending

Aestival Tide

Winterlong

THE BOOK OF LAMPS AND BANNERS

A NOVEL

ELIZABETH HAND

MULHOLLAND BOOKS

Little, Brown and Company

New York Boston London

Mulholland Books / Little, Brown and Company
Hachette Book Group
1290 Avenue of the Americas, New York, NY 10104
mulhollandbooks.com

First Edition: September 2020

Mulholland Books is an imprint of Little, Brown and Company, a division of Hachette Book Group, Inc. The Mulholland Books name and logo are trademarks of Hachette Book Group, Inc.

The publisher is not responsible for websites (or their content) that are not owned by the publisher.

The Hachette Speakers Bureau provides a wide range of authors for speaking events. To find out more, go to hachettespeakersbureau.com or call (866) 376-6591.

Camera Lucida: Reflections on Photography by Roland Barthes, translation by Richard Howard, translation copyright ©1981 by Farrar, Straus and Giroux, Inc. Used by permission.

ISBN 978-0-316-48593-7
LCCN 2020934680

10 9 8 7 6 5 4 3 2 1

LSC-C

Book designed by Marie Mundaca

Printed in the United States of America

To Henry Wessells, bibliophile and gentleman,
With love and thanks for introducing
me to an advanced philosophical artifact

For Death must be somewhere in a society... perhaps in this image which produces Death while trying to preserve life... *Life/Death:* the paradigm is reduced to a simple click, the one separating the initial pose from the final print.

—Roland Barthes, *Camera Lucida*

PART ONE

LONDON

CHAPTER 1

Much of the Tube was still shut down. Another car had plowed through a Go Happy London! tour group the day before, this time near Tower Bridge. I'd taken the night train from Penzance, nodding off between shots of Jack Daniel's before trying to resurrect my amphetamine jag with one of the Vyvanse I'd stolen a few days earlier. I overheard news of the attack from two train staff who stood beside the door as we pulled into Paddington.

"They'll be coming after us next." One of the uniformed women shook her head, her face pale from exhaustion.

Her colleague nodded. "That's what I been telling my kids. Get out while you can."

Inside the station, I pushed my way through crowds of people who stared hypnotized at their mobiles, or gazed in dismay at the images flashing across TV news feeds. More EU trauma, domestic terrorists here and in the U.S., images of rural food shortages and disintegrating governments on both sides of the Atlantic. The few people who took notice of me veered away.

I didn't blame them. I was gaunt and red-eyed from sleeplessness, wearing a battered black leather jacket and even more battered steel-tipped Tony Lamas, with a barely healed scar on one cheek and another scar, star shaped, beside my eye. Forty years ago, you might have thought I was a rock star after a bad night. Now I looked like what I was: an aging punk jonesing for a drink and a handful of black beauties.

Outside the station, the people around me didn't look much better. Shuffling hordes of black-clad commuters; a displaced army of homeless people dressed in black plastic trash bags that served as makeshift rain gear. Once, I might have seen the bleak light leaking from their eyes and photographed it. Now, the thought of my camera made me clutch the satchel that no longer held it.

Despair overwhelmed me like a fever. My old Konica, a seventeenth-birthday gift from my father, was gone, along with most of the stash of Tri-X film I'd carried like a talisman for years. I'd ditched camera and film impulsively the night before, back in rural Cornwall. Now in the broken-glass light of a London morning, the enormity of what I'd done made me sick.

I hurried down the street and into Paddington Underground, grabbed a free copy of the *Metro* from a guy bundled up like a refugee from the Shackleton voyage. His breath misted the air as he bellowed, "Terror suspect still at large! Secret neo-Nazi rally! New China virus named." Just in case I couldn't read the headlines on the placard beside him.

I scanned the paper as I waited for the train. The virus was long-running news by now, source of a constant simmering dread slow to abate. There was still only speculation about whoever had rammed the van into the crowd. The main articles were about a white supremacist gathering in East London and the even more dire situation back in the U.S., where two shooters wearing MAGA caps had burst into a sanctuary-city meeting in Portland, Maine, and killed two city council members along with representatives of the refugee community.

I barely skimmed the piece. I'm like one of those artificial eco-systems that creates its own bad weather: I don't need to read about the rest of the world's.

On page 5, I finally found the headline I was looking for: CROUCH END TRIPLE MURDERER STILL ON THE LOOSE. The killings were thought to be drug and perhaps gang related. No mention of me or any other suspects, so I made my way to King's Cross.

I wandered through the construction zone surrounding the station, until I found a side street where nondescript row houses had been converted into cheap tourist hotels with names like Hail Britannia and Windsor Arms. I settled on the Royal Garden, which was neither but cost only sixty-five quid a night.

I paid cash and went upstairs. The room was small and dank and, despite the NO SMOKING sign propped on the rickety side table, reeked of cigarettes and roach spray. I was so beat, I wouldn't have cared if I'd caught a roach puffing away on a Marlboro. I dropped my bag, pulled off my cowboy boots and tossed them into a corner, lifted my head, and saw my face reflected in a mottled mirror above the nightstand.

Along with my camera, my straw-blond hair was gone—I'd hacked it off, then dyed it black. I was a person of interest in several countries, but the passports I carried—my own and one nicked from a Swedish junkie named Dagney, who bore a passing resemblance to me—showed a six-foot blonde.

At the moment, I needed to distance myself from both of those women. I couldn't do anything about my height, but the rest could be dealt with, given enough makeup and a decent hairstylist. I combed my fingers through my ragged hair and shrugged out of my leather jacket.

For a few minutes I sat, trying to ignore the black sparks that spun across my vision, like specks on damaged film stock. They'd started after I first arrived in London a week before. I finally popped two Xanax from the stash of stolen pharmaceuticals in my bag, and collapsed into bed.

I woke to the sound of sirens and the brass-knuckled thump of bass from a car blasting grime in the street below. Ashen light filtered through the window. I clutched the coverlet around me as I sat up, still groggy from the Xanax. The digital clock beside the bed read 1:32 p.m. I had to keep moving. I took a shower, changed into a moth-eaten black cashmere sweater and black jeans, unpacked my bag, and took stock of its contents on the rumpled bed.

A dozen pill bottles stolen from the medicine cabinet of a small-time gangster in Crouch End, one of the three dead mentioned in the *Metro.* A couple of striped boatneck shirts. Socks and under-wear, another worn cashmere sweater, some T-shirts, all black. Two passports, my own and Dagney Ahlstrand's. A UK mobile phone that wasn't mine. Finally, a wallet containing my New York driver's license, a thousand euros, and the black-and-white photo I'd taken of the teenage Quinn O'Boyle back when "Walk on the Wild Side" first burned up the airwaves.

Even now, decades later, that photo made me shiver. Quinn had been the one constant in my life since we were lovers back in high school. He'd been my first muse, the boy whose face I still saw when I closed my eyes, the face I imagined when I stared through a camera's lens. We'd lost touch after he went to prison in the late 1970s.

For years, I thought Quinn was dead. We had reconnected just months ago, after I tracked him down in Reykjavík. Seeing him again had broken some kind of psychic ice dam—thirty-plus years' worth of emotions flooded me, everything I'd successfully frozen with alcohol and drugs.

And now Quinn was gone again. Three days earlier, he'd left the Canary Wharf flat where we'd briefly sought refuge, before my ill-fated excursion to Cornwall. Since then I'd had no message from him, no email, no phone call. Nothing but a two-word text message Quinn sent to someone else, after I'd last seen him:

rotherhithe darwin

Rotherhithe was in East London. Quinn had told me he knew a guy there who was supposed to help us get out of the country without running afoul of the authorities. But I'd never been to Rotherhithe, and I had no clue as to what "darwin" might mean.

I removed the old photo and stared at it, drew it to my face and inhaled, as though his scent might be imprinted there, some molecular code I could break that would help me find him. I smelled nothing but the hotel's cheap carnation soap and the chemical tang of my own fear.

I slid the photo back into my wallet, finished dressing, and stood. I kept five hundred euros in my wallet. The rest I sealed in a ziplock bag that I shoved into the bottom of my right boot, along with my U.S. passport. I zipped up my leather jacket and headed downstairs.

Outside, the cold wind froze my damp hair into stiff spikes. As the Xanax I'd taken wore off, paranoia and anxiety filtered back into my nervous system. I walked fast, boot heels echoing along the sidewalk, turned onto a crowded street. My hand moved reflexively toward my chest, reaching for the camera that was no longer there. I fought waves of vertigo by focusing on the only other thing that had ever made me feel alive—my obsessive love for Quinn, an emotion as corrosive as battery acid.

At the corner, people swathed in overcoats and scarves waited for the light to change, mobiles glowing in their hands. I didn't realize I was talking to myself until a woman stared at me, wide-eyed, then edged away. I cursed under my breath, elbowed my way to the curb to join the flow of commuters headed toward King's Cross, and finally halted in front of a hair salon.

Pink LED lights blazed from behind a wall of glass. Inside, banks of mirrors created an infinity of blondes in chrome chairs, all waiting to be young again. I felt a twinge of envy that these women could let themselves believe in such a futile ritual, if only for an hour.

A skinny white guy with long platinum hair glanced at the window. His eyes flashed disgust as he clocked me, then turned back to his customer. I shoved my hand into my pocket, touching my wallet, hefted my bag, and walked in.

Vintage Daft Punk blasted from the sound system. A young woman at the reception desk looked up from her mobile, displaying a Medusa's nest of snakes tattooed on her neck.

I said, "I'd like to get a trim."

Medusa's gaze flickered from me to the guy with the platinum hair. Almost imperceptibly he shook his head. The woman pursed lips glossy as pomegranate syrup and shrugged. "I'm sorry, do you have an appointment? We're fully booked."

I cocked my head toward the front window. "Sign says walk-ins welcome. And that looks like an empty chair over there."

"I know, but we're booked. Fully booked."

As my foot tapped at the faux-marble floor, a wad of brown hair stuck to the steel tip of my cowboy boot. I bent to pluck the mouse-colored clump and held it up, peering at it intently as I raised my voice.

"Oh my god, is that what I think it is?"

Several heads swiveled to stare as I extended the hand with the offending hair, as though holding a dead rodent. A redheaded woman craned her neck, horrified.

"Todd?" The receptionist called imploringly to the platinum blond whose mouth had become a perfect O of dismay. Before he could say a word, a woman stylist darted toward me.

"I'll take care of this." She touched my hand with one silvery fingernail, gesturing toward the back of the salon. "I'm Troya. Did you have something in mind?"

Half an hour later my ragged hair was a more polished version of the same, Chrissie Hynde circa 1981.

"This really makes your eyes pop," Troya said as we regarded my reflection in the mirror.

I couldn't imagine who would think that was a good thing. Still, I tipped her fifty pounds, making sure that Medusa and Todd got an eyeful.

"Where's the ladies'?" I asked.

Troya pointed toward the back of the room. As I headed there, I passed a counter crowded with hair products and noted a Mulberry bag gaping open to display its contents. Wallet, cosmetics bag, hairbrush, an iPad mini. In the restroom I splashed some water on my face and swallowed another Vyvanse. I only had a few left, medicinal speed similar to Ritalin. Not much kick but better than nothing. On my way back out, I nicked the cosmetics case from the Mulberry handbag, dropped it into my satchel, and headed onto the street.

A few doors down was a high-end boutique where I dropped a

wad on a black cashmere hoodie and slouchy black leather bag soft as a baby's instep. Next: Tesco, where I bought a bottle of Jack Daniel's.

Finally I returned to my hotel room, hurrying through streets slick with rain. I peeled off my worn sweater and replaced it with the one I'd just bought. I cracked the bottle of whiskey, did a pop, and checked out the cosmetics bag.

It was a good score—Charlotte Tilbury mascara and eyeliner, a shade of frosted lipstick called Poison Pearl, some Touche Éclat concealer, an enameled compact with a mirror and a reservoir for loose face powder. Stuff that would have cost a hundred quid if I'd bought it in Selfridges.

I don't bother with much makeup—who's going to believe I'm on the south side of forty, or even fifty? Still, I used the concealer on the star-shaped scar beside my eye, a reminder of a bad time I'd had three months earlier. Wincing, I took on the barely healed gash below it, sustained during my more recent, near-fatal trip to the Icelandic wilderness. When I finished touching up the scars, I made use of the eyeliner and mascara and Poison Pearl. I surveyed myself in the mirror.

I've spent the last thirty years looking like my own ghost. There was nothing to be done about my gaunt face and the dead, ice-gray gaze that people would cross the street to avoid. Still, if I was a living ghost, so were most of the people I saw walking the Lower East Side, filing in and out of the boutiques and high-end bars that had replaced CBGB and Brownies. If they weren't lining up outside burnt-out tenements for a hit, it was because they no longer needed to. Their suppliers had medical degrees. Mine couldn't afford to finish Bergen Community College.

But it's impressive what you can do with a good haircut and concealer that costs as much as a decent bottle of cabernet. I got a towel and did what I could to clean my boots. Then I carefully transferred everything from my worn satchel to the leather bag I'd just bought, including the now-empty satchel. Last of all I knocked back another mouthful of whiskey, and put the bottle of Jack Daniel's where I could reach it easily in the bag. I scanned the room to see if there was anything worth stealing.

Nope. So I left.

It was still cold out, but the rain had stopped. Between the looming construction cranes and half-built skyscrapers, fast-moving clouds streaked a mother-of-pearl sky. I headed for the Regent's Canal and walked along the towpath, dodging bicyclists and dog walkers, until I found myself momentarily alone in the dark passage beneath a stone arch.

I dug in my bag for the mobile phone I'd taken from a dead woman. It had seemed like a good idea at the time. Now the mobile was a liability. I glanced around, tossed it into the middle of the canal, and hurried on.

I left the towpath for the street. Within minutes I was lost. After wandering around for nearly an hour, I found myself at Russell Square, an area filled with cops and tourists headed to the British Museum. Lines of schoolchildren in matching uniforms, a cluster of well-dressed matrons who followed an Asian woman bearing a red umbrella like a standard. I made a wide detour around a couple of cops, stopping to buy a pair of knockoff Ray-Bans from a street vendor. I put them on, found an alcove where I sneaked a mouthful of Jack Daniel's, and cut over to a main drag where the street sign read SHAFTESBURY AVENUE.

Booze and cheap shades and pharmaceutical speed made the late-afternoon glow like burnished steel. Without the weight of my camera, my new bag felt preternaturally light, almost empty. I comforted myself by thinking that on the Wall of Death it's best to travel light.

CHAPTER 2

I walked until I reached a familiar marker—Charing Cross Road. I'd never been there before, but for decades I'd worked at the Strand Bookstore in Greenwich Village. After some early run-ins with customers, I was delegated to the stockroom. I'd remained there until the previous November, using my five-finger discount until security got beefed up. But I had enough contact with buyers and sellers to know that Charing Cross was where famous bookstores lived.

Or used to. The bookshops here had taken a hit. I slowed my steps, searching in vain for Neuman's or Blackwell's among the bakeries and cheap restaurants and souvenir shops. Finally I ducked into Any Amount of Books, stashing my bag with the woman behind the counter. I was neither stupid nor fucked up enough to try lifting anything from these shelves. I perused the photography books, then asked to look at a first edition of Nan Goldin's *The Ballad of Sexual Dependency* kept safely behind glass. A day ago, the girl behind the counter might have kept a raptor's eye on me as I handled it.

Now, makeup and my chic gamine hair gave me a new kind of invisibility. The girl unlocked the case and didn't bat an eye as I glanced at *The Grapes of Wrath*—five thousand pounds, not a bad price—and a mint first of *The Maltese Falcon* in dust jacket. You could buy a house for what that one was worth.

I picked up the Goldin with care. I had my own copy back in New York, boosted from the Strand when it first came out. I was curious as to what it went for now. Five hundred pounds: not bad.

Mine was inscribed—me and Nan shared a drug dealer. I thanked the salesgirl and set the book back on its shelf. She closed and locked the case, giving me a cheerful goodbye as I walked back into the street.

Early dusk had fallen. The streets were packed with people hurrying to the Underground, pretheater dinners, and pubs. I continued along Charing Cross till I saw another name I recognized from my days at the Strand: Cecil Court, an alley that had been made into a pedestrian way, lined with small specialty bookshops whose brightly lettered placards swung in the wind.

I entered the alley, the sounds of traffic diminishing to a soft drone. In the sudden hush my footsteps echoed loudly on the pavement. A young man glanced up at me, nodded absently, and went back to browsing a table stacked with antique prints.

I pushed my sunglasses to the top of my head and peered into the window of a shop that had just closed for the night. Children's books were displayed like sweets, with dust jackets in marzipan colors. The shop next door sold theatrical ephemera, its window crammed with black-and-white publicity stills of forgotten stage stars arranged like headstones, alongside books on Shakespeare and the glory days of music hall. Music wafted from an upstairs window. Lotte Lenya, "September Song," Tom Waits and "Hold On." A playlist for the death of the publishing industry.

At the end of the alley, I turned and retraced my steps, halting in front of a shop with a green placard in front:

WATKINS: SPECIALISTS IN MYSTICISM, OCCULTISM, ORIENTAL RELIGION, THE PERENNIAL WISDOM, CONTEMPORARY SPIRITUALITY

Back at the Strand, we used to special-order titles from this place for Sarah Lawrence students and aging musicians who played the theremin. Until recently, my own interest in the occult began and ended with a former lover who'd broken up with me after a bad night with the I Ching. I'm not a believer, and the last few months had made me increasingly gun-shy of those who are. The real world is weird enough.

Still, I found myself staring at a sign that advertised a talk and signing that night by Lawrence Caccio. Caccio had been a minor player in the Warhol crowd during the Factory's Union Square days, a not-bad photographer who'd had the unenviable distinction of being the guy who opened the door to Valerie Solanas the afternoon she shot Andy. Caccio had just released a tarot deck based on vintage photos he'd taken at the Factory, with an introductory note by Julian Cope.

I peered into the shopwindow, spied a clock on the wall. Almost six. Caccio's event started at seven.

I wasn't hungry, and I didn't feel like fighting the crowds to get a drink at a pub. Wind gusted down the alley, colder than it had been. I hunched my shoulders and entered the shop.

It was warm inside, with the musty, once-familiar scent of a place that traded in both new and used books. New paper, old ink, and leather bindings, with underlying traces of the store's clientele — weed smoke, a powerful base note of sandalwood incense shot with sesame oil. An old white hippie sat behind the counter, his gray hair pulled into a scraggy ponytail. He glanced up from his bowl of noodles and pointed his chopsticks at me.

"Can I help you with something?"

I shook my head and he went back to his udon. The room was surprisingly well lit for an occult bookshop. Maybe not so surprising, when I considered the number of shoplifters the Strand used to bust in the act of making off with paperback copies of Aleister Crowley's autobiography. I glanced at the prominently displayed stacks of the Factory tarot — at forty quid a pop, more than I was willing to spend on a novelty item.

I wandered toward the back of the store. There was less Anton LaVey than I'd expected, and more Asatru. Reprints of Éliphas Lévi and Elias Ashmole; a monograph on Guido Bonatti, a thirteenth-century Italian sorcerer who conjured a sailing ship from wax.

Crouching, I pulled out a cheap paperback dictionary of the occult. I leafed through it, stopping at random upon the entry for "onychomancy"—divination by means of reflection of the sun's rays, a fair description of old-school print photography. I replaced the book and straightened, bumping into someone behind me.

A tall, stoop-shouldered guy stood there. Gangly, his longish dark hair threaded with gray, wide mouth parted to speak, and a hand raised in apology, so that I could clearly see the familiar scrawl of scar tissue that ran from the middle finger down his palm to his wrist. He was maybe fifteen years younger than I was, with a beaky nose, wire-rimmed Lennon glasses, an amused expression that swiftly darkened as he stared down at me.

"Cass?" His voice rose in disbelief. "Cass Neary?"

Behind the wire-rimmed glasses, his eyes were topaz. A miniature nova bloomed above the pupil of the left eye, emerald striated with black.

Gryffin Haselton. I wanted to run, yet my lifelong curse held me. I couldn't look away.

"You look different." He touched my hair warily, as though it might emit sparks. "Jesus, it *is* you."

I started to turn, but he already had hold of my arm. Anger crowded out his astonishment as he pushed me against the bookshelf. "What the hell are you doing here, Cass? The police still need to talk to you—you know that, right? Where the hell did you go?"

Back in November, I'd met him on the remote Maine island where I'd gone to interview his mother, the legendary photographer Aphrodite Kamestos. Things did not go well. Not for Aphrodite, at any rate. I was complicit in—some might say guilty of—her death.

But I did get some beautiful shots of her, postmortem.

Now I looked toward the door, tensing to make a run for it. Before I could move, Gryffin's pissed-off tone grew thoughtful.

"You look good," he said. "What happened? You knock off a liquor store?" At my stony glare, he added, "Right, I get it. Too close to home. Seriously, you clean up very nicely. Want to grab a bite?"

"What, so you can call the fucking cops? Just let me go, okay?"

I pushed past him, but he followed me out into Cecil Court.

"Cass, wait!"

He caught up with me at Charing Cross, took my arm again, and pulled me close. "Listen—the autopsy said she died of natural causes," he said in a low voice. "She fell, she hit her head, she's dead. She was my mother, but she was also a drunk who lied to me her entire life. It was stupid not to talk to the cops, Cass. Now they *are* interested in you. Before that it was strictly pro forma."

I took a deep breath, fighting to keep my voice even. "What the hell were you doing in that bookstore? Are you stalking me?"

"Stalking you? Are you out of your mind? I was ready to pay cash never to hear your name again! As for what I'm doing here—"

He held up a battered leather messenger bag. "I'm a bookdealer, remember? I'm selling what's left of my mother's library, and later I have a meeting about another sale. Larry Caccio's one of my customers; I saw he was doing an event and decided to drop by and surprise him. What's your excuse?"

"I used to work at the Strand, remember?" I wrenched away from him, and he laughed. "What's so goddamn funny?"

"It's just so bizarre, that's all—what are the odds of running into you here in London?" He hesitated. "You want to get something to eat?"

"I'm not hungry."

"I'll eat, you can drink. Everybody wins."

"You just said you'd pay never to hear my name mentioned again."

He shrugged. "I changed my mind. Maybe we were supposed to meet up. Like, destiny."

"That would be just the kind of destiny I'd get stuck with."

"Come on, it's my treat." He gazed at me appraisingly. "Your hair—you look a lot better. Younger."

I resisted the desire to punch him. Barely. Still, while I didn't trust Gryffin, I knew, rationally, that he would have no reason to track me down in London, or anywhere else.

15

But stranger things had happened to me recently, including the fact that I'd lost Quinn so soon after finding him again. The last time I'd seen him, he was heading out to make arrangements for us to leave the UK incognito, on a barge owned by a guy he knew. Given Quinn's past work as an occasional hit man with the Russian mob, I wondered if he'd ended up on a slow boat to the bottom of the Thames.

The thought made me feel slightly nauseated. Now that I'd had it, I knew it would be difficult to push it away. Gryffin would be a distraction, at least. Let him indulge his bad-girl fantasies by buying me a drink or five.

"Yeah, all right," I said at last. "But enough about my goddamn hair."

CHAPTER 3

We went to a place that Gryffin knew, a mid-nineteenth-century pub called the Three Balls, now a gastropub. Inside, the old drinking establishment looked as though it had spent six weeks at the Hazelden clinic. Everything was sunlit and stripped down, the woodwork bleached and the original bar counter enlivened with vases of cut flowers and polite reminders not to smoke and to drink responsibly. I'd have preferred a dive, but once we were seated, Gryffin handled the menu as though it were a copy of the Magna Carta.

"I hope they still have that pig's cheek with watermelon pickle—oh, yeah, here it is. What do you want?"

"Single malt. Something I can't get at home. A double."

"I mean to eat."

I glanced at the menu. "Mr. McGregor's Rabbit Pie sounds nice."

Gryffin removed his overcoat and draped it on the back of his chair. He wore a gray herringbone jacket over a blue oxford-cloth shirt, unbuttoned at the neck, jeans, and knocked-up sneakers. When I kept on my leather jacket, he looked me up and down and made a face.

"The Ramones are dead, you know."

"Not Marky. Or CJ."

"Who's CJ?"

"The emergency backup Ramone. You getting me that drink?"

Gryffin ordered my whiskey, along with an expensive bottle of pinot noir. I raised an eyebrow. "Your mother's library must have found a happy home in the Hamptons."

"Nope. The really valuable stuff, she left all that to the Portland Museum of Art. She left almost everything else to the Center for Creative Photography in Tucson. Ansel Adams must be spinning in his grave. She didn't leave me much besides the Maine house, which is a wreck, and a couple of books I sold to another dealer this afternoon."

"She screwed you."

He shrugged. "She didn't owe me anything. And she'd be the first to tell you that."

I savored my whiskey. Gryffin waited until the waiter filled his wineglass, then raised it to me. "Cheers."

"Bottoms up." I finished the single malt and helped myself to the pinot. "I still think it's weird, running into you like this."

"Hey, we were in one of the last indie bookstores on the planet. You used to work in the Strand—soon that'll be the only one left. We'll all be fighting over the only surviving copy of *Infinite Jest*. It'll be *Left Behind* for bibliophiles."

"Very funny." I took a sip of my pinot. "You have another meeting tonight?"

"I'm brokering a sale for a dealer I know in Hampstead." He finished his wine and refilled his glass. "I'm celebrating. When this sale goes through, I'm done. Early retirement, new house in Monterey..."

"Aren't you kinda young for that?"

"Not that young, trust me."

"You *look* young."

He grinned. "It's the haircut."

Our food arrived. Gryffin ordered a second bottle of wine, and we tucked in. The rabbit pie was good, though I was disappointed it didn't arrive on a Beatrix Potter plate.

"So, is Caccio really into all that occult stuff? Tarot cards and crystals?"

"Dunno. Maybe. But a lot of people are, especially now—that's how Watkins stays in business. And my customer is. Not Harold—he's the bookdealer—but his client. She collects incunabula and volumes dealing with ancient magic. Alchemy, astrology. The real deal. Vellum manuscripts, fifteenth-century texts."

He sipped his wine. The emerald starburst in his iris caught the light and glowed, like that phantom sunset flare known as *le rayon vert*. He leaned across the table, lowering his voice.

"Have you ever heard of a book called *Picatrix*?"

I shook my head. "What is it?"

"The most influential text on magic ever written. The most influential one known to exist, anyway. It dates to the tenth or eleventh century, but it was probably written much earlier, somewhere in the Middle East. The English translation of the title is *The Goal of the Wise,* but no one knew of an extant copy of an edition in the original Arabic until 1920. Sometime around 1256 it was translated into Spanish, and a century or two after that into Latin."

"What does it mean, *Picatrix*?"

"No one really knows. Could be a transcription error, or a translation error. Some scholars speculate the author was a man named al-Majriti. His first name can be roughly translated as 'to sting,' which is similar to the medieval Latin word *picare,* which means 'to prick.' There's a famous passage in *Picatrix* about treating a man for a scorpion sting, with a tincture made of frankincense and the use of various talismanic seals.

"The book is filled with stuff like that—whoever wrote it compiled his information from hundreds of other texts on magic, everything that was known in the ancient world. It's a cross between an encyclopedia and a user's manual for astrology, talismanic charms, spells, poisons, obscure methods of torture and healing, you name it. Some of its ideas were later incorporated into Gnosticism, and the scientific method, and alchemy, and it was one of the earliest and most notorious banned books—the Inquisition arrested Casanova for owning a copy."

Gryffin took a gulp of wine. His face had grown flushed, his strange topaz eyes glowing with excitement.

"And I mean," he went on, stabbing a piece of watermelon

pickle with his fork, "there are really good reasons for this being a banned book. In one section, you get this detailed description of how you lure a man into a temple, then strip him and imprison him in a gigantic pot full of sesame oil up to his neck. You feed him nothing but dried figs—no water—and wave incense around him for forty days. By then he 'becomes as flexible as a candle.'"

I grimaced. "Nice."

"It gets better. After forty days, you remove the head, hang it up, and wave around some more incense, and it talks to you. Gives you information on the stock market, political uprisings, the arrival of merchant ships. It also reminds you of when you need to offer a sacrifice in the temple and answers any questions you might have."

"It's the prototype for Siri."

Gryffin laughed. "*Picatrix* is full of stuff like that."

"So, what? You have a copy of this book?"

"No. Better."

The waiter came to clear our plates. Without asking me, Gryffin ordered two Armagnacs. After the drinks arrived, he moved his chair around the table to sit beside me. I warmed my glass in my hands, eyeing him warily. Gryffin's father had been a brilliant, deeply damaged photographer turned serial killer, named Denny Ahearn. I was starting to wonder if Gryffin was following him into the deep end.

"In book three of *Picatrix,* there's a single reference to something called *The Book of Lamps and Banners.* It's an even more ancient and arcane work, rumored to have been written by Aristotle for his student Alexander the Great. Aristotle supposedly illustrated it, and there were handwritten notes to Alexander as well, and references to other people Aristotle knew. Eudemus. Plato."

"You're kidding me."

Gryffin shook his head.

"So why haven't I ever heard of this? Why hasn't anyone ever heard of it? Because this sounds like Dan Brown on really good acid."

"Because no copy was known to exist."

He reached down for his leather messenger bag and pulled it onto his lap. One hand rested protectively on the bag's handle; the other grasped his snifter of Armagnac.

"Until now," he said, raising his glass to me.

CHAPTER 4

I waited for him to continue. But Gryffin made no move to open his battered leather bag. He just finished his Armagnac and set the empty glass on the table. When his mobile pinged, he glanced at it, then at me.

"My meeting with Harold Vertigan's in an hour. Feel like coming along?"

"Not really."

"C'mon. Harold likes meeting new people. What, you got something better going on?"

I thought for a moment. Gryffin didn't seem like he was going to rat me out to Interpol. And I didn't have anywhere to stay. A place in Hampstead was preferable to the rathole where I'd bunked the night before.

"Yeah, okay," I said.

Gryffin signaled for the check. I headed for the loo, staggering a bit. I made a stop at the bar and asked for a glass of tap water, drank it and asked for a second, and downed that, too. In the restroom, I checked myself in the mirror.

Gryffin was right. I did look younger, unless you made the mistake of catching my gaze, which was more than a little crazed. My buzz had calcified into something hard and sharp. I fished among the pill bottles in my bag until I found what remained of my Focalin, a slower-release dose of pharma amphetamine. I popped the capsule, touched up my lips with Poison Pearl, brushed a bit of dried mud from one steel boot tip, and met Gryffin by the door.

He seemed a little worse for wear, fumbling to pull on his overcoat and nearly dropping his mobile as we walked outside. A lightweight.

I shot him a dubious look. "You sure you want me to come?"

"Yeah. I do." He grinned blearily, shading his eyes against a shaft of westering light that speared the sidewalk where we stood. "I want a witness! It's no fun celebrating if you're alone."

His mobile pinged again. "That's our car," he said. A minute later a Prius pulled over. Gryffin reached to open the door for me.

"I'm not your grandmother," I said as I made room for him.

"Boy, you're a tough sell."

"So I've been told."

The Prius crept through traffic. Cyclists whizzed past us, and I stared longingly out at an Underground station.

"We could have walked there faster," I said.

"This gives us more time to catch up. What are you doing in London?"

I gazed out the window, my stomach knotting. "Just seeing an old friend."

"Who?"

"A guy I knew in high school. I used to photograph him, kind of obsessively."

"Was he in your book? The one that got all the hype?"

"*Dead Girls*? No. I wish he had been." Near a crowded corner, people laden with carrier bags from Sainsbury's and Lidl surged toward a double-decker bus. "All the photos I took of him, they just disappeared. So did he. We only reconnected a week ago."

I stopped. I sensed Gryffin waiting for me to go on, but I remained silent. After a moment, he asked, "What happened to the prints from that book? Do you still have the negs?"

"Somewhere. In my apartment, probably, or my dad's place in Westchester."

"You should have another show. I found a copy of *Dead Girls* online—the price keeps going up. It's good. You know that, right?"

I tore my gaze from the window and turned to him. "What about you? Do you come here a lot on business?"

"Not anymore. I used to, up until about ten years ago. Internet's killed the book business, including mine. I dealt in mostly twentieth-century stuff. A lot of genre fiction, science fiction and classic crime novels. I started buying when I was a kid—Philip K. Dick, Arkham House. You could still find those books cheap back then. Eventually I began selling at flea markets, sent out a few lists, and got off the street, opened a little shop in San Francisco. The first wave of dot-commers, they were big on collecting science fiction. You make fifty million dollars when you're still a kid, you want to spend it on toys. The market got crazy—it's still crazy at the top end—but by then people weren't going to used bookstores to buy books. I had to close my shop. I still sell stuff online, but it's not the same."

He gazed past me, through the crawl of cars and buses to a Topshop, its entrance crowded with teenage girls in high boots and short puffer jackets. "That used to be Joseph's. Waterstones is still around, and Foyles, but the indie shops are dead."

"What about back there in Cecil Court? Those shops seem to be doing okay."

"That's toward the high end. And they cater to the tourist trade."

"Your friend Harold—I take it that's not his thing?"

"Not really. I mean, he's happy to entertain whoever walks through the door. But he deals in antiquarian stuff, the real deal—last year he sold a Shakespeare Second Folio for half a million pounds."

I whistled, and he nodded. "I know. I get altitude sickness in his place sometimes. But Harold's a sweetheart. I help him out when he has clients interested in the kind of books I specialize in. Like, if you want H. P. Lovecraft's *The Outsider and Others*—the 1939 Arkham House edition that has the first complete version of 'At the Mountains of Madness,' with the Virgil Finlay jacket—I'm your guy."

"So how did you come by that?" I tapped his leather bag. "It doesn't seem to fall within your remit."

"Everything's within my remit if someone's paying for it. But I wasn't the one who found this."

His hand tightened on the bag's handle, and he went on, "A friend of mine who's a business journalist went to Baghdad a few years after 9/11. Back then he was working for the *Washington Post*, but he visited the Bay Area a lot for work. That was when I still had a shop. He was a customer, not a dealer, but I'd find him things he wanted. Simenon novels—there's always one of those you haven't read. Anyway, he was in San Francisco and dropped by the shop before he left. I think he was a little concerned he might not make it back."

"Did he?"

"Oh yeah. He wasn't a war correspondent—he was covering the buildup there. Hazeldean, that whole pack of jackals. It was after Hussein was killed, a little golden moment when it seemed like Iraq might rebound. He asked if there was anything he could bring back for me. He was joking, but I told him that there is—was—a very famous book bazaar in Baghdad. Al-Mutanabbi Street. I've never been, but I used to dream about it—all those volumes dating to the Ottoman Empire, rare Arabic books, hookahs and mint tea at the Shahbandar café . . . a pipe dream.

"So I told him to visit it on my behalf, and if he came across a first edition of *The Arabian Nights*, to bring it back for me." Gryffin paused. "That was a joke."

"Ha."

"Because an actual first of that doesn't even—well, never mind. But he did visit al-Mutanabbi Street, just wandering around, since he had no idea what to look for. He thought it'd be good for his article, a little background. In and out of shops, browsing the books on tarps on the sidewalk, soaking up local color, all that. It's where Iraq's intelligentsia used to gather, scholars and book collectors, university students. Tourists, once upon a time.

"Late in the afternoon, he came upon a table heaped with books in front of a tiny storefront. He said it was about the size of a closet. Books on shelves and stacked everywhere. Nothing behind glass. Old books—ancient books. The kind of place you spend your whole life thinking you might stumble on, but you never do. *I* never do. Only, he did."

He stared out the window, his expression distant. "He started looking through the books. Some titles were in French or Greek, but nearly all were Arabic. Which, of course, he couldn't read. But he found a book, about so big—"

He measured out a small rectangle. "It was in black leather, not in very good shape, dating maybe to the early 1800s. But when he opened it, he saw that what was bound inside was actually a much older book. Handwritten in Greek and Arabic, with beautiful little illustrations throughout, animals and plants, and what looked like star charts. My friend thought it might have been a travel diary, dating to the late Renaissance. So, a somewhat valuable book, though mostly a curiosity.

"The shop's owner was out that day, and his son was minding the shop. When my friend asked how much the book was, he said seventy-five thousand dinars—about sixty dollars. A lot more than my friend wanted to pay for a souvenir for me."

Gryffin laughed. "So they bargained, and he got the guy down to fifty dollars. Which was still a lot of money for a souvenir, but my friend figured he'd get it back in goodwill and used-book discounts. Which he did."

"When he gave it to you, did you know what it was?"

Gryffin shook his head. "I had no idea. But it was a very beautiful little book, and it was obviously older than my friend thought it was. I thanked him, gave him a really good deal on some very early Simenons, and that was it. I figured I'd do some research on ancient Greek and Arabic texts and see what I could find out. That's well beyond my field of expertise—was, anyway.

"But I knew a guy in the Arabic studies program at Berkeley. I scanned a few pages of the book into my laptop and asked him to look at them and translate them for me. I didn't tell him I actually owned the book, I said I'd found the pages online and, as a bookdealer, I was curious.

"We met at Starbucks. He looked at the pages, and—I'm not kidding you—his face went pale.

"'Where did you get these?' he asked. I said again that I'd found them online while I was researching something. 'Yes, but where online?'

"I had to fudge that—said I couldn't remember, I don't read Arabic and it was a site somewhere in the Middle East. I think he knew I was lying.

"He said, 'This is from a book that doesn't exist. If it *did* exist, it would be priceless, because it could change everything we know about ancient history. There is one reference to it in a volume by a Sufi scholar, a book titled *Ghayat al-Hakim*. But this book, if it isn't some sort of hoax, is called *The Book of Lamps and Banners*. Are you sure you don't remember where you found it online?'

"I had to beg off. I thanked him and said I had to get back to the shop to meet a customer. I've always felt bad about that—we fell out of touch, and then I heard he'd died. Some kind of freak accident."

"What about your friend the journalist, the guy who found it for you?"

"He's gone, too." Gryffin's expression darkened. "He died in a car accident not long after—someone rear-ended him on Rock Creek Parkway, he went into a tree. They said he must have been speeding, but he wasn't that guy—I've been in a car with him and he'd never go more than five miles above the limit. It used to drive me crazy."

"The guy who sold it to him—the son of the shop owner—he must've caught hell when the old man came back and found that book was gone."

Gryffin shrugged. "If he even knew what he had. Probably he didn't. In the 1800s, books were often re-bound in morocco or calf, and few of those are ever very valuable. But that shop's gone now. They're all gone. In 2007 a suicide bomber took the entire block out. Fundamentalists have destroyed every part of their culture—the archaeological sites, the museums, university libraries. Why should we have thought they'd leave used bookstores in peace? Al-Mutanabbi's coming back, slowly. But it will never be the same."

I stared at the battered messenger bag. "Maybe I should just head back to my hotel."

"Oh for god's sake. Don't be ridiculous." He gave a sharp laugh. "None of this is connected. Harold wouldn't touch this book if he thought there was anything unsavory about it. He's strictly aboveboard."

"I thought *you* were strictly aboveboard."

"I am! It's an antiquarian book, Cass, not the Ark of the Covenant."

"People thought that didn't exist, either."

"Don't be a spoilsport. We're almost in Hampstead."

CHAPTER 5

The car dropped us off at a busy intersection, along a steep incline that overlooked Hampstead Heath. Gryffin extricated his long legs from the cab and joined me on the sidewalk.

"So what about you?" he asked as we walked. "You still taking photos with that antique?"

"No. I'm thinking I might get a digital camera," I lied.

Gryffin appeared amused. "Really? Well, good for you. Hell must have frozen over, huh?" He pointed at the building behind us. "That used to be a pub. Jack Straws Castle. Now it's posh apartments and a gym. Every bit of real estate in London's a link on some rich guy's key chain."

"Is that where your friend has his shop?"

"No. He's in the Vale of Health. That way." He pointed across the road, to gnarled and towering trees more suited to a national forest than a leafy part of London. "We're early, so I thought we'd walk a bit, burn off some of that wine."

Without a backward glance at me, he loped across the street, dodging a bus as it roared downhill. I followed, catching up with him at an entrance to the Heath. I'm tall, but each of his steps equaled two of mine. He turned and squinted through the trees.

"Does your end buyer live here, too?" I asked, trying to catch my breath.

"Nope. She's in Brixton. Has a bunker with a climate-controlled room to house her collection of vintage video games."

"You've been there?"

He shook his head. "Harold has. He says it's like a museum for stuff like Super Mario and Donkey Kong. Ever hear of FlightRisk? That's her—Tindra Bergstrand. She's a software designer. Started out with games like FlightRisk, now she's branching into VR apps. Made a ton of money, maybe not crazy rich, but crazy, from what Harold says. Only instead of collecting Birkin bags, she collects occult esoterica. Harold says she's working on a new app that incorporates the weird stuff she's into."

"What kind of weird stuff?"

"I know nothing. I want to know nothing. So should you."

"Why would I even be interested in a crazy software designer who collects books that the Taliban wants to blow up?"

"It was probably al-Qaeda. Anyway, she's made a fortune."

"Which she's going to spend on your book. How convenient."

"I'm starting to remember what a pain in the ass you can be."

"That's because you're starting to sober up."

"That's exactly what I mean." He grasped my arm. "Look, if you can't pretend to be a boring normal person for an hour, you better go. I cannot afford to lose this sale." His voice rose as his hold on me tightened. "You owe me this, Cass."

"I don't owe you shit."

I glared at him, and he touched my shoulder. I almost laughed. This guy had a thing for me—that, or a deeply buried urge to sabotage his own career. I shrugged, but made no effort to move away from him. After a moment, his hand dropped to touch my chin.

"You have the strangest eyes," he said.

"Takes one to know one," I retorted.

Despite my annoyance, I felt a flicker of desire for him. Not for the first time, either. For whatever reason, Gryffin Haselton had exerted a weird pull on me ever since we'd met in Maine the previous November. He was the anti-Quinn—a geeky straight arrow, with his glasses and rare books and untied shoelaces. But his weird mismatched eyes fascinated me, and so did his paternal heritage.

We continued walking. Around us, the early winter dusk deepened, a gray curtain falling across a stage dotted with twisted black trees and ghostly figures. Couples, nannies hurrying their charges home for dinner, kids entranced by whatever played on their earbuds or mobile screens. More dogs than I'd ever seen in one place, darting away from their owners to be recalled by a shouted command.

Also, more American voices than I'd heard anywhere else in London. It reminded me of Kamensic Village, where Quinn and I had grown up, sixty miles north of New York City. The flash of desire I'd felt moments ago dissolved into yearning for the pressure of Quinn's mouth on mine; for the two of us in another world, before we broke it.

I started as Gryffin pointed. "Look," he said.

Below us stretched a vast sloping field where lights burned against the darkening horizon—the Shard, the Gherkin, a black hair stroke of the Thames—the grimy city transformed by a complex algorithm of clouds, pollution, contrails, and scattered stars. My hand reached for the camera that was no longer there, and I swore softly.

Gryffin glanced at me. "What is it?"

"Nothing. Are we almost there?"

"Close."

We skirted the field and followed a maze of trails through stands of oak and holly and thickets of gorse. Finally we hit a well-trodden path. I could track other people on the Heath by the fuzzy blue halos of their mobiles, the yip of dogs, and occasionally a child's voice. After a minute, Gryffin announced, "This is it."

A service road led into a parking area crammed with rusted caravans and panel trucks and carnival trailers. The light from an old-fashioned wrought-iron streetlamp made it resemble some bleak outer borough of Narnia. As we passed the streetlight, my gaze snagged on something on the ground.

I crouched to see what it was. A dead pigeon, but larger than a New York pigeon, its buff-colored feathers shaded to cream and ivory, rose and iridescent green. One wing was awry, pinions outspread like fingers. There was no other sign of an injury.

I prodded the wing with my finger. Maybe a rat had gotten it. Or poison. I started to straighten when I saw a glint beneath the streetlamp: like a syringe but with a wedge of red plastic at one end, like a dart.

"You coming?"

I turned to see Gryffin waiting impatiently. "Yeah. Sorry."

At the edge of the parking lot, I paused again. Black feathers appeared to have exploded on the broken concrete, as though someone had dropped a balloon full of black ink.

I frowned. "Huh. An owl must've gotten it."

"More likely rats," said Gryffin. "Don't touch it."

We left the parking lot. Immediately it was as if we'd been transported to a tiny English village: winding streets so narrow it would have been difficult for two cars to pass at once, row houses of yellow London brick nestled alongside stone cottages still adorned with Christmas fairy lights. Cars were parked in front of some residences, late-model Priuses and Vauxhall hybrids, a vintage poison-green Karmann Ghia. Range Rovers dwarfed front gardens the size of a tablecloth. A single modest apartment building might have been an effort at council housing. You could live here and never know you were in London.

"Nice, isn't it?" Gryffin stopped in front of a cobblestoned alley where another antique streetlamp glowed. "Harold's just down that way."

We walked along the passage, my boots clattering loudly on the cobblestones. I felt like I'd trespassed onto a movie set. Any second, studio security would appear to throw me out.

"Who lives here?" I asked.

"Very small people with pointy shoes and hats." Gryffin snorted. "Who do you think? Normal boring people."

I stopped to regard a stroller parked in front of an orange door. The stroller resembled something ILM might design for a near-future movie featuring Googleplex employees in distress. I bet the door's paint color was called something like Misty Kumquat.

"You mean normal boring rich people," I said.

"Artists live here, too. One woman just celebrated her ninety-eighth birthday — she's still painting."

"Yeah, and when she croaks, they'll roll dice on her canvases for her studio space."

"Remember what I said about pretending? Look, this is Harold's house."

CHAPTER 6

A white picket fence bordered a pocket garden that in spring would be an explosion of roses and other flowers, now reduced to tangles of thorn and blackened leaves. The house was three stories high, its uppermost floor truncated, as though a giant had put his hand on top of the building and very gently pushed down. Wizened ropes of clematis clung to the whitewashed brick. A sturdy old bicycle leaned beside the front door, no Kryptonite lock or reinforced chain on its wheels. The door was painted a faded sailor blue. On the wall beside it a small brass plate read BIB-LIOTECA DE BABEL.

Gryffin pushed open the gate—hardly necessary, I could have stepped over it with no effort. But I was trying to pretend, so I diligently followed him to the door, where he knocked. From inside I could hear Scott Joplin, "Stoptime Rag." A rush of footsteps down the stairs, and the door was flung open.

A tall, beaming man stood framed in a rectangle of yellow light: thin and angular, with shiny, side-parted brown hair, bird-bright black eyes, and a wide laughing mouth. He wore a seersucker suit, creamy yellow and white, a buttercup-yellow button-down shirt, and a fastidiously knotted bow tie patterned with what appeared to be golf balls but which on closer inspection turned out to be eyeballs. His long, bony feet were bare.

"Come in, come in!" He beckoned Gryffin inside, shook his hand heartily, then noticed me. "Oh, hello! Is this your lady friend?"

"Just a friend." Gryffin's cheeks pinked, and I felt an unreasonable prick of jealousy. "Monica's in Malibu for some kind of sea lion summit."

"Harold Vertigan." Harold grasped my hand. Despite a youthful, reedy voice and that glossy caramel flow of hair, he must have been close to my age. "And you are?"

"Cassandra Neary. Cass."

"Well, please, come in!"

He held the door for us, and I followed Gryffin into a small, elegant entry hall. Everything had the same warm glow as Harold's hair—polished hardwood floor; plaster walls painted a soft umber; elegant bentwood chairs. On the walls, silver-framed mirrors reflected light from gas fixtures that had been retrofitted to hold LED bulbs. A striped Swedish rug ran the length of the hall.

Harold gestured to a closet. "You can hang your things in there. Is it cold out? It looks cold."

Gryffin tugged the lapel of Harold's seersucker jacket. "That's because you're dressed for summer."

"I live in hope, I live in hope."

He waited as we stored our coats. I dropped my bag on the closet floor, but Gryffin kept tight hold of his. There was plenty of room in the closet—I've slept in smaller places—but he was obviously taking no chances, not even with a trusted colleague. And he definitely wasn't taking any chances with me.

As we stepped back into the hall, Harold clapped his hands.

"What can I get for you? Some tea? Coffee? A brandy?" His gaze fell upon the messenger bag, swiftly moved to Gryffin's face. "If that's what I think it is—what I hope it is—there's a bottle of something we can open later, to celebrate."

He spun and headed down the hall. Gryffin shot me a grin and took off after him. I walked more slowly, casing the place. A half-open door gave me a glimpse of a powder room. There was a small, well-turned-out kitchen, with copper-bottomed pots hanging from a ceiling rack, an AGA gas stove, white pottery bowls lined up on a pink granite countertop. A beautiful old copper coffee machine and a wine rack that probably held a small fortune in claret and Sauternes. In the hall, old prints of parrots, beautifully framed. A small console table held six neatly stacked volumes. I picked up the top one: Edward St. Aubyn's *Bad News*. The inscription inside read *For Harold, who only brings good news.*

"I'm not a collector." Harold sounded apologetic. He glanced at Gryffin, waiting for us at the end of the hallway. "Some dealers, they use their shop as a way to maintain their own collections. The only books I keep are the ones I truly love. Everything else?" He flexed his fingers as though releasing handfuls of dry leaves. "This house is just a way station. The books, I provide them haven until they find their final home. Come, I'll show you."

He guided me into a room, brightly lit with a leaf-green rug. Custom-built bookshelves covered the walls from floor to ceiling. Several freestanding bookcases stood near windows half hidden behind green-and-white toile curtains. Beside the door, a small wall panel showed LED readouts for humidity and air temperature. I saw no sign of a security system, which might make Harold Vertigan's the only shop in London without CCTV.

Harold walked to a Gustavian desk, like everything else a model of restrained elegance. He leaned over a laptop, checking something, then nodded. "Looks like we're all set. Are you sure I can't offer you a drink?"

Gryffin put his messenger bag onto a low table and sank onto the sofa in front of it. "Maybe that bottle of celebratory something you mentioned."

"Absolutely. Back in a flash."

Gryffin shut his eyes. Seconds later, he began to breathe heavily. He'd matched me drink for drink, but obviously didn't have the stamina for it.

While he napped, I examined Harold's wares. There was a handful of volumes for the casual buyer, but most of this stuff would have been kept under lock and key back in the rare-book room on the Strand's fourth floor. Nineteenth- and twentieth-century firsts—Conrad,

Beckett, Lessing, Pynchon, Plath. As for the twentieth century, David Foster Wallace's stock still ran high—an inscribed *Broom of the System* went for four thousand pounds—but you could get a mint JT LeRoy for only fifty quid.

I crossed to where the toile curtains hid a set of French doors. I pulled aside a fold of fabric, peeked out at a walled garden bedded down for winter, and let the curtain drop. Beside the doors, a glass-fronted case held some older volumes, each housed in a bespoke clamshell slipcase, with the volume's title embossed on the spine in gilt letters. I gingerly opened a clamshell to display the treasure within, Roger Bacon's *Opus Majus.* There were also pamphlets—octavos and quartos, all in Italian.

I turned to Gryffin, dozing on the sofa as though in a hammock, his long legs stretched in front of him, fingers linked behind his head. I held up one of the pamphlets.

"What's this? *Nuovo Luciadario de Secreti.*"

He blinked awake, squinting at the pamphlet. "*Secreti italiani*—the mass-market paperbacks of the early sixteenth century."

I replaced the pamphlet on the shelf. "He seems to have a lot of this stuff."

"Something for everyone. Harold's a matchmaker—you fall in love with an antiquarian volume, he does his best to find it for you. Makes sure its hair is combed and it's wearing the right shoes. No missing pages, no illustrated plates removed to be sold off separately. No cheap morocco binding, unless that's the very last resort. The British Library deals with him. Patti Smith deals with him—he found her a copy of Swinburne's *Atalanta in Calydon,* inscribed to Arthur Rimbaud."

"And you deal with him."

"Right."

From behind us came the soft slap of bare feet on the floor. Harold appeared, bearing a bottle of champagne and three flutes. Gryffin stood somewhat woozily. "You're sure this isn't premature?"

Harold grinned. "I think it was your idea. But no. The time is always right for fine champagne with friends."

The bottle was Dom Pérignon, the glasses Waterford. I tried not to look impressed as Harold reverently opened the bottle, filled the flutes, and handed them round. He raised his glass and saluted each of us in turn.

"To *The Book of Lamps and Banners.* 'When a student understands all the wisdom and materials of all the world's devices and creations, all things will serve him and he will serve none.'"

Harold sipped from his glass. I downed mine and reached for the bottle, but Gryffin beat me to it. He refilled our flutes, set his on the low table, moved aside an issue of the *Times Literary Supplement,* and reached for his messenger bag.

"Time for the great unveiling," he announced. "All will be revealed."

He opened the battered leather satchel and withdrew a plastic shopping bag. Inside was a brown paper bag, and inside that a large green-and-white bag that had once held several pounds of Starbucks Caffe Verona but now contained a number of ziplock bags, one inside another. Gryffin opened each of these with the care and precision I associated with cocaine dealers in Alphabet City, circa 1983.

At last he withdrew a small object wrapped in rust-colored cloth. Painstakingly, he removed the cloth, revealing a book the size of a trade paperback. An unprepossessing volume, half bound in leather, its dilapidated covers held together with twine.

For a long moment he stared at it, his expression at once avid and utterly forlorn, as though he gazed into the face of a lover he was bidding farewell during wartime. With a sigh, he turned and handed it to Harold.

"There you go," Gryffin said. He picked up his glass and finished the champagne in one swallow.

Harold said nothing, only stared at the book in his hand. After a moment he glanced up at me. "There's another bottle in the fridge. Would you bring it in and do the honors?"

I did, and fast. For once I didn't bother to check the bathroom for a medicine cabinet. I was pretty sure there wouldn't be one. I popped the cork on the second bottle in the kitchen, gulped some down, and wiped my mouth before returning to the library.

Harold sat staring at the small volume while Gryffin paced unhappily by the French doors. I felt for him: Who wants to stick around and watch some other guy fuck your ex-girlfriend?

Or maybe he was nervous that Harold was going to find something wrong with the book, and the deal would fall through. I refilled our glasses and gave Gryffin his.

"Bottoms up," I said.

Gryffin forced a smile. "Cheers."

Harold ignored his champagne. He placed the book on the low table in front of him. For almost a minute he gazed at it, rubbing his chin. Finally he reached into a pocket of his seersucker jacket and withdrew a pair of white cotton gloves. He pulled them on and undid the twine, gingerly grasped one leather board and opened the book. Reaching into another pocket, he withdrew a magnifying glass. He leaned over the volume, examining the endpapers.

"Whoever re-bound this did a good job," he said. "Two-thousand-year-old papyrus is tough to match—they must have found some in an Egyptian sarcophagus for the endpapers and frontispiece. That's one thing the Victorians were good for. Stealing things from other people and putting them to their own use."

Gryffin seemed to relax. "That's what I thought," he said, and sat next to Harold.

I squeezed in beside Gryffin. "So this belonged to a Victorian collector?"

"Among others," replied Harold, still peering through the magnifying lens. "Probably many, many others. If this is authentic, it would have been valuable even when it was first written. Aristotle and Alexander were rather well known in their own lifetimes." He laughed. "My guess is that it was in private hands after Aristotle's death, and then in a library—probably the library at Alexandria, until Julius Caesar burned it down."

"So someone saved this one book?"

Harold shrugged. "Many people may have saved many books, though not enough of them. The library at Alexandria was burned more than once—by Romans, by Coptic Christians, by Muslims. This—"

He set down the magnifier to hold the volume in both hands, raising it toward us like an offering. "This was probably passed down from one scholar to another. Or stolen from one by another, for hundreds of years. Thousands. At some point it fell into the hands of a nineteenth-century English antiquarian, who took it upon himself to rebind it. Thus the somber black morocco."

Harold stopped to eye my brimming champagne glass with mild dismay. "Would you mind terribly?"

"Sorry." I downed my champagne and set the glass aside. "So, is it legit?"

Gryffin winced. I waited for Harold's reply, but he had once again picked up the magnifying glass and was now poring over the cover. Eyes widening, he turned to Gryffin.

"The binding's not morocco—it's anthropodermic. Did you know that?"

Gryffin shook his head. "Jesus, no."

"Just as well. Bad enough you brought this into the country in your hand luggage."

I frowned. "What's anthropodermic?"

"Human skin," said Harold. "It's not exactly common, but there are quite a few in private collections and university libraries. One or two medieval Bibles, and it seems to have been popular among anatomists going back to the sixteenth century. After the French Revolution, copies of the French Constitution were bound in the skins of aristocrats. Then there are the murderers—after they were hanged here in England, the cadavers of several convicted men were used to bind accounts of their trials."

I pointed at the book. "Any idea who that might be?"

Harold's mouth twisted into a wry smile. "I'll leave the carbon dating and DNA tests to Tindra. That might tell us more about how old it is. Some of your more gruesome Victorians went in for that kind of thing, like Richard Burton and his friends in the Cannibal Club. But this binding could be much, much older."

He rested one gloved hand gently on the cover. "This is a very advanced philosophical artifact. And I can guarantee you that some of the people who've owned it over the years knew exactly what it was."

He turned several pages, all blank, before halting at what appeared to be a title sheet. Harold sucked his breath in, and I felt my skin prickle.

The page was biscuit colored, its deckled edges darker. It appeared thick and soft to the touch, like heavy silk. Feathery Arabic calligraphy covered the page, as well as Greek letters. At the top was a delicate rendering of hares leaping over three scarlet candles, each alight with a minute flame that must have been drawn with a single filament of sable. Seven circles of varying sizes and colors hung above the hares' long ears. Dull red and indigo, watery yellow, a lovely fresh violet; orange and black and the brown of crushed mulberries.

"Be careful."

Harold placed a hand on my arm: without realizing it, I had bent my head to within inches of the page. I stared at him, then at Gryffin, and knew that each of our astonished faces mirrored the others'.

"Extraordinary," murmured Harold.

He turned to the next page, Greek words scrawled alongside a column of Arabic. The page following was crowded with esoteric symbols and another illustration, a beautiful naked woman with a vermilion scarf bound across her eyes. She had seven arms, and each of her seven hands grasped something: a candle, a mirror, a sword, a fish, a tendril of ivy, a skull, and a book whose cover, no larger than my pinkie nail, bore the same image as that in the book in front of us.

"These pages are parchment, not papyrus," said Harold. "It looks as though they were bound into the original manuscript. They're in Arabic, with Greek annotations. Which might make this the oldest example of an illustrated Arabic text, on top of everything else. Oh, dear..."

A loose page protruded from between the others. Delicately, Harold pinched it between his fingers and gazed at it. I could see lines of text that resembled bird tracks, but no illustrations.

"What is it?" Anxiety crept into Gryffin's voice. "Is it damaged?"

"No, nothing like that," Harold replied with a reassuring look. "It's part of the original Arabic text, I think."

He turned the sheet to peruse the other side. Brightly colored images covered the page now facing me, with a single line of written text across the top: incredibly tiny words, black ants marching across the page. Only these words weren't in Arabic, or Greek, but English. I leaned closer so that I could read them:

He that doth professe such dessire as to see the Devvill must seek Him yre and no further

"Good heavens," Harold murmured, still scrutinizing the bird scratchings on the other side. "These are runic."

I shook my head. "Runic?"

"I think so. It looks like an early form of the writing used by some ancient Germanic tribes. Which is remarkable, because the rest of this is an Arabic book. Except for the tipped-in pages, it's made of conjugate bifolia—five folded sheets that, when cut, would result in twenty pages. Arabic books were usually made from groups of conjugate bifolia bound together. But sometimes a leaf comes loose, and I think that's what's happened here. Most of the time, the missing page is lost."

He turned back to the volume on the table, his brow furrowing. "Yes. The other pages in this section are all illuminated. Which means that this one has detached from bifolia bound elsewhere in the volume."

"Do you know what it says?" I asked.

"I can make out a bit. I sold a fragment of a ninth-century Bible once, from Iceland. One of the only examples we have of a biblical text transcribed in runes." He squinted at the leaf. "'Angar's work, beware, this is power...' I think the rest is some kind of formula, perhaps for metalworking.

"Or maybe not," he added, and touched one of the runes with a gloved finger. "This doesn't look like ink, but blood. So, a spell? Spectrographic analysis will sort that out. God knows, they might even be able to run DNA tests on it."

He sank back onto the couch, looking faintly shell-shocked. "Do you know what this means? It establishes a link between the ancient Middle East and Mediterranean and the far north, centuries before anyone thought that existed. It's unbelievable."

He turned to Gryffin. "This is it," he said, and reverently set the loose leaf back where he'd found it. "*The Book of Lamps and Banners.* I would stake my life on it."

Gryffin looked back at him. For the first time since the volume had changed hands, he smiled.

CHAPTER 7

For the next few minutes, Gryffin and I sat and watched as Harold paged through *The Book of Lamps and Banners*. As with Gryffin earlier, it seemed less a formal inspection than the kind of anguished scrutiny that anticipates a wrenching farewell. I got a fleeting glimpse of lapidary images that reminded me of when I'd smoked opium: faces with more than two eyes, trees giving birth to legless creatures, maps of unrecognizable constellations. Handwritten notes in Greek vied with the pictures and Arabic text for attention.

There was more, too. The volume had been heavily grangerized—additional pages, drawings, notes, and annotations had been stuck in throughout. Some were papyrus, others parchment or paper, the latter covered with Latin words or the eccentric English spelling I associated with facsimile editions of Shakespeare. Later additions looked Victorian, the pages filled with neat, cramped penmanship. The notes looked like recipes—or, more likely, alchemical formulas or spells.

Watching Harold leaf through them was like watching a scrambled time-lapse film of the history of magic, unfolding in a language at once dreamlike and naggingly familiar. The remnants of speed and alcohol in my brain gave the symbols a strange metallic sheen. The hand-written letters seemed to shift on the page. I found myself squinting, as though I might actually understand what they spelled out.

"Aristotle." I pointed at a line of Greek underneath several arcane symbols. A swastika, horned circles, an eye bisected by an arrow. "You think that's actually his handwriting?"

"I don't know," replied Harold. "And I don't know how they could begin to figure it out. I don't care. This is what I love—"

He tapped the page with a gloved finger. "The possibility that it *could* be. That something this extraordinary could have survived for over two thousand years, that we're part of the chain that has kept it intact—that's more than enough."

That and a million pounds, I thought.

Harold looked at Gryffin. "You haven't scanned any of this, have you?"

"No. I should have, no matter what she said. If something were to happen to it . . ."

I watched to see if Harold caught him in the lie, but he only shook his head. "Nothing will happen to it," he said. "Though I wish you'd scanned it, too. But I always try to observe the buyer's terms—mine is not to reason why. I'm trying to convince her to make it available to the British Library at some point. So far she's recalcitrant. I'll see what I can do."

When he at last closed the volume and set down the magnifying lens, he looked slightly heartbroken.

"Well." He continued to stare at the book on the table in front of us. I felt a powerful urge to touch it, to feel its textured pages beneath my fingertips and breathe in the ancient dust it exhaled. As though he sensed my desire, Harold turned to me.

"Would you like to look at it? Go ahead." Like a magician pulling a scarf from the air, he produced another pair of white cotton gloves and handed them to me. "Just take care turning the pages."

I put on the gloves and picked up the book. As I touched it I felt a slight shock, as though I'd touched something metal while wearing wool.

"Be careful," Harold murmured again.

The volume's binding felt no different from one made of ordinary leather—slightly softer, maybe, though it was hard to tell through the gloves. I opened to a random page. It showed a stylized, leafless tree, the base of its trunk encircled by a creature like a legless dragon. Each of the tree's limbs ended in a cluster of slender branches like cupped hands. Tree and serpent had been drawn in delicate, swooping black lines, then painted in subdued shades of green and brown: everything except the serpent's eyes, which were flecks of gold leaf. At the very top of the tree a black bird perched in profile: a raven. Its single eye was gold, and stared out as though challenging me to look away.

I tore my gaze from the raven to examine the rest of the page. Three strands of letters wove above and below the tree. Arabic and Greek; the third was unrecognizable. As I examined it more closely, the raven's wing appeared to move. I heard a rustle that became the sound of my own name, whispered in a dark alley in downtown New York.

Cass, Cass...

"Cass!"

I jerked upright as Gryffin yelled at me. Quickly Harold slid the book from my hands as I sank back into the sofa.

"What the hell was that?" demanded Gryffin. I stared at him blankly. "You looked like you were about to pass out."

I glanced at Harold and remembered how he'd warned me earlier when I first touched the book. I said, "What was that? You tell me."

He only gathered the volume, folded it back in its cloth wrapping, and stood. "I must let Tindra know her treasure has been unearthed."

He crossed to his desk, opened a drawer, pulled out a black morocco slipcase, and placed the wrapped book inside it. Gilt lettering on the slipcase's cover read *The Book of Lamps and Banners.* For a long time Harold remained at his desk, staring at it.

At last he stood and embraced Gryffin. They spoke for a moment, too low for me to hear. Payment arrangements, I assumed. At last Gryffin nodded. Harold laid a hand on his shoulder. His other hand gestured at me, then the door into the hall.

"You'll have to excuse me," he said, "but would you both mind waiting in the dining room? I have to deal with a few formalities. This shouldn't take too long. Then we can see about dinner."

He closed the door, and Gryffin and I stood in the hall.

"Congrats," I said, peeling off my cotton gloves. "I hope you have a good accountant. And a good lawyer."

He flushed. "There's nothing illegal about this."

"Who said there was? Who even suggested there might be something illegal about taking advantage of some poor Iraqi bookseller during wartime, and then taking advantage of the guy who smuggled the book into the U.S. and gave it to you, without having a clue as to how much it was worth? Not to mention selling it to some Silicon Valley geek rather than a museum, so a bunch of scholars can argue about whether or not Aristotle was playing footsie with Alexander the Great. Who could even imagine such a thing?"

I leaned over to whisper in his ear. *"Not me."*

"Stop it," Gryffin snapped. He tore off his gloves and stuffed them into a pocket. "I knew this was a mistake. You're a mistake."

"Yeah, and you fucking love it."

He gave me a disgusted look. "What the hell happened back there? When you looked at the book?"

"I don't know. It was like I was having some kind of flashback."

"You know what your problem is? You seriously need to sober up. Go to AA. Or rehab. If they'll even take you." He slung the messenger bag over his shoulder and headed for the kitchen. "I thought maybe you'd gotten your shit together."

"What, because I got a haircut?"

Gryffin knew his way around the kitchen. After dropping his bag on the counter, he opened the door to a pantry retrofitted as a liquor cabinet. I stepped in with him, watching as he looked over the shelves and selected a bottle of Lagavulin. The fact that this guy had good taste in Islay single malts seemed further proof of . . . something. I reached for the door, and softly pulled it closed behind us.

"Hey, I can't see," complained Gryffin.

"That's the point." My hand found his unshaven cheek, and I pulled his face toward me.

"Stop," he whispered. "Cass, don't."

I kissed him, his tongue tasting of champagne and Armagnac, his skin warm as I slid my hand beneath his shirt and tugged it from his jeans. I pulled him to the floor, unbuttoning his shirt. He didn't put up a fight but held me tightly, his mouth covering mine as he turned onto his side and pulled me close. He was bigger than Quinn, taller, his hands pinning me easily to the floor; gentler than Quinn. When he came, I could feel his heart pounding in time with my own. After he drew away from me I thought he'd fallen asleep, but then he spoke softly.

"Why did you do that?"

I traced the corner of his eye, imagining the tiny emerald flame the sun would spark there. *Because I could,* I thought.

"I wanted to know you in the dark," I said. "Don't overthink it."

He sat up and quickly began to dress. "What about your boyfriend?"

I looked away and thought of Quinn, that subcutaneous sense of him within me always, his poison-green eyes and scarred face, the saline taste of his skin and his harsh laugh.

" 'You can't put your arms around a memory,' " I said, and pulled on my shirt.

Gryffin stood and opened the door. "Did you just make that up?"

"Johnny Thunders."

"Who's that?"

I shook my head. "I can't believe I just fucked you."

Gryffin peered out into the kitchen before stepping cautiously from the pantry. I grabbed the bottle of Lagavulin from the shelf and stuck it behind the waistband of my jeans, tugging down my shirt to cover it, and joined Gryffin.

He stood staring at his reflection in a darkened window, smoothing down his unruly hair. The door to the library was still closed. As Gryffin started toward it, I made a quick detour to the hall closet, where I shoved the bottle of whiskey into my bag and cursorily

THE BOOK OF LAMPS AND BANNERS

checked the pockets of Gryffin's overcoat. They held nothing but wadded Kleenex, credit card receipts, and business cards. One of the latter was matte black, superimposed with the image of an eye. Silvery sans serif letters burned through the black:

Tindra Bergstrand
CREATOR, LUDUS MENTIS

I pocketed the card and slipped back into the hall. After two steps I heard a strangled cry. Gryffin stood framed in the open doorway of the library, shaking his head.

"No, no, no..."

I ran to his side, gazing into the room. Even then, I couldn't look away.

CHAPTER 8

Harold's chair was half turned toward the rear of the room. He sat in it, head thrown back as if in surprise. His left eye was intact, but seemed to have been replaced by a crimson marble. I stepped behind the chair to get a look at the back of his skull but saw no exit wound. I shot a glance at the French doors. Closed. One toile curtain was awry.

"Cut the light," I called to Gryffin, still standing in the doorway. He did, though the desk lamp remained on.

I crossed to the French doors. Had someone jimmied the lock? Was it possible Harold didn't bother to lock them? I fumbled the cotton gloves from my pocket and pulled them back on, turned, and held up my hands so Gryffin could see them. Quickly he did the same.

I turned back to the doors, gingerly touched one's handle. It was open. I tugged the curtain back into place, and again stepped over to Harold's chair.

All I know about forensics comes from watching cop shows. But I can calculate shutter speed, distance, and time, and working in a darkroom taught me how certain chemicals, metals, and gases interact with one another, and with human physiology. You don't want to be inhaling mercury or spilling silver nitrate on your skin.

The gases and trace elements of heavy metals discharged by firing a bullet interact with certain media—like human flesh or blood—not unlike the way that old-fashioned photo chemicals interact with sensitized paper. At very close range, the combination of gases, smoke, and metallic residue can cause flesh to blacken. They also alter the chemistry of blood—the color changes from dark crimson to that cherry-candy red you see in Hammer horror flicks.

This wasn't a contact wound. And it wasn't a bullet wound. There was no telltale blackening of lacerated skin where the projectile had entered his eye socket. Which ruled out suicide. Plus, why would a guy who'd just made the sale of his life off himself?

I peered more closely at the eye. Other than the crimson orb itself, I saw no trace of blood, no torn flesh. The pupil of the other eye had contracted to a black speck. Otherwise, it appeared undamaged.

What could have done this? A high-velocity weapon? That would suggest someone outside in the overgrown garden; someone with very good aim. I looked around for damage to furniture or a wall or the floor. Nothing. I groped for the camera that was no longer around my neck, then turned to Gryffin.

"Your phone," I whispered. He slipped across the room and gave it to me.

I'd never handled a mobile's camera before. I found it insultingly easy to use. I crouched to shoot Harold head-on, getting as close as I could to focus on that swollen eye. As I withdrew, I noticed something on his forehead. I tentatively moved aside a lock of hair and saw a symbol drawn on the skin in blood: three interlocking triangles. Just above it, blood seeped from a small, deep gash—soon the symbol would be unrecognizable. I took a quick photo of it, shoved the mobile into my pocket, and stood to survey the room one last time.

A piece of paper had slipped under Harold's desk, the color of strong tea and splashed with indigo and scarlet—a loose page from *The Book of Lamps and Banners,* maybe the same one Harold had examined earlier.

I hesitated, feeling a superstitious unease. Finally I picked it up. I darted into the hall, retrieved my bag from the closet, and returned to the library. I grabbed the copy of the *Times Literary Supplement* from the coffee table, slipped the page inside, and once more looked around.

Absolutely nothing seemed to have been disturbed. On one side of

Harold's desk, stacks of papers were lined up neatly beside his laptop. On the other side sat the black morocco slipcase containing *The Book of Lamps and Banners*. Whoever killed Harold had neglected to take the most valuable thing here. I grabbed the slipcase, slid it and the *TLS* into my bag, then nudged Gryffin into the hall, shutting the door behind us.

We ran to the closet. Gryffin halted to stare at me, glassy-eyed. "Is Harold—he looked dead."

"He looked dead because he is dead." I tossed Gryffin his overcoat. He made no move to catch it, and it fell to the floor at his feet. I snatched it up and shoved it at him, along with his mobile, then grabbed my leather jacket.

"Listen to me." I pulled him close. "Put on your coat and walk slowly out that door with me, now."

"What are you even saying?" Gryffin's panicked voice echoed through the empty hall. "We have to call the police—"

"No, we don't. Let's go."

I started for the door, but he remained frozen. I took a deep breath.

"Gryffin—listen to me. Your friend's dead. I don't know what kind of arrangement the two of you had, but I bet it doesn't have much to do with the IRS or Inland Revenue. If you call the cops, you're fucked."

He blinked, and I could see the lights go back on inside his skull. "The book—where's the book?"

"I have it," I said, and he finally pulled on his coat. "Is there CCTV inside the house?"

"No."

"What about outside?"

"Not here. Other places, probably."

"Well, keep your head down and stay with me. Look like we're a couple."

I linked my arm through his and we slipped outside. "Gloves," I said, yanking off mine as we headed into the shadows.

The narrow street was empty. A cold wind rustled the branches of a holly tree. On a neighboring doorstep, a tortoiseshell cat regarded us, unblinking. Mellow lights shone in nearby houses. There was no sign of any disturbance, no sirens or raised voices or alarms.

"Get us out of here. Not the way we came." I tightened my hold on his arm, inclining my head toward the darkness that was the Heath. "There."

He nodded, and we followed the road through the Vale of Health, past all those fairy-tale buildings with their blue plaques and hybrid vehicles, the muffled sounds of conversation and television from behind curtained windows, a glimpse of a teenage girl hunched over a tablet. I felt dazed, no longer drunk but dreaming. Was this still the real world? If it was, what did that mean for me?

I pushed away the question. The chilly air braced me. My racing heart began to slow, and after a few minutes I relaxed my grip on Gryffin's arm. The sidewalk became a path of beaten earth that skirted the edge of the Heath. From the high street, headlights shone through the trees, the murky globes of streetlamps. I heard a dull rumble of traffic, the rush of wind in the trees. Still no sirens.

"What if we're on CCTV?" asked Gryffin.

"Nothing we can do about it. But we're innocent."

"Not of stealing the book."

"We're not stealing it. We're protecting it." I tried to remain calm. "You've never been arrested here, right? Me neither. As long as they don't have our fingerprints or faces in their database, we're good. That's why you don't want to go to the police. One reason, anyway," I added. "I can think of more."

Because once the cops got hold of me, they'd know I was in the country illegally, using a stolen passport. Maybe the police back in the U.S. no longer wanted to question me, but I was connected to a trail of other killings that stretched from Helsinki to Reykjavík to London. As the line of headlights drew closer, Gryffin steered us onto another path, crashing through knee-high brush.

"Do you know where you're going?" I asked.

"No," he said, panting. "But I think the big meadow's down there, the one that overlooks Parliament Hill."

He paused to catch his breath. Enough gray light leaked from the sky that I could see his face was streaked with tears.

"What happened?" He tore off his glasses and wiped his eyes. "Why would someone do that?"

"You tell me."

He didn't reply, or move. I reached into my bag for the bottle of Lagavulin, took a long pull, and handed it to him. He stared at me like I'd offered him a live chicken, but recovered enough to knock back a healthy mouthful.

"Better?"

He nodded. I capped the bottle and dropped it in my bag. "How could you do that?" he asked.

"Do what?"

"Take pictures of someone dead."

"It's what I do." The whiskey had loosened the fear coiled in my chest. "It's what all photographers do, unless you're just shooting landscapes. Weddings, birthday parties, selfies—sooner or later, they're all photos of the dead. That's what photography is. A massive necropolis. The dead, we carry them with us everywhere we go."

"You're crazy. No photographer thinks like that."

"You're wrong," I said.

He pushed past me and began to run, stumbling through the gorse. I caught up with him at the edge of the woods. The sound of grass rippling in the wind might have been that of the sea. Flickers of light indicated where people made their way across a vast field, like winter fireflies. Overhead, a dark fragment broke away from the trees and arrowed toward us. Gryffin stared at it, frowning.

"Is that a bird?"

My reply died in my throat. It wasn't a bird, but an object with two sets of whirring propeller blades and a squat rounded body, so compact I could have held it in my hands. It stopped, hovering in the air above us, and I saw its single black eye and glowing red light. A drone.

CHAPTER 9

I turned to race back into the woods, but a figure blocked my way.

"Hang on there," a woman's voice said. Casually offhand, as though we were in a subway car. "Tommy, can you get her? Watch your head."

Someone else grasped my shoulder—a man, his hand large enough it could have circled my thigh with ease. When I tried to move, his grip tightened. I gasped, hearing my neck pop.

"Don't do that," he murmured. He shared the woman's East End accent, a trace of Caribbean uplift. His other hand grasped Gryffin's shoulder, holding the two of us as though we were ill-behaved children.

"Hey, this is how you bring it down, right?" The woman stared at the remote in her hands, then at the man, then me. "You don't know how these work, do you?"

"No. But you've made a mistake, me and my boyfriend were just—"

"Shhh." The man shook me the way a terrier shakes a rat. "The button on the right—near the top, Ly—yeah, that one. Slowly. Wait till it's on the ground, then you can grab it."

With a soft thump, the drone fell onto the grass. The woman swept it up, depositing it in a backpack. She was stocky, a few inches shorter than me, wearing a black anorak, black pants, lace-up black leather boots. A constellation of freckles on her dark skin. Around her neck hung a pair of night-vision goggles.

"Don't hurt them." She gave the man a scolding look, turned to me, and shrugged. "Steroids. Tommy, I'll take over with her."

The man released me. He was dressed identically to the woman and shared her freckled skin and light brown eyes. Like her, he was a bit shorter than I was. They looked so much alike that they must be twins, I realized, though where she was stocky, he was massive, with broad shoulders and the chiseled, impassive features of an Easter Island monolith. Former military or maybe a onetime cop. A sinuous line of Arabic script was tattooed around his neck. He smelled of vitamins and beer.

"Good enough," he said.

He retained his hold on Gryffin, who, despite having a good six inches on him, stood rigidly at his side, gazing at the ground. I stared at him, willing him to look at me. After a few seconds he raised his head and shot me a look of utter loathing. I quickly turned away, and the woman slid an arm companionably around my neck.

"Car's over there." She gestured toward a break in the trees.

"I really think there's a mistake," I said.

"I really think you should shut up." Her tone was good-natured, but her gloved hand slipped under the collar of my leather jacket, trailing along my neck until it stopped. One finger traced a line from my temple. "That's your external carotid artery. It supplies blood to the brain. If I do this——"

She gradually exerted pressure, and fiery pain streamed from my neck to my eyes. The air turned red. "After a minute or two, you start to suffer brain damage. A little longer and it affects your executive function. Painless, though, relatively speaking. I was premed at King's College London, but I had to drop out. No dosh. Also, Tommy there has a gun."

She released my throat and I fought to breathe again.

"You'll make a great doctor, Lyla." The huge man shook his head. "Fucking Tories. We'll get you back to school."

"That's the plan," she said. "All right, here we go."

They led us to a side street where an SUV with tinted windows was parked. An approaching couple lifted their heads when they saw us.

"Now give me your keys, mate, you know you're in no state," Tommy said loudly, for the couple's benefit. He slid a hand into Gryffin's pocket and mimed pulling something from it, opened the back door, and pushed Gryffin into the SUV. "There you go!"

Lyla held the door for me. "After you."

"Fuck you." I tried to twist away, but Lyla shoved me inside, then closed the door. I heard the click of locks engaging as I pressed my face against the dark window and saw Tommy shrug apologetically to the couple hurrying past the car.

"Some people just don't know when they've had enough," he said, and mimed raising a glass.

He and Lyla slid into the front of the SUV. Lyla took the driver's seat, and moments later the car pulled away from the curb.

Gryffin slumped against his door, messenger bag between his knees. "Where are you taking us?"

"Relax." Tommy pulled off his gloves and dropped them on the seat. He reached into a pocket for a small blue box. "Gum?"

"No, thank you," said Gryffin as Tommy helped himself to a piece.

I dug into my bag for the slipcased volume. "Is this what you want?" I said, holding it up. "Because——"

Lyla raised a hand. "Talk to Tindra."

We left Hampstead's posh puzzle of Georgian blocks and mid-Victorian mansions and headed into an unfamiliar part of the city. Lyla wove in and out of traffic, shooting occasional glances into the back seat. After a while she put the radio on. A newscaster reported the latest news about the terrorist car attack and the new virus in China, then segued into a piece on a planned gathering by English and European nationalists. Tommy scowled.

"Fucking Nazis," he said, and switched the radio off.

I stared out the window, looking for familiar landmarks. After thirty minutes we passed Westminster and the towers of hierarchic London. Lines of black-clad police stood in front of barriers, some in riot gear. I desperately wanted a drink but was afraid Gog and Magog would confiscate my bottle. I licked my cracked lips, watching the play of light on black water as we crossed Westminster Bridge, winding our way around Waterloo and past more barriers where police stood guard as crowds walked to and from the station.

About fifteen minutes later, we passed another Tube station. A small group stood on the sidewalk across the street, taking selfies in front of a mural: David Bowie as Aladdin Sane, lightning bolt splitting his face. We were in Brixton.

Another few minutes and the SUV made a sharp turn, then another. At last it came to a stop on a block of nondescript midcentury houses. Behind a security gate, a short driveway led to a garage below street level.

"Home again, home again," said Lyla. She glanced into the back seat at Gryffin, and shook her head. "Ah, it's not so bad. First-world problems. We'll get this all straightened out."

Tommy tapped the SUV's touch screen. The security gate swung open. The telltale emerald thread of a laser snapped from sight as the car rolled forward and the gate closed behind us. Three miniature boxtree topiaries lined the driveway: Ms. Pac-Man, Mario, Donkey Kong. Tommy tapped the touch screen again. The garage door opened, and we drove inside.

I clutched my bag with *The Book of Lamps and Banners* inside it. I tried to summon Quinn's voice in my head, telling me to run or play dead or fight. I felt numb, the need for a drink like a drill to my temple.

I couldn't stand it anymore: I opened my bag and gulped down a few mouthfuls of Lagavulin. The SUV came to a halt. I heard the door locks disengage. Lyla hopped out, opened the door, waited as I extricated myself. She gestured at my bag.

"Open that, please."

I no longer cared what happened. I held it out to her.

Lyla barely looked inside. She flicked at my rolled-up clothes, her nose wrinkling at the bottle of whiskey. She shot me a look, reached to touch the star-shaped scar beside my eye.

"Hurts, does it?" she said as I flinched. She glanced at the bottle. "That'll kill you good as cancer. You set, Tommy?"

A few feet away, her brother cursorily inspected Gryffin's bag, nodded. "All good. Tindra wants to see you," he said, tapping Gryffin's shoulder. "Both of you. This way."

They steered us through the garage, past a bicycle and some flattened cardboard boxes, to a door with a security screen. Lyla pressed her hand against it. The door opened onto a corridor lit by a line of LEDs on the floor, like an airplane's safety lights. The corridor was empty, save for a metal bookcase crammed with old paperbacks.

At the end of the corridor, a second door led into a large, windowless room with tiled floors. A small open kitchen occupied one corner; ten-gallon jugs of water filled another, along with some free weights. The red eyes of CCTV cameras blinked from the ceiling, and I heard the hum of a filtration system. Two Ikea arm-chairs, a couch, a coffee table. Everything white, except for the vintage video-arcade consoles lined against one wall. Gorgar, Missile Command, Space Invaders. The place looked like a bomb shelter built for a computer whiz kid in 1984.

I checked out Space Invaders—an original Bally, the first pinball machine inspired by one of the video-arcade games that would soon eclipse them all. I hadn't seen one since 1980.

"You like that game?"

I glanced over my shoulder to see a young white woman with dark buzz-cut hair and a single long blue dreadlock studded with sequins. She held a chain leash attached to a black-and-white Staffordshire terrier that looked like the convict twin of the dog from *The Little Rascals:* spiked choke collar, black lips pulled back to show white teeth and pink gums.

I shrugged. "Been a while."

The girl handed the leash to Lyla, walked toward the console, and slapped it. Lights flashed, and a silver ball dropped into the charger as the machine chirred awake. She worked the table with the nearly immobile stance of the longtime player, leaning slightly into the machine, fingers tapping the controls ceaselessly.

It doesn't take much to score big on Space Invaders. After a few minutes with the first ball still in play, the girl seemed to lose interest. She lifted her hands, watched the ball spin into the gutter, and turned to me.

"Where's my fucking book?" she said.

CHAPTER 10

Gryffin was right. Tindra Bergstrand wasn't a rich chick lugging a crocodile Birkin with a hamster-sized dog inside it. She looked like she could crack walnuts in the crook of her elbow. Not tall but solidly built and square shouldered, wearing a white T-shirt, black cargo pants, white thick-soled Vans. Muscular arms, no tattoos or piercings that I could see. Other than the spangled dreadlock, her only concession to ornament was a single earring—a flattened disk of amber the size of a quarter. She had a wide, unsmiling mouth, sharp nose, uptilted fawn-colored eyes beneath a high forehead. Swedish accent. I pegged her as twenty-five or thereabouts.

She didn't offer her hand or return my gaze. After a moment she repeated her question. "Where's my book?"

I pulled the slipcase from my bag and handed it to her. Without a glance at me, she opened the slipcase and removed the book, letting the case fall to the floor with a dull crack. She stared at the book's cover, opened it, and flipped the pages. Then she turned and threw it at me.

"What the fuck is this?"

I caught the book, confused. A volume somewhat larger than *The Book of Lamps and Banners,* with light green boards and the title stamped in gilt:

Youth

I opened to the title page—*Youth: A Narrative, and Two Other Stories, by Joseph Conrad*—and swiftly turned to the table of contents:

Youth: A Narrative
Heart of Darkness
The End of the Tether

"Shit." I handed Gryffin the volume. "They had a sense of humor, anyway."

"Where's my fucking book?"

Tindra snatched up the Conrad and smashed it on the edge of the Space Invaders game. Gryffin cringed as the book's spine exploded. The air filled with white pages, like scores of moths, as Tindra turned to the twins.

"Check their bags."

Lyla handed the dog's leash back to Tindra, took Gryffin's bag, and rifled through it. Tommy did the same to mine. He looked at Gryffin, then me. "Where's her book?"

"I don't know," said Gryffin. "I delivered it to Harold, we were there, we saw him—"

Tindra cut him off. "I know what happened."

She pulled out a mobile, held it up so we could see shaky time-stamped footage of the two of us exiting Harold's house.

"Then you know it wasn't us." Gryffin sounded far more calm than he looked. "If you were actually watching us with that drone, you know we didn't kill him."

"I wasn't watching. I was waiting. No one's looked at anything." Tindra turned to Lyla. "Kill him? What's he saying? You didn't..."

She began to scroll frantically at her mobile. Lyla looked at me. "What're you on about?"

Gryffin groaned. Tindra's dog whined softly.

"Who got killed?" Tindra suddenly sounded much younger. "Where's Harold? He was supposed to call me."

I said, "Harold's dead. If your two friends here had been paying attention, they'd've known that."

"Who else was there?" asked Tindra.

"No one. Just us," Gryffin insisted. "It was my book, I——"

"Your book?" Tindra turned to Lyla. "Who are these people?"

"I told you, we saw them leave his house." Lyla's voice cracked. "After you texted me. You said you hadn't heard from your book bloke. I thought he'd scammed you, him and these two."

Tindra raised a hand to silence her. The dog whined louder, tugging at its leash.

"Listen," I said. "We didn't kill him. You know that, you——"

Tindra gave a low whistle. The leash slithered to the floor, and the snarling dog was at my side. I froze.

"Bunny, down," Tindra said without raising her voice.

The dog dropped as though tased. After several seconds it scrambled onto its haunches and I heard its low growl, like the hum of an old tube radio warming up.

"I'll transfer your money back," said Gryffin. "I don't even know if it's gone through, I haven't——"

"I don't want my money back," she said. "I want my book."

She walked up to Gryffin and jabbed him with her finger. "Who are you?"

"Gryffin Haselton. A bookdealer. The book belonged to me, I was selling it to Harold. He's one of my oldest friends."

Tindra glanced at me. "You his girlfriend?"

"No," said Gryffin.

"We just met," I said. "I'm a photographer. I never heard of this book until a few hours ago. He's telling the truth, far as I know."

Tindra shoved her mobile into a pocket, eyes half closed as though listening to music. The room fell silent, except for the air system and the dog's panting. Finally Tindra spoke.

"I want someone to tell me what the fuck happened. You——" She pointed at Gryffin.

He recounted everything, from the two of us arriving at Harold's house to discovering his body in the chair. He left out the part about us having sex in the liquor closet. When he finished, Tindra pointed at me.

"Do you have anything to add?"

"No."

"You should call the police," said Gryffin.

Tindra shook her head. "No police," she said. Gryffin started to protest, and she turned on him furiously. "I said no police! Maybe they want something—a ransom. They might call or come here. I'm going to wait. I don't care about the money."

I saw Lyla and her brother exchange a glance. Gryffin ran a hand across his face. "Cass," he said. "This is crazy—tell her it's crazy."

"I don't think it's crazy. What are the police going to do? They're caught up with all this terrorist Nazi shit. They're not going to send a bunch of cops out after a book no one even knows exists."

"That's not the point! Someone murdered Harold—that's what they should be investigating."

"They'll get to it," Tommy broke in. "Someone'll find the body and notify them. Happens nine times out of ten."

"This is bullshit." Gryffin started for the door, reaching for his mobile. "I'm calling 999, then the U.S. consulate. Cass, you do whatever the hell you want." He yanked fruitlessly at the doorknob, held the mobile to his ear, and swore. "She's blocking it."

Tindra turned to me. "You can go."

Gryffin gaped at her. "What are you talking about?"

Tindra gave me a once-over, her gaze lingering on my battered leather jacket and steel-tipped cowboy boots. "*She's* not going to the police."

She gestured at Lyla, who escorted Gryffin back to the couch. Tommy sat beside him, hands folded on his lap. His nails were bitten to the quick. "You're safer here than outside," he said to Gryffin. "Trust me."

Tindra whistled. The dog raced to her side, and the two left the room, the door closing after them with a click.

Lyla set her backpack on the coffee table and removed the drone. "Sorry. She went off her meds," she explained, peeling off her anorak. "Sometimes she gets paranoid."

Tommy shook his big head. "I had a mate did that in Lashkar Gah. Started listening to ZOG podcasts and talking to UFOs."

I frowned. "What's ZOG?"

"Zionist Occupied Government." Tommy opened a drawer in the coffee table and withdrew a Parcheesi set. "White supremacists, they think there's a Jewish conspiracy to rule the world."

"They're the ones marching in Victoria Park tomorrow," his sister added as Tommy unfolded the Parcheesi board. "Among others."

Tommy nodded. "Anyway, Tindra always says she can't code on her meds. So she stops taking them, and it's all Scientologists and MI6 tapping her mobile."

"Shouldn't you be getting her help?" said Gryffin.

"I've tried a dozen times," said Lyla. "She's gone through some bad stuff. But she's crazy obsessive. She's got her app ready to launch, but she says she needs that book before she can do it. I wish I could help her, but..."

"You do what you can," said her brother.

"Maybe." Lyla sighed. "It doesn't ever seem like enough. And now this."

Her voice trailed off again, and Gryffin turned to her imploringly. "You both realize how crazy this is, right? Your drone video, it'll show who the real killer is."

"That's not our problem," said Tommy. "Our problem's Tindra, and her problem's the book."

"You're obstructing justice!"

Tommy gave him a hard look. "If I was you, I'd shut up about all that. First thing the cops are gonna want to do is talk to you. And her." He pointed at me. "Your alibi's for shit, both of you. In the kitchen, getting champagne. Meanwhile someone shoots your friend in the head. Who doesn't hear that?"

"It wasn't a bullet," said Gryffin.

"We were having sex in the pantry," I said. "On the floor, with the door closed. Harold's room was down the hall, and that door was shut, too. He didn't hear us, we didn't hear him. End of story."

Lyla and Tommy absorbed this. After a moment, he said, "That's pretty good."

"It doesn't matter." Lyla started to arrange gaming pieces on the Parcheesi board. "She truly doesn't care who killed him. All she wants is that book. She's obsessed with her books. Alchemy, early science. That's how we met, she was doing a year at UCL; we were in the same neurochemistry class. I couldn't afford to stay, but she just got bored. Went back to uni in Uppsala, then to study computers and neuroscience at Stanford. She dropped out to play World of Warcraft full-time. She hit level sixty in about a week and decided to start designing her own games. FlightRisk, that was the first. She was just twenty-one."

"Impressive," I said.

Tommy nodded. "She's brilliant. But." He tapped his head.

"She's been working on this app for years. But every time she goes off her meds, she starts prepping and buys all this retro shite." Lyla gestured at the video games. "You're stuck in the panic room, do you really want to be playing Missile Command?"

"World of Warcraft, the Rabbit Hole, Majora's Mask. And Space Invaders." Tommy recited what was obviously a familiar litany. "It all bores the fuck out of me. But I don't know what I'll do if she doesn't keep me on."

"Eh, there'll always be work for you, Tommy." Lyla handed him the dice. "You go first."

CHAPTER 11

T ommy moved one of his gaming pieces and glanced up at Gryffin. "Want to play? Might help pass the time."

Gryffin shook his head, and the siblings bent over the playing board.

I stood and watched them, brooding. Tindra said I was free to go,
but I was reluctant to leave Gryffin. I knew he'd rat me out to the
cops in a heartbeat once he had the chance.

And who was Tindra Bergstrand? All I knew was that she had
enough money to purchase a rare book that was worth more than I
cared to contemplate; a book that, so far, had left more bodies in its
wake than the Maltese Falcon. I didn't want to be another one.

I stared at my feet. I wished I'd never seen Gryffin again. I wished I
was back in Reykjavík with Quinn. I wished I never bought that posh
leather bag or the cashmere hoodie. Now I only had five hundred
euros left.

But if I could find the book before Tindra did—or Gryffin, or the
cops—and if I could find Quinn, and if Quinn could find a buyer, the
two of us would finally have enough money to get away someplace
safe. I wouldn't have to return to a landlord waiting to boot me out
of my rent-stabilized crib so he could sell the building to a developer
who'd raze it and put up a high-rise that would block the sun for
whatever poor schmoes were still holding out on Houston Street.

And Quinn wouldn't have to return to living in a sheet-metal
Quonset hut in Reykjavík, selling off his dwindling collection of rare
vinyl. We could go to Greece. We could go anywhere.

If we found the book. If I found Quinn. Except I had no more idea where Quinn was than Tindra's stolen book: only the words *rotherhithe darwin,* a persistent taunting whisper in my head.

I took a deep breath and walked over to the Space Invaders console, motioning for Gryffin to follow. After a glance at the twins, he joined me.

"Give me your mobile," I said.

"What?"

"Your mobile—give it to me."

"Forget it."

Lyla glanced at us, frowning. I gave her a little wave and leaned into Gryffin.

"Gryffin, do not be an asshole. They're not letting you out of here, not anytime soon. This way I can use your contacts, people you know who know Harold. Maybe someone has heard something."

"You don't even know how to use a smartphone."

This was true. Before he could move, I snatched the mobile from his pocket. "What's your password?"

I thought he might finally lose it. Instead, after a moment he muttered it under his breath.

"Are you freaking kidding me?" I rolled my eyes and tapped in "BOOKS." "Okay, show me your contacts in London. Bookdealers, runners, anyone who might help me."

"No one's going to help you, Cass. You don't know anything about books."

"I worked at the Strand for thirty-three years."

"In the stockroom!"

"Listen to me. Who else knows about *The Book of Lamps and Banners?*"

"No one."

"Bullshit. The guy who bought it in Baghdad, he knows. Your guy at Berkeley suspected something."

"They're both dead."

"Right, and I'm trying not to see a pattern there. Harold's

accountant must know something, if he just wired money. Tindra knows. And them."

I cocked a thumb at the twins. "That's three dead people and six live ones, counting us. Which is a lot of people to know about something that's supposed to be a secret. Did Harold have any enemies? A rival?"

"The book business doesn't work like that."

"Well, something fucking works like that. Come on, Gryffin! Anyone who knows Harold, anyone who might know about this book? Dealers or, I dunno, alchemists."

Gryffin removed his glasses and pinched the bridge of his nose. "Let me think." He took the mobile from me and began to scroll through his contacts. "Nathan Ballingstead, he lives in Wapping. A runner."

"Who else?"

"Lucy Ryman-Briggs used to have a shop in Farringdon. But she only sells online now, I haven't talked to her in a while. Malloy Townson—another runner, he's pretty sketchy. I don't have an address for him, and I don't know if that phone number's still good."

"Who else do you know who's sketchy? Because those are the people who might actually be useful."

He tapped the mobile's screen. "This guy. And maybe him, he's in Clerkenwell." He sighed. "That's it. Not many people still doing business."

"Do any of these people know you're here?"

"No."

"That's good."

Gryffin's scowl suggested he thought otherwise. I let my lips brush his ear.

"Gryffin," I murmured. "If they don't know you're here, they won't know you're missing, and they won't call the cops. *We do not want to call the cops.* Got that?"

I slid the mobile into my pocket, and he grabbed my hand. "What the hell are you doing? Give me that!"

"No way. Hey," I called over to Lyla and Tommy. "Can one of you let me out of here?"

As Lyla stood, Gryffin turned to me. "Goddamn it, Cass. Go to the consulate. Or call them anonymously. Something. You have to do something."

"I am doing something. Look at the bright side—maybe Tommy will teach you how to play Missile Command."

Lyla escorted me to the underground garage. "Don't do anything stupid," she warned. "My brother served in Afghanistan. He came back different. Episodes. He couldn't find work. Tindra's my best friend, she hired him. Both of us. Now go."

She gave me a push and closed the door.

CHAPTER 12

After the filtered air in Tindra's bunker, the corridor smelled musty and neglected. The LED floor lights and CCTV cameras made me feel as though I was fleeing a downed plane. I slowed when I saw the rickety metal bookcase, shoved against the wall like a discarded dorm relic, and glanced at the books it held.

Computational and Mathematical Modeling of Neural Systems. Ancient Christian Magic: Coptic Texts of Ritual Power. The Rise of Magic in Early Medieval Europe. Synaptic Self: How Our Brains Become Who We Are. Transient Global Amnesia. Anglo-Saxon Runes and Magic. Trauma and Memory: A Neurological Approach.

I pulled out a cheaply produced hardback. The boards had pulled away from the spine, and the pages were loose. The cover had no title or author listed, just a color photograph of a naked man. Tattoos covered his arms and torso: swastikas and runes, stylized dragons and hammers and crosses. In his hands he held a horned animal's skull that obscured his face.

A clichéd image of masculine defiance, except for the rust-colored ribbons of dried skin and strands of what looked like human hair that clung to the skull. The tips of the man's fingers were bloodied. I turned to the frontispiece and title page, careful to keep the pages from falling out:

Skalltrolleri: Fotografier producerad av Big Delusory Whim

The photographer had a sense of humor, anyway. The book consisted of photos depicting skulls in various stages of decay: mostly color, a few black-and-white. The latter were more interesting, the interplay of light and shadow canceling out the lurid subject matter. Another time, I would have kept it, but I didn't want Tindra's CCTV to capture me stealing a book, especially one with a white supremacist on its cover. I stuck it back on the shelf and continued on.

The garage was empty save for the SUV and that lonely bicycle. A slant of security light illuminated a figure sitting cross-legged on the floor. Tindra, her face glowing green from the laptop on her knees. Her blue dreadlock coiled around her fingers, its stray hairs like bits of frayed rope. The dog Bunny lay beside her. He growled as I approached, falling silent when she covered his muzzle with her hand.

I glanced at the computer, its screen filled with lines of code as incomprehensible as the symbols in *The Book of Lamps and Banners*. Tindra quickly closed it and set it on the floor beside her mobile.

"Your app?" I asked. She said nothing. "Lyla said that's why you want the book."

Her expression grew blank as a sleepwalker's. I set down my bag, squatting so we were closer to eye level, and got a whiff of the dreadlock. It smelled like a long-dead animal. I gazed at her warily, trying to determine if that decay went deeper.

I can sense damage. It's a toxic chemical that radiates from some people, their sweat and skin and saliva and sex. Whatever neuro-chemical alchemy creates it, I have the receptors to pick up on it, the way a dog can sense fear, or attacking bees home in on the person who kills their queen. I can read it in photographs, embedded in the emulsion or superimposed on an image, a blurred outline like the fake ectoplasm in nineteenth-century spirit photography. I wonder sometimes if that's what I am: an analog ghost haunting the digital world, invisible to anyone born after the millennium.

Tindra saw me. She returned my gaze—not challengingly, but with the resigned patience of a sober person being subjected to a

Breathalyzer, as though she knew what I was looking for and knew I wouldn't find it.

I didn't. No acrid taint rose from her. I felt no dark energy like a pent-up electrical charge waiting to be released if I were to brush against her bare skin.

Instead I felt something stranger and more disturbing: a kind of emptiness, the psychic rift caused by the profound disassociation I connected to my own rape on my twenty-third birthday. For me, it had been a sense of myself splitting into three distinct selves: one being assaulted on the rubble-strewn ground; one floating above the scene and watching with calm detachment; the third embodying a silent scream sucked into the void.

It was the last of these that still gave me night terrors. It was what I sensed in Tindra: a profound absence, the human equivalent of the hole on a piece of emulsion that has been exposed to direct sunlight.

Yet she sat less than two feet away from me, quiet and alert. Her pale brown eyes regarded me with detached curiosity that gradually became recognition. Her eyes widened and she nodded, as though I'd answered a question.

She said, "That's why I need the book."

"How'd you hear about it?" My voice came out in a parched whisper.

"It's the kind of thing I know."

I waited for her to go on, but she just stared at me with that preternatural calm. I tried a different tack. "Did you know Harold Vertigan before this?"

"I've bought a few things from him."

"Was there anyone else who knew about this book? Another dealer, someone who might want to rip him off?" I pointed at the laptop. "Your app—it has something to do with magic, too? You can't seriously believe in that shit."

Anger flared in her tawny eyes. "It's not 'magic.' It's an ancient language, using symbols and images. A kind of code. We're

73

returning to that mode of communication. Everything is code. No more words."

"Yeah? Then how come I can hear you now?"

"That's changing." She held up her mobile as though displaying a piece of evidence to a jury. " 'They drift between the shores of perception, between sign and image, without ever approaching either.' Sartre."

I laughed. "Props for that. But Sartre was talking about photographs, not words."

"Who cares?" A smile flickered at the edges of her mouth. "Who cares what it even means. See this?"

Without warning, she thrust the mobile toward my face. Its screen was a molten whirlpool of insignia: horned circles and crescents, wheels and crosses and swastikas, teeth and birds that seemed to spell out a message I couldn't decipher. I recoiled, hands in front of my face, and shut my eyes.

Yet I still saw those symbols, a pinwheel galaxy of blue and green and crimson, the poisonous yellow of a liqueur you know you'll regret tasting but can't resist. Pain exploded inside my skull as the symbols spun, fragmented into brilliant pixels that rearranged themselves into a series of freeze-frames, and began to move.

Horrified, I stared at the image of my younger self on a dark downtown alley, the black silhouette of a car pulling alongside me.

"No," I whispered.

A knife glittered, a voice hissed my name.

Cass, Cass...

The car door opened. Something moved, someone moved, a man, two men. A running girl. Someone else screamed: not someone else. Me.

"Stop!" I shouted. *"Stop it..."*

I had seen this before; I had been here before. I had never left this place.

On the ground in front of me, light bounced from a spar of jagged glass as long as my hand. My fingers dug into the cracked cement as I dragged myself forward, summoning all my strength to grab it.

"No! Don't touch it—"

Knife, car, glass, all vanished. Tindra knelt in front of me. As my hand closed around her mobile, the dog leaped at my face.

"Bunny, drop!"

The dog fell back. Phantom images reeled across my vision, green and violet, that terrifying molten yellow. A curve of glass like a displaced grin. I fought to catch my breath, stammered, "What the fuck was that?"

Tindra watched me, one hand tight on her dog's collar. "A new language," she said. "I invented it for my app, Ludus Mentis. It's from *ludus mentis,* 'play' and 'mind.' So, Ludus Mentis—like a mind game.

"I got the idea from the Orphic mysteries," she went on breathlessly. "And some other stories. When the Titans wanted to destroy Dionysus, they gave him toys. A ball, a wheel, a top. A mirror. Dionysus had never seen one before. When he looked into it, he couldn't look away. He didn't realize it was a trap. The Titans tore him limb from limb and ate him."

She thrust the mobile at me again, and now its screen reflected my own face. "You see how it all ties in? The way we're all sucked in by this? We can't look away, none of us, no matter how hard we try…"

Her voice trailed off as she lowered the mobile. "But no one's even trying. And that's how Ludus Mentis is going to change everything."

CHAPTER 13

I felt the hairs on my neck rise. I thought of photographing Harold's corpse back in the Vale of Health, of all the other terrible things I've shot over the decades, because I can't look away.

"Interesting," I finally managed. "Though I think an app based on ritual cannibalism is gonna be a hard sell."

Tindra fixed me with a cobra stare. "The code is in us already. All those paintings on cave walls—the oldest ones, with all those crosshatches and dots and zigzags, like you see when you're tripping? Those symbols are hardwired into our brains. *They mean something.* Cave drawings, runes, numerals, alphabets, Linear B, Linux...it's all code. *We're* all code."

She rapped her skull with her knuckles. "It's already in here: Ludus Mentis just opens a path to access it. Like those apps where you change your brain waves with biofeedback. Only Ludus Mentis taps into a different part of your consciousness—it mimics the neuroelectric impulses your brain sends when it reacts to powerful emotional memories. Basically, I figured out a way to use optogenetics and the Fourier transform to rewire your brain."

"Opto-what?"

"Optogenetics is a way of controlling living cells with light. There are neurons which specifically store memories of fear. Scientists experimented with rats and made those neurons light sensitive, so that the rats would respond to certain patterns of light. When those neural pathways were triggered, the rats would act frightened. Do you get it?"

I nodded, wishing I didn't get it.

She continued, "Those scientists had to use a virus to make the neurons sensitive to light, but I figured out a way to bypass that. Certain symbols used in conjunction with specific light patterns can trigger the same neural response. And if they can trigger one response, it makes sense that a different combination could trigger a very different response. Not fear but forgetfulness, maybe, or remorse, or excitement. There are endless combinations and endless possibilities."

I fought to keep my voice level. "You really *are* talking about rewiring the brain."

"Yes! Because if we erase their traumatic memories, people can get better. We can retrain their thoughts, reprogram the neurons to let go of fear. Or stimulate fear when it's necessary."

"What about the other thing, the transform?"

"The Fourier transform? It's actually a wavelet transform, derived from a mathematical theorem that describes a means of separating any signal into a series of circular paths, or patterns. That's all our brains are, that's all consciousness is: a series of electrical and neurochemical signals. A kind of code. And because it's code, it can be rewritten. I think that *The Book of Lamps and Banners* is the earliest expression of the Fourier transform, recorded in ancient symbols as well as mathematical ones."

"But how can you control what happens? How do you know how someone will react?"

"It doesn't matter," she snapped. "I mean, it does, but that's what I'm working on now. I just need to test it, to get different reactions and compare them. But once I get the bugs worked out, the app can be used for all sorts of things. Trauma, insomnia, ADHD. Regulating mood disorders without drugs. Addiction. Libido. Everything."

She fell silent, eyes glowing, and I wondered how the app was working on her own mood disorder, which was clearly fully operational.

Yet I could still see that vision of my twenty-three-year-old self projected on my mind's eye, drunk on a downtown street after partying all night at CBGB; a man whispering *Miss, miss* and me hearing *Cass, Cass;* the flash of a zip knife and blood mingling with semen as I ran screaming down the alley, bare feet slashed by broken glass. Whatever Ludus Mentis was, it had unlocked a gateway to the single event I'd spent decades trying to forget. I looked up to see Tindra watching me intently. She nodded.

"I know," she said softly. "Me too."

I stared at her with a shiver of apprehension. "How could you know?"

"I could tell, when I met you. Don't you find that sometimes? That you just know?"

I recalled what I'd sensed within her, a hole where trauma had been. Had she burned away her own memories? If so, what had replaced them?

I hesitated, then asked, "What happened to you?"

She didn't reply but continued to stare at me with that unnerving, nearly unblinking gaze. I felt like I had as a teenager, playing some stoned game with a friend: If you stared long enough into another's eyes, could you tell what they were thinking? Could you make them see what you saw in your mind's eye?

Only Tindra really did seem able to intuit something. Not what I was thinking at that moment, but the underlying strata of damage and rage, grief and loss, which were at my core. As I stared back, there was an instant when I sensed the same thing within her: a limit to the abyss behind her eyes, a place where the darkness stopped and something else, someone else, survived. Then she blinked, and it was gone.

"When I was thirteen," she said, "a friend of my father's—we started having sex. It went on for a long time before someone at my school reported it to the police. They did nothing. Someone must have threatened the teacher, because it never came up again. But people in school knew, my friends knew. They said I was *slampa,* a slut."

THE BOOK OF LAMPS AND BANNERS

"That's horrible."

"The worst was my father not believing me. Or, he believed me, but it didn't matter. He acted as though nothing bad had happened. He and . . . the man, they stayed friends. That was when I left. I haven't talked to him since I was fourteen." She fell silent.

"Where was this?"

"In the town where I grew up in Sweden."

"I didn't think stuff like that happened in Sweden."

"Of course it does. It happens everywhere."

"What about your mother?"

"She died when I was much younger. Cancer."

"And the guy who raped you?"

"He's still alive. But it doesn't matter. It's gone now." Her fingers splayed across her white T-shirt. "Almost gone. I'm not afraid of him anymore. When the code is finished, I'll be able to make him disappear completely."

"Bugs." I forced the word out. "The app, you said you're still working out the bugs."

Tindra leaned back to sit on her heels. "That's why I need *The Book of Lamps and Banners*. It's like a beta version of Ludus Mentis. Whoever wrote it had figured out how a combination of lights and symbols can change the way we think. Their book drew on knowledge that had already been around for thousands of years, things the ancient Egyptians knew, and the Sumerians, the Minoans. So 'lamps and banners' is just shorthand for what we call code."

"But no one's really ever seen the book," I broke in. "How can you know any of this is true?"

"Because I've researched it more thoroughly than anyone ever has. Once I have the actual book, I'll incorporate everything inside it—every detail, every thumbprint, every bit of DNA on every page. It's all there, not a line missing. I'll be able to complete writing a code that was begun thousands of years ago."

Tears spilled from her eyes. She looked exhausted, all that manic energy spent. The dog Bunny whined, put its paws on her lap, and licked her cheeks.

"I've been working on it since I was fifteen," she whispered. "It will change everything."

It already had changed everything for Harold Vertigan, yet Tindra seemed barely to have registered his murder. I bit my tongue and asked, "What are you going to do now?"

"I don't know." Her voice was a child's. "I don't want to go to the police right away."

"Because you and Gryffin and Harold did the deal under the table?"

"No," she insisted, but her pale cheeks flushed. "I told you. Whoever stole it, they might want to sell it back to me. Or if I can find out who they are, I can track them down. I have Lyla and Tommy. And Bunny." A spark glinted in her eyes. *"It's my book."*

I thought of the loose page I'd nicked from Harold's place and slipped into a copy of the *TLS*. Tindra didn't know it was missing. If I somehow managed to find *The Book of Lamps and Banners,* the fact that I retained that page would mean the book was intact. If Tindra located the book before me, she'd desperately want the missing page. Maybe she'd pony up serious money for it.

And if the book was never found, I could sell the loose page—worst-case scenario, to some random collector on eBay.

I knew these ideas were crazy. Whoever wanted this book had no compunction about killing for it, and there was a good chance Tindra wouldn't, either. The only person who might be able to help me was Quinn, whose black-market connections might extend to some shady corner of the antiquarian book trade. Long shot, but the only one I had. And I still had to find Quinn: another big if.

"Look, I know you want it for your app," I said at last to Tindra. "But do you have any idea how much that book is worth? It's like the Rosetta stone and the Dead Sea Scrolls and the Quran all rolled into one. It's worth a fucking fortune. Whoever has it is not going to just hand it back to you."

Tindra buried her head in her dog's neck. For a long time

neither of us spoke. All the booze and speed had leached from my system. Along with a throbbing headache and the memory of the nightmarish flashback triggered by her app, I had the familiar sense that I was staring through the windshield of a car about to plow into a brick wall.

When at last Tindra looked up again, the tears were gone. An odd expression played across her face—appraisal, contempt, and, again, a strange recognition. "What kind of photography do you do?" she asked. "Digital?"

"No. Analog. Old-school."

" 'Old-school.' " She gave me a derisive smile. "You're one of those analog saints."

"More like a shaman. And what about your old computer games?"

"People like to play games. No one cares about photographs. Or books."

"You're obviously wrong about the books."

She laughed. "You really are an immutable object."

"A what?"

"A piece of code that doesn't change. Or it changes incrementally, and that change has an unanticipated effect on subsequent lines of code. And you know the dead," she said, as though this were a logical thought progression.

I shook my head. "I only met Harold for a few minutes."

She stood, and I could see that her pupils had shrunk to poppy-seed specks. "That's not what I mean. I can see it, there—"

Her finger extended toward my right eye. The scar beside it started to ache. "It's why I showed you Ludus Mentis."

She withdrew her hand, as though suddenly afraid of some contagion. Her mobile chimed. She glanced down at it, did a double take, swiped at the screen, reading a series of texts, then furiously tapped out a response. Seconds later, another chime. Her eyes widened as she stared at whatever had appeared on the screen. Disbelief, horror, relief, all flickered in her eyes, along with a yearning so pronounced it resembled fear.

She looked up at me, and immediately her features resolved into that same disturbing composure. The mobile disappeared into her pocket, and she picked up her computer.

"I have to go," she said.

"Wait—"

I whipped out Gryffin's mobile and found the photos I'd shot of Harold, zooming in on the one that showed the emblem on his forehead, three linked triangles drawn in blood.

"You know about symbols. Do you recognize this?"

Her face went from pale to paper white. "Who is that?"

"Harold Vertigan."

She took the mobile from me and scrolled through the other photos, barely glancing at them before she returned to the close-up of Harold. "Have you sent these to the police?"

"No."

"Good."

Her fingers tapped at the screen. The photos disappeared, all save the close-up. Then that, too, was gone.

I grabbed the mobile from her. "What the fuck?"

"I deleted them from the phone. And the cloud." Tindra shrugged. "Better this way."

She turned, Bunny at her side. I started after her, ignoring the dog's soft growl.

"You didn't tell me what it means," I called. "That symbol on his forehead."

"You'll figure it out."

She slipped through the door to her flat. I got my bag and waited as the garage door silently opened, then the security gate, and walked out onto the dark road. When I glanced back, the gate to Tindra Bergstrand's house had already closed behind me.

CHAPTER 14

I wandered the streets of Brixton, head pounding from the virulent speedball of fear, alcohol, drugs, and sheer weirdness I'd absorbed over the last few hours. I needed to find Quinn. But I had only a vague idea as to where Brixton was in relation to the rest of London, and no idea how to find my way to Rotherhithe.

And I had no assurance that Quinn was still in London. He'd fled to Reykjavík decades ago. Now that he'd left Iceland, he was in danger of being extradited to the U.S., and probably several other countries as well. It would be disastrous if the cops found him.

The thought of losing Quinn terrified me. For decades I'd assumed he was dead. I'd found him around the same time I picked up my camera after nearly thirty years, and for a few weeks it seemed like it might be possible for me to have some semblance of a life again. Not a normal life, but I don't expect miracles.

My shivering got worse, a bad sign. It was cold, but not that cold. I paused in front of a shuttered halal butcher to gulp down more whiskey, kept walking.

The shaking subsided, but not the dread that had gripped me since my encounter with Tindra's app. Bad enough to have the experience of my assault replaying in my brain like a skip on scratched vinyl. Even more disturbing was the sense that there was something I'd missed all those years ago—a flash of forgotten light or shadow at the corner of my vision that Ludus Mentis had revealed. Every time

I thought of it, my stomach knotted, but the image never resolved into anything I could recognize or name.

After about twenty minutes, I reached the high street. The drum of traffic and distant music calmed me, along with the sight of people on the sidewalks, the familiar stink of diesel and cigarette smoke. I ducked into a Starbucks, got a latte, and sat at a table in the back.

I pulled out Gryffin's mobile, hesitated, then entered Quinn's number. The call rolled directly into voice mail.

You've reached Eskimo Vinyl in Reykjavík. Leave a message, I'll get back to you.

I disconnected and sipped my coffee. After a few minutes, I googled the two words that were my sole clue as to where Quinn might be:

rotherhithe darwin

A quick Google search told me that Rotherhithe was in East London—not too far from Canary Wharf, which was where I'd last seen Quinn, but a long way from Brixton.

"Darwin" presumably meant . . . Darwin? My search brought up a brasserie in Southwark, now closed for renovation, and not much else. No other pubs or restaurants, no Darwin memorials, no one by that last name.

I finally gave up. I found an online Tube map, figured out how to get to Rotherhithe, and headed for the Brixton station. On the train, I nodded out till I had to change to the Overground, nodded out again, and didn't wake until a recorded voice announced we were approaching Whitechapel.

I stared out at the malign pageantry of Canary Wharf. Blindingly lit construction cranes loomed over the city like an army of alien mantids, another marker of the slow apocalypse. Cataclysmic storms and epidemics, mass extinctions, and bizarre viruses, mass entertainment indistinguishable from mass graves. When I was a teenager, I dreamed of dancing at the end of the world. Now it seemed I'd have my chance.

The train pulled out of the station. Several skinheads had boarded, along with three bearded guys who looked like they'd materialized from Sunset Park. The skinheads were a decade or more older than their hirsute companions and wore leather jackets or hoodies emblazoned with Iron Crosses, swastikas, band names heavy on the umlauts. Their hands and necks were tattooed with stylized hammers or severed heads. One guy had the words BURN EM inked above the knuckles of both hands. They spoke animatedly, switching between English and German.

In contrast, their younger companions across the aisle might have stepped out of a craft beer ad: Timberland boots, barn jackets, knit caps. All three sported T-shirts emblazoned with the word SVARLIGHT beneath an S-shaped lightning bolt bisecting a scarlet oak leaf. Pinned to their jackets were large buttons that showed a blue eye, its iris a stylized sun. They pored over a Tube map, consulting one another in what sounded like Swedish.

The symbols on their T-shirts and buttons reminded me unsettlingly of Ludus Mentis, and Svarlight's lightning bolts resembled those in the Nazi SS symbol. Then again, so did the twinned S's in the Kiss logo. Maybe Svarlight was a band.

I watched as the few other passengers checked out the newcomers. Two young black women whose faces twisted in disgust, a middle-aged white businessman who glanced up, then quickly returned his attention to a book.

After a minute, the youngest-looking skinhead leaned across the aisle to say something to one of the bearded guys, who laughed. As Canary Wharf's towers disappeared behind us, a voice rang out from the other end of the car.

"Friends, I have two children and nothing to feed them. If you can help, please..."

A slight brown-skinned man stood at the rear of the train, white plastic bucket in one hand, head bowed as though afraid to look up. Beneath his nylon windbreaker, an oversize Wembley T-shirt hung almost to his knees. His filthy sneakers had no laces and flapped open as he walked down the aisle.

"Please, we have nothing. Anything you can spare, please . . ."

As in New York, most of the passengers ignored him. A white girl toting a laundry bag dropped some coins into the bucket as the man worked his way down the car. Two of the skinheads nudged each other and stood. Like pit bulls snapping to attention, the others removed their headphones, slid their mobiles into pockets, stood, and headed toward the panhandler.

"Get the fuck out of here."

A barrel-chested skinhead towered over the slight man and pushed him toward the back of the car. I pulled up my hood, stood, and followed, slipping behind the skinhead.

"Leave him alone," I said.

The skinhead turned. He did a double take when he saw my face just inches from his own. Few guys ever get the chance to gaze eye to eye with a six-foot androgyne in a bad mood. This one obviously didn't know how lucky he was.

"You fuck—" he spat. Before he could go on, two of the Swedes marched toward us.

"Hey, man," one said. He gestured to a woman who'd raised her mobile to record the fracas. "Calm down."

The train slowed, approaching the next station. The panhandler elbowed past his tormentors, dropping his bucket as he raced toward the doors. The skinheads watched him but didn't move. Several more people had now whipped out their mobiles.

I quickly turned and headed toward the back of the car. The last thing I wanted was to show up on anyone's amateur video. The train pulled alongside the platform; the doors opened. The skinheads hopped out, shoved through passengers waiting to board, and disappeared. I saw no sign of the man in the Wembley T-shirt.

But the three Svarlight guys stood on the platform, talking to a transit cop. One held the white plastic bucket: he pointed at the train, then turned to gesture toward the exits. The transit cop nodded, began speaking into his walkie-talkie, and headed in the direction the Swede had indicated. I had no way of knowing what the Svarlight crew had told him, but I suspected it wasn't a complaint about neo-Nazis.

The train's doors closed. I sat. The car was now almost empty. The other passengers kept their heads down, and I did the same. After a short time, a recording announced the next stop: Rotherhithe.

CHAPTER 15

Much of this part of London had been destroyed during the Blitz. What remained was a combination of old brick warehouses and postwar construction, all repurposed as housing for those who could afford a view of the Thames and the gleaming forest of skyscrapers and ancient landmarks on the other side of the river: a desolate if striking palimpsest of a city devouring itself.

For the hundredth time, my hands reached for my camera. I sighed, withdrew Gryffin's mobile, and stared at the black screen. Digital photography held no magic for me. I'd rather shoot one perfect black-and-white photo than thousands I'd never look at. I dropped the mobile back in my pocket.

I halted to lean against the railing above the river and gazed at the dark water far below. I could count the things that defined me on the fingers of one hand: photography, Quinn, booze, drugs. I'd lost half of them. I removed the Lagavulin from my bag and swallowed a mouthful, then another, waited for the familiar warmth to dissolve my anxiety.

At last I turned to gaze at the foreshore. I could always buy another camera, or steal one. I had a few rolls of Tri-X left in my bag. Finding a place that still processed black-and-white film would be more of a challenge. But I might find a darkroom, too, if I looked hard enough.

Quinn was another matter.

Shoulders hunched against the cold, I crossed the street and continued walking. I scanned street signs and buildings for anything named for Darwin, a blue plaque or boutique or car park. Nada. Despite the dystopian surroundings, most of the pubs here valorized London's maritime past with names and signs that favored anchors and compasses and clipper ships. I chose a place called the Bollard and walked inside.

It was close to eleven, but the pub was still crowded. I elbowed past Barbour-jacketed drinkers, ordered a pint, and slipped along the bar counter to where several women stood chatting. I sipped my beer, scrolling through the email on Gryffin's mobile in hopes he might have received something about the book, or Harold. Other than some special travel offers and announcements from Advanced Book Exchange, it was a wash. I turned to the woman beside me.

"Hey, is there a place around here called the Darwin?"

The woman frowned. "I don't think so. Sylvie?"

Her friends shook their heads. One pulled out her mobile, did a quick search, and came up with the same brasserie I had. I finished my pint and left, hit up two more pubs before I got lucky at an Indian takeaway.

"Darwin? Not that I know of." The guy behind the counter bagged me a kebab and an onion bhaji, took my money, and yelled into the kitchen. "Noni, is there a Darwin bar around here?"

A young woman stepped out from the kitchen, wisps of curly hair escaping from a hot-pink hijab. "Darwin bar? I don't think so."

"Not necessarily a bar," I said. "Any place named Darwin."

"Darwin?" She wiped her hands on her apron, thought for a moment before nodding. "Oh yeah, there is. But it's not a pub. It's a boat."

The man behind the counter said, "She's not looking for a boat. Are you?"

I ignored him and turned to the woman. "Where's the *Darwin*?"

"Down that way." She pointed out the front window. "Big piece of junk. You can't miss it."

I thanked her and hurried out, eating my kebab and bhaji on the fly. When I'd finished, I crossed back to the river walk. A concrete barrier ran alongside the pedestrian way, separating me from the foreshore.

It was high tide. A twenty-foot drop ended in black water and the bilious yellow wake churned up by a River Bus carrying passengers to Greenwich. Squat black barges cruised along with surprising speed. I squinted at them, trying to make out a name that might be DARWIN. If things had gone according to plan, Quinn and I would have been sequestered on one of those barges, already on our way to Greece.

I wandered farther along the river walk. The wind carried the estuarine reek of exhaust fumes and dead fish, the roar of aircraft far overhead. I gulped more whiskey, stumbling on a chunk of broken concrete; called Quinn's number again but disconnected before the voice mail kicked in.

I rubbed my eyes, wondering if I should cut my losses and find a cheap hotel. Years ago my father had given me the number of an attorney friend, in case I ever found myself in real trouble. Maybe the time had finally come to call him.

In the near distance, a shadowy bulk rose from the shore. As I drew near, I saw that it was a boat—a commercial fishing vessel of some kind, long retired from the looks of it. White paint flaked from its hull. Rusted sheet metal peeled from the stern, where rivets protruded from a makeshift repair job. A length of chain dangled from the aft deck, heavy enough to shackle an elephant. Below, murky water lapped at the base of scaffolding that held the boat upright. The smell of fuel was so strong I was surprised that the boat hadn't been torched by a stray match. The vessel seemed out of place amid the gentrification: one of those vicious, red-eyed drunks who can't be evicted from the street corner where they hurl abuse at passersby.

A makeshift rope bridge extended from the bow to the seawall. An artificial Christmas tree stood on the small deck, along with several folding chairs and a plastic fuel tank. Light glimmered from a porthole window. On the hull, barely visible in the shadows thrown by the seawall, faded words were painted in block letters:

DARWIN'S FAULT

LEIGH-ON-SEA

CHAPTER 16

A fter a quick look around, I tucked my bag under my arm and hoisted myself over the seawall railing. The rope gangway sagged beneath me as I scrambled across, until I reached the deck and clambered on board, ducking into the shadows by the door.

Light fell through a grimy porthole. Through the pitted glass I could see the pilothouse, gutted of controls, and hear thrash metal. Stale cigarette smoke cut through the smells of piss and fetid water. I remained in the shadows, waiting for someone to appear in the doorway. When no one did, I counted to fifty, and knocked.

Inside, the music fell silent. A face filled the porthole, and the metal door creaked open.

A sixtyish white man stood in the doorway, his nimbus of gray hair aglow from the overhead light. A paint-stained sweatshirt hung loosely from his bony frame, and a lit cigarette dangled from fingers crosshatched with dirt and pale scars. Sun-worn face, sunken cheeks, a nose familiar with the wrong end of a fist or a barroom floor. One eye was a pure sea blue. Pale skin sheathed the other's empty socket, the flesh drooping in soft, waxy-looking pockets.

"Yeah?" He squinted at me with his good eye.

"I'm looking for Quinn O'Boyle. Is he here?"

The man took a drag from his cigarette, twisted his head like a bird's to look me up and down with his one blue eye. "No one by that name."

"I'm a friend. Cass. Cass Neary. Has he been here or called or something?" I dug my fingernails into my hand to steady myself. "I thought you might know him."

"No one by that name," he repeated. The door closed in my face.

"Goddamn it." I pounded on the steel frame. "Just talk to me!"

Music blasted from inside, even louder than before. I tried the door handle—locked. Abruptly it turned in my grasp and the door opened. Someone else stood there, lankier than the first man and bare chested, glaring at the floor with bloodshot eyes.

"Who the fuck is it?" He did a double take when he saw my boots, looked up into my face. "Cass?"

He dragged me inside, kicking the door closed, pushed me against the wall, and ran his hands across his stubbled scalp, shaking with anger.

"Goddamn it, Cassie, what the fuck happened? I told you to wait at Bruno's place!"

Before I could answer, he took my chin and lowered his face to mine, his fingers digging into the flesh as he kissed me. His mouth tasted of rust and ash, a sweeter undercurrent of beer and whiskey. He withdrew and I pressed my face against his bare chest, felt beneath my fingertips the ravaged map of scars there, the rope of puckered flesh that ran down his side and the imprint of the brand upon his left breast—three creatures whose entwined limbs and teeth formed at their center a human skull: the Gripping Beast.

"Cassie." He tilted my face up to his. "Jesus, what happened? Your hair . . ."

"I needed a change."

"I like it." He grinned, pinned me against the wall again, and traced a finger along my arm. "You look hot."

"Get a fecking room, O'Boyle."

The one-eyed man loomed behind Quinn, reached past us to throw the door's dead bolt. Quinn lit a cigarette, pinched the match between his fingers, and dropped it into a beer can on the table.

"Wink, this is Cass. We've known each other since we were

kids. Cass, this is Wink. We've known each other since we were in Pentonville. When was that? 'Eighty-three?"

"Nineteen eighty-four. My girl bailed us out, night before the wedding. Remember that?"

"She came through." Quinn sat at the galley table. "But she was wicked pissed."

Wink nodded. "I don't blame her. All that blow was for our honeymoon."

"She was a bitch." Quinn pushed a chair toward me. "What was her name? Reba?"

"Rhonda."

"Right. Help me, Rhonda, help me get the hell out of jail."

Quinn laughed. He picked up a half-full bottle of Myer's dark, sloshed a few inches into a grimy coffee mug, and handed it to me. Wink tugged down the window shades, went to a small refrigerator, and hooked two bottles of Bud between his fingers.

"I'll leave you two romantics," he said, and stepped into the adjoining room.

The thrash metal resumed, but at a lower volume. Quinn poured himself some Myer's while I surveyed the room. A Formica-topped table and three folding chairs, boxes full of empty beer and liquor bottles, some nautical charts on the wall. I turned back to Quinn.

"Who is he?"

"Old friend." Quinn took a final drag of his cigarette, his pale green eyes glittering. "So what the fuck happened?"

I gave him the short version of what had gone down since he'd left me four days earlier in Canary Wharf, omitting the details as to what I was doing when Harold Vertigan was killed. Quinn listened, lit another cigarette, and smoked nervously, flicking ashes onto the floor. The roar of diesel engines rose from the river whenever a large boat passed, drowning out the chain-saw roar of Slipknot and Motörhead.

Quinn's gaze never left mine, his mouth twisted into a permanent, mirthless smile by two horizontal black lines tattooed on either side of it: relics of his time in Alaska, along with the three vertical red lines incised between his eyes. I'd asked him once what the lines signified.

"They mean I killed a man."

Now the flickering fluorescent light turned his gaunt face into a mask as ominous as the image of the Gripping Beast. A four-day growth of gray stubble covered his skull and chin. As I poured myself another jolt of rum, he leaned across the table to press his fingers to my mouth.

"Stop. My fucking head is going to explode. If you were a cat, you'd be on your sixth or seventh life by now."

I drank my rum. "Good thing I'm human."

"Jury's still out on that one."

"So what the hell happened to you? You were supposed to be gone for three hours."

Quinn sighed, closing his eyes. "I ran into someone I know. Things got problematic."

He opened his eyes, and I was confronted by the same icy don't-fuck-with-me gaze I'd first seen decades ago, when I'd photographed him holding a spoon over a lit candle in a Kamensic Village bedroom. When he didn't continue, I asked, "What about Greece?"

"What about Greece. Like I said, things got fucked up. Wink's contact got detained in Marseilles, they found a bunch of dead refugees in the hold of his barge. So scratch that. I can think of seven guys here in London who'll kill me if they find me. And that's before Interpol enters the picture. Why I quit shaving. I oughta do what you did and dye my hair. Get tinted contact lenses."

He lurched to his feet, picked up the bottle of Myer's. "I should never have left Iceland. Come on, I'm beat."

I followed him through the next room, where Wink sprawled on a vinyl couch surrounded by empty bottles, a laptop on his stomach. He stared at it with his Cyclops eye, riveted by a field of exploding Humvees.

I followed Quinn down a metal ladder. Below, the only light came from an overhead fluorescent bulb. The cabin was barely ten feet wide and maybe twice as long, its walls pleached with mold. Nylon nets suspended from the ceiling held sprouting onions and potatoes. A faded school photograph of a young girl in a soccer uniform was taped above the metal sink. The air reeked of cigarette smoke and gasoline, with a pervasive note of burnt plastic. I didn't want to think about what the wiring looked like.

Opposite the galley, a door opened onto a tiny cabin, with clothes strewn on the floor.

"That's Wink's berth." Quinn pointed to a stained bedsheet that hung from the ceiling. "This is mine. Luxury quarters."

He pulled aside the sheet to reveal a pair of bunks, the top one crammed with tools and electrical equipment, a backpack I recognized as Quinn's. A sleeping bag took up most of the lower bunk, where Quinn's leather jacket hung from a nail. He tossed the jacket onto the upper bunk, took off his biker boots.

"Make yourself at home." He crawled into the lower bunk and lit a cigarette, its tip glowing like an emergency beacon.

"Is that safe?" I pointed at the cigarette and set my bag on the top bunk.

"None of it's safe. Wink pays off someone on the local council so he can stay here, guy owes him a favor. They've been trying to get him out for years."

He took a drag on his cigarette, pinched it out, and flicked it into the near darkness. I peeled off my leather jacket and draped it over Quinn's, removed my boots, and slid into the bunk beside him. There was barely room for both of us. He pulled me close, his breath warm against my cheek.

"Damn it, Cassie," he whispered. "I thought something bad happened to you."

"Something bad did happen to me."

He pressed his mouth to my temple. His tongue flicked at the star-shaped scar beside my eye as he unbuttoned my jeans. He slid his hand down my stomach, to the snarl of scar tissue left there by a zip knife when I was raped. He kissed me, then drew back to stare at me with his green-glass eyes.

"You been fucking someone?"

"Yeah. But that wasn't something bad."

"Not as good as this, though . . ."

He yanked the bedsheet drape across the opening to the bunk and tugged down my jeans. We fucked like we did as teenagers, with half our clothes on, covering each other's mouths so we wouldn't cry out. Later, Quinn cradled my cheek in his hand.

"What is this, Cass?" he murmured.

I ran my finger along his upper lip, a drop of blood where I'd kissed him. "What do you mean?"

"All these years and we're still like this. How come?"

I kissed him gently. "Nobody else thinks *Berlin* is a better album than *Transformer*."

He rested his head on my shoulder. My fingers splayed across his chest so I could feel his heart thumping beneath them.

"Hey," I said. But he was already asleep.

CHAPTER 17

I dozed fitfully for an hour or two before I gave up. Wink's train-wreck soundtrack had gone silent. I watched Quinn's chest rise and fall, and thought of my lost camera. Until the last few months, I'd gone for decades without shooting anything. Picking up my camera after so long had been like the first line of coke during a lost weekend, an arrow right into my visual cortex. Losing it was as close to withdrawal as I'd ever been.

I forced myself not to think about it, pulled on a T-shirt, and retrieved Gryffin's mobile. I opened the camera app and stared at the dim rectangle that framed Quinn's sleeping face, the tip of one eyetooth where his lips parted, the frozen grimace carved into his cheeks. I saw all these things, and tasted the sour aftermath of all the damage he'd sustained over the decades, a damage inextricable from my own.

Yet gazing at the thumbnail of Quinn on the mobile's screen, I sensed nothing. Tindra might practice alchemy with silicon sensors and electrical pulses, millions of pixels and photons and electrons. For me, the mobile held as much magic as a chunk of Styrofoam.

I shot a dozen photos anyway, Quinn's broken face no more peaceful asleep than awake; then deleted them all.

"What are you doing?" His eyes opened and he sat up, rubbing his jaw.

"Taking pictures."

"With that?" He frowned. "Where's your camera? The one your dad gave you?"

"I gave it away."

"What?"

I turned away. "I don't want to talk about it."

I knew he was still watching me. After a moment he swung from the bunk, tugged on his jeans, and lit up. While he smoked, I got my bag from the upper bunk.

Quinn shook his head. "New hair, new bag. What else new you got, girlfriend?"

"I dunno. Some drugs."

"Goddamn it, Cass! I'm trying to lay low, and you should be, too. You spend thirty-something years hiding in a downtown bunker, and now that you're out, you can't stop pulling shit that's gonna bring the cops down on you. And me."

"Fuck off. What the hell did you expect?"

He glared at me, but then his expression softened. "When's the last time you got some sleep? Or ate?"

"I can't sleep. And you don't eat when you live too long."

He slid a hand under my T-shirt, tracing my rib cage. "Christ. You're nothing but bones, Cassie."

"You said I looked hot."

"Yeah—a hot skeleton. You need to quit that speed. You're gonna give yourself a heart attack."

I pulled away and picked up Gryffin's mobile again, scrolling through his contacts.

"Whose phone is that?"

"Gryffin's."

"Is he the one you fucked?"

"I told you back in Reykjavík, he's a rare-book dealer. His mother was a famous photographer, that's how I ended up in Maine. His father was a serial killer. As it turns out."

He peered over my shoulder. "Whose numbers are those?"

"People Gryffin knows. Bookdealers, runners—people who scout books to sell to dealers. This guy Ballingstead, he's a runner, lives in Wapping. That's close to here, right?"

"Close enough."

He began to pace. I had a flashback to when we were kids and did a handful of black beauties, and Quinn thought that knocking off the local drugstore would be a really good idea. He halted beneath the fluorescent bulb, his face the same sickly green as his eyes.

"Why do you have that guy's phone? You steal it?"

"No. But this book—if we find it, we can sell it ourselves and keep the money."

Quinn laughed. "That's insane. There's no way we could sell it. It'd be like unloading a Picasso. Like unloading the world's *only* Picasso."

"There's no way to sell it *legally*. You know people, and any guy you don't know, you know the guy who does. People like that, they have more money than they know what to do with, and they hire people to acquire stuff for them. If we can find the book, you can pass it on to someone. We take our cut and disappear."

"What about this guy Gryffin?"

"If he goes to the cops—and he will go to the cops as soon as he can—I'm fucked. If we're going to do this, we need to move now, before Tindra decides to call the police. Or we could just bail," I added. "Leave now and start over someplace else. Can't we just bail?"

Quinn ran a hand across his grizzled scalp. "We could try. But with all this new border-control shit, one of us might get detained at the airport. In which case we'd be screwed."

"We're kinda screwed now."

"Yeah, I know. What're you thinking?"

"Gryffin says he didn't tell anyone about this book, or the deal with Harold. He's either lying or stupid. I'm thinking he's just stupid. Someone got wind of it, either through him or Harold."

"That chick Tindra?"

"I don't think so. She's too isolated. I don't think she has any friends, except her dog. And her bodyguards."

"Why does she need bodyguards?"

"I don't know. They have—I don't know what they have. Some kind of weird ménage à trois or something. She's definitely emotionally fragile. But she wouldn't have told anyone else about the book—she's obsessed with getting it for her app. She wants to, I dunno, scan or photograph the pages. She says the book is like an ancient form of computer code."

"Weird with a beard." Quinn lit another cigarette. "But the app might be a little moneymaker."

"No," I said. "She tried it on me. It's horrible. Like mainlining angel dust. I had a flashback to when I was raped—it was like I was actually there again. It *causes* PTSD instead of curing it. Trust me, we'll be doing the world a favor if we find the book before she does."

"How're we gonna do that?" Quinn resumed pacing. "She's got her bodyguards and your guy Gryffin, who knows all about this book shit. What do we got?"

I held up Gryffin's mobile. "His contact list."

"What if he's already called them?"

"I'll risk it. I'll see if I can find Ballingstead, he's closest. You see if you can find out who put a hit on Harold. Someone nailed him right in the eye; how many people can do that?"

"You'd be surprised."

I went to the galley, splashed water on my face, and raked my fingers through my hair. Quinn was right: I looked like I'd crawled out of a car wreck. I gingerly touched the scar beside my eye, still an angry red. I wasn't sure if Boots had enough concealer to hide that, but I got out the overpriced makeup I'd nicked and tried to make myself look less like my own ghost.

When I returned to the bunk, Quinn looked me up and down, then shot me a vulpine grin. "That's an improvement. I thought you were taking off."

"I'm gone." I picked up my bag. "What time is it?"

"A little after seven. You're not gonna roll this Ballingstead guy out of bed, are you?"

"No. But I have to figure out where he lives. And I want to check the news to see if Harold's there."

"You can do that later. Stay, baby." He pushed me onto the bunk. "Thirty-seven years, we got a lot to make up for."

I couldn't argue with that.

CHAPTER 18

Afterward, I dressed quickly. Quinn watched me, smoking a joint.

"You look good, Cass. I kinda miss the blonde, though."

"Well, now you get two for the price of one."

"Yeah, and I'm the only guy on the planet who could handle that."

He held the joint out to me. I shook my head. "I need fast drugs. You got a line on something?"

"I gotta do my best to stay clean. I thought you had some crank?"

"I used it up in Iceland." I pulled on my boots. "Come on, you have to know someone."

Quinn scowled. "You're out of your fucking mind. Want me back in prison? Plus I keep telling you, that shit'll give you a heart attack. You're too old for this, Cassie."

I turned and grabbed his leather jacket, dug into the pockets until my fingers closed around a pill bottle. Quinn wrenched it from me, but not before I saw the label.

"Cialis?" I said. "Seriously?"

"Man's gotta do what a man's gotta do. Here." He reached into the sleeping bag for a small object and tossed it to me. Another mobile.

I tossed it back. "How many of these do I need?"

He put the mobile in my hand, folded my fingers over it. "This is a TracFone, a burner. Use it to call me and anyone else you need to talk to. Do *not* use your little friend's mobile to make any calls. Once he goes to the cops, you'll be traced and it'll be game over."

"Can I go online with it?"

"Bad idea. Which guarantees you'll do it." He sighed. "Look, if anything happens, ditch the phones in the river."

"Will I see you later?"

"Yeah, but not here. I don't want Wink dragged into this."

"Then where?"

He thought for a moment. "If you don't hear from me, meet me at Victoria Embankment Park. Get off at Embankment or Waterloo or Charing Cross Underground. There's a big statue of some guy in the park, I'll meet you there around three."

"What if something bad happens?"

"Like you said, something bad already did happen. Nothing we can do if it happens again." He pulled up his shirt to display the brand of the Gripping Beast. *"Hver er sinnar gæfu smiður."*

"Meaning?"

" 'We forge our own fate.' "

He pulled out his mobile and turned away. "Do what you can, baby. I gotta get to work."

I picked up my bag and split. Not until I reached the Overground station did I realize I hadn't mentioned the loose page I'd taken from Harold's library.

CHAPTER 19

Wapping was one stop north, on the other side of the river. Overnight, the cold front had blown itself out. News crawls warned of the poisonous air as a blanket of smog descended upon the city. The Overground platform resembled a scene from a zombie flick, crowded with people wearing face masks.

My eyes watered as I stumbled onto the sidewalk, the inside of my nostrils stinging as though I'd just snorted low-grade crank. Pus-colored haze obscured the tops of cranes and high-rises. The air smelled like burning tires and hand sanitizer. I put on my shades and found a newsstand. In front of it, a plastic sign with the headlines shuddered in the breeze:

NAZIS ON THE MOVE: WHERE WILL THEY GO NEXT?

MAYOR WARNS OF DEADLY FOG

VIRUS DEATHS MOUNT

I bought a couple of papers and wandered aimlessly till I found an American-style diner that was open. I barricaded myself at a table in the far corner, ordered rare steak with a side of bacon and a pot of coffee. The bacon was English bacon, fatty and more like ham. The steak was well done and mostly gristle. In New York, a place like this would last about a week. Here it was packed. Still, I finished everything off, ordered more coffee, and took my last Vyvanse as an eye-opener.

The carbon-based media had nothing about Harold Vertigan's

murder. Either his body hadn't been discovered yet or the neo-Nazis and toxic fog, the Chinese virus and the most recent terrorist attacks in the U.S., had kept him out of the news, for now.

After the waiter brought more coffee, I furtively poured a slug of whiskey into my mug, set aside the papers, and began scrolling through the online news on Gryffin's mobile. Within minutes I hit pay dirt—not only news of Harold's death, but a guy named Nathan Ballingstead.

Harold's murder had just been made public on a Hampstead news site. His body had been discovered by his cleaning lady around seven that morning. Neighbors claimed to have heard nothing, and police were scrutinizing surveillance video in the area. The police suspected robbery—a year earlier, a man had murdered a bookseller for a first edition of *The Wind in the Willows,* valued at fifty thousand pounds.

But until someone did an inventory of Harold's stock and library, there'd be no way of determining if anything had been stolen from the shelves. There was no sign of forced entry, and no mention of the symbol scrawled in blood on his forehead, a detail I assumed the police would keep to themselves as long as they could. The thought of being captured on CCTV footage made my skin crawl, but there was nothing I could do about that now. Another good reason Gryffin and I had parted, anyway.

On the upside, the London book-collecting world was small enough that at least one reporter had already spoken to the guy I'd targeted:

"The world has lost a prince among booksellers," said Nathan Balling-stead, himself a noted figure in the rarefied sphere of antiquarian book collectors. "This isn't just a heinous crime directed against a single human being: this is the wanton slaughter of an entire world of literary wisdom and insight." When asked as to the ultimate disposition of Vertigan's library, Mr. Ballingstead said that would "depend on how the investigation unfolds, of course. But myself and several others close to Harold are in discussions with his solicitor."

Based on what I'd seen of high-end dealers at the Strand, Harold's cronies would be swarming around his shop like great whites butting a shark cage. I found several other articles on the murder. Nathan Ballingstead was quoted in every single one. The guy was a news whore.

I settled up and went back outside, found a quiet side street where I made the call on the burner Quinn had given me. Ballingstead answered after one ring.

"Hello, who's this?"

"Hi—my name is Shelley Wilson, I'm a journalist with the *Tribune*." I tried to smooth the rough edges from my New York accent, which might be recognizable if anyone questioned Ballingstead later. "I wanted to know if you had a few minutes to talk about Harold Vertigan's death, and maybe a bit about the antiquarian book business in general?"

"Yeah, I thought so—my mobile's been going all night." An orotund voice, like a self-satisfied Stephen Fry's. "What would you like to know?"

"Actually, I wondered if you might be able to meet with me. I'm in London covering another story. I could come by your flat, or we could meet somewhere else if you'd like."

"Sure, come on by." He gave me the address and directions. "Ring when you get here, and I'll buzz you in."

It took me a while to find his place. I crossed paths with countless dog walkers, then a group of uniformed children, all wearing too-big surgical masks that revealed only their eyes. After a few blocks I realized I'd gone the wrong way. I retraced my steps, brooding.

I knew several runners when I worked at the Strand. All men, they were a vital element of the book trade back when it was part of the city's creative and sociocultural DNA. They served the same function that a lobster does: bottom-feeders who sucked up dross and repurposed it for folks higher up the food chain as something highly desirable, and more expensive.

Runners spent their days scouring used bookstores, flea markets, estate sales, tag sales, church bazaars, and dumpsters, looking for something to sell. Ace doubles and old paperbacks with lurid cover art; *Famous Monsters of Filmland* and *Black Mask* magazines; volumes bound in morocco or vellum or gilt-lettered cloth that were worthless as literature but looked nice on people's shelves.

The guys I knew were extraordinarily knowledgeable. No one buys crap, no matter how cheap it is. More than once I saw some junkie or wino get the bum's rush for toting a shopping bag full of Reader's Digest Condensed Books. The best runners could spot a copy of *Amazing Fantasy* #15 — better known as *Spider-Man* #1 — or Poe's *Grotesque and Arabesque* on a white-elephant table at a distance of thirty feet, then talk a church volunteer into selling it to them for fifty cents instead of a buck. At the end of a week or month, they'd gather bags full of books and vintage pulps and make the rounds of dealers.

That's a lost world. Everyone does business online now, and there's only a handful of runners left. I was about to meet one of them.

CHAPTER 20

Ballingstead lived in an unmemorable five-story building, drab red brick and concrete, with scraggly plane trees planted out front. Every runner I'd known lived on the first or basement floor—easier to lug books in and out—and Ballingstead was no exception. He buzzed me in, opening the door to greet me.

"My god, I've been up all night with you lot! Never tire of it, do you? Blood and circuses, all those hungry ghouls online craving meat. How can you live with yourselves? Come in, come in."

Ballingstead resembled an Arthur Rackham gnome who'd gotten lost at the Glastonbury Festival years ago and never found his way home. He barely came up to my chin, a wizened, spidery-limbed man whose round face seemed to have been plopped atop the wrong body. He had a shoulder-length fringe of lank gray hair; flushed, bulbous cheeks; a receding chin; and protuberant blue eyes. He wore faded jeans and a windowpane-check shirt, open at the neck to display a red plastic rosary worn as a necklace.

We walked down a short hallway devoid of any furnishings save shelves crammed with books. The place smelled like a teenage boy's room, of sweat and weed and unwashed sheets. "Tell me again who you are?" he asked.

"Shelley Wilson. I write for the *Tribune*. I just happened to be in London when this story broke and—"

"Yes, everyone's very excited about it. Well, I shouldn't say *excited*," he added, though he obviously was. "We are heartsick, just heartsick, every one of us who knew Harold. The *Tribune,* that's on-line, isn't it? Or is that the other one? So far I've talked to the *Metro Morning News, The Telegraph, The Independent, The Guardian.* News Six just now, I told them they could send someone over, but they won't. Who else?"

"The police?"

"Oh yes, the police! No, I haven't gotten in touch with them yet, I suspect they may call me as well. Or just drop by."

I glanced uneasily back at the door, but Nathan prattled on without noticing. "I'm not a person of interest, so I imagine I'm pretty far down the totem pole as far as that sort of thing goes. *Pretty far down,*" he repeated with emphasis, and gestured me into a room.

There's a very thin tightwire that separates collectors and hoard-ers, and Nathan seemed to be barely maintaining his balance there. Boxes covered the floor, stacked so high they obscured the walls. Any bit of free space was piled with books like a frozen game of Jenga. Here, the pervasive odors were old paper and Earl Grey tea.

"Welcome to the Fortress of Bookitude." Nathan indicated a metal folding chair alongside a leather recliner with a blanket draped across it, the only proper furniture I could see. "Pardon the sordid state of affairs, you're the first to actually visit in a while. I don't spend much time here, to be honest."

I sat, after making my way past a wasteland of takeaway boxes filled with dried-up tea bags and an Anglepoise lamp perched on a carton marked DOCTOR WHO. Nathan settled into the recliner, tossing a pillow into the canyon of boxes behind him.

"So," he said.

"So how long have you——"

"Aren't you going to record this?" Nathan stared at me quizzically. "Or take notes?"

"Oh yeah, right." I fumbled inside my bag for a pen. "You, uh, got a piece of paper or something?"

Nathan's brow furrowed. He pushed himself from the recliner and puttered around the room, returned to hand me two sheets of lined notepaper. "You don't use a recorder? Or your mobile?"

"I'm old-school." I smoothed the paper on my knee. "Okay. You've known Harold a long time?"

He nodded, touching the rosary around his neck. "Yonks. I used to see him at George's stall in Farringdon every Saturday. There were a hundred bookstalls there once, extending all the way to High Holborn, all passed down through families. It's all gone now—they ended up building an awful Thatcherite office block there. There's still a bit of the original brick wall, if you know where to look."

He shook his head sadly. "It would be around 1971 when Harold and I first met. Farringdon wasn't closed to anyone, but ninety percent of the people there were runners or dealers or scouts. Not many women, sorry. There was no bullying, but it was a genuine scrum—you needed to be fast and strong, which in those days I was.

"George had four long tables, covered with books. When you arrived they were all covered with tarpaulins. Each table was priced differently and, for years, the best table had every book on it priced for a pound. But you never knew which table would be the best table. George switched them every week, and you never knew what was under the tarp. He uncovered them one at a time, and he wouldn't unveil the next one till the first was empty.

"It was like watching a cardplayer for tells. He'd walk back and forth between the tables, stop in front of one, and everyone would cluster around it. Then suddenly he'd make a break to another table and whip off the tarpaulin like a stage magician. Everyone would run for it and start grabbing books as fast as possible before they disappeared."

"Sounds like a madhouse."

Nathan smiled. "It was."

I remembered I was supposed to be taking notes and scribbled on the sheet of paper. *Madhouse.*

"Within half an hour, he'd have sold two thousand books," Nathan continued. "In forty-five minutes, everything would be gone."

"And that's where Harold learned his job?"

"Oh yes. Harold had a marvelous eye, one of the best. He sold enough to private collectors to lease his own place in Islington, and eventually did well enough to set himself up in Hampstead."

His eyes blurred with tears. "I still can't believe it's true. Can you?" He gave me a pleading look, as though I might reveal some elaborate hoax.

"No." I recalled Harold's expression as he gazed at his treasure for the first time. "I can't."

Nathan took out a red bandanna and blew his nose, shaking his head.

"Do you know who might have killed him?" I asked. "Some kind of professional rivalry?"

"The book business isn't like that. Or it wasn't until now."

"What about something personal? Love affair gone bad, something like that?"

"There were rumors..." He stopped himself and stuffed the bandanna back into his pocket. "Not my business."

"What about a guy named Gryffin Haselton. Do you know him?"

"Gryffin? He's one of my American customers, lives in California. Why do you ask?"

"No reason," I went on quickly. "Just, someone told me he's a friend of Harold's."

"He is. Lovely chap. He used to stay with me when he visited London. Not much room for him now," he admitted with a glance around the room.

I fought to recall another name from Gryffin's contact list. "What about Malloy Townson. Know him?"

Nathan rolled his eyes. "Everyone knows Malloy, though some wish they didn't. He has some strange ideas, Malloy."

"Could he—"

"Not unless he'd lost his mind completely. Which is possible, I suppose. But Malloy has enough trouble keeping track of all his conspiracy theories, without something like this. He and Harold were good friends. Opposites attract—Harold's open-minded as they come. Whereas Malloy..."

He held out his hand and mimed a shaky boat. "He runs with a different crowd. Folks who have 'the right to offend.' I have a different word for them."

"Is there anyone who holds a grudge against Harold?"

"I'd be very surprised." He mused, frowning. "But you know, now that I think of it, I did hear something. Where was it? Wait!"

He snapped his gnarled fingers triumphantly. "I know! A launch at Maggs for Iain Sinclair a few months ago. I was there chatting with someone, can't remember who. But whoever it was mentioned he'd heard that Harold was negotiating for something extraordinarily rare."

"Really?" I kept my voice even. "Do you have any idea what it was? Or who you were talking to?"

Nathan sighed. "Not a thing. My memory's going, that's the sad truth. But that's interesting, isn't it? If Harold had come across something unusual. I wonder if anyone else has mentioned it?" He thumped the arms of his chair. "I don't think they have! You have a scoop there, my friend."

I gave him a conspiratorial look. "Can you please not mention this to anyone right away? Just so I have time to file the story?"

Nathan thought for a moment. "Yes, all right. Though I can't lie to the police if I see them. This might break the case."

There was a ping, and Nathan dug in the recliner for his mobile.

"Speak of the devil," he said, reading a text. "Here's Malloy now. They're headed to the Bolt—we meet there once a month with Harold. Thirty years we've been doing it." He tapped in a reply, sighing again. "Now it's just me and Malloy and William and Birdhouse."

"Gwilym Birdhouse?" I did a double take. "The singer?"

"The very one. He dabbles a bit as a collector. English esoterica, Elizabethan, mostly. Fancies himself a modern antiquarian. Are you a fan?"

"He was after my time. I didn't even know he was still performing."

"I'm not sure he is. But he made enough to keep himself happy. He raises sheep in the Hebrides or Faeroe Islands, one of those places. Orkney. Sheep for wool, not eating—he's a vegan."

"So is Birdhouse his real name?"

"Haven't the slightest. He's Malloy's friend more than mine. Harold could get along with anybody. And Birdhouse was a customer, so . . ."

Nathan made a show of pinching his nose. "You learn to make excuses for differences of opinion. I think he's a crackpot. You can make up your own mind about his music. Handel, that's my style."

Nathan's mobile pinged again. This time his eyebrows shot up when he looked at the screen. He raised a finger to me, spoke to whoever was on the other end, and wended his way into the hall.

As soon as he was out of sight, I grabbed my bag. The conversation had been a washout. I'd wave goodbye as I left.

I made a cursory inspection of the boxes as I left the room. Most seemed destined for Oxfam. But near the door, a stack of books caught my eye, the top one a volume of Mick Rock's work. I paused to scan the other titles. Lillian Roxon's *Rock Encyclopedia*. Madonna's *Sex*. All in pretty bad shape, spines cracked, dust jackets missing. If I looked inside, I'd probably find seeds and stems left from back in the day.

Then a familiar title caught my attention. I stooped and carefully removed an oversize volume from the pile.

The cover was a black-and-white night shot of five people standing in an alley slick with rain. Battered metal trash cans, a junked car. The light from a streetlamp bleached their faces a featureless white. Jean-clad pipe-cleaner legs, cowboy boots, and filthy Keds. One figure faced the camera, his hand extended warningly, mouth a smeary wound.

The others were turned sideways, staring at something on the wet pavement, just out of the camera's line of sight. If you knew where to look, you'd see a bare foot protruding from a black puddle at the edge of the frame.

I saw it, because I knew where to look. I knew where to look because my name was on the cover.

CHAPTER 21

*D*ead Girls was the book that had made my reputation. Photos of the nascent downtown punk scene: outside and inside Max's and CBGB, reeking alleys, the back seat of Chevy Impalas where kids huffed Carbona. Pictures so grainy and underexposed you didn't know if you were looking at a living person or a mannequin or a corpse. Musicians and artists whose drug habits lasted longer than their careers; a beautiful girl whose boyfriend tied her off and split when her eyes rolled back in her head and her skin turned blue. A line of hunched-over figures waiting to score amid charred box springs and burning tires. Black-and-white photos I'd taken of myself, dressed up like Salome, or Judith beheading Holofernes.

The book got rapturous reviews. A year later, I was broke and broken, working in the Strand's stockroom to keep myself in speed and Jack Daniel's.

The sound of footsteps echoed from Nathan's hall. I jammed the book into my bag and scrambled to my feet.

"Well!" Nathan walked back into the room, flourishing his mobile like he'd just won the lottery. "Now, who do you think that was? Metropolitan Police—they're coming to talk to me. Saves me a trip to the station house. Though I always wanted to be in one of those interrogation rooms. See if it's like the movies."

"I'll get out of your way." I pushed past him into the hallway. "Thanks again for your help."

"My pleasure," he said as he opened the door. "Send me a link to your piece when it goes up. Did you want a photo?"

From the corner of my eye, I saw two policewomen heading up the sidewalk. "Not now. Gotta run if I'm going to make my deadline."

I shoved on my sunglasses and left with studied nonchalance, turning in the opposite direction from the cops. One of them stared at me as Nathan ushered her inside. When I reached the corner, I broke into a run, stopping at the first bus shelter I saw. I joined the queue to board a red double-decker, and slumped into an empty upstairs seat.

Quinn was going to kill me. The cop who'd seen me leaving Ballingstead's place would ask who I was: if she googled me, she'd find there was no Shelley Wilson at the *Tribune* or anywhere else. If CCTV had captured Gryffin and me in the Vale of Health, the same cop might recognize a six-foot woman with cropped black hair, wearing a motorcycle jacket and cowboy boots.

Plus I'd jogged Nathan's memory so that he recalled hearing something about Harold Vertigan and an exceedingly rare book—information he'd certainly pass on to the police. I reached into my bag for the whiskey and took a long swallow, finishing the bottle, and gazed out the bus window as we passed Trafalgar Square.

Quinn and I should bail, now, before I was recognized or Gryffin went to the cops. I tried calling Quinn on the burner. No answer.

I ran through my options. Ordinarily I'd opt for killing time in a bar, but Quinn would be royally pissed off that I'd screwed up my meeting with Ballingstead. Showing up drunk wouldn't be a good idea.

Still, Ballingstead had mentioned a place called the Bolt, which I assumed was a pub. I took out Gryffin's mobile and tried to figure out the best way to get there. Nathan would no doubt entertain the cops for as long as he could, reliving glory days of the London used-book trade. If I was lucky, I could get in and out of the Bolt before he arrived to meet his friends.

And, I had to admit, I was curious to see what Gwilym Birdhouse looked like now. I hadn't thought about him in decades. Not that

I'd ever thought of him much, or thought much of him. He'd made his reputation as a teenager in the late 1980s, long after my hey-day, an English singer/songwriter who had a foot in two camps: the moody psych-goth of bands like the Jesus and Mary Chain, or Love and Rockets, and the kind of low-key, slightly jazzy folk-rock that harkened back to Traffic's "John Barleycorn Must Die."

Birdhouse got lumped in with other eccentric English musicians—Robyn Hitchcock, Roy Harper, Julian Cope. Like Cope, he was more like a genuine, and genuinely odd, throwback whose songs, despite their psychedelic trappings and postpunk energy, reflected a deep yearning for an earlier time. An era that had never really existed, outside of village festivals where Morris dancers performed for American tourists hungry for a vision of Ye Olde England that never was.

Birdhouse had never gone out of fashion, because he'd never been *in* fashion. His lyrics involved puns and clever wordplay; he was a keyboard player, not a guitarist, and one of the few musicians who played a harp. I saw him perform only once, in the mid-nineties, when he opened for Alejandro Escovedo at the Bottom Line. Bird-house played his sole hit, a lachrymose ballad called "No One Knows You Like the Rain." He didn't endear himself to the audience by showing support for the Gulf War.

Still, Birdhouse continued to record albums like *Tree Songs* and *Houdini of Harrogate,* playing English summer festivals like Green Man and narrating podcasts about endangered species in the Hebrides. The last time he'd been on my radar was when he came out in favor of Brexit. Not the sort of company I wanted to keep. But beggars can't be choosers.

CHAPTER 22

I found the Bolt in a cobblestoned mews slick with moss and smelling faintly of garbage. A plaque identified the pub as the site of a former stable. In 1747, lightning struck the building; the horses managed to escape from their stalls and raced in flames through the nearby streets.

The Bolt's exterior appeared recently remodeled. Inside, women with Tesco bags at their feet chatted over lunch plates that had yet to be cleared away. Three men sat at a table by the window, too young by several decades to be Harold's friends. Behind the bar, a cheerful girl with an Eastern European accent and a shamrock tattooed above her wrist hovered over the register. I ordered a large whiskey and made a slow pass through the pub.

It was larger than it first seemed. A chalkboard listed the week's events—karaoke, darts tournament, 1980s Quiz Night. Near the restrooms, an arched doorway opened onto a second room. I stepped inside.

Two white men in late middle age sat at a long wooden table covered with empty pint glasses. One man, grossly overweight, wore a pink-and-green flannel shirt. Wisps of white hair streamed from his scalp like smoke. The other man had brush-cut iron-gray hair and blue eyes. The ruddy skin around his eyes was crinkled, as though he'd spent decades staring into the sun, and he had a tattoo on his neck of a red cross. He looked more like a long-haul truck driver than a bookdealer.

I wondered if these were Nathan's colleagues. The only other customers were an elderly man and woman with a dog lying placidly at their feet. I strolled past the two middle-aged men, feigning interest in the faded equine prints and old photos of mounted policemen on the walls.

"...have forgotten about it in a week. It's all just unbelievable. The police rang, I couldn't tell them a thing." The fat man jabbed a finger at his companion. "Not a thing. Sheila told them they could drop by, but they didn't."

I settled at a neighboring table, sipping my whiskey as I pretended to read my mobile.

"This will be ISIS, William," said the man with the brush-cut hair. "Up in Birmingham, they have a cell."

"Don't be daft. It's not the damned ISIS, Malloy!" the fat man exclaimed. "What the hell would terrorists want with Harold?" He reached for his pint glass. "You need to stop reading the Internet. This was a robbery. Someone wanted a book."

"You're wrong about that," his companion said. "It'll be the camel fuckers, mark my words."

The fat man—William—leaned across the table. "Shut your mouth, Malloy, you'll get us tossed."

Their conversation resumed at a lower volume. I caught snatches of it—Harold's name; the uselessness of the police; Malloy's theories about terrorism. Nothing useful.

After a few minutes of drinking and eavesdropping, I reached for my bag. I withdrew the copy of *Dead Girls,* then the *TLS,* and removed the page from *The Book of Lamps and Banners* from the magazine. It felt oddly supple beneath my fingers, more like suede than papyrus. I wanted to examine the manuscript text without being observed, so I opened *Dead Girls,* slipped the leaf inside, and lowered my face to the page.

It exuded a very faint scent. Not the dusty smell of old books or paper, but a strange, smoky odor, like charred wood and grilled meat, and also of carrion. I remembered what Harold had said about the volume's anthropodermic binding and quickly closed the book. A wave of nausea hit me, as when I first stared at Ludus Mentis.

After a few moments, the nausea passed. I glanced at Malloy and the fat man, who gazed into their pint glasses in stony silence. Harold must have been the peacemaker between the two. I sighed and again opened *Dead Girls,* taking care to avoid the papyrus sheet as I flipped to the introduction by Chris Makos:

> *At the age of twenty, Cassandra Neary is already an expert chronicler of the dark side of downtown. Look at these photographs if you dare. You won't easily forget what you see.*

There was Dee Dee onstage, pummeling his bass; Leee Childers flashing his Cheshire cat grin; Mickey Ruskin arguing with a drunken socialite at Max's. My then-girlfriend Jeannie reeled in the aftermath of a catfight with Sable Starr, blood streaming from her nose as she flipped off the camera. Stiv Bators. Jerry Nolan. Jim Carroll. A dozen people whose names I'd forgotten, and even more whose names I'd never known. All of them were dead.

I turned to a self-portrait—me as Joan of Arc beside a blazing trash can, my gray eyes incandescent with the glory of speed. Leather jacket at my feet, halo of flaming ash around my head. My scuffed Tony Lamas, their steel tips already battered from bar fights. I was nineteen years old and immortal.

"Ah, here he is," exclaimed the fat man, William. "Tweet-tweet."

I looked up to see a man heading toward the other table. He wore felted boots and a heavy shearling jacket and carried a bottle of Pellegrino. As he drew alongside Malloy, he unwound a long gray scarf from his neck, his head emerging like a turtle's.

"Hey, Malloy. William. I came as fast as I could, it's impossible to get anywhere from the island."

His round cheeks had coarsened with rosacea, and his narrow blue eyes now gleamed moistly behind horn-rimmed glasses, but he was unmistakably Gwilym Birdhouse. Same wild thatch of hair, more gray than blond; same ripe baritone.

William gave him a curt nod and muttered, "Gwilym."

But Malloy stood to embrace the newcomer and drew him into the empty seat beside him. "Gwilym! I'm surprised you got here so quickly."

Birdhouse shrugged. "Well, circumstances. Can you believe it? I always thought it'd be you, Malloy." He grasped Malloy's arm with a fond look, barely acknowledging William. "A sad day."

"Nothing to drink?" asked William, taking a sip from his own pint. Birdhouse lifted his bottle of sparkling water, and William snorted. "What about all your John Barleycorn blather? That just for the punters?"

Malloy slapped his palm on the table. "Leave off, Will."

Birdhouse waved as though dispersing a bad smell. "No offense taken. He's upset. I'm upset." He looked around the room, glancing from the elderly couple to me. "Where's Nathan?"

"Still talking to the police. Just texted he won't make it. Have you heard from them?"

"Not yet." Birdhouse extracted himself from his shearling coat. Underneath he wore baggy black jeans and a long-sleeved black turtleneck. "I'm hoping to avoid that."

William picked up his glass and raised it to the others. " 'Shall we never see a picture of "We Three"?' "

"Should be five," said Malloy. "To Harold."

CHAPTER 23

The three men leaned across the table, speaking quietly. Now and then Malloy boomed out an epithet, to be *shhh*ed by William. The older couple with the dog had left. Birdhouse retreated to the bar and returned with another bottle of Pellegrino. He settled back alongside Malloy, joining the conversation in between bouts of texting and reading on his mobile.

I didn't hear much other than Malloy's continued insistence that ISIS was behind Harold's death. William inevitably rose to the bait, but Birdhouse only regarded Malloy with faint amusement, as though watching the antics of an ill-behaved toddler. I decided I'd give it another fifteen minutes, then split. I'd wasted enough time.

And if Nathan unexpectedly showed up, I didn't want to be seen. I'd find another bar and kill the next hour or two, till it was time to meet Quinn.

Yet I doubted there was enough whiskey to kill my growing dread. I blinked, trying to dispel the spidery black threads that knit and unraveled across my vision. After a minute I realized I was grinding my teeth—the beginnings of withdrawal. I licked my lips, tasting blood, picked up *Dead Girls,* and opened it to the leaf from *The Book of Lamps and Banners.*

I've seen reproductions of medieval manuscripts in books. These pictures had the same saturated pigmentation, eerily unfaded by the centuries. Or millennia, if the book was as old as Gryffin claimed it was. Lapis and scarlet; saffron and iridescent green; a delicate lavender that looked like the first flush of spring in a crocus that has yet to fully open.

Most striking was a flame-bright crimson that resembled a screenshot of an actual fire, not something created with ground pigments. Again, I felt a shiver of the same terror that had sickened me when Tindra unleashed her app.

My apprehension wasn't eased by the illustrations embellishing the unreadable text. One showed a woman with the lower body of a squidlike creature. Her face was that of a lamprey, and her tentacles ended in talons that grasped squirming figures that might have been human.

The illustration was no more than two inches square. Yet its background was meticulously, psychedelically, rendered. Myriad branches grew from a single trunk, each branch crowned with a human head. Multiple suns blazed in the lapis sky, along with swastikas and arrows that, close-up, looked less like arrows than rockets, complete with fins and contrails.

The longer I stared at the page, the less crazy Tindra's theory seemed. Symbols and images repeated in a manner that seemed commensurate with some kind of code. But I had no idea what, exactly, I was looking at. One moment, it would all be in focus. The next, an image would blur, or even seem to change shape and color: the lamprey now a crimson poppy, the tentacles folds of a long robe.

Same with the picture of a decapitated head with too many eyes to count. First it was a head. Then it was the cratered surface of the moon. Then a head again. Then the moon.

Drugs and booze make me crazy, but not that crazy. I wondered if the papyrus had been impregnated with a hallucinogen, or even a poison. Could a poison still be active after two thousand years? I didn't think so, but there was definitely something strange and frightening going on, something that seemed to defy the little I knew about medieval illumination, and maybe physics.

And also history: When this book was written, did anyone, even Aristotle, know there were craters on the moon?

This is a very advanced philosophical artifact. And I can guarantee you that some of the people who've owned it over the years knew exactly what it was.

I turned the sheet over. Compared with the phantasmagoric images on the other side, the runic lettering here appeared crude and much older—it was easy to imagine someone scratching it onto the page with a sharpened stick.

And Harold had been right. Unlike the other written text, the runes weren't inscribed in black, but a very faint rusty brown. If it was blood, the effort to write must have been painstaking, each line barely a hair's breadth. Harold had speculated that this was a formula, or perhaps a spell.

Beware, this is power...

I jumped as someone pounded on the neighboring table.

"Listen to yourself! That's shite talk and you know it, Malloy!" the fat man shouted. "Gwilym, don't encourage him!"

"Shite? How many white faces did you see on the Tube getting here?" Malloy stood to yank a windbreaker from a wall peg. "White genocide, that's what this is."

He barreled toward the door. William got to his feet and called after him. "That's right, do a runner."

"Let him go, Will," said Birdhouse mildly.

"Go back to your bloody sheep," William retorted. "All you do is wind him up, and you know it."

The fat man snatched up his overcoat and stormed out. Birdhouse remained where he was, unfazed by the outburst, sipping Pellegrino as he scrolled through his mobile.

I looked back down at the papyrus sheet. I knew I should put it away, but the images drew me like a drug. If a single page could have such a powerful effect, what would it be like to look through the entire *Book of Lamps and Banners*?

And if Tindra was right, and it really was an ancient manual for mind control—what would her app be capable of, if she used this to upgrade Ludus Mentis from the beta version?

I glanced up to see Gwilym Birdhouse watching me. I quickly closed *Dead Girls,* straightened, and stared back at him, trying to appear composed. Birdhouse's expression betrayed no sign that he'd seen what I'd been looking at. His narrow blue eyes were watchful, slightly amused. Not the gaze of a man in the throes of grief; more like someone waiting to see if a slightly thick friend had finally figured out the punch line of a joke.

"Birdhouse, right? Big fan," I said, and finished my whiskey. "Your friends there seemed upset."

Birdhouse nodded. "Yeah. We had some bad news."

"Sorry to hear that."

"A good friend was killed. Murdered." He reached to scratch behind one ear, exposing a neck tattoo similar to Malloy's: a rippling flag, a red cross on a white ground. "It's quite a shock."

"That's horrible. Did they catch who did it?"

"Not yet. Not as far as I know, anyway." He glanced at his mobile, shook his head. "Metropolitan Police are useless. They'd have to bring in Scotland Yard or Interpol. And they won't do that, not now. Waste of resources with everything else going on."

I hesitated, then asked, "Who was he? Your friend?"

"A bookseller."

Birdhouse's mobile pinged. He read the incoming text, set down his mobile, and again stared at me. His gaze shifted from my face to the copy of *Dead Girls.* He picked up the bottle of Pellegrino and stood.

"See you," he said. As he walked past, I caught a powerful whiff of something redolent of wet dog.

Other than me, the room was empty. After a minute the girl from behind the register entered and cleared away the empty glasses. She returned to wipe the tables down, and the doggy odor dissolved into ammonia and lemon. I tugged on my leather jacket, got my bag, and went outside.

The sulfurous haze had deepened to a bruised green. Spatters of rain struck my face. I pulled up my collar and hurried toward the street.

After a few steps, I remembered the Aran sweater my father used to wear when he was out raking leaves, its strong animal scent when it got wet. Lanolin. Gwilym Birdhouse smelled like that. Unsurprising, given his shearling coat and felted boots, and the fact that he raised sheep. What was it with musicians retreating into country life? Paul and Linda McCartney holed up on Kintyre in Scotland. Ian Anderson overseeing a salmon fishery. Birdhouse and sheep...

Halfway down the cobblestoned alley, I looked up to see a figure blocking my way. Someone put an arm around my throat and yanked me into an abandoned entryway.

"Quiet now," a voice murmured in my ear.

CHAPTER 24

S hush. You're fine. Don't make a scene." Lyla covered my mouth with her palm, looked at Gryffin beside her. "Tell her, go on."

"Tindra's gone," he stammered. "Sometime last night, she just took off."

I grunted in dismay, and Lyla nodded. "That's right," she said, and I felt the pressure on my windpipe relax. "You're not going to shout, are you?"

I shook my head. She released me, and I turned to Gryffin, fighting to catch my breath. "Took off where?"

I saw then that his lip was split. Dried blood flecked his chin. "Christ, what happened to you?"

I reached for his face, and he knocked my hand away. "I told you. Tindra's gone. Lyla found her. Or didn't find her. She thought I did something." He gingerly touched his lip. "I think *she* did."

"You shut your mouth," said Lyla. She carried a backpack and wore the same clothes as when I'd last seen her—black anorak and trousers, black boots.

I looked at her, confused. "So where is she?"

"I don't know." Lyla sounded scared. "She's always up early, five at the latest. Some nights she doesn't sleep at all. I didn't see her by six, so I texted her, then again at half past. When I went to her room, she was gone. Her and Bunny."

"Maybe she took a walk," I said. "Did she leave a note?"

"She didn't answer my text. Not a word." Her voice broke, and she clutched her arms to her chest. "Something's happened to her."

"What about your brother?"

"He's gone, too. Before I woke. I think he must have heard her leave and gone after her." Her eyes filled with tears. "If something happens to her, I'll kill myself."

I frowned. "How'd you find me?"

"She tracked my mobile on the Find My Phone app," said Gryffin. "You're a goddamn genius, Cass. Give it back to me."

I shoved the mobile at him and stepped away, raising my hands.

"I'm done," I said, looking from Gryffin to Lyla. "This is none of my business. Not my book, not my friend, not my brother, none of it. So fuck off."

Gryffin blocked me as I started toward the street. "She has a gun," he warned. "I wouldn't mess with her, Cass."

"I don't want to mess with her. I just want to get the hell out of here."

"You can't do that. Neither can I. It's gotten out of control. If Tindra's gone to the police—"

"Why would you care?" I retorted. "That's what you wanted to do."

"You were right. It would be stupid." He removed his glasses, stared at them as though trying to remember their purpose, then shoved them back on. "I'll be all over Harold's phone records, his computer. Someone may have seen us. Or CCTV."

"We're innocent. Call a lawyer."

"Tindra wouldn't go to the police." Lyla edged between us. "She must have gone to meet someone."

"Who?"

Lyla shook her head. "I have no idea. But it's the only thing that makes sense. Whoever has the book...they got in touch with her, and she's gone to meet them."

I remembered Tindra in her garage. Her mobile had chimed, and she'd seemed agitated by whatever message she'd received. I averted my gaze from Lyla and Gryffin.

"Look, just let me go, okay?" I said. "You know I'm not talking to the cops."

"I'd rather you stayed with us." Lyla pointedly slipped her hand beneath her anorak. "You were the last person to see her—she came back into the room, she said you'd left, and then she went to bed. Did she say anything to you? I wouldn't have let you go, you know," she added, a veiled threat.

"She seemed fine. We didn't really talk. She seemed tired, is all."

The sound of church bells echoed from the street as a clock tolled two. I was supposed to meet Quinn in an hour. My stomach turned at the thought of losing him again. "Shit! I've got to be somewhere and meet someone."

"Me too." Gryffin glanced at Lyla. "I'd rather not deal with the cops, either."

I snorted. "You've changed your tune."

"After everything in Maine, I had to hire someone to scrub my connection to my father online. If news gets out about this, it'll all come up again."

I wanted to point out this wasn't a matter of if but when. I headed toward the street, trying to ignore the sound of their footsteps behind me.

CHAPTER 25

We rode in the same subway car without speaking. I'd decided against trying to make a break for it. Lyla wouldn't pull a gun in the Underground, but pointing me out to a transit cop would do the job.

She dogged my every step, a black-clad phantom. Gryffin stared at the floor. Now and then he'd withdraw his mobile and try fruitlessly to get a signal. When we reached Embankment, Lyla jerked her head toward the door, and we followed her out.

Yellow mist enveloped us as we left the station. Above us loomed Hungerford Bridge, spanning the Thames. Helicopters circled noisily overhead, and a siren wailed in the distance. I squinted through the haze to see police officers in riot gear among the pedestrians heading across the bridge.

"What's that about?" I asked.

"The Nazis," said Lyla. "They're gathering by Mile End."

"Is that near here?"

"No. But that's South Bank." She pointed to the buildings that lined the other side of the river. "It's a huge tourist area. No one's taking chances."

"Are they even allowed to march?"

"No. But they can gather in a public space if they call it a private barbecue or picnic. Anti-fascists drive themselves crazy, trying to figure out where they'll pop up—they organize everything peer-to-peer, on social media mostly. But late last night, someone twigged that they'll be having an outdoor party today, to honor 'English and Italian friendship.'"

I laughed. "Honoring what?"

"Mosley meeting with Mussolini in 1932. They call it 'the right to offend.' I think you have something similar in your country," she added, "only you call it 'freedom of speech.'"

Gryffin drew up next to us. "Have you heard from your brother?" Lyla shook her head.

We walked toward the park entrance, Lyla at my side, Gryffin falling a few steps behind. My jaw clenched involuntarily; needles scratched my retina, leaving black streaks. Despite the steady infusion of Vyvanse over the last few days, I was going into amphetamine withdrawal. Haze reduced the park to a grayish-yellow scrim. I saw no sign of Quinn.

I slowed to let Gryffin catch up with me. "What do you think is going on?" I asked.

"I don't know." He looked miserable. "I keep thinking I'll wake up. But then I haven't gone to sleep yet."

"You think Tindra was kidnapped?"

"How? You saw that place — it's a bunker."

"Yeah, but why is that? The three of them holed up with all those arcade games, it's like living in a bomb shelter with Oddjob and Gogo Yubari."

I looked up as another copter droned above the river. "Wouldn't a tech lord have better security? I thought all those Silicon Valley gurus have Gulfstreams to escape the apocalypse. Fly them off to New Zealand or some missile silo in Kansas."

Ahead of us, Lyla had stopped to check her mobile again. I looked at Gryffin, then lowered my voice. "Look. Tindra's developing that app — it's why she wants *The Book of Lamps and Banners*. She thinks the book is actually a code, like a beta version of what she's working on."

I half expected him to laugh. Instead he cocked his head, musing. "Well, it makes sense, kind of. Back then they didn't have scientific language for metallurgy, or winemaking, stuff like that. I've seen fourteenth-century manuscripts filled with pictures of severed heads being boiled in pots, dragons and burning towers, people chopped to pieces. It looks like a depiction of a murder, but it's actually an alchemical recipe for extracting base metals. *The Book of Lamps and Banners* predates that, but it's entirely possible that it contains its own visual language. Like a secret code that only a very few people would understand."

We both glanced to where Lyla stood gazing at her mobile. "What if it really was written by Aristotle?" he said. "It could change our understanding of everything we know. It might contain not just ancient knowledge, but forgotten knowledge. Things we never knew. Maybe things we wouldn't want to know."

My neck prickled as I recalled Tindra saying almost the exact same thing. "Then why the fuck did you sell it to Harold and not a university or museum?"

"I messed up. I got greedy. The longer I had it, the more I looked at it...all I could think about was how much it might be worth. But then I got nervous about hanging on to it—it seemed like bad luck, like..."

"'The stuff that dreams are made on.'"

"Or night terrors."

CHAPTER 26

Victoria Embankment Park was nearly empty, trees and outbuildings shrouded in fog. A few dog walkers strolled along the damp pavement, charges straining at their leashes. A man lay stretched out on a bench, carrier bags full of clothing on the ground in front of him.

Otherwise the park seemed deserted, except for a lanky figure in a black watch cap, black leather jacket, and battered biker boots, pacing in front of a large statue.

"That your friend?" asked Lyla.

I said nothing. As the three of us drew closer, the figure looked up. He took a drag from a cigarette, tossed it onto the grass behind him, and fixed me with a cold stare.

"Surprise," I said.

Quinn started toward us. "What the fuck, Cass?"

Gryffin shot me an alarmed look. Ignoring him, Quinn gripped my arm.

"Hey!" Lyla called out.

I raised my free hand. "It's okay." She halted beside Gryffin as Quinn pulled me behind the statue.

"What the hell are you doing, Cass?"

I stared at his face. One cheek was badly bruised. Blood trickled from a puncture wound on his chin. "Jesus, Quinn — what happened?"

"Nothing." He gestured angrily toward the others. "Who are they?"

"She's the bodyguard for the girl who bought the book. Lyla. That's Gryffin."

"Gryffin? The guy you fucked? Why's he looking at me like that?"

"You're looking the same way at him."

Quinn gave a sharp laugh. "This is like that club nobody wants to belong to if they let you in. Only the club is *you*."

I reached to touch his chin, but he took my wrist and lowered it.

"I ran into some friends."

His voice dropped. "Listen to me, Cassie. Your guy got nailed in Hampstead? I checked around and came up cold. Out-of-network killing. It was no one I know, and no one that anyone I know knows. My guess is it was a simple robbery. Or someone had a beef with your guy—owed him money, deal gone bad, who knows."

"Gryffin says that's not how the book business works."

"The fuck does he know? Maybe *he* killed him. Oh, wait—he was banging you in the wine cellar. So scratch that."

"So now what?"

"Now nothing. If it's a professional hit, forget about it. We do not want to get involved. If it was an amateur, they'll catch him." He pulled me close. "You better hope they don't catch *you*. You and Mister Rogers there must've left prints all over—once they dust it, that flat is going to glow like it's radioactive. But I do have a line on a couple people interested in that book, if we can find it. Serious money, Cass."

I touched the puncture wound on his face. "Who did this?"

He laced his fingers with mine. "Someone who's sorry. Don't worry about it."

I leaned against him, slid my hand under his jacket and shirt. As I felt the complicated topography of scars on his chest, I stiffened. Quinn looked down at me. "What is it?"

"The guy who was murdered? Someone drew something like the Gripping Beast on his forehead."

"What are you talking about?"

"When I found the body, there was a symbol drawn on Harold's forehead in blood. I forgot about it till now—the Gripping Beast reminded me. It wasn't exactly the same—"

I snatched up some twigs from the ground, broke them into similar lengths, and crouched to arrange them on the sidewalk at Quinn's feet. Three overlapping triangles, all the same size.

"Like this," I said. "It's not that exactly, but close. Do you recognize it?"

Quinn stooped to move a stick so it aligned more neatly with the others. "Are you sure?"

I nodded. He fumbled in his pocket for a cigarette, dropped it, and scooped it up. I'd seen Quinn nod out, seen him bleeding after being pistol-whipped, watched him garrote a man with a guitar wire. But I'd rarely seen him genuinely disconcerted.

"What does it mean?" I asked.

"It's a valknut. An Odinist symbol, like the Gripping Beast. It's big with the Brand." I gave him a blank look. "The Aryan Brotherhood."

"The prison gang?"

He nodded. "But Odinists, yeah, with them the valknut can be a religious thing. Remember Iceland? Like that. And sometimes a gang will use the valknut, too, especially in prisons. A lot of Odinists are just pagans—you know, like Asatruars. But some are definitely white supremacists."

"I saw a bunch of them in the Tube last night—they're organizing some kind of Nazi march."

"That's why all the cops and copters are out, dollface. Why the hell didn't you tell me about seeing this on your guy Harold's face before now?"

"Too much other shit came down too fast." I pointed at the sticks at our feet, triangles within triangles. "Do you have one?"

"A valknut tattoo? No. Too many neo-Nazis use it now. Like I said, I'm not a believer."

"So what would it mean to someone who was?"

He sucked at his cigarette, hollow cheeked. "Shit, I don't know. I knew a guy was into it—an Odinist, not a Nazi. It's something about being among the chosen, so when you die, the Valkyries recognize you and take you to Valhalla. But I've also seen it carved on a corpse, as a warning."

"Will the police know what it means?"

"How obvious was it?"

"Not much. By the time the cops got there, it probably just looked like smeared blood."

"Well, they monitor far-right groups here. The Defenders of Albion, Combat Eighteen—a lot of groups use symbols like this. But a neo-Nazi symbol won't be the first thing the cops are looking for, if they're investigating a stolen rare book."

Quinn tilted his head back as another helicopter droned overhead. "God, these fucking Nazis, they're everywhere now. Cassie, how the hell do you get into this shit?"

"Does it matter?"

Quinn sighed. "Not at this point." He tossed his cigarette and grasped my shoulders, turning me so that my back was to Gryffin and Lyla. He withdrew something from his jeans pocket and took my hand.

"Here." He hesitated before sliding something into my palm—a tiny bag of white powder. "I called in a favor. Against my better judgment. It was definitely more trouble than it's worth."

I leaned into him, opened the plastic bag, and scooped some powder into my pinkie nail. No telltale blue glitter or crystalline spark to indicate this was anything but low-grade crank. Not an awful lot of it, either. I ducked my head and inhaled, scooped out a second hit, and snorted it. It was like taking a blowtorch to my nostrils.

"Jesus!" Tears streamed from my eyes as I closed the bag and shoved it into my pocket. "What's that cut with, Comet?"

"Probably."

Garbage or not, within seconds I felt a familiar hole blasted inside my skull. My entire body vibrated. I stared up through the yellow haze, waiting for the rush to fade before I spoke.

"Thank you, baby," I whispered.

Quinn regarded me through slitted eyes, already regretting what he'd done. "You won't thank me when they have to jump-start your heart."

I laughed. I was immortal again. And I didn't need a camera—I saw everything the world had been hiding from me. Cracks in the pavement opened to reveal what lay beneath, a spangled map mirrored what was burned against my eyeballs...

"Cass? Cassie?"

I blinked. Quinn held my face in his hands, staring at me in concern. I grinned. "That's pretty good shit."

"I thought you were checking out on me."

I laughed again. "Uh-uh. Checking in."

"Christ. Maybe we should just split now, Cassie. I'll figure something out."

He kissed me, hard. I closed my eyes, riding another rush, when Lyla's voice cut through the rumble of helicopters and traffic. I turned to see her staring at her mobile in horror. Gryffin grabbed it from her, looked at the screen, then at me. Even from where I stood, I could see his face had gone pale.

"Cassie, don't," Quinn pleaded. But I'd already run to pry the mobile from Gryffin's hand.

CHAPTER 27

The screen showed a picture of a sleeping animal surrounded by underbrush. It was a few seconds before I realized the image was not a still frame, but a video clip: the animal's chest moved very slightly as it breathed. Then it grew still.

"What the fuck." I glanced at Quinn. "That's her dog. Tindra's."

I played the clip again. The time stamp was barely two hours earlier. There was no indication as to where it was recorded.

I looked at Lyla. "What is this? Who sent it?"

"My brother. It came from Tindra, she forwarded it to him."

She took the mobile, swiping so I could read a series of texts:

found book
erik svarlight
need help

"Someone poisoned the dog?" I asked Lyla. She nodded. "But if the dog was with her, how could they poison it?"

"I don't know!"

Gryffin frowned. "Who's Erik Svarlight?"

"Svarlight—it's not a person, not necessarily. It could be a band or something." I glanced at Quinn. "Look, I don't know what it is. But I saw some white supremacists wearing Svarlight T-shirts, in the Underground. Swedish guys."

"Tindra's saying this guy has the book." Gryffin turned to Lyla. "Right?"

"I told you, I don't know! Let me think!"

She strode toward a shuttered outdoor café, found shelter beneath its awning, and bent over her mobile. Quinn pulled me to his side.

"Come on, Cassie," he said. "This is done."

"Done?" The crank lit up my synapses like a sparkler. "It's not done—she found the book! This guy Erik, he's kidnapped her or something."

"Doesn't sound like that to me." Quinn watched Lyla, now frantically texting. "Do you know him? Erik whoever?"

"No. But Tindra said he has the book."

"No, she texted *found book*. It doesn't mean he has it."

I pushed at him in frustration. "Bullshit. He killed her freaking dog. She needs help."

"So she got herself in over her head." Quinn touched his bruised cheek, scowling. "Why the hell do you care?"

"The book," I snapped. "Remember? You said you can find a buyer, we can get serious money. Now we have a line on where she is, so we *can* find it."

"You're out of your fucking mind, Cass. If she has the book, you think she's gonna give it to you? And it doesn't even sound like she does have it—this guy Erik does, maybe. And if a bunch of Nazis are wearing his T-shirt, he's over there—"

He pointed across the river. "At the demonstration. And if you think going there's a good idea, you really *are* out of your mind. We're pulling the plug on this."

He grabbed my arm. As I started to argue, Lyla came running back.

"Victoria Park," she said breathlessly. "Tommy just texted, that's where he thinks Tindra and Erik are."

"I thought this was Victoria Park," said Gryffin.

"Victoria Embankment Park," said Lyla. "Victoria Park's in the East End. That's where they're marching."

She started back toward the Underground station. Gryffin watched her as another helicopter roared east into the haze. "I guess I better go, too," he said reluctantly. "If there's a snowball's chance in hell my book shows up."

"*Your* book?" I retorted. "You sold it to Harold, and he sold it to Tindra."

"There's a hold on the transaction." He shook his head. "And why would a Nazi even want it?"

"Why not? Everyone else does."

He turned and headed after Lyla, and Quinn tugged at my arm. "Cassie."

I twitched away from him. The copter's drone grew into a thundering pulse as a man hissed my name in a darkened alley.

Cass, Cass . . .

A knife glinted in the man's hand, and his arm extended toward me. I froze as a ghostly car cruised past, disappearing into the Thames beneath Hungerford Bridge.

I could tell, when I met you, Tindra whispered in my ear. *Don't you find that sometimes? That you just know?*

"Cass." Quinn's tone was urgent. "Cassie, come on."

The roaring in my head diminished to a dull buzz, a wasp trapped inside my skull. I took a few deep breaths, my jaw clenching as I struggled to speak.

"I can't just leave her."

"Why not?"

"I can't explain. Just . . ." I looked up into Quinn's cold green eyes. "Look, I have to go. And we need the money."

"I don't give a fuck about the money."

"That's not what you said this morning."

"This morning all this shit hadn't exploded in our hands, Cass!"

"We're broke and here illegally."

"I can find work here."

"What work? Killing more guys for the Russians? You want to go back to prison?" I scanned the horizon above South Bank.

"Cassie, baby. Nobody is going to find that book." Quinn spoke slowly and barely above a whisper, warning signs that I ignored. "It's on a plane to Miami or Moscow or Dubai or——"

"It's not. He has it, and Tindra's with him."

"Who the hell are you talking about?"

"Erik or whoever killed her dog."

I stared at Quinn, razor-eyed: the only way he was going to stop me was by force. I knew he wasn't beyond that. But after half a minute, he let go of me. "Goddamn it, I should never have gotten that shit for you. You're crazy enough when you're not tweaking."

I punched his arm. "I'm not tweaking. Where's Victoria Park?"

"Near Mile End. The Tube goes right there." He gestured toward the station entrance. "That chick Lyla, she seems to know what she's doing. Try to stay close to her. Jesus." He tugged at his watch cap. "I should have my head examined."

"Come with me." My lips brushed his bruised cheek. "We can do it together. It'll be fun."

"That ain't gonna happen, baby. There'll be cops all over. And I might run into some people I know, which would not be a good thing. If they start kettling, get the hell out. Your burner still got juice?"

"I think so."

"Whatever you do, don't lose it. I'll call or text where to meet me later. You do the same."

He stared into my eyes, his battered face a reflection of my own. "Do you really want to do this, Cassie? It sounds like the crank talking." He kissed my forehead and pushed me away. "Go fast."

I nodded and loped toward the station. When I glanced back, Quinn lifted a hand to me, turned, and walked off into the fog.

CHAPTER 28

I found Gryffin and Lyla waiting on the platform. Lyla didn't acknowledge me, but Gryffin appeared relieved. "You're here," he said.

I didn't reply, just kicked at a discarded vaping capsule until the train arrived and we hopped on. Lyla stood by the door. Gryffin pointed to a pair of empty seats, and I joined him. As soon as the train rattled back into the tunnel, he turned to me.

"Who the hell is that guy?"

"None of your business."

"No, I mean it. Who is he? Quinn, right?"

"Just shut up, okay?"

"I'm not going to shut up." His voice rose, and an old man in a white thobe glanced at us warily. "Tell me—"

"I already told you—if you don't shut the fuck up, I'm getting off at the next stop."

"Okay, then just tell me what you're doing with him," he whispered. "He looks like a thug. He *is* a thug. He looks like trouble, Cass."

"He is."

"I thought you were cleaning yourself up."

"Because I got a haircut? Are you some kind of idiot?"

"He gave you drugs, right? What was that, heroin?"

"You really are an idiot. Heroin puts you to sleep. Do I look like I'm asleep?"

"Tell me why you're with someone like that. You're smart, you could have a career again. This is like a death wish, Cass."

I said nothing. He lowered his head until it was barely an inch from mine. *"Tell me."*

My attempt at silence lost out to crank-fueled logorrhea. "Because he's the only thing I ever cared about. Because when I met him we were seventeen and I couldn't take my fucking eyes off him and after that I couldn't keep my camera off him. We were together for a while, then he took up with someone else, and then he got popped for breaking into a pharmacy and went to prison and I never saw him again. I thought I'd go crazy and then I *did* go crazy. The floor dropped out of my whole fucking life and I haven't stopped falling since. All this time I thought he was dead and then a few months ago he gets in touch and . . ."

I stopped, sucking in air like I'd just been saved from drowning. "And he's gone, he keeps leaving and every time I think it's the last time. You think heroin is a drug?" I jabbed Gryffin with my finger and he flinched. "*Quinn's* a fucking drug and if he's dead I'm dead, too."

Gryffin stared at me, let his breath out in a low whoosh. "But he's not dead, Cass. And Quinn's not a drug. He's just a person, a screwed-up person, and you're letting him screw *you* up."

I shook my head. "He's keeping me alive. He's—"

I lurched to my feet and stumbled over to Lyla by the door. "Who's Erik? Do you know? Does she know him? Tindra?"

"I lost my signal before I could check."

Lyla stared stonily at an ad for cheap flights to Spain. I continued without pausing for breath.

"And someone killed her dog—that's fucked up, right? Why would she agree to meet someone who'd kill her dog? I don't get it. Is she, like, a secret Nazi? Is it even safe for you and your brother to be at this rally?"

Lyla looked at me like I was something she'd peeled from her shoe. "What, you think a colored girl shouldn't walk into a Nazi parade?"

"I mean, yeah."

"You don't know what the fuck you mean."

"Yeah, okay, I get it, I totally get it. Stupid white American. But this guy Erik, do you have any idea who he might be?"

Silence.

"Okay, but not someone good, right?" I felt my face flush, my rant morphing into amphetamine rage. "Someone bad. Fucking Nazis. Maybe that's who killed Harold, fucking Nazis—"

"You freak, you're so spun you can't even see straight," she murmured, and stepped on my foot, hard. She stared pointedly at two white couples sitting across from us, the women wearing ankle boots and puffer coats, the men in flannel shirts and barn jackets. All sported buttons that featured a red oak leaf intersected by a lightning bolt. Svarlight.

One of the women saw me looking at her. She pushed a lock of brown hair behind her ear, glanced at Lyla, then turned to whisper something to the man beside her. He said something under his breath and they both laughed. Beside me I felt Lyla stiffen. I clenched my hands into fists. Neither of us spoke again.

CHAPTER 29

Mile End station was in the East End, north of the river. As the train slowed, Lyla pulled up the hood of her anorak to hide her face. Gryffin shoved his hands in his pockets and made a point of not meeting anyone's gaze. I stared back defiantly and wild-eyed at anyone who glanced my way.

"Stop it," Gryffin said nervously. "You look like one of them."

"Good," I snapped. "Maybe they won't fuck with us."

As we exited the station, a steady stream of people filed onto the escalators, nearly all white. Boisterous young men sporting shaved heads and motocross jackets, older people who would have fit right into the audience at a midwestern NPR fundraiser. A few small groups displayed the Svarlight logo, though they were outnumbered by guys supporting DOA, Defenders of Albion, or other UK groups. Several families had kids in tow, which made it look less like a nationalist march than a Waldorf school picnic, without the angst.

A lot of people carried hand-lettered signs with messages like MY JOB WENT TO EU, BRING IT BACK!, or ADJUNCT = NO FUTURE. There were counterdemonstrators, too, flaunting slogans like NO TO FASCISM, HOPE NOT HATE, and DOA IS DOA. For the moment, the two factions kept a safe distance from each other.

A tall black woman strode past us, murmuring an invective. "Great," Gryffin said. "They really do think you're one of them."

Lyla whirled to poke him with a gloved finger. "No one told you to come. Keep your mouth shut or fuck off, both of you. I mean it."

I met Gryffin's gaze, willing him to leave. He was nothing but deadweight; Lyla might lead me to Tindra. But Gryffin just jammed his hands in his pockets and walked on.

A greenway had been constructed around Mile End, incorporating a retired overpass and landscaped with leafless birches and plume grass. It reminded me of the High Line, only with the Regent's Canal running alongside it. Despite the greasy fog and chill wind, children's playgrounds lent the scene a festive air, as did the sounds of distant laughter and an occasional burst of applause.

Lyla headed toward the canal towpath. After fifteen minutes, we left the path for a well-trodden stretch that led to a busy street. On the other side was a vast expanse of green lawns and plane trees, benches lining a broad walkway.

I ran to catch up with Lyla, who was scanning her mobile.

"She's done something to her mobile, or he has—I can't track her. And I still have no signal." She glanced at a helicopter hovering in the near distance. "Might be they're jamming the signals for crowd control. But you were right..."

She indicated two blond guys sporting Svarlight's oak leaf and lightning bolt on their shirts. "If this Erik is connected with them, maybe he won't be that hard to find. He might be one of the speakers."

"Hiding in plain sight?" I shot her a dubious look.

"I don't know. Maybe my brother's already found her. That's what I hope."

We crossed the street and joined the crowd entering Victoria Park.

The explosive exhilaration I'd felt with the first few hits of crank had settled into a steady, shining buzz. I craved more but needed to pace myself. Gryffin walked ahead of us, messenger bag slung over one shoulder, his tall frame stooped like a disconsolate commuter's. Lyla remained focused on her mobile.

"Any news?" I asked after a few minutes.

"No." Her hood slipped back, and I saw her eyes were red. "It was so fucking stupid of her to come here. She knew Tommy would go after her. She knows it's not safe for him."

" 'Safe'?"

"Since Afghanistan? He has issues. Tindra hoped her app would help him. That was one of the reasons she developed it."

"Ludus Mentis?" I felt a bolt of panic. "He hasn't tried it, has he?"

"I don't know. Does it matter?"

It might, I thought. *A lot.* But I said nothing.

The park was so big that, once inside, the demonstrators hardly seemed an organized crowd, just scattered groups making the best of a dreary afternoon. There were definitely many more cops here. Many more scary-looking people, too, including a lot of heavily tattooed, booted men who chanted and carried signs with that distinctive white flag with a red cross.

JOBS-FIRST!

3,000,000 ISLAMISTS IN ENGLAND

100%

TAKE BACK CONTROL

WHITE GENOCIDE

I looked at Lyla. She'd drawn the hood back around her face so that she resembled a huge black bird. "What's 'one hundred percent' mean?"

"One hundred percent white."

"What about the red-and-white flag?"

"Saint George's flag. It symbolizes England, as opposed to the United Kingdom. The right wing's made it a racist thing. Him and the dragon..."

She gestured at two teenagers carrying a banner that displayed a knight in red armor thrusting a sword into a dragon emblazoned with a crescent moon. "ISIS talks about Crusaders, and they play right into it."

I sidestepped an elderly woman who glared furiously at the teenagers. "Tindra told me what happened to her when she was a girl."

147

Lyla drew up short. "What did she tell you?"

"That she was assaulted by a family friend, and her father did nothing. Is that who Erik is? Her father?"

"No." Lyla's tone was adamant. "She would never have agreed to see her father. She despises him. A Swedish Democrat—a white supremacist, though he never called himself that."

"Isn't everyone in Sweden white?"

"It's not funny."

I glanced over and saw Gryffin waiting for us beneath a tree. Lyla began to walk again. "He's on HNN," she said. "Her father. She can see him anytime she wants."

"What's HNN?"

"White supremacist website, biggest in the world after Stormfront. Herla Network News. He has a regular podcast, *Vali's Hour.*"

"I thought they shut down Stormfront."

"They did. HNN, too. But they just find another server that doesn't mind taking Nazi money. I mean, your fucking FBI claims it lost its records on Stormfront. So the white supremacists just burrow into the Dark Web. You can find anything there—Nazi propaganda, how to make bombs. HNN pretends to be a site for heathens, but that's just a front. That mosque firebombed in Berlin? They were behind that. And those murders at that crèche in Denmark."

"So Tindra's father is a Nazi?"

"Of course not." She laughed bitterly. "Just a good Swede promoting free speech and northern European folk culture. Like them." She gestured at the people around us.

"You think he's here?"

"I sincerely doubt that."

We caught up with Gryffin, his shoulders hunched against the wind as he hurried toward us.

"Hey, what took you so long?" He pointed to the crowd gathered around a monument a few hundred yards off. "That seems to be the main event. Any idea what this Erik looks like?"

Lyla shook her head. She withdrew a pair of compact binoculars from her backpack and focused them on the crowd. I heard her curse softly.

Hundreds of people had assembled here, along with police in riot gear who stood watching them impassively, arms behind their backs. A large group of men marched in orderly formation toward the monument, two by two, close enough that I caught whiffs of their aftershave. All wore identical white polo shirts and brown khaki pants. Most had close-cropped hair, and their ages ran from older teenagers to white-haired men well past seventy.

There must have been a hundred of them. A few carried home-made cardboard shields crisscrossed with black duct tape that formed crude lightning bolts and symbols like deconstructed swastikas. The shields resembled something a kid would make for a school project, which only made them more disturbing.

"Jesus." Gryffin shuddered. "It's Oswald Mosley's grandchildren."

I watched, nervously zipping and unzipping my leather jacket. My skin felt brittle, as though I'd shatter if someone touched me. Finding Tindra or Tommy or an unknown Erik here seemed as likely as finding my long-lost photos of Quinn. The police observed but made no move to intervene as the white shirts headed toward the front of the crowd. I ran my tongue across my cracked lips, fighting the urge to run.

After the last of the white shirts passed, Lyla lowered her binoculars. "We need to split up. If you see Tindra or my brother, text me if you can get a signal. Otherwise we'll meet back here in half an hour."

As Gryffin nodded and started toward the monument, Lyla turned to me. "You'll want to keep an eye on that," she said, indicating my bag. "And don't take off, right?"

It was as much a plea as a warning. I zipped up my jacket and walked away without looking back. I didn't intend to see either one of them again.

CHAPTER 30

Immediately I lost sight of Lyla and Gryffin. Wherever I looked, I saw angry white people waving signs. WHITE GENOCIDE, ENGLAND FIRST, BAN THE BURKA. Union Jacks, Saint George's flags, a good number of Svarlight followers, a few news crews. An amplified male voice rang out to cheers, his words too garbled for me to catch. The crowd had grown to perhaps a thousand or more, and the counter-demonstrators were far outnumbered. I saw no evidence of Antifa or other aggressive anti-fascist organizations. I couldn't decide if that was a good or bad thing.

Another group marched by in formation, smaller than the first, bearing green-and-white flags superimposed with an upward-pointing black arrow. A few people cheered as they passed. Most quickly looked away. Nazism cloaked as free speech was okay; more overt displays, not so much.

Clutching my bag, I pushed my way toward the monument, scanning all those white faces for a young white woman with a blue dreadlock. Tommy, a brown-skinned man, would have been easier to spot, but I saw no sign of him, either. He was a war vet: he'd know to keep a low profile. Or maybe he'd been smart enough not to come here in the first place.

Or to leave. I hoped Lyla would do the same.

The crank gave everything a gray blistered shimmer, like an old black-and-white TV on the fritz. Cold wind bore the dank smell of crushed grass and mud churned up by countless feet. Fifty yards away, the monument's stone spire poked above the throng like a ship's mast. I elbowed past a knot of men arguing about soccer and a woman who cradled a yapping Jack Russell terrier, finally halted near a half-dozen kids huddled together. They looked like college students, the guys with curated beards and long hair, the girls' faces shiny with sweat.

"I don't think they're here," one of the girls announced. Beneath a rain jacket she wore a red STOP RACISM T-shirt. She checked her mobile and stood on tiptoe, craning her neck. "I still can't get reception. But there's a gazebo or something—I think that's where they went."

A wave of feedback washed over the crowd. The college kids began pushing their way out. I moved into the spot they'd vacated and angled myself to get a better look at the action, trying not to get knocked over in the process.

"Sorry!" a middle-aged woman exclaimed, and smiled in apology. There were deep grooves beside her mouth, and her graying hair hung in a long braid down her back. "Wild, isn't it? I haven't done this since the Greenham Common Peace Camp."

I shifted my bag to my other shoulder and cocked a thumb at the monument. "Who's talking?"

"Ronald Morton. I heard him in Sheffield last month. I don't agree with everything he says, but…" She gave a rueful shrug. "We have to start somewhere, right? Put the wheels back on the bus."

"What about someone named Erik? Is he one of the speakers?"

She shook her head. "I've never heard of him, sorry."

A helicopter momentarily drowned out her voice and everyone else's. I kept going in hopes of getting a look at Ronald Morton.

After a few minutes I succeeded. A nondescript man stood on a dais in front of the monument. He looked just shy of forty, with thin brown hair, wearing an overcoat with a large Union Jack pin on the lapel. He spoke into a wireless mike as he scanned the crowd, occasionally grinning and giving a wave when he recognized a face. But he never broke his stream of talk.

"…not that *we* don't want them here. *They* don't want to be here.

No human being wants to feel unwelcome! No one wants to be torn away from their own roots, their own culture and family and history and identity."

He had a bland mid-Atlantic accent, with a trace of a country burr. He paused often, to let his words echo out into the crowd and stare pointedly at one of the TV cameras focused on him.

"They're right to want a home. But not here. Not amongst folk who aren't their own kind, hardworking folk whose roots go back a thousand years, folk who are watching their way of life inundated by unfamiliar languages and beliefs . . ."

The crowd erupted into cheers and chanting. Morton grinned and lifted his hands.

"Ronnie!"

"Ron-nee, Ron-nee . . ."

As people surged toward the monument, I stood my ground, ignoring shoves and muttered expletives. Another blat of feedback reduced Morton's speech to word confetti.

" . . . every day . . . new opportunity . . . restore our . . ."

A burly man placed his hands on my shoulders to push me out of his way. Instinctively I turned and kicked him, and he collapsed. I started to kick him again, then realized people were staring at me.

"What the fuck you doing?" someone yelled.

I turned and bolted.

CHAPTER 31

P eople started to shout, hurtling in every direction. I froze as the ground seemed to tilt. The drone of voices became a chain-saw scream. Many screams. Something struck me in the stomach, a fist or boot. I doubled over, gagging, finally looked up again.

The demonstration had exploded into a riot. Everywhere people ran, or tried to, pushing others to the ground and trampling them as lines of helmeted figures, black and neon green, raced from behind the monument, wielding riot shields. A man shrieked, a child's thin wail grew abruptly silent as a woman screamed. I stumbled backward, turning to flee in another direction.

But there was no other direction, no up or down or left or right; only a heaving ocean of limbs and faces.

The crank's quicksilver halo fragmented into a world like a damaged negative, eyes, mouths, faces all obliterated. The ground seemed to shiver, as though a huge hive hummed furiously beneath my feet. Blurred hands, gaping mouths, a thicket of jerking knees and feet and the stink of vomit. It was like falling into hell's own mosh pit. I choked, tasting blood where I'd bitten my lip. Snatches of robotic-sounding speech echoed as a helicopter circled overhead, its rotors sending up waves of grit and mud.

If they start kettling, get the hell out.

I pressed my bag against my face, in case someone lobbed a tear gas canister; kept my head down and zigzagged through the mob. Not far away, a woman with a Union Jack painted on her face screamed obscenities at a cop. Beside her, a heavyset man swung a DOA sign like a battle-ax. A mounted policeman wheeled and galloped toward him, people fleeing from the horse as though it were a tank. My inchoate terror dissolved into a more practical fear: not of tear gas but getting arrested.

I lurched toward a break in the crowd, finally halting in a patch of grass. Gasping, I lowered my bag. The crowd was sparser here, mostly people like myself struggling to catch their breath. A few onlookers ran toward the melee, mobiles held up to record the event. Four old black women followed them with arms linked, their hair hidden beneath brightly colored turbans. A loudspeaker blared a warning as sirens sounded in the distance.

A few yards off stood a man, short, white, bald, in a faded green parka with ratty fake-fur trim. A laminated card hung from a lanyard around his neck. He held an SLR camera, its lens pointed to where an arm punched upward through the crowd, wielding a police baton. The baton fell, and I heard a thump, then more screams. The photographer had barely lowered his camera when someone lunged at him—another cop with a baton.

I watched as the crank sizzled in my brain and everything around me began to slow. The photographer's mouth gaped wider and wider as he fell, but no sound came out. His hands opened and the camera floated into the air, as though he'd released a black bird.

With dreamy slowness, the photographer rolled onto his side. The policeman loomed above him, baton raised. The camera dropped onto the grass a few feet from where I stood, its lens pointed skyward. The photographer covered his head with his arms as the baton came down on his skull with a dull *crack*.

Someone shouted. The four old women stopped to look back, then with shrill voices raced toward the cop. As they surrounded him, I snatched up the camera and darted through the crowd, which had begun to scatter. It was a long time before I slowed to a walk and glanced behind me for signs of pursuit.

No one appeared to have taken any notice of me. The demonstration had broken up so swiftly that it scarcely seemed as though it had ever happened. The Nazis in their distinctive white shirts and brown pants were gone, along with almost everyone else. A pair of mounted police officers made slow figure eights around the monument, circling those who remained, like cowboys rounding up cattle. Onlookers stood at a safe distance, along with several TV crews, recording the riot's aftermath on mobiles and videocams.

Two police helicopters hovered above the monument as a police van drove across the grass, lights flashing, and stopped near a group of policemen who stood in a half circle, staring at something on the ground. A woman hopped out of the van, followed by two white-suited figures, and all three walked to join the others.

Out of nowhere, a small black shape appeared and swooped above them, low enough that the woman looked up in alarm. *Another drone,* I thought; then saw it was a bird, a crow or raven that abruptly banked and headed in my direction before veering off into the trees, where I lost sight of it.

CHAPTER 32

The bird had disappeared into a thick stand of ancient yew trees, which seemed as good a place as any for me to sit and absorb what had just happened. I trudged toward it, passing a group of weary demonstrators dragging their battered placards in the mud. They tossed them into a waist-high pile of discarded signs and kept going.

Here, near the outskirts of the park, several groups had set up makeshift information booths. Defenders of Albion, Mothers Against Fascism, Free Speech Legal Defense Council, England First! I searched for Svarlight's telltale red oak leaf with no luck. I'd long since given up on looking for Tindra or Tommy, along with any hope of finding a stolen book in the wreck-age of a nationalist rally. I might be wasted, but I wasn't *that* wasted.

I had a camera again. It seemed like a good time to cut my losses.

I sank onto the cold dirt beneath the yews. A huge limb hung so close to the ground that its branches formed an impenetrable curtain of black-green dotted with crimson berries. I crawled till I was out of sight of any passersby and shut my eyes, counting my heartbeats until they seemed normal for someone wired on crank and a flood of adrenaline. Minutes passed before I opened my eyes, exhaled, and allowed myself to relax. My back ached, my head. The split on my lower lip felt hot, skin stretched like that of an overripe plum. I found some Kleenex in my bag and did my best to clean my face.

From outside the park echoed the thrum of traffic, louder than it had been earlier. It must have been rush hour. Two young boys walked past, kicking at the gravel path and laughing, shadow puppets behind the yew's green-and-black scrim. When they were gone, I reached beneath my jacket and pulled out the camera.

It was an older Nikon F2, late 1970s, with a bayonet-mount lens, its frayed leather strap wound with electrical tape. A white label on the back bore a printed name and address in Barnes: a professional photog's rig. The lens cap hung from an elastic band secured behind the focus ring. I checked to make sure the lens hadn't been damaged in the fall. It was heavier than my old Konica, a more expensive camera than I ever would have bought for myself.

I carefully peeled off the address label, took off the lens cap again, stared through the viewfinder, then wound the exposed film onto the take-up spool. I popped open the back of the camera and removed the film roll. I stuck the address label back on the protective casing, wiped it all off with another piece of tissue so there'd be no finger-prints, and tossed it into the shadows. If someone ever found it, maybe they'd return it to its owner. I'd have to wait until I had access to a closet before I could load the camera with my own black-and-white Tri-X.

I looked through the viewfinder again, playing with the focus, gently touched the shutter release waiting to be triggered. I felt as I had lying beside Quinn, not exactly safe but suspended, the city beyond the curtain of yew branches as distant and unreal as the images I'd glimpsed in *The Book of Lamps and Banners*. The grief that had infected me since giving away my Konica faded, replaced by a familiar sense of urgency and yearning.

I recalled when I'd seen that raven arrow above the police van, the woman followed by two white-clad figures, the line of cops staring at something on the ground in front of them. A body. I could have shot it. I might even have been able to capture the moment when it was transformed from a man or woman into something beautiful and terrifying, eyes reflecting a sky no longer seen, mouth open to gasp or cry out or whisper a secret never to be told. I ran my fingers across the focus ring, pressed and released the shutter release, then carefully placed the Nikon in my bag.

I knelt to gaze out through the branches at the park. Afternoon had waned to early evening. The air smelled acrid, but I didn't catch any whiff of tear gas. The helicopters were gone, also the Metro Police van. The demonstration might as well have happened a thousand miles away. It was as if the city had fought to suppress the sudden outbreak of a virus, and won. London was vast: it could seemingly swallow hundreds of rioters, leaving no trace save footprints in the mud and a few bloody faces. The rest would be dealt with in courts and prison cells and, perhaps, the morgue.

My shadowy refuge grew darker as the temperature dropped. My headache had become a solid brick of pain. I was badly dehydrated, sweating despite being chilled. The speed still sparked in my brain like a fistful of firecrackers, but it had been hours since I'd had a drink.

To ease the craving, I got out the copy of *Dead Girls* and opened to the leaf from *The Book of Lamps and Banners*. I was wary of touching it, of even looking at it for too long—whenever I did, it seemed as though the images had rearranged themselves. I knew this wasn't the case, but there was something about the brilliant pigments and grotesque figures that defied any attempt to impose order upon them.

In the Bolt, I'd been absorbed by the tiny illustrations—the monstrous tentacled woman, the severed head that turned into a moon. Now what seized my attention was the way the images were arranged on the page, a pattern that reminded me of the intricate arrangement of frames in a graphic novel, or the schematic in a set of blueprints that showed where the wiring would be in a high-rise.

I could make no sense of it. Yet there was undeniably order on the page. The same colors and motifs repeated themselves in varied combinations. The sinuous appendages no longer resembled tentacles, but letters. What I had taken for random stipples of scarlet or indigo were in fact a kind of punctuation.

Dizzy, I raised my head, and in the shifting world of branches and sky read the same grammar. There was meaning in the yew's needles; meaning in a contrail's scrawl, in the tattoos on a passing girl's arm, and the logo on a jogger's sweatpants.

Tindra was right. *The Book of Lamps and Banners* was a code, a secret language composed of colors and shadows and chimerical creatures. The page was an attempt to capture the transient beauty and strangeness of the world around me. Like Tindra's app, the images had the subliminal power to change the way one saw the world.

I felt a rush as potent as a line of uncut cocaine, followed by a wave of nausea. The scene in front of me shivered into an unintelligible mass: I had a flash of the raw terror I'd experienced when I looked at Ludus Mentis. Gasping, I lashed out at an unseen attacker.

My fist struck the tree, hard enough that the pain brought me back. I caught my breath and recalled Tindra's avid expression when she first told me about her app.

A mirror... When he looked into it, he couldn't look away... You see how it all ties in? The way we're all sucked in by this?

Yet what happens when the mirror doesn't reflect your own face, but the void behind it? I looked down at the page from *The Book of Lamps and Banners*.

It's all there, not a line missing. I'll be able to complete writing a code that was begun thousands of years ago.

But the book wasn't intact, so neither was Ludus Mentis. The app's incomplete code was worse than meaningless: it provoked a neurological response that unraveled one's consciousness, reducing the world to a primal soup of fear and rage.

I quickly closed *Dead Girls*, entombing the papyrus sheet inside it, and stared at the book's cover, my night shot of a bunch of kids staring at something that lurked in the darkness, just out of sight. A moment in time, ephemeral as the cigarette smoke rising above the kids' heads.

And yet I had captured it on a piece of cellulose coated with gelatin and silver. Human figures, most of them now dead, immortalized through an alchemy of light, silver, salt.

Ludus Mentis wasn't the only portal to the past. Whatever meaning that fleeting moment on the Bowery had held, I had put it there.

CHAPTER 33

stuffed *Dead Girls* into my bag and stood. I had the hollowed-out feeling that follows a long acid trip, a sense that my singed neurons were slowly regenerating. I was ready for a drink, maybe even an early dinner. I checked the burner to see if Quinn had texted me. Nothing. Trying not to panic, I popped three ibuprofen and stepped out from beneath the trees.

The sun hung just above the horizon, turning the hazy air rose pink. I zipped up my leather jacket, started to walk. The park was nearly deserted, though I saw a few stragglers carrying protest signs under their arms. I wondered if Lyla and Gryffin had been arrested. I couldn't imagine they'd found Tindra or Tommy, though I'd have no way of knowing if they had.

I felt a pang, thinking of Tindra as she cradled her fierce-looking dog as though it was a stuffed animal. It was a good-sized Staffordshire terrier, well trained and capable of bringing down someone my size. Who could have killed it, and how? Poisoning didn't make sense—Tindra would never have let it eat something unfamiliar.

And, despite what Lyla believed, the dog didn't look like it had been poisoned. When I was ten, a friend's dog, a bad-tempered bullmastiff who'd once killed a German shepherd by snapping its neck, had been killed—rat poison in a chunk of meat. I'd been with my friend when she discovered the writhing mastiff in the woods. The dog had snapped at her viciously and mindlessly as a snake—an agonizing death.

Yet in the video Tommy had texted to his sister, Bunny appeared to be sleeping peacefully. Surely if the dog had been shot or stabbed, Tommy would have noticed and texted that to Lyla. So yeah, maybe poison.

But how do you poison a big, well-trained attack dog walking beside its owner in a large, crowded park? Where was the dog's corpse now?

And where was Tindra?

My thoughts outran my steps as I stared distractedly at the ground, kicking at gravel. I hoped I'd find an exit from the park soon. I had no clue how to get back to the Underground. When I looked up, the rosy haze had darkened to bloodred fog: a toxic magic hour, the few passersby ghostly shapes that flickered in and out of sight.

I kept walking. After a short while, I saw three boys crouched around something on the gravel. A fourth boy stood above them, poking the object with a stick. I drew closer, and he glanced at me. His friends scrambled to their feet.

"It was just here," one said.

A small dead bird lay on the path. It looked like a sparrow, tiny legs straight as matchsticks, claws curled as though grasping an invisible perch. There was a tiny depression in its breast.

"It's the fog," explained the boy with the stick. "Makes 'em sick." He tossed the stick into the shadows, and he and his friends hurried off.

I stared down at the little corpse, then used the steel toe of my boot to nudge the sparrow onto its side, so that it gazed at me with one poppy-seed eye.

I resumed walking. The greasy haze made my face feel as though it had been smeared with Vaseline. Two women in park uniforms ignored me as they passed, speaking loudly into their mobiles. When the fog swallowed them, I paused beside an overflowing trash bin.

Something glinted amid the foil wrappers and takeaway containers on the ground. I bent to see a dart with a red feather at one end, like a tiny powder puff. Straightening, I prodded it with my boot. I'd seen something like this before.

I shook my head: I needed to stay focused. Tindra, dead dog, dead bird, the book, the app, Quinn, a drink... the only one of these things that mattered to me now was Quinn.

And a drink. And maybe another bump. I reached into my pocket for the crank, and froze.

Two white guys in red Svarlight hoodies were headed toward me on the path, hands in their pockets. I shoved the bag of crank back in my pocket and called out to them.

"Hey, are they still around?"

They halted. Young, fair-haired, and blue-eyed, their cheeks raw with windburn. The older of the two regarded me cautiously. "Who?"

I pointed at his sweatshirt. "Svarlight."

"Oh, yeah." His companion gestured at some benches a short distance away. "You'll just catch them, they're getting ready to go home."

"Thanks," I said, and they left.

I stared at a heavyset gray-haired woman perched on one bench, spooning food from a takeaway container. If I hadn't looked up, I would have walked right past her. Above her dangled a limp plastic banner, held aloft by two plastic rods. It was emblazoned with a scarlet oak leaf and lightning bolt. A large tote bag at her feet displayed the same logo. A few feet away, three young men stood talking to a burly middle-aged white guy with a long, braided salt-and-pepper beard. He wore dark work pants, work boots, a fleece-lined black denim jacket.

The wind tugged the jacket open, revealing a Svarlight T-shirt. One of the young men wore the same T-shirt. Another sported a Defenders of Albion knit cap. The third, dressed in a plain white windbreaker, waved a CD at the bearded man.

"Been looking for this for weeks! What happened to the download?"

The bearded man shrugged. As I approached he gave me a nod, turning to resume his conversation.

"That was only up there for a week," he explained. He sounded

Swedish. "Read the small print. Are you on the mailing list? We send out a list of new downloads every Sunday night. Freya tweets them, too. When she remembers."

"You're lucky I remember your dinner," the woman on the bench called. She looked at the young man and added, "There's two songs on that CD weren't on the download. That's your reward for buying it."

Like the bearded man, she sounded Swedish. The others all seemed to be Brits. They nodded amiably as I joined them.

"A lot quieter now," the Defender of Albion said, smiling.

I glanced at the woman's tote bag, trying to discern its contents.

"Come take a look if you want," the woman, Freya, said.

She finished whatever was in the takeaway box, dabbed her chin with a paper napkin, then hauled the tote onto the bench, scooting over to make room for me. "Sit," she urged.

I did. Her long hair was more silver than gray and loosely braided, her face sun weathered and deeply lined. Her blue eyes were so pale they almost looked white, making her appear blind. Her loose cotton dress hung almost to her ankles. She had big hands, the knuckles swollen from work or arthritis. No rings. No coat, only a popcorn-knit wool sweater that looked handmade. For an instant I met those eerie pale eyes and saw a glint of fear, or maybe just exhaustion.

"Help yourself."

She pointed at the tote and stood, yawning, then walked over to the bearded man, leaving me alone on the bench.

CHAPTER 34

The tote held dozens of CDs, a few Svarlight T-shirts, a stack of brochures held together with a rubber band. I removed one of the brochures:

Nordiska Motståndsrörelsen

It was illustrated with photos of men marching in formation, clad in black trousers, white shirts, black ties. Each man carried a green flag with an arrow at its center. There were a few lines of Swedish text, a URL, phone numbers. I glanced up and saw the gray-haired woman watching me.

"You may have that," she called.

I muttered thanks and dropped the brochure back into the tote, then began sorting through the CDs, all packaged in illustrated cardboard sleeves. Bands with names like Jötunn's Egg, Bloodwinter, Den Sorgen. The artwork ran to photos of moody rural landscapes and pine forests under a clouded moon, or woodblock prints from nineteenth-century volumes of Teutonic folktales. The Wild Hunt was a popular motif, along with archaic farm implements and snow. The back of each album bore the same lightning-bolt-and-oak-leaf logo.

Svarlight wasn't a political fringe group, but a music label. I picked up a Bloodwinter CD.

"That's the last one," the woman said, returning to the bench.

"If you're looking for Harrow the Wind, or Tessa Sowen, I'm afraid we sold out. But we'll be streaming Tessa's album Sunday night, once we're back home and settled. Are you on our mailing list?"

I shook my head. "Well, go online and sign up," she said, and glanced over at the bearded man as if for approval.

I continued to pore over the CDs. Based on the album and song titles and cover art, I'd guess that Svarlight's list ran to alt-folk or post-rock. I didn't see anything that looked like Nazi symbolism. No swastikas or Iron Crosses, no stylized eagles; just a few band names spelled out in variations of the elaborate medieval black-letter typeface favored by metal bands.

But that stack of brochures was definitely neo-Nazi propaganda, and Svarlight was here to hawk their wares to white supremacists. Why?

I put aside Bloodwinter and picked up *Stone Ships,* the album by Jötunn's Egg. The cover art showed an animal skull on the grassy verge of a rocky beach. Some of the vertebrae were still attached, protruding onto a swathe of grass studded with tiny yellow flowers. Horns curled from either side of the skull. A yellowish tube trailed from one eye socket, blossoming into a fist-sized growth that resembled the blossom of an underwater plant. Tendrils and a ragged flap of skin or muscle clung to the other eye socket, where another, tongue-shaped growth bulged. Delicate periwinkle-blue shadows dappled the vertebrae and coiled horns, as though petals had fallen there.

I turned to the back cover, a black-and-white photo of rocks arranged in the shape of a boat, the stone ship of the title. It sat in a clearing, surrounded by evergreens and white birches, rings of autumn ferns. The stone ship looked desolate but not out of place, adrift on grassy hummocks like stationary waves.

The track list was in English. "Within the Petrified Darkness We All Disappear" and "I Scream, You Laugh, I Bleed" were the highlights. All songs were credited to Kirsten Manus, the cover art and production to Big Delusory Whim and Svarlight Studios.

I stared at the name. At last I placed it: the book of photos I'd seen in Tindra Bergstrand's hallway. I turned to Freya and held up the CD.

"The person who shot this cover. Do you know who he is?"

"Of course." She reached past me into the tote. "Here's his book. We published it a few years ago. It didn't sell many copies."

She handed me a hardbound book, its cover featuring a man's elaborately tattooed torso, his face obscured by the horned skull he held in front of it. I turned to the title page:

Skalltrolleri: Fotografier producerad av Big Delusory Whim

"*Skalltrolleri*," I said. "What's that mean?"

"'Skull magic.' It's not a real word—he made it up."

"The photographer?"

"Yes. He took those pictures, he made up the word."

"What's his real name?"

Freya picked at her wool sweater. "He likes to be anonymous."

Mindful of the cheap binding, I opened the book. I flipped past the title page and a brief introduction in Swedish, to the first photograph.

A black ram stood alert in a field of wildflowers, its horns like a pair of nautilus shells, each golden eye bisected by a horizontal pupil. In the foreground a sheep's skull lay alongside a mound of earth, its coiled horns black with dirt. A green tendril emerged from one eye socket, like a baby grass snake. The color reproduction was off—the greens bled into the sky's summer blue, giving it the sickly hue of a faded 1970s Kodachrome.

I wondered if that was intentional. The scene itself was hackneyed, placid ram paired with sinister skull. What saved the photo was the way one of the ram's eyes caught a sliver of light, so that its flattened pupil wore a corona of gold. It made the creature look otherworldly, slightly ethereal. Whoever had taken the shot had a good eye and a knack for capturing sideways details that most people wouldn't even notice.

I examined the other photos. Skulls in varying stages of decomposition; young men, some barely teenagers, sporting Nazi and racist insignia as tattoos and scarifications; T-shirts with S-shaped lightning bolts, Iron Crosses, sun wheels. One photo showed two white teenagers, no older than sixteen, pointing guns at a third, darker-skinned figure bound to a chair, his face covered by a flowered pillowcase.

"That was a game." I glanced up to see Freya watching me. "They were all friends."

As I turned to the next photo, the book's spine cracked, and the page drooped between my fingers. I looked at Freya. "Can I buy this?"

"Of course. That's twelve pounds, or fifteen euros."

I picked up the *Stone Ships* album and a CD by Bloodwinter, fumbling in my pocket for money. "How much for the book and these two CDs?"

"The CDs are ten pounds apiece. Ten euros, if you'd prefer."

"Give her both for ten, Freya," the bearded man called out. "And five for the book. We can't give that one away."

I held up a note. "I only have ten."

Freya gazed at her husband, who gave her a curt nod. "You can have them all for ten," she said as the bearded man joined us.

"New customer?" he asked. At my nod he smiled approvingly. "Good. That's what we like, new blood. Here, wait—"

He reached into the tote, pulled out a red T-shirt, and handed it to me. "Here you go."

"That's okay, I don't—"

"Keep it!" He waved me away. "Anything we don't sell we have to carry back."

"That's right," said Freya. She took my money, tentatively touched the bearded man's arm. "Erik, we need to be going."

I froze, staring at the red lightning bolt and oak leaf printed on the T-shirt.

found book
erik svarlight
need help

"Thanks," I croaked, and stashed the book and CDs in my bag.

The guy with the Defenders of Albion cap walked up to Erik. "What was that title on the show last week? The one about folklore and racial memory. *Blood Harvest,* something like that . . ."

"You mean *Reaping Blood*?"

"Yes, that's it! Who's the author?"

"Markus Thierke. Message me and I'll send you a link." Erik clapped a hand on the young man's shoulder, turned to shake hands with the other two. "We need to catch the ferry. Thanks for supporting us."

The three men ambled off. Erik yanked up the plastic poles holding the Svarlight banner, collapsed them, and stowed everything in the tote. He glanced irritably at Freya.

"Aren't you done yet?"

"Almost."

She reached into a pocket of her dress for a money pouch, unzipped it, and slipped the cash I'd given her inside. As she did, her sweater's sleeve rode up.

Tattooed just above her wrist were three linked triangles: a valknut. It bisected a circular band of raw skin, as though she'd been wearing a too-small bracelet.

Before I could get a better look, Freya turned away. As Erik hefted the tote, I saw the same symbol tattooed on the back of his hand. He grabbed Freya's wrist, asking her a question in Swedish. She removed a mobile, swiped at it, then nodded. "It's coming."

She gave me a farewell nod. "You have a good evening."

"I'll try." I looked past them to the street. "Is there a Tube station near here?"

"West Ham station," said Erik. "It's the rail line."

A sedan pulled up to the curb, and the two of them went to meet it. I sank back onto the bench, trying to make sense of the last few minutes.

Erik had to be the guy mentioned in Tindra's text. His wife or partner, Freya, bore a tattoo of the same symbol I'd glimpsed on Harold's forehead. And Svarlight published that book of photos of young white nationalists.

Tindra's message suggested Erik had *The Book of Lamps and Banners,* and Tindra had gone to meet Erik. So where was Tindra? Where was the book?

This guy Erik didn't appear as though he'd had any sort of confrontation earlier in the day, let alone arranged a kidnapping or murder. If anything, he and Freya seemed to have kept their distance from the demonstration, setting up near the edge of the park. If they did have *The Book of Lamps and Banners,* where was it? They were traveling light—a tote containing some T-shirts, CDs, and copies of *Skalltrolleri.* I'd seen no sign of the stolen book.

I drummed my fingers on the bench. Maybe Tindra had never come here at all. She might be anywhere by now, including dead.

But why did she own a copy of *Skalltrolleri*?

If I'd been straight, this would all be simply crazy. Since I was still blasted on cheap crank, it seemed on the brink of making sense. I recalled the vortex of Ludus Mentis in the split second before it triggered my flashback. It seemed to represent a language I couldn't understand, unfamiliar symbols, but also swastikas, sun wheels, crosses.

What if it was some kind of dog whistle directed at white supremacists? Could Tindra secretly be a neo-Nazi? Maybe she was in collusion with Erik. Or maybe she'd been kidnapped by him. Either way, he seemed like the only lead I could follow.

My reverie broke as a dog barked. A man in a plaid anorak strolled across the grass, holding aloft a golf club, as a small white terrier danced around him. I heard the sound of a door slamming and children's voices. Soon it would be dark.

I picked up my bag and got to my feet. The man in the anorak stood silhouetted against a sky molten with sunset. As I watched, he raised his golf club, swung, and hit a ball I couldn't see, shading his eyes as he traced its trajectory.

"Get it, Lucy!" he yelled as the white dog raced after the ball, and I started toward the West Ham rail line.

CHAPTER 35

I had to ask for directions twice before I found the station. Once there, I called Quinn. He answered on the third ring. I could hear music in the background, Johnny Hallyday.

"I need to see you," I said.

"I'm at Derek's. Get your skinny ass over here."

"Is that safe?" Derek owned the Banshee, a pub in Camden Town, which had been a nexus for some shit I preferred not to think about right now.

"'Safe'?" Quinn laughed. He sounded drunk. "Just come. I'll protect you."

The Banshee was nearly empty. The usual superannuated folk beardies sat at their table by the window, nursing their pints. Hallyday had given way to "Looking for a Kiss" on the vintage Seeburg that Quinn had supplied with old 45s from his stock of thousands in Reykjavík. He sat at the bar, the black watch cap pushed back from his forehead as he spoke to Derek across the zinc counter. Derek glanced up at my approach. His expression cooled as he gave a nod to Quinn, who turned to beckon me over.

"There she is. Hurricane Cass."

Quinn pulled me to him, tipping my face to kiss me. He tasted like candy, Coke, and Myer's dark. Even after decades of being clean, he had a junkie's penchant for sweet stuff. I dropped my bag and pressed against him, sliding my hand beneath his cap to feel the soft stubble on his scalp, the ridged scar in the shape of a cross.

"Hey, baby," I murmured. For a moment everything that had

happened in the last twenty-four hours fell into the black bottomless pool that was my need for Quinn. I traced his bruised cheek with one finger, and he put his arms around me.

Derek stalked to the other end of the bar. I swayed with Quinn while David Johansen shouted in the background, and for a few minutes I imagined we were back in New York and twenty years old and Johnny Thunders was still alive.

"Okay," Quinn said at last. He pushed me away and turned to pick up a brimming pint glass that I knew held rum and Coke. "So what you got for me?"

I looked around. The place was empty except for us and the Furry Freak Brothers. I turned back and told Quinn what had happened since I'd left him that afternoon.

"Erik." I repeated the name for the twentieth time. I knew I should slow down, but it was like my mouth had caught a fast train and left my brain at the station. "I asked Lyla who he was, but she wouldn't answer me. She's lying. Or not lying, but not telling me what she knows."

"I don't blame her. You're running on no sleep and enough crank to keep you wired for another three days. 'Paranoia strikes deep,' baby." He took another swallow of his drink.

"I'm not paranoid."

"You're spun. Look at your eyes—they're dilated like crazy."

"That doesn't matter." I pulled out the book I'd just bought and dropped it on the bar beside Quinn's mobile. "Check this out. It's produced by the same people as those CDs. Svarlight. They're a music label, but they've done at least one book, this one. Be careful, it'll fall apart—"

Quinn gingerly turned the pages. "Guy likes his skulls."

"No kidding. So why would Tindra have a copy of this?"

Quinn pushed the book toward me. "Why would anyone?"

"Because it's by a guy who's a white supremacist or neo-Nazi or something. It has some connection to them, anyway. Maybe through her father. Tindra hates him—they haven't had any contact since she was fourteen. Lyla told me he does a podcast for some kind of white supremacist site, Perla News, something like that."

"Herla Network?"

"You've heard of it?"

"Yeah. Some of the guys I do business with are fans." Quinn squinted at the book's cover photo, swallowing a mouthful of rum and Coke. "But this guy—his body looks too young to be her father's. So maybe the photographer's her father, and this is some guy he took a picture of?"

"But if Tindra hates him, and he's a neo-Nazi, why would she have a copy of his book?"

Derek returned and silently set a shot glass of Jack Daniel's in front of me. Like Quinn's, his face was scarred, a ridge of tissue that ran along his jaw like a hinge, bluish gray against his ebony skin. Years earlier, his right-hand ring finger had been cut off at the joint. I knew who'd done that, but we didn't have to worry about him any longer.

I downed the whiskey. Derek swapped out a pint glass of water for my empty shot glass. "You want something to eat?"

I shook my head, and Derek walked over to check on the bearded ones. I pushed the mobile toward Quinn, tapping the cover of *Skalltrolleri*. "Google it."

Quinn scowled and picked up the mobile, shoving it into his pocket. "Why? What about the book we're actually looking for? Did you look in Erik's magic bag for that?"

"It wasn't there."

"You sure?"

"Yeah. I had a good look at the bag, and it wasn't there. Plus they wouldn't be lugging it around with a bunch of CDs."

"You sound awfully sure of that." I knew he really meant *You fucked up*. "This girl Tindra—what does she look like?"

I swiveled on my stool, holding out my hand. "Maybe this tall. Kind of big-boned. Strong, she looks like she works out. She has black hair, a buzz cut."

"Any identifying marks—tattoos, stuff like that?"

"Not that I saw. But she has a long dreadlock. Blue, with glitter stuck in it. Sequins."

"She a black girl?"

"No. I told you, she's Swedish."

"There are black people in Sweden, Cass."

"I know," I snapped. "But Victoria Park wouldn't have been a good place for a black girl this afternoon."

"What about her bodyguard? And your boyfriend Gryffin? How'd they make out?"

"I don't know. I ditched them."

"That's my girl." He glanced at the book again, shook his head dismissively. "Well, we got squat. You have any idea what the hell is going on?"

"She could have been kidnapped, but I don't see how anyone could have gotten into her place without Lyla or Tommy knowing."

"Maybe she went for a walk and someone nabbed her."

"Yeah, I thought of that. She had her dog, though."

"Her dog's dead. Who'd kidnap her?"

I tried without success to catch Derek's eye to get another drink. "Same person who killed Harold?"

"So why kidnap her? The book's already gone."

"Maybe it doesn't have anything to do with the book."

"Don't give me that. There's some connection. Think, Cass."

Exasperated, I stood and peered over the bar, looking for a bottle within reach. Quinn pushed me back onto my stool. "Stop it. Derek!"

Derek slid me another shot. I took a sip, closed my eyes, and tried to recall everything I could about the Swedish couple. At last I pointed at the pocket holding Quinn's mobile.

"Okay, look up that Herla site. Her father's show is called *Vali's Hour*, something like that."

Quinn retrieved his phone. "Here it is," he said after a moment. "'*Vali's Hour*. Activist news and neo-*Volksmusik*.'"

"What's that?"

"European alt-folk. In this case, probably with a Nazi twist."

He held up the mobile to display a thumbnail photo of a man in his forties. Long black hair swept back from a high forehead; uptilted eyes fixed the camera with a confrontational stare. His resemblance to Tindra was striking.

Longtime commentator Valî keeps you up to date with current events along with little-known history, folklore, and new progressive Volksmusik every Sunday night at 23:00 and streaming online at Herla.org.su.

"Valî," I said. "Valî Bergstrand?"

"Probably a pseudonym. They're less common than they used to be. Nazis aren't afraid anymore."

I removed the Bloodwinter CD from my bag and slid it toward Quinn. "Do you know the label? Svarlight?"

He glanced at the title and track listings, did the same with the Jötunn's Egg album, *Stone Ships.* "I've never heard of these bands. But I know the label. I don't keep their stuff in stock, but sometimes people will special-order it. They do some limited vinyl pressings, but mostly they just rip CDs on demand."

"Was it founded by a guy named Erik Svarlight?"

"Beats me."

"You know some Swedish—what does it mean, 'Svarlight'?"

Quinn stared at the album, shrugged. "I think *svar* means 'reply' or 'answer,' something like that. But 'light' is English. It's a made-up word. Svarlight, starlight . . ."

"So it's a pun?"

"I guess." He examined both albums. "Looks like they put out the same kind of music as Heathen Harvest. I bet most of their business is streaming downloads. I doubt they make much money."

"What's Heathen Harvest?"

"Indie label, mostly an online presence. European nationalist music, some of it—you know, updated folk music about the good old days and the old ways. The rest is heathen-related stuff."

"Black metal? I hate that shit."

Quinn reached to touch the scar beside my eye. "I remember. But Svarlight is more postindustrial and neo-folk. Post-rock. And definitely DIY—the studio's probably a laptop in this guy Erik's basement."

"So this is neo-*Volksmusik*? Like what's played on *Vali's Hour?*"

"Maybe. I don't listen to it much. Some of it's okay, just not my taste. But just because a band's on a label like Svarlight doesn't mean they're white supremacists. If you listen to the lyrics, yeah, sometimes there are code words and racist dog-whistle shit. But most of the bands are just, you know . . ."

He moved his hand back and forth, mimicking a rocky boat. "Kinda woo-woo. Like, fire up a bowl and go out and dance naked around a bonfire. Good old-fashioned pagans. Like those guys," he added, indicating the folkies by the window.

I picked up the Jötunn's Egg album, *Stone Ships,* and examined the back cover. At the very bottom, beneath the photo credit, were two lines of very small print. I read the first:

Recorded at Kalkö, Sweden
Photo Credit: BDW

"Where's Kalkö?" I asked.

"Little island in the Baltic Sea."

"Erik and his wife were going to take a ferry somewhere. Can you get to Kalkö by ferry?"

"Not from here. But from Stockholm, sure. Takes a few hours."

He looked past me toward the jukebox, one of those thousand-yard stares I knew better than to ask about. He shook his head. "Kalkö's a long way to come to sell a couple of CDs at a fringe Nazi rally. Expensive, too, if they took the ferry to Stockholm and then flew from there. Why would they bother?"

"That's the million-dollar question. I think they were here for Tindra. And the book. Though this is the thing..."

I felt my synapses burn as though I'd just done another bump. "I'm not sure this really *is* about the book. I told you she designed an app. She showed it to me on her mobile—all these colors and weird symbols, like in *The Book of Lamps and Banners*. Hieroglyphs, things like that. When I looked at it, all of a sudden I had a flashback to when I was raped. Not just a flashback—it was like I was actually there. It freaked the hell out of me."

"Jesus. What the hell kind of app is that?"

"She calls it Ludus Mentis, it means 'mind game.' She told me it's supposed to control PTSD. She was abused when she was a kid; I assume that's what got her interested. And her bodyguard, Tommy—he was in Afghanistan. Sounds like he has PTSD, too. I think she wanted to help him."

"So this app is like therapy? Biofeedback?"

"Tindra says it can rewire your brain. All I know is when I looked at it, I thought I was going crazy. It's like it *induced* PTSD."

Quinn gently grasped my chin in one of his scarred hands. "This old world really fucked you up, didn't it?" he murmured. "I wish I'd been there. I should have been there."

"You were in jail."

His expression hardened. He turned away, drank what was left of his rum and Coke, and got unsteadily to his feet. "I'll be right back."

He headed toward the men's toilet. I finished my whiskey, held up my empty glass to Derek. He refilled it and watched as I took a sip.

"Don't take him down with you," he said.

"I'm not taking him anywhere."

"Let him go back to Reykjavík. He was safe there. Whatever you're up to, keep him out of it."

"Quinn's a big boy, he can make up his own mind."

"Not with you around. You're like heroin to him."

"Fuck you," I said.

I looked up to see Quinn approaching. Derek busied himself with cleaning a tap. I picked up the Bloodwinter CD and scanned the personnel info on the back.

Two acoustic guitars, one a twelve-string; female singer; drums; something called a *nyckelharppa.* I searched for the photo credit— again, BDW—then swore under my breath.

"Check this out." I handed the CD to Quinn, pointing to the final credit line:

Album produced, engineered, and mixed by Gwilym Birdhouse at BDW and Svarlight Studios

CHAPTER 36

G wilym Birdhouse." Quinn rapped his knuckles on the bar counter. "The eighties singer?"

He hummed the opening of "No One Knows Me but the Rain," and I dug my nails into his arm. "Ow! What the hell?"

"I hate that song."

"Everybody hates that song." He stared at the CD, musing. "So, he's producing stuff for a shoestring label. So what?"

"It's a link, right? Nathan told me that Birdhouse collects esoterica—old manuscripts, shit like that. So it's possible he'd have at least heard of *The Book of Lamps and Banners*. But I can't imagine him killing Harold Vertigan for it. Or kidnapping Tindra," I added. "He's a vegan."

"Vegans—you'd be surprised." Quinn withdrew a cigarette from a crumpled pack. "But yeah, it seems a little extreme. And if somebody killed her, where's the body? That's always the challenge, what you do with the body. It's harder than it seems."

"Okay, so they kidnapped her."

"Then where are they keeping her?"

"I don't know!"

The three folkies turned to me in disapproval. I ignored them and stared into my glass of Jack Daniel's. I thought about Ludus Mentis tapping into the memory of the one experience I'd devoted my entire life to blocking, the chemical wall I'd erected since then between myself and the dark. I raised my head to look at Quinn.

"What if she went along willingly?" It was an effort not to slur my words, but Quinn stopped playing with his cigarette and waited for me to go on. "Or not willingly, but because they have the book and her app. That's what the real hostages are."

"A book's not alive."

"An app is. *This* app is."

I finished my whiskey, but it no longer warmed me. Quinn stuck the cigarette behind his ear.

"But why would someone want it?" he asked. "It sounds horrible."

"Yeah, but think what something like that could do if it went viral." I talked way too fast, trying to keep up with my thoughts. "Like if some fascist got hold of it and used it like a weapon. Or if a whole bunch of people used it. White supremacists, nationalists, politicians, terrorists—whoever. Like in Rwanda, they did all those radio broadcasts and brainwashed people into committing genocide. I mean, look at Fox News. Or Stormfront, or Herla. This thing could be all over the Internet in a day."

"Huh." Quinn contemplated this. "Seems like a long shot, unless someone knew what they were doing."

"Tindra knows what she's doing. She just might not want to actually *do* it. Unless she's forced to."

I took out *Dead Girls* and set it on the bar. "And there's still this."

I opened it to the page from *The Book of Lamps and Banners*. Quinn didn't even register the illuminated leaf: he reached for the copy of *Dead Girls*. "Hey, wait—that's your book! I want to see—"

"Fuck that." I snapped the book shut. "It's not worth a million dollars."

Quinn bared his teeth, more menace than smile. "Why are you like this, Cass? Every time you have a chance to pull yourself out of the hole you've dug, you fuck it up on purpose. You could do something with your photography again." He gestured at *Dead Girls*. "Take more photos instead of getting wasted."

My face grew hot. "You gave me that crank."

"I know I did. I'm an asshole. But look at yourself—" He reached for my hand, but I pushed him away. "You're a walking skeleton. You don't eat, you're either tweaking or drunk, twenty-four seven."

"What?" I laughed in disbelief. "*You're* telling *me* to straighten out?"

He leaned back on his barstool. "Yeah, I am. Until I hooked up with you again, I was keeping it together. I have the vinyl business, I have a place to live. I have a life. I can't afford to be shit-faced all the time, Cass. I can't afford to be a fuckup."

My eyes stung. I waited till I could talk without my voice shaking. "If we find the book. Or Tindra, and the app—"

"Cass, listen to me—*nothing* is going to happen with that app. The only thing worth pursuing here is the book, and I don't see us finding it. I say we call the game and split. Come with me back to Reykjavík. I have the vinyl business, we can get by. I'll get you another camera."

"I already have another camera."

"So what the hell are we waiting for?" He stared at me, his expression torn between fury and pleading. "You've still got that Swedish passport you nicked from Dagney, right? We can get the red-eye. Or leave early tomorrow."

I turned to look at the Seeburg, its flickering ice-blue aurora imprisoned in glass and Bakelite. "I can't stay in Iceland," I said. "Not permanently. You know that."

"So we'll work something out. All this time, we can figure something out, right?"

His big hand covered mine, and I nodded, thinking of his place outside Reykjavík: a shell of rusting corrugated metal and plywood nestled beneath a hive of cell towers, furnished with thousands of vinyl albums and not much else. Not much different from my place back on Houston Street, when you came down to it.

I leaned toward him till our foreheads touched. "I'd still like to go to Greece."

"Maybe we can do that."

"If we had the book, we could sell it and buy a place there."

Quinn sighed. "Christ, you just don't give up. You don't know about this kind of stuff, Cass. I do. This kind of thing never ends well. It hasn't even begun well. We need to leave London. You've already got a footprint here the size of a truck. Let's go to Reykjavík."

"I can't stay in Reykjavík."

"So don't stay. Go back to New York on your own passport, you can come see me in a month or two."

"We'll be three thousand miles apart."

"It's the twenty-first century, Cass. People live in different places."

"I don't want to live in a different place. I want to go somewhere warm, together. I want to go to Greece."

"Greece costs money," he said. "I need to get back home so I can take care of business there."

"*Business.*" I sneered.

"That's right." He reached for his backpack and dumped its contents on the counter. Vinyl records, their cardboard sleeves wrapped in clear plastic. "My *legal business.* Because if I get involved in something else and I'm caught, I'm fucked. I owe money, and this is the only way I can make it legally."

He grabbed one of the albums, a limited pressing of a band I'd never heard of. For a moment I thought he'd hit me with it. Instead he tossed it onto the others.

I said, "That's chump change." Quinn's mouth tightened, but I couldn't stop. "If we find this book, I can cut a deal with Gryffin. I'll give him the book, he can transfer money into my account. You and me can be gone in a heartbeat, Greece or anywhere else we want to go."

"'*If* we find this book,' '*if* we find this book.' Cass, you have no fucking clue where that book is."

"Yes, I do. We go to Kalkö and look for Erik or Gwilym Birdhouse. Or Tindra's father, whoever he is. You said it's a small island—all we have to do is find one of them."

"And then what?"

"I don't know. We'll think of something. *You'll* think of something. That was your job, right?"

"Watch it, Cassie."

"It's worth a shot." I swiveled to stare out the Banshee's rain-streaked windows. "But you're right. I need to get out of London. The weather sucks."

"Kalkö's not going to be an improvement."

"I don't care. You speak a little Swedish, right? From your junkie girlfriend."

"Ex-girlfriend. You oughta thank her, you're using her passport."

He stared at the Seeburg. "We could go to Kalkö," he said at last. "I went a few times with Dagney—it's a big tourist place in the summer. Right now, not so much, so probably it wouldn't be hard to find these people, and probably I could convince them—if they have your book. If the girl went with them of her own accord, it could get tricky. Like if she's somehow in on this. But we can try."

"Will you be able to leave London without trouble?"

"Leaving's not the problem—it's the other end, them letting me in. But I got here, right? I have a Scandinavian travel card, I'm a legal resident of Iceland, I'm white. I think I'll be okay. But . . ."

He stroked the hair at my temple, pushing it behind one ear. "You need to do something about your hair. Too many variables—at least you need to look like that passport photo. Can you make it blond again?"

I nodded, and he traced the barely healed gash on my cheek, adding, "And you need to cover that with makeup or something."

"I know. I just need a few things from Sainsbury's." I pushed away my empty glass. "So now what?"

"Keep moving. If we're gonna do this, we need to do it fast. Not tonight—only a few flights a day from Stockholm to Norderby, we don't want to be on the same one with your friends. I'll find a hotel at the airport, we can leave first thing tomorrow. Go buy your stuff and meet me at the Tube. I'll settle up. And listen to me, Cass—"

He grasped me by the wrists, his gray-green eyes icy. "This is it. Last dance. You fuck it up, I'm done."

I glanced over to see Derek standing at the jukebox. He punched in a song, turned, and stared at me as the ringing chords and sledge-hammer drums kicked in. The Gun Club, "She's Like Heroin to Me." I gave him a sardonic smile. He didn't smile back.

CHAPTER 37

Three hours later we were at a chain hotel near Heathrow. Quinn checked us in, using a credit card and Irish driver's license, both featuring a name other than his own. I waited till we were alone in the elevator to comment.

"Nanker Phelge? Are you kidding me? How many fake IDs do you have?"

He didn't answer.

Our room came with a view of a freight company garage. I had my overloaded leather bag, Quinn the worn L.L. Bean backpack that held some vinyl records, a change of clothes, and his laptop. He pulled out the computer as soon as we arrived and settled on the bed to book our tickets.

I went into the bathroom with the supplies I'd bought at Sainsbury's: a large box of baking soda, a bottle of the strongest dish detergent I could find, and some expensive hair conditioner. I made a paste out of the baking soda and dish detergent, then spent the next forty-five minutes working it through my hair and rinsing it out, a trick a stylist friend had taught me on the Lower East Side back when Limelight was in its prime. By the time I was done, my hair was the color and consistency of shredded October leaves. I went through all of the conditioner before I could stand to touch my scalp.

But I was blond again. I showered, dressed in clean drainpipe jeans and a boatneck shirt, and went to sit on the bed beside Quinn. I pulled out Dagney Ahlstrand's passport and stared at her photo, compared it with my own pallid face in the wall mirror.

"What do you think?" I asked Quinn.

He glanced up. "Better. You look like you."

"Is that good or bad?"

"Good, if it keeps you from getting stopped at border control." He swiveled to look at me properly. "No, it's good."

I turned away, pulled the stolen Nikon from my bag, and raised it to my face, adjusting the lens.

"That your new camera?" I nodded. "Nice. What is it?"

"A Nikon." I stared at him through the viewfinder. "It's a good rig. Expensive."

I flicked the shutter release and Quinn stiffened. I lowered the camera. "Don't worry. It's not loaded."

I set the Nikon on the bed and went through the rest of my stuff. I sorted my few remaining pills into prescription bottles with my name on them, doling out three Percocets for later. I'd need something to offset the crank if I was going to get any sleep.

Last of all I opened the cosmetics case I'd nabbed in the hair salon and removed the little enameled compact. I pried open the empty compartment designed to hold face powder, tipped most of the contents of the ziplock bag of crank into it, and snapped the compact shut.

"Okay, I'm good," I announced.

Quinn put his hand around my bare ankle and squeezed. "You sure you want to do this, Cassie?"

"What else are we going to do?"

"Jesus, I dunno. Act like normal people?"

"Normal people don't do what we do." I peered over his shoulder at the laptop. "What're you looking at?"

"Trying to track down your friends in Kalkö. Svarlight has a post-office address in Norderby, but I think they may live by Slythamn. Norderby's the tourist deal, it was some kind of trading post for thousands of years. Baltic amber, stuff like that. The northern part of the island is more industrial. There's a big quarry and a cement plant. That's where Slythamn is."

"What makes you think they're there?"

"Not too many other places they could be on Kalkö. Plus, there's an old listing for a Bergstrand in Slythamn."

"Have you been there?"

"I drove through once. It's pretty grim."

He gestured at his laptop: a photo of dun-colored factory towers and dark clouds billowing from smokestacks, with a row of small, barn-red buildings in the foreground. "The main cement plant cut back its workforce a few years ago. There's a lot of unemployment, even though officially no one in Sweden is unemployed."

"Why would Tindra's father live there?"

"Why do people live anywhere? Maybe he has family. Maybe he works in the cement factory. I don't even know for sure that's where he lives. If they're there, we'll find them."

"So will Lyla and Tommy." It was the first time I'd thought of them in hours. "There's no way they won't have figured this out, too."

"I thought he was MIA. You think his sister would go there without him?"

"I don't know."

"Would he go without her?"

"I told you, I don't know." I rubbed my eyes, my thoughts colliding like pinballs.

" 'Don't know,' 'don't know.' What *do* you know, Cass?"

He stood and started pacing. I slid over to his laptop and clicked on another photo. It showed a group of protesters with the cement plant in the background. Winter—everyone wore heavy clothing and held handwritten signs with gloved hands.

I pointed at one of the signs. "What's this mean?"

" 'Sweden first.' "

"What about this one?"

"*Blott Sverige svenska krusbär har.* It's a saying—'Only Sweden has Swedish gooseberries.' Meaning keep your dark-skinned fruits to yourself."

"What about this?"

He shook his head. "No clue. I don't know that much Swedish—'where's the bathroom,' 'how much is this,' 'I think you're hot.' Beyond that you're on your own."

I clicked to translate the article. Employees and concerned locals were protesting the fact that the cement factory had recently hired a dozen immigrants. The dateline for the piece was not even two months ago:

We have a housing shortage on the island and not enough jobs. Why are they going to foreigners and not to genuine Swedes?

A related article was a year older and more disturbing. Someone had set fire to refugee housing outside Slythamn. No one died, but a thirteen-year-old refugee girl had gone missing in the confusion. There was a blurry accompanying photo of a skinny kid, dark hair, braces, no head scarf. A phone number to call if you had information.

I lost interest and searched for news about the rally in Victoria Park. The more liberal sites appeared to be downplaying it. They cited fewer than a thousand participants; online tabloids and nationalist sites represented the gathering as having been more heavily attended. HNN called it "a triumph."

Today's event was a rousing show of support on the part of citizens who wish to preserve our way of life. Representatives from the U.S., Sweden, Germany, Denmark, and France underscored that this is an international problem, with repercussions that extend beyond our own shores to those of other nations that share our core values.

I clicked through news photos, looking for anyone who resembled Tindra or Lyla, Tommy or Gryffin. Or me. Finally I yawned and gave up.

Quinn had turned on the flat-screen TV and was sprawled on the bed, watching a soccer match. I lay beside him. When a commercial came on he switched channels, clicking through news, weather, another commercial, more soccer, more news . . .

"Hey." I sat up, pointing at the screen. "Go back."

"What?"

"The station you just passed, go back to it."

He pointed the remote at the screen. A Sky News newscaster read from a teleprompter while footage of the rally played behind her. The video switched to an enlarged photo image. Cops stood around the body of a dark-skinned man as two hooded figures in white coveralls approached from a police van.

"Son of a bitch," I whispered. "That's Tommy."

CHAPTER 38

A headline flashed across the screen—SUSPECT DOWNED BY METRO POLICE—then cut to a John Lewis ad. I snatched the remote from Quinn's hand, ran through scores of stations, but saw no other related news. I grabbed the laptop. In seconds I found the story.

BREAKING NEWS

An unidentified man died late this afternoon at a nationalist rally in Victoria Park. Described as dark skinned and wearing military-style clothing, earlier he had been observed near the front of the crowd during Conservative MP Ronald Morton's address, according to a Metro Police spokesperson. Witnesses later claimed to have seen him arguing with a woman about a mobile phone, immediately before he attacked another man without provocation. When on-site police intervened, the assailant attacked them. An officer responded by using a Taser. The man died shortly afterward at the scene. Human rights activists have denounced the police action as being racially motivated.

I scrolled to another brief article, and another. All the information was the same. "Jesus Christ," I said, and ran a hand through my hair.

"You sure it's him?" asked Quinn.

"I think so, but..."

He leaned over my shoulder and clicked the top of the screen. Rows of photographs appeared. Most were the same shot I'd seen on

TV, but Quinn jabbed his finger at one originally posted on Twitter. "Let's see that one."

He enlarged the digital image till it filled the screen, so underlit it resembled a sepia photograph from the early twentieth century. I still recognized Tommy immediately.

"That's him," I said. I felt sick.

"You sure?"

I nodded. I remembered that massive head bent over a Parcheesi board. *Want to play? Might help pass the time.* "Tommy. I don't even know his last name."

"He's a pretty big guy to die from being tased. Maybe he had a bad heart."

I stared at the photo and let my eyes adjust to the distorted play of light and shadow, as though adjusting to a darkroom. Tommy lay on his back, his arms thrown out, mouth and eyes wide as though staring at something wondrous.

I enlarged the image. "Does getting tased hurt?"

"Fuck yeah. It's like being electrocuted. You seize up—"

Quinn demonstrated, drawing his arms to his chest. "If you get hit in the arm, I mean. Your legs spasm if you get it in the thigh. It's pretty bad."

Again I peered at the photo, that rapt expression. Tommy didn't look like he'd been in pain. "But people die from it?"

"Sometimes, sure. But a guy that big? Like I said, that would be tough, unless he had a bad heart or was fucked up on drugs. Was this guy an addict?"

"I don't think so."

I reread the account of the attack, then flipped back to Tommy's photo. Who had he attacked? Erik? The man who'd met with Tindra, or kidnapped her?

I was still scrolling for news when an update popped up. Tommy hadn't yet been ID'd, but his victim had—a sixty-three-year-old black man from South London who'd been part of a church group protesting the white nationalists.

"He came out of nowhere," the pensioner stated, obviously still shaken. "Never seen him before, I have no idea why he singled me out..."

I turned to Quinn. "This doesn't make any sense. Why would he attack some old guy protesting the Nazis?"

I enlarged the photo to get a better look at Tommy's face. His upper lip had curled back slightly from his teeth, as though he was starting to smile. Both eyes were wide open. One shone glassy white, its pupil shrunken to a nearly invisible pinpoint. Darkness occluded the other eye. I thought of Harold and the crimson bloom in his eye; of the dead bird and the dart I'd seen near his house, the dead bird the boys had been toying with in the park.

I peered at the photo of Tommy more closely. Was that darkness caused by a shadow? Or some flaw or damage to the eye itself? I looked at Quinn. "Have you ever seen someone get electrocuted?"

"Yeah, once. Guy wasn't cooperative, I had to give him a nudge."

"Do you remember what his eyes looked like? Like, were they dilated?"

"'Dilated'?" Quinn rubbed his chin. "I dunno. Maybe. It wasn't a lot of voltage—too much and you go into cardiac arrest, and I wasn't being paid for that. I remember he looked like shit afterward, more like he'd OD'd. Except for the burns."

"But you think maybe his eyes were dilated?"

Quinn raised his hands. "I told you, I don't know. They could have been. I'm not an EMT."

I zoomed in and out on the photo, until I was certain that there was no object or figure that might have cast a shadow across Tommy's right eye. Whatever darkness was there came from the eye itself.

The pupil of the other eye was definitely constricted, not dilated. I enlarged the image until it fragmented into gray ash and snow. Even digital images decay if you distort them enough.

After a minute I stood and took a step back, still staring at the computer screen. I let my eyes go in and out of focus. When the image blurred, I slowly moved my head back and forth, until the image grew clear again, like a photograph emerging from the toner bath in a darkroom. My thoughts snapped into focus along with my vision. I knew what I was looking at.

With digital photography, there are no chemicals or recombinations of physical elements—no alchemy—unlike traditional print photography, where light interacts with the emulsion to alter its chemistry. Ionization occurs, charging and changing crystal silver to metallic silver, and this creates a latent image in the film's emulsion.

But you need an impurity for the process to work. That's where the chemical developing agent comes in. The random agent acts like the grain of sand in an oyster, only instead of growing a pearl, the presence of the chemical allows the metallic silver within the film's emulsion to expand. The photograph develops, and the latent image becomes visible. Tindra had called me an immutable object, something that doesn't change. Maybe I was also the random agent.

"That." My finger stabbed at the laptop screen, the eye like a dark planet striated with branching lines that might have been rivers and tributaries. Capillaries. I gestured excitedly at Quinn. "They shot him in the eye, like Harold."

Quinn stood behind me. "I don't see it."

"You don't have to. *I* see it. And I bet by now the police have, too."

Quinn pushed me aside, scrutinizing the image like it was a racing form.

"I don't buy it," he said at last. "There's no bullet small enough. Nobody could get in a shot that clean."

"Someone already has—it's how Harold died."

"The body wouldn't look like this. This guy's face, you'd see where the bullet entered. And exited. Look at his eyeball—there's no bullet hole! And there's no mention anywhere of him getting shot."

"I didn't see an exit wound with Harold, either. Or the dog."

"You wouldn't know what to look for." Quinn sounded irritated. "And the frigging dog was poisoned."

"What if it wasn't?"

"Listen to me. There's no way someone could drill that guy's eye in broad daylight, not without someone seeing him. He was in a public park. There was a demonstration going on."

"Uh-uh." I perched on a corner of the bed. "I found a spot. I needed to lay low, I hid under this gigantic tree. No one could see me, but I could see them."

Now Quinn just looked pissed off. "You're being stupid. There wasn't a shooter hiding under your tree."

"There are other trees! Somebody found a perch or a place in the bushes and nailed him. Just like Harold. And maybe the dog, too."

"Shot him with what? You need to sober up, Cass. And sleep."

"I'm right," I said. "I know I'm right."

I stormed into the bathroom, stood over the sink, and ran the cold water, splashing it into my face. I *was* right; I was certain of it. But I knew there was a piece missing, something out of focus or just beyond my range of vision; something a camera's unblinking eye would have captured, but that I'd missed.

Quinn was right about one thing: I needed to sleep. I turned the water off and dug out the three Percocets, swallowed them with some water, and squeezed my eyes shut. I recalled Harold's astonishment as he gazed upon *The Book of Lamps and Banners*, his delight morphing into a corpse's gaze, and Tommy's swollen eye, its pupil lost in a web of burst capillaries. Freya's tattoo. Children poking at the carcass of a tiny bird. A dead dog. Lamps and banners and a language with no words. Skull magic.

I drank another mouthful of water, returned to the other room, and sat on the bed. I picked up *Dead Girls* and opened it: not to the illuminated page but a black-and-white photo. Me at nineteen, naked, my fingers clasping the bony hand of a life-size model of a human skeleton draped with a white sheet, as though it were a bride. Beneath the photo was Odilon Redon's caption for his *Temptation of Saint Anthony*, the drawing that had inspired my self-portrait:

Death: I am the one who will make a serious woman of you; come, let us embrace.

Minutes passed. Quinn slumped in the chair, watching me. I closed the book, stood, and walked to the window.

"You okay?" Quinn asked.

I gazed down at the freight company's loading dock. Two fourteen-wheelers with the same bright orange logo sat side by side, their engines idle. Black turbines spun atop the freight garage, blades flickering like the shadows thrown by an old-fashioned film projector. A blue-and-white Learjet descended toward rows of green lights on the runway, a red wind sock billowing in its wake.

The mundane scene was a metaphor for something I couldn't understand. Yet the meaning was there, if only I could stare at it long enough; if only I could break the code.

A new language . . . lights and bright colors and symbols—it's all lamps and banners. It's all code.

I turned from the window, returned to the bed, and stared at my book of photographs. I thought about how a lost world hid inside it, conjured from sunlight and salted paper. What had changed in all those years?

Not me. Not enough, anyway.

The storm in my brain began to subside, lulled by Percocet. I tugged my shirt off over my head.

"Hey," I called to Quinn. "Come here."

He looked at me, then stood, reaching to close the window blind.

"Leave it open," I said.

I lifted my face to his as he sank onto the bed and touched my cheek.

"You smell clean," he said. "You smell like you."

"I am me," I said, and pulled him to me.

PART TWO

KALKÖ

CHAPTER 39

It was still dark when we woke to the sound of Quinn's phone alarm. He stumbled around, cursing as he made his way to the bathroom. I sat up groggily, hoping I wouldn't be sick, switched on the light, and confronted my reflection in the mirror across the room. Four a.m. hangover: never a good look. I drank some water from a glass on the nightstand, found the compact in my bag, dug out two tiny scoops with my pinkie nail, and snorted them. It was so caustic, I felt like I'd shot the stuff directly into my eyes.

By the time Quinn returned from showering, I'd dressed and done my best to clean up. He stared at my eyes and tossed his towel onto the bed.

"What the hell, you don't even want coffee first? That shit's gonna ruin your pretty teeth."

"Now there's that much less if they search my bag."

"Not funny, Cass."

"It's mostly B$_{12}$ and Epsom salts. No one's going to search my carry-on. I'm more worried that I have a Swedish passport and don't speak Swedish."

"No one's going to care on this end. Over there, just speak English. Anyone asks, tell them you've been living in the U.S. for a long time. *Tack* means 'thank you,' *snälla* means 'please.' *Hej* means 'hi.' You ready? I need a smoke."

Outside, Quinn wandered in circles, chain-smoking until the airport shuttle arrived. There hadn't been time to go online and check for more news about Tommy or Harold. When the shuttle van arrived, I collapsed into a plastic seat and stared out at the wasteland of loading docks and service ramps, lines of cabs and black hire cars already choking the access roads. Quinn elbowed me. "Stop grinding your teeth."

I chewed my thumbnail instead.

At security, my stomach clenched as I watched two guards pull an elderly woman in a hijab from the line, ignoring the protests of her daughter, a young woman carrying a Vuitton bag, her dark hair pulled into a neat chignon. The old woman said nothing, only walked with the guards down a long corridor.

We got through security with no trouble.

"You hungry?" Quinn asked.

I shook my head, staring at that long, now-empty corridor. Quinn pulled me after him.

"Come on," he said. "Nothing you can do."

We found a Boots so Quinn could stock up on nicotine gum for the flight, then a place for me to buy a coffee, hoping it would dissolve the bitter film that coated my tongue. It didn't.

In the crowded terminal, we sat and watched the infinite news cycle on TV. The sound was turned off, so I read the news crawl. Mass shootings in a Wisconsin Walmart and a Reno parking lot, another UK politician faking his own death. A machete attack in Finland. In Chile, an eight-year-old girl had survived an avalanche that buried her village. In Greenland, a melting glacier had revealed the intact skeleton of an immense pliosaur. There was more info about the new virus that had emerged in China.

Then up popped footage of yesterday's demonstration. Quick montage of Morton delivering his speech to rapt onlookers, token shot of a skinhead with a swastika tattooed on his neck, a few seconds of the melee that brought the rally to its end. A scene of uniformed figures moving around an area marked off with police tape, which quickly segued to a police news conference. I followed the news crawl:

VICTIM IDENTIFIED AS AFGHAN SPECIAL FORCES VETERAN THOMAS LEWIS OF BRIXTON.

WE HAVE NO SUSPECTS IN CUSTODY AT THIS TIME.

ANYONE WITH INFORMATION IS ENCOURAGED TO CONTACT THE METROPOLITAN POLICE.

I turned to Quinn. "You think they know more than they're saying?"

"Hell yeah. But my guess is they don't know much more than we do, except how he died."

"Like this."

I made a gun of my hand and pointed it at my eye. Quinn turned away in annoyance. We didn't talk again until our flight was called.

CHAPTER 40

We landed at Arlanda late morning and passed through border control, again without incident, the agent barely glancing at me before she returned my passport. We'd lost an hour traveling east; it was midafternoon when we boarded the small plane for Norderby.

The other passengers all seemed to be commuters or residents returning home after a visit to the mainland. A deadheading flight attendant, a couple of young guys in T-shirts and skinny jeans who discussed an IT merger, switching back and forth from English to Swedish. A leonine old man shepherded three small towheaded grandchildren into their seats. Beside me, Quinn chewed nicotine gum and read a Jo Nesbø novel.

Within minutes of takeoff, heavy clouds obscured the world below, a veil that occasionally thinned to allow a glimpse of the Baltic Sea, gray as wet granite. I shifted uncomfortably in my tiny seat, grateful the flight was only half an hour. Lack of booze and sleep, coupled with hours of increasingly hectic thought, had left me feeling as though the skin was being peeled from my face, layer by layer.

"Stop it," Quinn said for the hundredth time as I twitched.

I tried to focus on Greece: being there with Quinn, photographing some Cycladic cliffs. Sun and heat and ouzo. I'd go cold turkey from speed, drown my cravings in the sea. It could happen. I raked my fingers through my hair, drummed them on the armrest. It could happen.

After about twenty minutes we began our descent. A gap opened in the clouds, as though someone had cleared a dirty windshield. I leaned over to peer down at the medieval walled city of Norderby: orange-tiled roofs and a small cluster of white houses. More a village than a city; a candy village, small enough that I could bite down and shatter it in an instant. Outside its walls, an ugly industrial building marked the ferry terminal, where a large white ship was docked. An eyeblink and it was all gone, blotted out by clouds.

I watched idly as the flight attendant strolled down the aisle, checking seat belts and tray tables. The three towheaded children stared at a picture book, lips moving in unison. When the flight attendant reached the rear of the plane, she stopped beside a man with a thatch of gray *Eraserhead* hair staring intently at his laptop. I swiftly looked away, waited several seconds, and glanced back again. The flight attendant gestured at the gray-haired man's computer.

"Holy shit," I whispered.

Quinn glanced up from his book, irritated. "What?"

"That guy back there—don't look! It's Gwilym Birdhouse."

"Gwilym Birdhouse?"

"Shut up! Yes," I hissed. "He's on the plane."

"So?"

"Just, he's here, too."

Quinn craned his neck to look behind us. "You're right—that guy kinda looks like Gwilym Birdhouse."

"It *is* Gwilym Birdhouse."

The flight attendant strode down the aisle as the recorded announcement played, first in Swedish, then English. I tried not to look toward the back of the plane.

"Why's he here?" I asked.

Quinn shrugged. "You saw that CD—he's a producer for Svarlight."

"Yeah, but—"

"But nothing. Don't hear zebras when it's horses, Cass."

"What the hell does that even mean?"

"The most obvious answer is usually the right one." He picked up his book again.

I sank into my seat and buried my face in the in-flight magazine. Quinn made sense, but I wasn't buying it. I could think of another reason Birdhouse was here.

The Book of Lamps and Banners. He might have heard it had been stolen and was interested in buying it. He was friends with that guy Malloy, who was definitely a racist. And he worked with Svarlight. That was still a big jump to being involved with a plot to kidnap and perhaps murder for a rare book.

Then again, musicians are notoriously susceptible to crazy belief systems, including fascism. Maybe Birdhouse simply wanted *The Book of Lamps and Banners,* but knew nothing of its dicey provenance. He wouldn't have to be a Nazi to buy a stolen rare book from a white supremacist; just a collector with a wiggly moral compass.

Or maybe Quinn was right, and Birdhouse was here for a recording gig at Svarlight Studios. I stared out the window, hoping for another glimpse of Norderby. I saw only flat yellow fields and red barns, an array of big-box stores, and finally the airport runway. After we touched down, I retrieved my bag from the overhead bin and put on my fake Ray-Bans. Quinn slung his backpack over his shoulder.

"It's raining," he said, indicating my sunglasses.

"I don't want Birdhouse to recognize me."

"How long were you with him?"

"Only a minute or two."

"I think you're safe. Stop being so paranoid."

People started to move in the aisle in front of us. I touched Quinn's shoulder and pointed toward the back of the plane. "Let me out first—you wait and try to see where he goes. I'll meet you inside."

The airport terminal was a modular building, not much bigger than the plane. I staked out a spot near the exit, keeping my head down as I clocked everyone walking past. Gwilym Birdhouse ambled by, talking on his mobile, Quinn a few steps behind him. He followed Birdhouse out of the terminal and returned several minutes later, shaking rain from his leather jacket.

"He got a cab. It turned left onto the access road. That's all I know."

"Could you hear anything he was saying?"

"Yeah." He gestured impatiently at me to follow him back outside, walked several yards from the door, and stopped to light a cigarette. "Dinner tonight with someone in Norderby. I think he's here on vacation."

"Vacation? Are you kidding me? That makes no sense. One of his best friends was just murdered back in London. Why would he come here? Plus it's winter—who comes here in winter?"

"We're here."

"We're not on vacation!"

Quinn took a long drag on his cigarette and sighed. "That's for goddamn sure."

CHAPTER 41

A taxi pulled up to the curb, discarded a passenger, then sat, idling. Quinn stubbed out his cigarette.

"Let's grab that," he said. "I rented us a car. There's a hotel in Slythamn where we can stay tonight, it's about an hour away."

"Slythamn? Where the cement plant is?" I thought longingly of the confectionary city I'd seen from the air. "Why can't we stay in Norderby?"

"Because we aren't on vacation," Quinn retorted, and hopped into the cab. "I told you, I looked up Svarlight online. There's a postal address in Norderby and another in the boonies, out by Slythamn. We'll check that out first. If we don't find anything, we can go to Norderby and see if there's anything there. After that, I'm done."

"What about Birdhouse? Don't you think that's weird?"

"Just because you think it doesn't mean it's real, Cass. Especially when you're spun."

We picked up the car at a Swedish Rent-A-Wreck a few miles south of Norderby, alongside a muddy field populated by black sheep who watched us suspiciously from behind a wooden fence. The car was an older VW Jetta, dinged up but clean. The hose used to wash it down still sputtered in a puddle by the trailer that served as an office. The guy who ran the place barely spoke to either of us. He glanced at Quinn's license, then ran a credit card through his mobile, handed Quinn a set of keys, and walked back into the trailer.

"In summer this place is filled with people," Quinn said as we pulled back onto the main road. "Surfing's big. And windsurfing. I think there's a map in the glove box, if you want to see where we're going. I know the way."

I barely glanced at the map before tossing it into the back seat, instead stared out the window.

The rain had let up. Charcoal clouds surrendered to soft blue sky edged with lavender and gold. The late-afternoon light gave the countryside a comforting glow: fields and tidy houses, sturdy barns, a few small modern apartment blocks in seaside colors: maritime blue, lichen green, lighthouse red and white. I gazed into the distance at Norderby, where cars emerged from an ancient stone gate, orderly ants exiting a well-fortified nest. People bicycled and walked home from work or school. Children ran along greenway trails. It was a bucolic dream of twenty-first-century life: wind farms and winter pastures, cell towers and ancient stave churches; gulls above the indigo reach of the Baltic Sea.

The dream broke outside of Norderby, where we stopped at a congeries of big-box stores and gas stations. We made a quick run into a government shop to stock up on whiskey and cigarettes, a bottle of Myer's dark for Quinn; then a supermarket for flatbread and cheese, Coke, and a few bags of chocolates to sate his sweet tooth. By the time we hit the road again, early dusk had fallen.

We headed north along the coast road. Quinn pointed out five tall stone pillars at the edge of a west-facing cliff. "That's Galgkapt—Gallows Head. They used to hang criminals there and leave the corpses as a warning to approaching sailors."

With the sun poised above the Baltic Sea, the stone gallows glowed crimson, fingers of a bleeding hand; then turned black against the sky. I shivered and reached to turn up the heat.

"How old are they?" I asked.

"Twelve hundreds? I told you, this was a Viking settlement before it became a trade center. There are Viking ruins everywhere. Older ones, too. Picture stones, graves. That CD, *Stone Ships*? The island's famous for those. Graves shaped like boats."

"Sounds like you liked coming here."

"Dagney really dug it. She used to vacation here as a kid. But yeah, I did, too. More in summer than now," he admitted.

I turned to stare moodily out the window. The mention of Dagney put me out of the mood to talk.

Norderby was on the island's western coast. Our destination, Slythamn, was on the east coast and a bit north. The car radio didn't work, so we drove in silence on nearly empty back roads, through a twilit landscape that resembled something out of a tale by the Brothers Grimm. Fields gave way to forests of evergreen and birch, interspersed with neat wooden cottages, whitewashed limestone houses with metal roofs, derelict homesteads collapsed into heaps of silvered wooden beams.

Then more fields, where an occasional solitary windmill stood sentinel—real windmills, with wooden sails and squat barrel-shaped housings—the pastureland divided by disintegrating stone walls and fences made of neatly latticed boards or branches. Watching it through the rain-streaked windows, the rumble of the car's studded tires the only sound, I felt as though I'd fallen into that shadowy place between dreams and waking. When Quinn braked suddenly, my head snapped up. I'd nodded off.

"Sorry," he said. "See that?"

He pointed into the gathering darkness at something hanging from the ghostly white limb of a birch. *A shabby brown coat or sweater,* I thought; then saw it was an animal. A fox, suspended by its jaw so that its mouth gaped open, black gums and white teeth and a shriveled curl of tongue. Its abdomen had been slit, exposing the rib cage and a snarl of intestine. I rolled down my window to get a better look.

"What the hell is that?"

"Like Galgkapt. A warning to the other foxes not to mess with someone's sheep."

The cold air smelled like Christmas, pine boughs and a promise of snow. We'd left the main thoroughfare for a rutted gravel road, not much more than a trail, surrounded by forest. No fields, not even a clearing that I could see. I shook my head, perplexed. "But there's no sheep here. Where are we?"

Quinn lit a cigarette. "Svarlight has a post-office address in Norderby, and there was also that old address for a Bergstrand in Slythamn. I thought we'd check it out in case it's Tindra's father. The road didn't have a name, but I think I can find it."

"Are you sure?"

"Of course not. But it's worth checking out."

I gazed at the mutilated fox. "Do people do stuff like that here? Torture animals?"

"Not that I ever heard. Swedes are big on animal rights."

"Then why hasn't someone reported this?"

"Maybe no one's seen it. Road doesn't look like it gets much traffic."

He backed up the car, turned it around, and drove off slowly. In the last few minutes, night had fallen like a guillotine blade. I saw a few specks that might have been snow. I felt an inordinate relief when we turned back onto what passed for the main road.

"We almost there?"

"Almost. Though I wouldn't be in so much of a hurry if I were you."

Within ten minutes, the fairy-tale landscape of forest and meadows butted up against an industrial one: corrugated-metal sheds, blocks of sagging prefab structures and one-story houses, their white stucco flaking off to reveal gray concrete. The few streetlamps illuminated no trees—no vegetation at all, save for patches of dead grass protruding from the concrete like hair. Lights shone behind the lace curtains in some windows, but the town had a joyless air.

"So people do live here," I said.

"Sure. Cement plant's still open, though they lost most of their workforce when they closed the big processing facility. A lot of people left then, to the mainland or Estonia. That's why no one's happy they moved refugees in. But yeah, people live here. People will live anywhere."

"Where are the refugees from?"

"Not sure. It was good for the school—they worried it might have to close. Not enough kids."

"How come you know so much about this place?"

"I told you, I used to come here with Dagney."

"But for what? The windsurfing?" I laughed.

"There's a horse track outside Norderby."

I stayed mum. When I first tried to find Quinn in Reykjavík, the only thing I'd had to go on was that he spent a lot of time in seedy casinos. I suspected people here would do the same, given the option.

Slythamn was a bleak pocket universe tucked into a Nordic Arcadia. There was no demarcation between residential areas and the factory grounds. Red lights blinked from power plants and a cell tower. Storage silos reminded me of guard towers in a prison block, linked by an Escher-like network of conveyors. Everywhere were yellow warning signs: FARA! superimposed on a lightning bolt.

Quinn turned onto a street more like a tunnel, hemmed in by chain-link fences topped with razor wire and more warning signs. These showed the silhouette of a man plummeting to his death. I couldn't see what we were being warned against until the car stopped, and Quinn pointed out his open window.

"That's the main quarry. Or was—it's the one they shut down."

A single pole light illuminated the quarry, which was more like a canyon, its sheer walls plunging well over a hundred feet to a vast dark floor. Abandoned machinery and vehicles stood everywhere, axle-deep in standing water. The roof of a long narrow warehouse had collapsed, the structure resembling a crushed caterpillar.

Yet the ravaged landscape had a sinister beauty, too, like the fox's corpse, or those photographs of sheep's skulls and deserted beaches. I wished I'd put film into the Nikon.

"I want to come back here tomorrow," I said.

"You should see the rauks—the rock formations down on the beaches," Quinn said as he shifted into first gear. "They're beautiful."

"Beautiful is overrated."

"Hold that thought," said Quinn. "We're almost at the hotel."

CHAPTER 42

We drove past an exit ramp blocked off by sawhorses, dodging potholes and toppled construction cones. Overhead, corkscrewed rebar and a twisted girder dangled from an overpass like metal viscera. Chunks of concrete littered the road in front of us.

Just past the ramp loomed a black mound the height of a house. In its shadow stood a limestone building painted baby-shit yellow. A vertical sign hung from one corner: SLAGGHÖGEN. Quinn stopped the car and let it idle.

"Nice," I said. "It's the Gulag Inn."

"Close." Quinn pointed at the sign. "It means Slag Heap Hotel."

"You're shitting me."

"I shit you not. I got us a room in the main building."

"What the hell?"

"Or we could stay there—probably a little cheaper."

He pointed to another structure, set back from the empty parking lot: two rows of metal shipping containers stacked one atop the other. There were eight in all. Each had a metal door with a single window and a spotlight above the door. Three of the spotlights were lit.

"There's more privacy in the main building," Quinn went on. "I don't think anyone else is staying there."

"Why are *we* staying there?"

"Don't go all Westchester on me, Cass. You got a wild hair to find those people—this is the closest place to where they might be."

"And you don't think anyone is going to remember two Americans staying in this dump?"

"Forgetting comes with the room charge. Trust me: no one here ever wants to remember anything."

He pulled the car around back and parked, out of sight of the road. I sat fuming as he got out and walked toward the entrance. Finally I picked up my bag and followed.

Inside, the place looked like a time capsule entombed in the early 1980s, possibly somewhere in the Soviet bloc. Fake-wood paneling, black rubber mats on the floor, unshaded fluorescent lights. A square opening cut into one wall framed a closet where the receptionist sat. Young, probably still a teenager, her pert freckled face crowned by a black Mohawk that reinforced the sense that we'd entered a time tunnel. She wore too-tight clothes on a fleshy frame. She smiled as Quinn sidled up to the window, setting down her mobile.

"*Hej hej!*"

They spoke in Swedish, Quinn occasionally fumbling over a word. I wondered if his accent gave him away as American and hoped he could pass for a Brit or Canadian. With gray stubble hiding his facial scars and the black watch cap pulled low on his forehead, he might have been a fisherman or carpenter. I assumed there were plenty of both on the island.

"*Tack.*" He rapped his knuckles on the counter and said something to the girl in a low voice. She laughed and handed him two metal room keys.

"What's so funny?" I asked as we climbed the stairs to the second floor.

"I told her if my wife comes looking for me, I'm waiting for her in our room with a special treat."

"Who comes here to have a threesome?"

"Hey, we might get lucky."

Our room was in the front of the building. It was small but clean, and so warm I immediately peeled off my leather jacket. The double bed had two duvets on it, neatly folded down. There was a Formica-topped table and Ikea chair, a single bedside table with an ancient clock radio, a Magnavox TV on a rickety stand, and a radiator too hot to touch.

Quinn tossed his backpack onto the bed and went into the bathroom. I opened the window and stared out at the slag heap, close enough I could have lobbed the TV at it.

"At least we have a view," I said as Quinn emerged from the bathroom, holding two glass tumblers. He filled each with a few inches of whiskey and handed one to me.

"Skål."

"Skål."

The whiskey tasted good. I finished it and reached for the bottle. Quinn put his hand around mine. "Not now. We need to eat. *You* need to eat."

"I'm not hungry."

"No shit, Sherlock. You've snorted your body weight in speed over the last week. C'mon, we'll grab something, then come back."

He turned my hand over, staring at the backs of my fingers, the bones sticking up like they'd puncture the skin if pressed too hard. He shook his head and gazed at me in concern. "You're a fucking mess, you know that?"

The only restaurant in town was called Viking Aztec Pizza and Tex Mex. Inside, the walls sported a sombrero, a plastic two-headed ax, faded tourist posters with aerial shots of Norderby, windsurfers, a black ram. Half a dozen people sat in the plastic booths. After turning to give us a cursory glance, they paid no attention to us.

Quinn ordered a sausage pizza and red wine. The sausage was lamb and not bad. The pizza crust tasted like it had been extruded from a tube of foam insulation. The wine came in those miniature plastic bottles you get on a plane. I poured it into two plastic cups, then picked off the sausage from the pizza and ate it, leaving the rest to Quinn. He polished it off and went to get more wine.

I stared at the poster beside our booth. A photo of a stone boat like the one on the Jötunn's Egg album, and another photo of what looked like a very large gravestone with crude figures carved on it.

None had any facial features to identify them as male or female, or even human.

There were other symbols carved on the rock. Ships with up-turned prows; snaky-looking creatures; a triskele of an animal with a long muzzle and prominent eyeteeth. A figure wearing a robe with a long, pointed hood, holding what might have been a scythe or a crescent moon. Beneath it was another figure, with a valknut inscribed upon its torso.

Quinn returned with the wine.

"What's this?" I indicated the poster with the carvings. Quinn refilled our cups and pushed mine toward me.

"Picture stones. You only find them in a very few places, mostly here and Gotland."

"What does it mean?"

"Something about Vikings. That's a longship, and a dragon." He reached to tap a line of circles on one of the ships. "Those are shields, so some kind of battle."

"So this is death." I touched the mysterious hooded figure. "Like in *The Seventh Seal*. Didn't Bergman live here?"

"No, he lived on Fårö. And I don't think that's death." He leaned over to examine the poster. "Nope. That's a Valkyrie."

"How do you know?"

"There's a room in the museum that explains it."

"A Valkyrie?"

"Yeah. See? That's her drinking horn. She's bringing it to the dead guy with the valknut — she's taking him to Valhalla."

"I thought that was a scythe."

"No. Look, here's another one —"

He pointed to a figure I hadn't noticed, larger and more detailed. The object it held was clearly not a scythe but a ram's horn.

"Wait." I traced an invisible line from the drinking horn to the valknut. "Why is this here?"

"It's some Viking thing. You okay?" Quinn glanced at my plate and frowned. "Damn it, Cass, you need to eat something."

"I just did. The valknut—"

"I told you all I know," he broke in, exasperated. "It's something about being chosen. Why does it matter?"

I continued to stare at the poster. My head began to pound, precursor to the explosion of pain I'd felt when I looked at Ludus Mentis. I sank back and covered my eyes with my hands. "Can we go?"

"Go? We just got here."

"I feel sick. And this place creeps me out."

"That's the crank, Cass. But yeah, come on."

Outside, the cold air made me feel better. Once I'd pushed the image of the valknut and those carved figures from my mind, it was easy to believe that Quinn had nailed it. Too much crank, not enough food or sleep.

There was no one in the office when we returned to Slagghögen. Propped up on the desk was a small card with a phone number for after hours. Presumably the receptionist slept somewhere on-site. I hoped it wasn't in one of those shipping containers.

I poked my head through the window where the girl had checked us in. A computer sat on a desk, along with a plastic rose in a Starbucks mug. On the wall was an old-fashioned mailbox, rows of pigeonholes with names taped beneath them. I jiggled the knob to the office door. It was locked.

"What're you doing?" Quinn asked. "She's gone for the night."

"Curious who else is staying here."

"Doesn't look like anyone."

I pointed at the mailboxes. Three had envelopes and magazines stuffed into them. "Someone's here. Or there, maybe..."

I stepped to the window and stared out at the hotel annex, each metal unit as welcoming as a prison cell. When we'd checked in, three of the units' spotlights had been on. Now only one was lit.

"Who cares?" said Quinn. "I'm going to bed."

When I heard his steps on the second-floor landing, I boosted myself through the office window, hopped onto the floor, and pulled a handful of envelopes from one of the pigeonholes.

All were addressed to Ranim Elbaz. One had a return address at Refugees Welcome Stockholm. There was also a children's magazine with a cartoon bear on its cover, and the latest issue of *Damernas Värld,* a women's magazine.

The other mail slots held similar items—official-looking envelopes from government agencies or refugee services, a few handwritten addresses postdated from Athens and Aleppo. I grabbed the women's magazine, hopped back into the foyer, and went upstairs. Quinn was already in bed, his laptop in front of him.

"Check this out." I tossed the magazine onto a pillow.

"*Damernas Värld*? You can't even read that."

"Check out the name."

"Llorde?"

"The address label!"

"Ranim Elbaz. You know them?"

"No. But it's not a Swedish name. Some of the refugees must be staying there. I checked their mail downstairs—all the names sound Arabic."

"Wake up, Cass! There are refugees living here! We already knew that. Leave them alone. Last thing they need is you dicking with them." He set aside the laptop and turned off his light. "Get some sleep."

There was no way that was going to happen anytime soon. I picked up the laptop and typed in Birdhouse's name. I ignored his Wikipedia entry and his website and went straight to the online videos. There were more than I'd expected. Some were from his brief MTV heyday, before Nirvana and grunge pushed performers like him off a cliff.

I focused on what came later—he'd done some recent shows in Helsinki and Stockholm in smaller venues. An American tour sched-uled a few years earlier had been canceled due to poor advance sales. He'd made an appearance at a UKIP rally in Sheffield, and another in support of Brexit, where he shared the stage with Roger Daltrey and the lead singer of Iron Maiden. Both Birdhouse performances were shambolic, like watching your drunken dad sing an off-color song at a wedding.

It was a different thing when I clicked on various cuts from an album that came out in 1991, *Sheaf and Knife*—a compilation of some of the more gruesome Child Ballads, from the nineteenth-century compendium of more than three hundred collected by Francis James Child.

Birdhouse's renditions of the ancient songs were straightforward and stark. No 1980s histrionics or drum machines; just Birdhouse's reedy voice and a piano, sometimes a harp. His voice had started to go by then, but the occasional missed note and uneven delivery suited the archaic words and melodies. The result was eerie and unexpectedly powerful. More than once I felt the hairs on my neck stand up, and I finally had to close the laptop.

Sheaf and Knife tanked, the wrong songs at the wrong time. It was Birdhouse's final commercial album. Just five years later, Nick Cave would do much the same thing with his *Murder Ballads,* and make a big splash. I couldn't blame Birdhouse for slinking off to the hinterlands to lick his wounds and raise sheep.

As I put the laptop on the nightstand, Quinn turned over, growling, "For Christ's sake, *go to bed.*"

I got up, clenching my teeth, gathered the magazine I'd taken from downstairs, my room key and leather jacket, and split. Black energy buzzed inside my brain like a giant fly. I needed to discharge it, but doing so in the same room where Quinn slept wasn't a good idea. I went downstairs and replaced the magazine where I'd found it. Then I went outside and walked to the back of the building, shivering as the wind sliced through me.

There were no streetlamps here, just a single floodlight hanging from the eaves. All of the hotel windows were dark, and a few broken. A car rattled by, slowing as it maneuvered around potholes, gunned its engine, and roared off into the night. I kicked a chunk of asphalt and walked to the far corner of the lot, out of reach of the floodlight. The cold air burned my nostrils: particulate from the cement plant. I bet the cancer rates around here were impressive.

I stopped to stare at the hotel's annex. In the dark, it looked even more like a meat locker. The same solitary light shone outside a door on the second level. I shifted from foot to foot, pulled up my collar. Gray vapor misted the air every time I exhaled. I shoved my hands into my pockets, staring at the lunar stretch of rock dust and broken glass.

Desolation flooded me, a ghostly aftershock from Ludus Mentis: the bone-deep memory of that October night on the Bowery. My twenty-third birthday. A broken streetlight, a car slowly driving up behind me in an empty alley. My ears still humming from the waves of feedback and jackhammer guitars back in CBs. It was cold. I was barefoot. There was shattered glass everywhere, empty syringes in the gutter.

The car pulled up beside me and stopped. I thought somebody whispered my name, *Cass, Cass.* It was only much later I realized he must have been hissing *Miss, miss.*

A knife. Glass bit my knees as I knelt in a vacant lot. My fingers clutched my abdomen as I staggered down the street, blood in my mouth, blood streaking my bare legs and feet. The cop who found me thought I was wearing striped tights. Afterward, always the same two questions from police, my father, friends.

Why didn't you run? Why didn't you fight?

They were the same two questions I never stopped asking myself.

I glanced down, saw a shimmering crescent moon reflected in black water. But there was no moon, only a shard of glass from one of those broken windows. I picked it up and tossed it into the shadows. I began to pace, the crank a wire twisting behind my eyes.

I needed to get out of here—not just here but every place I'd ever been, every place that reminded me of what I couldn't escape. I couldn't stay in Reykjavík with Quinn. I was being evicted from my apartment in New York. I could barely afford a return ticket back to the U.S., let alone airfare to visit Quinn in some unimaginable future. I shut my eyes and pictured blue Aegean water and a rocky islet where no one knew us, a refuge we could reach if only we had enough money.

A door creaked. I looked up to see someone walk out onto the second story of the annex. A boy, thirteen or fourteen. He'd left the door open behind him, and I could see the glow cast by a computer screen and hear the *ack ack* of a video game.

The boy leaned over the metal railing in front of the unit and gazed out at the street. The sleeves of his hoodie were pulled down so only his fingertips showed, but the hood was thrown back so I could see his face. Straight dark hair cut short, dark skin, a wistful expression at odds with his grim surroundings.

From inside the apartment came a blast of artificial gunfire, followed by a groan. A moment later, a second, smaller boy poked his head outside and spoke to the first.

"Okay," the first boy said.

The younger boy went back inside, closing the door behind him. The older remained where he was, leaning on the rail with his chin on his hands. The wind gusted and sent an empty beer can rolling loudly across the lot. I took a step back as the boy looked down.

When he saw me, his eyes widened. I thought he might cry out. Instead he smiled, a child's smile, and spread his fingers in a wave. I lifted my hand and did the same.

Behind him the door opened again. A woman called out words I couldn't understand with frightened urgency.

The boy's expression shifted to alarm. He turned and slipped inside. I walked back across the parking lot, thinking of how swiftly the boy's expression had changed, as though he'd recognized me as someone to fear. Maybe I was.

CHAPTER 43

Very early the next morning, I untangled myself from Quinn. I staggered into the bathroom and retched, took a quick shower, did a bump, and stumbled back into the other room. My blinding headache subsided. I dressed and left Quinn still sleeping as I went downstairs. In the office, the girl with the Mohawk sat folding towels as she sang loudly and out of tune.

"Oh! *Hej hej*." She smiled and removed her earbuds. "I didn't hear you."

"Is there someplace I can get coffee?"

"Oh sure." She pointed to a table in the lobby. "I just made some this morning, help yourself. Or there's a café at the harbor."

"This is fine, thanks."

She returned to her towels. I poured some coffee and sipped it, black, willing my hands to stop trembling as I gazed out the window. Cars drove past, sending up yellowish spume from the potholes. I finished the coffee and poured myself another cup, stepped to the side window to stare at the annex.

"Are those shipping containers?"

The girl plucked out her earbuds again. "Sorry?"

"That building looks like it's made of shipping containers."

"It is. The former owner, he won them in a bet. They used to be for visiting workers at the cement plant. Now we rent them out."

"Must be popular for honeymoons."

The girl laughed. "We don't get too many lovers staying here."

"I saw someone up there last night. Kids."

"Yeah, there are some refugee families. Their house outside town burned down, they're only here temporarily."

"I thought that was over a year ago. You'd think if someone firebombed your home, they wouldn't put you in a meat locker."

The girl reddened. "It wasn't a firebomb. It was an accident."

"That's not what I read."

"No one has proved anything." She began folding a towel with surprising vehemence. "I don't know why they are here. We have no jobs on Kalkö. And Sweden has more refugees than anywhere in Europe, did you know that? The most, for a country of this size. Since I was born, there are twenty-five percent more Muslims here. The government pays for them—"

She gestured at the stairs. "But I live here with my brothers because we can't afford our own flat."

She gave me a challenging look. I just shrugged.

"Thanks for the coffee," I said. "Do you have a pen and a piece of paper?"

She yanked open a drawer and produced a pen and a small pad of paper. "You can keep that."

I stuck them in my pocket, refilled my mug and poured coffee into a second one, adding a splash of milk and four spoonfuls of sugar for Quinn, and made my way back upstairs. Quinn was in the shower. I set down the coffee and sat cross-legged on the bed, pulled out pen and paper, and stared at the blank sheet.

My nerves blazed like a lit fuse, the memory of symbols tumbling through the air in front of me, red and violet and indigo.

Wavelet. Fourier transform. Svarlight. Valknut. Ludus Mentis. Mind game. Lamps and banners. It's all code.

I scribbled down the words and shut my eyes, trying to concentrate on just one of them.

Valknut.

Where had I seen it? Written in blood on Harold's forehead, tattooed on Freya's wrist, and Erik's hand; carved onto an ancient Viking stone with figures of dead men and Valkyries.

What did it mean? *Something about being among the chosen.* Valknut, Vikings, Valkyrie...

I flashed to when I was in Reykjavík, searching for Quinn, and a bartender had spoken to me of Valkyries, quoting from an ancient saga.

"We sisters weave our cloth with the entrails of men, their severed heads: corpse carriers, our bounty chosen from the bodies of the slain."

Someone else in Iceland had said much the same thing, a woman whose brother had just been murdered.

"On all sides she gathers hordes of the dead, back bent to bear them homeward to Hell. Shield-maiden, skull-heavy." That is you...

So had a serial killer on an island off the coast of Maine.

You and me, we carry the dead on our backs...

And so had I, without even realizing it. *That's what photography is,* I'd told Gryffin. *A massive necropolis. The dead, we carry them with us everywhere we go.*

If Tindra was right, and humans were all code, or coded, then we each might hold some meaning within us and some symbol to represent it.

Like a Valkyrie. Because what is a photographer but a chooser of the slain, someone who decides who or what is destined for immortality.

You'll figure it out, Tindra had said of the valknut.

A Valkyrie would know which corpse to bear to Valhalla because it was marked with the valknut. That was why Tindra had turned white when I showed her that photo on Gryffin's mobile. The symbol drawn on Harold's forehead had not been meant for me or Gryffin or the police. It was a warning for Tindra.

CHAPTER 44

I was still staring at the piece of paper when Quinn walked out of the shower. He sank onto the bed, naked, toweling his head. "Where'd you go?"

"Nowhere. Just downstairs."

I handed him the coffee I'd brought him, now lukewarm. I poured some whiskey into my mug, sipping it as I sat on the bed behind him. If I told him about the valknut and Tindra, he'd think I was crazy. I *was* crazy.

"Shit." I crumpled the paper and tossed it across the room.

Quinn looked over at me, set aside his towel, and took a sip of coffee. "What is it, baby?"

"Just thinking."

"You think too much."

I trailed my fingers across his thigh, then buried my face in his shoulder. He put his mug aside and turned to wrap his arms around me. I stripped and lay next to him, breathing in his heat as we fucked, the scents of burnt coffee and sugar. The stubble on his face and scalp hid some of the scarifications, but not the ones between his eyes. I could feel them beneath my fingertips.

They mean I killed a man. I'd never asked how many.

We lay together after, Quinn snoring softly. I got up to take another shower. Despite the heat blasting from the radiator, I couldn't get warm. When I returned to the bedroom, I found Quinn dressed and standing by the window, cracked open so he could smoke. His laptop sat on the table behind him.

I finished drying myself and pulled on my clothes. "Any news?"

"See for yourself," he said without looking at me.

On the *Daily Mirror* home page was a photo of Tommy in uniform, dun-colored hills towering behind him. A red scarf was wrapped around his head in a loose turban.

POSSIBLE ISIS AGENT "WENT ON RAMPAGE" AT PEACEFUL RALLY

"ISIS?" I snorted. "This is a damn tabloid."

"Keep reading," said Quinn.

Thomas Lewis, 29, Brixton, died of injuries sustained after he attacked unarmed demonstrators at a peaceful rally organized by Saint George Heritage Foundation founder and Conservative MP Ronald Morton.

"I saw him get into an argument with a woman about a mobile. Then he charged a man out of nowhere," recounted Angeline Bow of Beckton Park. Onlookers wrestled Lewis to the ground, but he escaped and fled into the crowd, where he was subdued by Metro Police. While the authorities have offered no motivation, Morton has stated that "this is clearly a terror incident, possibly linked to ISIS." Lewis was employed as a private security guard for Swedish software magnate Tindra Bergstrand, who could not be reached for comment at this time.

I gazed at the picture, Tommy's dark skin contrasting with the red scarf wrapped around his head. The Arabic letters tattooed on his neck were clearly visible. "He's from the East End. He was in the military, for Christ's sake! They don't even mention he was a British soldier who served in Afghanistan."

"Of course not. But this might buy us some time. The police will want to question his sister, especially if they can't locate Tindra. They'll advise her not to leave the country for a bit, which means she won't show up here in the next twenty-four hours. Not that she'd want to."

"Why?"

"Because of the funeral arrangements. She's his sister, right? Any other family that you know of?" I shook my head. "So she'll have to manage that before she goes anywhere. And if they run toxicology tests, which I'm sure they will, that can take a while, too."

"Will the cops hold her?"

"Why would they? More likely she'll start legal action against the police. She didn't kill her brother—the cops did."

"I meant because of Harold. Once they look at their cell-phone records, it'll all be linked. Tindra buys the book from Harold, Harold's murdered. Tindra's bodyguard freaks out and dies. Tindra disappears."

"I know. It's a mess." Quinn opened the window wider and leaned out, letting a blast of cold air into the stuffy room. "At some point your name is going to come up. When they question his sister, and when they question your boy Gryffin. Not if: when. And those two will have a physical description of me, even if they don't have a name."

He rubbed his scalp. I started pacing the cramped room, trying to think my way out of this.

"No one knows we left the UK," I said at last. "No one knows we both have stolen passports. I can't see Gryffin lying to the cops about me. But he wants that book, and I don't think he'll say anything that might screw up his chances of finding it. He'll do what Lyla tells him to do, which will probably be to keep his mouth shut."

"That's good. It still means they both might end up on Kalkö. The bodyguard, anyway. She'll figure out this guy Erik lives on the island. How long it takes for her to get here depends on how long the police detain her, and what arrangements she makes for her brother. I give us forty-eight hours, tops."

He withdrew from the window, closed it, and leaned against the wall, arms crossed.

"I'll wait till tomorrow night," he said after a long silence. "I booked this place and the car for two days. After that I'm going back to Reykjavík. I want you to come with me," he added, fixing me with that green-glass stare.

I bit down on a retort and looked away.

CHAPTER 45

I couldn't sit still. I killed time by dumping the contents of my new handbag onto the bed, including the weather-beaten satchel I'd had since high school. I needed to lighten my load.

Dead Girls was a heavy souvenir to keep lugging around. Then again, it was starting to feel like the sole connection I had to my former life. I put it and the copy of *Skalltrolleri* into my worn satchel, then loaded a roll of Tri-X into the Nikon. I stuffed the remaining rolls of film, the camera and pill bottles, and most of my clothes into the satchel—basically, what I'd packed when I left New York.

Everything else I dumped into the leather bag. I kicked it under the bed, a present for the girl with the Mohawk, and looked at Quinn.

"I want to go back to that place where we saw the fox."

I thought he'd argue or at least ask why, but he only nodded. I knew he was going through the motions till we could leave for Reykjavík. He already had on his leather jacket and watch cap.

We walked out to the car. All the lights were off in the annex. An old Saab pocked with rust was parked in front. I gave it a quick once-over. No stickers or decals, nothing inside but empty pizza boxes and plastic energy-drink bottles. I circled back to where Quinn waited in the Jetta.

"See anything?" he asked as I slid into the passenger seat. I shook my head.

A steady line of traffic filled the opposite lane as we left Slythamn: people heading to work at the cement plant. The day was much colder and very windy, the eastern horizon banked with graphite clouds.

"Snow," said Quinn. "Weather here comes down from Siberia."

Once we left the town limits, we got stuck behind a school bus. Quinn rolled down his window to smoke, impatiently flicking ashes until the bus pulled over to let us pass. After a mile or two, pastures and tidy farm buildings surrendered to evergreen forest. Trees leaned over the road, their branches touching to form a tunnel that seemed to breathe around us.

The wind rose. Without warning a rippling wall of white moved across the road like a threadbare curtain—a snow squall.

Quinn hurriedly closed his window and downshifted. Ghostly runnels swept the road around us. Another blast of snow, and the air grew calm once more. The dark spruces straightened, all the snow blown from their limbs.

Quinn squinted up at the trees. "Why do you want to go back there?"

"That fox . . . it was a weird scene." It was the first time I'd spoken since leaving Slagghögen. "And you said someone connected to Svarlight might live there."

"I said I saw an old address online. That's not much to go on."

"If nothing's there, we can check out the other address in Norderby."

"That's just a post-office address. And I don't want to be wandering around asking questions about some crazy Swedish nationalist who works out of his basement." He sighed. "I'd still like to know why he'd want this book."

"Because it's worth a shit ton of money. But I don't think he wants the book. He wants the app."

I tapped my fingers on the dashboard like it was a keyboard. "Stop that," Quinn snapped. "Even if this is your guy, he lives in the middle of nowhere."

I knew he was arguing with me because he wanted to pull the plug and head back to Iceland. I gritted my teeth, then said, "It doesn't matter where he lives. He puts up a link through his podcast, every racist nutjob in the world can download it."

"Will he even know how? And you said the app doesn't work."

"It worked on me, only not the way it was supposed to. And . . ."

I stopped. People who'd witnessed Tommy's death said that there had been an altercation over a mobile phone. Yet what if that witness hadn't seen an altercation, but Tindra's app being deliberately deployed as a weapon against someone vulnerable? A veteran with PTSD, a black man surrounded by a threatening crowd. The beta version of an app meant to treat PTSD, which instead caused traumatic flashbacks.

"She needs *The Book of Lamps and Banners* to fine-tune it," I said. "That's why the beta version's not working. But someone wants to use it just the way it is, to mess with people's heads."

Quinn groaned in exasperation. "But if it goes viral, it could fuck up all kinds of people, not just people targeted by white supremacists. What would be the point?"

"Maybe there is no point. Or maybe that *is* the point—just set it loose and see what happens. Let it come down. Helter Skelter," I went on, growing agitated. "Like Manson. Or Dylann Roof. You think you're using it to start a race war, only you end up killing everyone exposed to it."

"But you didn't kill anyone, Cass—it just freaked you out. And Tommy didn't kill anyone, either."

"What if it works different on different people?" It all began to make sense, the staticky logic of methamphetamine. "So I flashed back to getting raped; Tommy flashed back to the war. So he *might* have killed someone—he might have killed a lot of people, if the police hadn't tased him." I recalled the explosion of blood and optic nerves in Tommy's eye, and Harold's. "Or if someone else hadn't stopped him first."

"C'mon, Cass! This is like *The Terminal Man*." Quinn laughed. "You don't think that could actually happen?"

"You want to find out?"

"It would be crazy."

"Is there anything about these people that isn't crazy? Witnesses said they saw Tommy arguing with someone about a mobile. What if it was Tindra's phone? What if someone deliberately provoked Tommy and used Ludus Mentis, just to see what would happen?"

"They'd have to know he was a vet with PTSD."

"Yeah, and maybe they did know that—if they have the app, they have Tindra, too. Though she wouldn't have told them about Tommy..."

"She would have if the conditions were right."

I stared at my hands, the little red half-moon where a fingernail had broken the skin. I longed to say, *Maybe I'm wrong.* Maybe whatever I'd seen in Tindra's garage had been a manifestation of drugs and my own damaged psyche and nothing else. Maybe this was all my own delusion, and Quinn was just going along for the ride, out of love or inertia or whatever it was that connected us.

I stared out at the snow. I thought of the dead fox; of Tindra's dead dog, Bunny; of Lyla and Tommy moving brightly colored pieces across a Parcheesi board. I thought of the papyrus sheet hidden between the pages of *Dead Girls;* of sitting with Gryffin and Harold with *The Book of Lamps and Banners.* Words marching across a page, resolute and unstoppable as army ants.

He that doth professe such dessire as to see the Devvill must seek Him yre and no further.

"The book," I said. "When I first saw it, in Harold Vertigan's house. There was a page with a drawing, a tree and a black bird, a raven. I was staring at the raven, its wings started to move, and I heard the same voice..."

"What voice?" asked Quinn. I didn't reply. "Cass? Cassie, what is it?"

He eased the car off the road, onto the frozen ground beneath a huge spruce, put the car into neutral, and took my shoulders, gently but firmly turning me to face him. "Cass. Do you want to go back to the hotel? We can get our stuff, go to the airport—"

"No." My breath came in shallow bursts, but I forced myself to go on. "When I looked at Ludus Mentis, I heard the guy who raped me, it was like I was right there again—him saying my name, trying to get my attention. And when I looked at *The Book of Lamps and Banners,* I had the same flashback, just like with the app. And the page I have in there—"

I pointed at my satchel. "It fell out of the book at Harold's place and I grabbed it. But every time I look at it, it makes me feel sick."

"Cassie, this is the crank."

"It's not the drugs! Don't you get it? It's this!" I pulled *Dead Girls* from my satchel, opened it to the papyrus leaf. "*This* is the drug. This is the final piece of code. Tindra wasn't crazy. Once she scans the entire *Book of Lamps and Banners,* everything changes."

"No, Cass." Quinn's face grew expressionless. "What changes you is meth and alcohol."

"Listen to me! If you were to look at it, the same thing would happen to you. She tried to explain it to me, something about wavelets and a mathematical theorem—how you can use it to rewire the brain. I don't know how it works, but it *does* work. And if somebody manages to finish what she started . . ."

Quinn's brow furrowed, his concern at last giving way to curiosity. "Let me see that."

He reached for the book, but I slammed it closed before he could touch it.

"No. You said we have till tomorrow night." I placed his hand back on the steering wheel. "Drive."

CHAPTER 46

H ang on." Quinn gazed into the rearview mirror. "Someone's coming."

I slumped into my seat, out of sight. Quinn picked up his mobile and held it to his ear as though listening. I heard the metallic rumble of studded tires as a car drove past us. It was the first vehicle we'd seen since the school bus.

I sat up. "You see anyone?" I asked as Quinn steered the Jetta back onto the road.

"Lady with a couple of kids in back. We're good."

"How many people live here in the winter?"

"Maybe four hundred. Why?"

"Just running the odds that we'll actually find these people."

"Maybe you should worry that they'll find us." He tipped his head toward an unmarked gravel road. "That's where we were yesterday. You still want to do this?"

"Yeah. Drop me off and pull over where I can find you. I'll walk down and see what's there and meet you back at the car."

Quinn looked doubtful, but after checking to be sure there were no other cars in sight, he stopped to let me out. "Don't get lost."

I slung the Nikon around my neck, hopped out, and headed quickly down the gravel road. Quinn did a U-turn and drove in the direction we'd come from, back toward Slythamn.

Once I was out of sight of the road, I clambered up a sharp incline, into the woods. Frozen reindeer moss and dead leaves crunched beneath my boots, and branches tore at my hair. I looked back and muttered a curse. I'd left a trail of footprints on the thin skin of snow dropped by the squall. I hoped that another squall might cover my tracks before someone noticed them.

The wind was frigid, and I wasn't wearing gloves. I jammed my hands into my pockets. It felt like years since I'd had a camera with me, and I didn't want my fingers to be numb when I used it. The air smelled of pine and raw earth and decaying leaves, with an underlying brackish scent. We weren't far from the shore.

After a few minutes of pushing my way through overhanging limbs and past mossy stones, I reached a clearing. I ran my fingers through my hair, dislodging bits of bark and lichen, then cradled the camera against my chest. The Nikon may have been heavier than my old Konica, but its heft and shape were as familiar as my own hands. Despite my underlying dread and my brain ticking like an overheated engine, I felt exhilarated. Those few days without a camera had left me feeling as though I'd lost a sense more deeply embedded than sight, the sense that I can see everything at once, past and future and present, before choosing the precise moment to hit the shutter release and capture the single image that best represents the truth.

Digital photography expands that notion. Immediately and endlessly manipulable, it offers the illusion of infinite choice and recall: by constantly shooting or recording everything, one freezes the present, making it recoverable.

And yet the present is always lost. Film photography creates images from the stuff we're made of: salt, traces of metal, water, carbon. Digital process makes us believe that we can control time. Film reminds us that we dissolve in it, like salt in water or bone in acid.

I halted, trying to get my bearings. The trees all looked the same, an endless progression of spruce, birch, beech, scraggly hemlock, which formed a shifting, vaporous web of vegetation. Yellow leaves carpeting the ground gave the illusion of sunlight. I walked by instinct, hoping I'd eventually come across the dead fox. Failing that, I'd backtrack to find Quinn.

After several minutes, a pale object appeared in the shadows. It looked uncannily like a body, or part of one—an arm or a leg suspended from one of those black trees. Then the wind shifted, and for an instant the sun broke through. What I'd mistaken for a body was the white column of a birch. Bark peeled from its trunk in long strips. Something moved in its upper limbs—a raven, fluttering to where the dead fox dangled from a branch.

The raven halted, its black beak stabbing with precise, impartial patience at the fox's exposed rib cage. I froze, holding my breath; then raised the camera to my face, opening the aperture as far as it would go. I waited. Three heartbeats, and the raven cocked its head to stare at me with one yellow eye. I pushed the shutter release, its gentle click more the memory of a sound than a sound itself.

The raven hopped and twisted its head to regard me with its other eye. The feathers on its neck rippled as though another creature moved beneath them. It clacked its beak, gave a low gurgle.

Not a sound of alarm—it continued to stare at me, as though waiting for a reply. I remained still and it repeated the gurgling cry. At last it raised its wings and flapped away from the fox's carcass, flying so close above my head that I could hear the whistle of air through its feathers before I lost sight of it among the trees.

CHAPTER 47

I realized I was clutching the Nikon as though someone had tried to snatch it from me, and lowered the camera. Somewhere overhead a bird clacked. Other than that and the scratching of branches in the wind, the forest was silent. I walked toward the birch tree, the spongy earth releasing a whiff of fungus and leaf mold with each step. I stopped to stare at what remained of the fox.

The raven had done its work. Strips of matted fur hung from its abdomen like ruined velvet. Despite the cold, beetles crawled within the stomach cavity. Most of the animal's flesh was gone. So were its eyes, picked cleanly from their sockets so that the bone gleamed in the gray light. I didn't bother to raise my camera: the carcass was neither beautiful nor sinister but simply dead.

I walked a few more steps into the forest, but saw nothing more unusual than some scattered black feathers on the carpet of dead spruce needles. I picked up a long, blue-black quill—a raven's. More littered the ground nearby, pinion feathers, and also tufts of down.

Ravens weren't the only predators here. But did owls eat ravens? I dropped the feather and looked around. A few feet away, something white protruded from the ground, a bone from the dead raven. I crouched to get a better look, then picked it up warily.

It wasn't a bone but a dart, with a red plastic fletch and translucent plastic cannula. The steel tip looked lethal. I pinched it between my fingers and held it to the light. As the needle caught the sun, I flashed to that overflowing garbage can in Victoria Park and a dead sparrow, and before that the dead pigeon in the parking lot in the Vale of Health, with what looked like a syringe nearby.

It hadn't been a syringe, but a dart like this one. A half inch of clear liquid still remained in its plastic chamber. I held it with the steel tip well away from me, scanning the ground as I walked. After a few minutes, I came across a second cannula, at the base of a tree. This one was spent, its chamber empty. I nudged it with my boot, then looked up.

That tree was the most immense birch I'd ever seen, mottled bark no longer white but cement gray, encrusted with lichen and old-man's beard and the stalactites of some pale fungus. It must have been hundreds of years old. Just above the level of my head, its papery outer bark had peeled away, exposing a patch of smooth trunk the color of sherry.

Someone had scratched three concentric circles here to make a target, the outermost circle slightly flattened into an ovoid. The target and the surrounding bark were pocked with hundreds of tiny holes, as though the tree had been attacked by a miniature wood-pecker. I ran the fingers of my free hand across the bark, scrutinizing the crudely etched target; drew my head back to get a better look.

The target represented a human eye. I inserted the dart's tip into one of the pinholes, as though probing a rotten tooth. It fit perfectly.

I withdrew the dart and looked around. I saw no one, but couldn't shake a sense of being watched. The raven, perhaps, or some other animal. I picked up the second, spent dart, and with extreme care tucked both into my pocket. I shot a few frames of the homemade target, trying to capture the details of the crude eye. As I replaced the lens cap and stepped away, the wind whipped up to shake the evergreens, and a rain of dead needles stung my face. I turned and quickly retraced my steps.

CHAPTER 48

What happened?" asked Quinn as I slid into the passenger seat. "Somebody see you?"

I shook my head, out of breath, flapped my hand to urge him to drive. He put the car into gear and pulled onto the main road, peering into the rearview mirror to make sure we weren't followed.

I looked behind us. The road was empty. "Find another place we can pull over," I said. "Not near here."

After a few minutes we veered down one side road, then another, driving past farms and villages that weren't much more than a few houses clustered near a neat white church or café. The Jetta slowed as Quinn made another turn, down a lane bordered by wooden fences thick with blackened rose vines. We passed an overgrown cemetery, its gravestones nearly lost to weeds and creeping ivy. Maybe fifty feet away were the ruins of an ancient stone church, its roof gone and windows gutted. Beech trees grew where its nave had once been.

Quinn stopped the car, switched off the ignition, and turned to me. "So?"

I held out the first dart. "Look at this—careful, it's still got something in it. I found another one, but it was empty."

He took it from my fingers, frowning as he studied it. The wintry light made him look younger despite his four-day beard, the scarifications hidden so that it was easier to imagine the face of the teenage Quinn beneath. I touched his cheek, and he flinched.

"Careful," he warned. He twisted the dart back and forth. "Where'd you find this?"

"On the ground, in the woods. Can you tell what's in it?"

"No, but I don't want to find out the hard way." He glanced into the back seat. "See if you can find something to put this in."

I found a wadded-up bag that had contained the groceries we'd bought and handed it to him. He wrapped the dart in it.

"Put that in your bag," he said. "Let me see the other."

He scrutinized this even more closely, cautiously removing the fletch and sniffing at the empty tube. He covered the cannula's open end with his finger, tipped it upside down, and checked to see if any residue remained on his fingertip.

"So?" I asked.

"I'm not a chemist. But with a dart like this, my best guess is that it's some kind of animal tranquilizer. Ketamine or fentanyl. Don't get any ideas," he added, and returned the dart to me. "Anything else?"

"Yeah." I told him about the crude eye carved into the birch tree. "Someone was using that tree for target practice. I found feathers, too, like they'd shot a bird, probably more than one. A raven." I hesitated. "Look, I know you won't believe me, but I've seen those darts before—one in Victoria Park, one in a parking lot near Harold's place. Dead birds, too."

"So, some dead birds, and some darts."

"And two dead people shot in the eye with no sign of a bullet's exit wound, and maybe a dog. And a target—"

"That looks like an eye. That is a weird fucking MO, Cass."

"As opposed to what? Whoever murdered Tommy wanted it to look like an accident. When Ludus Mentis made him freak out, they plugged him with a dart so he couldn't tell anyone what had happened. Getting tased by the cops was icing on the cake. If that's fentanyl, he was probably already dead, or close to it."

"Toxicology will show if he had drugs in his system. Your book-seller, too. And maybe the dog. Frigging amateurs," Quinn muttered, taking out a cigarette.

We returned to Slagghögen. Back in the room I went onto

Quinn's computer. Quinn made himself a rum and Coke, heavy on the Myer's, and sipped it while I scrolled for news. Other than the obligatory hand-wringing over the circumstances of Tommy's death—person of color, white nationalists, when would there be a stop?—I came up cold.

"There's nothing." I felt like throwing the laptop out the window. "How can there be nothing?"

"It's London," said Quinn. "You're talking nine million people, one dead book guy, one dead black guy. Oh, and a dead dog."

"And Tindra."

"A missing girl ain't news."

"It will be when someone makes the connection between all of them."

"For Christ's sake, give it a rest, Cass!" Quinn's green eyes were bloodshot, his face more haggard than I'd seen it since we'd met up. "Your book is gone, that girl is gone. You've got at least two dead people killed by stupid people. If the girl's dead, too, that's too bad. I don't give a fuck about your boyfriend Gryffin."

His icy gaze held all the things he'd lost to prison and his work as a contract killer, to heroin and alcohol and despair. I knew he was ready to add me to that list.

"You're spun, Cass. It's crazy, all this stuff about voices and the app and pictures moving on the page. None of it makes any sense. You wanted to find that book because it's worth money and we'd have a nut. So let's find it. Otherwise we can leave now. Or I will."

I took a deep breath, trying to stay calm. "Yeah, okay," I said, and closed the laptop. Quinn's expression didn't exactly soften, but the cold rage in his eyes gave way to resignation.

"You know it doesn't add up to much, Cass. Your darts and some feathers—actually, it doesn't add up to anything."

"It does if someone used a tranquilizer gun to kill Harold and Tommy and the dog. And Tindra, for all we know."

"You can't prove anything. You got zip, Cassie." Quinn drained the rest of his drink. "They'll claim Tommy got taken out in self-defense.

A brown-skinned guy at an alt-right rally—witnesses say he swung at somebody, and why wouldn't he? No one's come forward to state otherwise." He poured another shot into his mug. "And where's his sister in all this? Any mention of her?"

"I don't know. No."

I went to the window and stared out at the slag heap. Quinn flopped onto the bed, yawning.

"We can drive to Norderby," he said. "Have lunch and walk around. If the museum's open, we can go there. But I gotta catch some z's. You got me up way too goddamn early."

Even with his eyes closed, his expression signaled that he was done. He'd given up any hope of us finding the book. He'd given up on me. He was trying to salvage the trip. Pretend we were on vacation, act like normal people. Tomorrow we'd be on a flight back to Reykjavík. He'd remain there. I'd return to my rent-stabilized shithole until I got booted out, go on unemployment and cadge money from my father, use whatever cash I could scramble together to buy booze and drugs so that I could pass out and pretend that I'd never found Quinn again, never lost him, never gave a fuck about him or anything else.

I sank beside him on the bed, placing my hand on his chest. "I just wanted us to be happy," I whispered.

"People like us aren't happy, Cass," he said without opening his eyes. "It's enough that we're alive." He rolled over and didn't speak again.

CHAPTER 49

I couldn't rest. After a few minutes, I got up as quietly as I could and paced the room, waiting until Quinn began to breathe deeply. I stood over him and watched him, his arm flung out above his head, mouth slightly open to show one eyetooth.

Quinn slept like the dead when he napped, an hour, sometimes longer. The rum would help push that limit. When I was sure he wouldn't wake, I took the car keys from where he'd tossed them on the nightstand. I wasn't signed on the rental agreement as a driver, but I didn't plan on going far, or for long. I grabbed my leather jacket and camera and left.

I hurried downstairs and through the lobby. No sign of the girl behind the hotel desk. I strode to the car, glancing up at the shipping containers as I slid into the front seat. A young woman in a head scarf stood in the open doorway of the same apartment where I'd seen the boy the night before. When she noticed me, she went inside and shut the door.

I followed the route that Quinn and I had taken earlier. There was hardly any traffic. All of the snow had blown off the road, and gashes of blue sky showed through the unsettled clouds overhead. When I reached the gravel road, I did a U-turn. I drove back a short distance and pulled onto the shoulder, parking beneath a dense overhang of conifers. I sat, waiting to make sure no cars came into view. The sun was already a third of the way above the horizon. I'd track its passage and give myself half an hour before heading back.

I slung my camera around my neck and got out, ran across the road and down the gravel drive to clamber up the embankment and into the trees. I passed the dead fox, another raven picking at the ground beneath it, and kept going. Beech and birch gave way to more recent growth, ash and conifers that formed a nearly impenetrable thicket with lethally sharp branches. I fought my way through, trying to keep my camera from getting snagged. Every few minutes I paused to listen for any sound: a car, footsteps, voices. I heard only a few birds and the steady patter of dead evergreen needles dropping to the ground.

The trees began to thin. The spruces had been cut, and their stumps formed a treacherous maze, slick with acid-green moss. Dead ferns rattled in the wind. The smell of fresh manure overwhelmed the resinous scent of spruce.

I halted, debating whether to continue. A few yards to my left, the gravel road turned to packed earth, wide enough for one vehicle and cratered with potholes and frost heaves. Directly in front of me, a fence made of woven branches marked the edge of a field of close-cropped, yellowing grass and wind-stunted trees. Their trunks and limbs all pointed the same way, so that they appeared to be crawling across the field. Half a dozen boulders stood in the pasture. Then one of the boulders moved, and another, until all had turned to stare at me. Not boulders but sheep, five black ewes and a black ram with an imposing set of curled horns. They seemed not to blink, each of their eerie amber eyes slashed by a horizontal black pupil.

I held my breath. Those woven branches wouldn't be much of a barrier if the sheep decided to charge. But they remained motion-less, their gaze never leaving me. After a minute, I slowly lifted my camera, staring through the viewfinder at the black ram. I focused the lens until the viewfinder held nothing but a single iris, its flattened pupil a portal into an unknowable darkness. I adjusted the focus a hair's breadth, pushed the shutter release.

The ram snorted and bolted toward me. I fled, keeping to the woods bordering that rough one-lane road.

When I was a safe distance from the sheep, I cautiously hopped down onto the road. Behind me, it wound between trees and fields, disappearing from view. Ahead, it curved out of sight, fences and fields dissolving into black spruce and white birch. There were tire tracks in the dirt at my feet, deep ruts where a vehicle had gotten stuck and churned the mud into a knee-high ridge, now frozen.

I assumed the road led to a house or farm. But the only structure I could see was a small wooden outbuilding tucked into a pine grove—not much more than a shed, painted white with a red metal roof, small windows with lace curtains, and a red door. I couldn't see any lights or flicker of motion; caught no sound of voices, TV, or radio or computer. If anyone was inside, they would have seen me by now and confronted me.

My head ached from the steady cold wind. Clouds hid a sun the color of solder. I thought of Quinn asleep in that dismal room, waking to find me gone. I should head back. I should eat, but the crank had long since burned any hunger from me. I should do what Quinn had told me to do, forget all this and return with him to Reykjavík.

Instead I headed for the shed, ducking beneath pine boughs until I reached the back of the structure. The white clapboards were veined with black mold. A door with a small window sagged from its hinges. I wiped cobwebs and grime from the glass and peered inside.

Dim light filtered through lace curtains webbed with dust. A surfboard rested atop the rafters. Hand tools lay in neat rows on a worktable against one wall, and glass jars filled with screws, nails, nuts, and bolts. Knives glinted on a piece of leather, arranged by size, the smallest as long as my finger, the largest a wicked crescent, like a scimitar.

I jiggled the doorknob. It was unlocked. I stepped inside, closing the door behind me, and clapped a hand over my mouth and nose against the reek of mildew and a fainter odor of decay, like a dead mouse trapped beneath the floorboards; also a choking chemical smell that reminded me of high-school biology class. Formaldehyde or some type of solvent. Eyes streaming, I cracked open the back door, letting in a waft of cold air, and looked around.

Open cardboard boxes covered the floor, all filled with dirt. Posters had been tacked to a wall—a white singer named Saga, the logo for the band Skrewdriver. As I drew closer to examine a third poster, my skin crawled.

It was the back-cover art for *Stone Ships,* the album by Jötunn's Egg. The same ancient monument made of sharp-edged stones; same moody background of a mist-bound evergreen forest. Whoever spent time in this shed knew the Svarlight label.

I turned away. On another wall, more implements hung from a pegboard: shears, forceps, hammers and saws, trowels, a hatchet. Stacks of feathered masks covered a worktable, wings jutting above eyeholes punched in the leather. I stepped through the maze of cardboard boxes and picked up one of the masks.

It wasn't a mask but a skinned bird, its boneless torso soft and pliant as a glove. I set it aside to examine another bird, with a long slender black bill and dangling twiglike legs. In addition to dozens of birds, there were skinned rabbits, squirrels, voles, shrews, bats. A tiny hedgehog; mice. All eyeless.

I picked up a rat, its jaws parted in a toothy snarl, and sniffed. It smelled musty, but it wasn't the source of the fetid odor that permeated the shed. Neither were the birds or small mammals.

I glanced out the window and did another lap around the room. A dead raven lay on a small table, its outstretched wings pinned to a piece of cardboard and exuding the stink of decay. A recent kill. The eye staring up at me had shriveled to a dull gray seed. When I grasped the raven's beak and gently turned it, flies rose in a dizzying swarm.

In the raven's other eye was a minute hole, as though an insect had burrowed to the skull beneath. I lifted my camera and zoomed in, tightening the focus until I could see a telltale black pinprick in the iris, then let the camera fall back against my chest. The raven's eye had been penetrated by a dart's tip, just like Harold's, and Tommy's.

CHAPTER 50

I searched the room, pushing aside coils of wire, boxes of nails and thumbtacks, fine-gauge screens. At the back of one shelf, I found plastic containers plastered with FARA! labels—enough toxic preservatives to take out a small household:

ARSENIK. ALUN. SVAVEL SYRA FORMALDEHYD

On the next shelf was another box. Inside were ziplock bags full of empty darts, identical to those I'd discovered in the woods.

I continued searching until I spotted a knee-high refrigerator nearly hidden behind a large carton. A nautical chart was taped to the fridge door, along with a list of names and phone numbers, several curling photographs, and a Swedish flag magnet.

I stooped to open the fridge. On the top shelf were three bottles of Falcon beer, a box of milk, and a plastic container filled with earthworms. On the lower shelf was a large plastic bottle:

IMMOBILON: ETORPHINE HYDROCHLORIDE

I whistled softly. Whenever you see documentary footage of an elephant or rhino getting nailed by a dart, etorphine's what got the job done. Thousands of times as powerful as morphine, it's toxic to humans in even small amounts, and extremely difficult to obtain anywhere in the world—including the U.S. and, I assumed, Sweden. That hasn't stopped people from snorting or injecting it.

My old dealer Phil got his hands on some a few years back. I didn't buy any, but others did, resulting in a spike in fatal ODs that week. Narcan can reverse the effects, but etorphine's so powerful that cops and EMTs weren't toting around enough of the antidote to bring anyone back.

The warning label on this bottle was in English. It had been imported from the UK. Why? As far as I knew, there were no rogue rhinos roaming Kalkö.

I took a photo of the bottle, closed the fridge, and got back to my feet. I photographed the table with its macabre menagerie, also the dead raven, focusing on where its eye had been before an etorphine dart turned it to jelly. Then I quickly turned to leave.

As I stepped away from the table, I bumped against one of the dirt-filled cartons on the floor and swore as my boot's steel toe poked a hole in the side of the box. I reached to push the torn cardboard back into place, then recoiled.

Inside the box, dirt rippled like water, as though a wave was building beneath the dark surface. I watched as a minuscule yellow finger thrust through the dirt and began to writhe. Then another, and another emerged—dozens of them, hundreds, maybe thousands—until the entire box seethed.

Maggots.

I could hear them moving against one another, a sound like rustling paper. I backed away as they wriggled through the soil, attempting to crawl up the sides of the carton. A few escaped and I crushed them beneath my boot, but within seconds most had burrowed back into the dirt.

I grabbed a screwdriver from the table behind me. Taking a deep breath, I used the screwdriver's tip to probe the quivering mass inside the carton, flicking aside maggots and dirt as a storm of blowflies whirled up around me.

A pale dome appeared inside the carton, flecked with writhing black threads—more maggots. With the screwdriver, I moved aside as many larvae as I could, until I exposed what they were feeding on. A ram's skull, shreds of flesh peeling from its jaws. Fine white dust adhered to its coiled horns, lime, maybe, or some kind of enzyme powder.

I shoved the screwdriver through its empty eye socket and lifted the skull, yellow larvae raining from the rows of square teeth. I lowered the skull back into the carton and picked up my camera. I trained it on a beetle crawling along the skull's lower jaw, its black wings holding a glint of iridescence, each antenna topped with a minute onyx bead.

The beetle paused, wing carapaces unfolding as I snapped the picture, and then it scuttled into the skull's mouth cavity. I lowered the camera and used the screwdriver to smooth out the dirt, hoping the box's contents would appear undisturbed.

I went to the next carton and prodded at the soil. Again the screwdriver struck something hard. This skull was much smaller—a lamb's. Only a few larvae emerged from the soil. The maggots had been at work longer here.

I checked two more boxes. One contained another ram's skull, the other that of some kind of carnivore with long incisors, a small dog or fox. I hurriedly swept the dirt back with my hands and stepped over to the window, pulling aside the curtain a fraction of an inch.

Outside, woods and road seemed unchanged beneath the curdled gray sky. The sun had crept a finger's width closer to the horizon. I had no idea how much time had passed. An hour?

I turned and counted six more boxes in the shed, but I didn't dare take any longer to examine them. I replaced the screwdriver where I'd found it, flicking off a larva that still clung to the handle. Despite the cold, I'd broken into a sweat.

I turned to leave, flies buzzing around my face. I swatted at one, stepping over a carton near the back door. Something glinted in the soil inside the box: a copper coin, like an oversize penny. I hesitated, crouched to get a better look, and saw several long black filaments protruding from the earth.

Hair.

I brushed at the earth to reveal more hairs, one twisted around a writhing maggot. I snatched my hand back, then gingerly plucked the copper coin from the soil.

It was smooth and almost weightless between my fingers. Not a coin, but a small amber disk threaded with wire, a hook that had been twisted out of shape. Two long hairs clung to it, electric blue. When I held it to the window, it glowed in the wintry light, a golden eye that winked at me as it turned. Tindra Bergstrand's earring.

CHAPTER 51

I fought nausea even as my free hand grabbed my camera to take a picture of the earring. Before I could, another sound joined the flies' buzzing inside the shed: car wheels on gravel, approaching from the direction of the main road. My fist closed around the earring as I drew alongside the window to peer outside.

An old blue Volvo drove slowly past, expertly navigating around potholes. Someone familiar with the road. The sheep glanced up, then lowered their heads and continued to graze. I held my breath, waiting to see if the Volvo would stop. The car continued on at a snail's pace, avoiding ruts. Eventually it rounded a curve and disappeared from sight.

I slipped the earring into the pocket of my leather jacket and swallowed, tasting bile; opened the back door; stepped outside; and began to run through the trees paralleling the road. My boots skidded on the wet ground and I barely kept myself from falling, desperately clutching my camera.

In the field, the ram gave a warning snort that sounded more like a growl. As one, the sheep raised their heads to stare at me, the black slits of their pupils glistening in eerie golden eyes. I froze, but they didn't move; just fixed me with their unwavering gaze, as though willing me to stay. I backed away, turned, and continued to walk through the forest, careful to keep the road in sight. When I glanced back, the ewes had returned to cropping grass, but the ram continued to stare after me.

By the time I reached the car, my face and fingers were numb.

I could barely feel the plastic bag of crank when I dug it from my pocket, jabbing my pinkie into the white powder, then snorting it. It might last me another day if I rationed it carefully. I sat, waiting for the rush to explode behind my eyes. Finally I shoved the key into the ignition and drove back to the hotel.

At one point, a van's silhouette appeared in the road behind me. I kept my face down, lifting my foot from the accelerator to let the Jetta slow to a crawl. The van passed me in a spray of grit. Once it was out of sight I touched my jacket pocket, reassuring myself that the earring was still there, hit the gas, and kept going.

When I walked into the hotel room, I found Quinn in a chair by the window, his mouth a grim line.

"Where did you go?"

"Nowhere." My fist tightened around the car keys, hoping he hadn't noticed they were gone. "Just out."

"Don't lie to me, I know you took the car." Before I could blink he was in front of me. He pried my hand open, and the keys fell to the carpet.

"I didn't lie."

He snatched up the keys, pushing me roughly aside. "Goddamn it, you're not signed on as a driver. You could have gotten us both arrested."

"But I didn't."

He stared at me, his face livid. I stared back, daring him to touch me again, the crank boiling inside my veins, behind my eyelids. When he didn't move, I let my breath out and sank onto the edge of the bed.

"Where'd you go?" he repeated.

I shrugged off my satchel and camera, withdrew the amber earring from my pocket, and held it up. "I found this."

Quinn barely glanced at my hand. "What is it?"

"Her earring. Tindra's. There's a shed further down that road where we saw the dead fox, it must be some kind of farm. There were sheep. This was inside the shed." I held the earring out toward him, and he reluctantly took it. "That's her hair, see? I told you she has a blue dreadlock."

"Where was it?"

"In a cardboard box in the shed. There were all these boxes filled with dirt. And dead animals, like a taxidermy shop, only it was just their pelts and skulls. That's what was in the boxes—skulls and maggots. Someone's cleaning the skulls, using maggots or some kind of beetles to eat the dead flesh. That's where I found the earring, in one of those boxes. Not buried, it looked like it might have just fallen there. Or..."

I stared, mesmerized by the amber disk pinched between Quinn's thumb and forefinger. It rotated slowly, the long blue strands wisps of cloud around a tiny sun.

"I saw hair in the box, too," I went on. "Black hair coming out of the dirt. It might have been from one of the sheep, or a goat. But it might be hers. But the earring—that definitely means she's here, on the island."

Quinn scrutinized it, handed it back to me. "No. It means the earring is here. She might or might not be, just like she might or might not be dead."

"Maybe she's dead, but..."

"Why would she come here? If Erik is the same guy who assaulted her—and somehow he's also the same guy who stole the book and killed Harold and her bodyguard—why would she come here? She'd have to be crazier than you. And that's a stretch."

"Why would she come here? The book, for starters. And revenge. She told me what she planned to do when I met her, only I didn't understand what she was talking about. But now I do."

"She came back to find the man who raped her when she was a kid. She told me she wasn't afraid anymore. That when the code was finished, she'd make him disappear completely. She wasn't kidnapped. She came here of her own free will. She came here to confront him."

Quinn clapped a hand to his head. "Can you even hear yourself?

You met her for what, ten minutes? Five? Enough to scramble your brain, that's for sure. *This makes no sense.*"

He pointed at the earring. "Put that fucking thing someplace safe. Or lose it. Your prints will be all over it."

"I'm not going to the cops. We need to go back and see what else is in that box."

"Are you out of your fucking mind? That's someone's private property. You'll get popped for trespassing. And that's the *best*-case scenario. Even if you're right, I've seen enough heads in boxes for one lifetime."

He stormed to the closet, yanked his leather jacket from a hanger, and jammed on his watch cap. "Come on, we're going into town to get something to eat."

"I'm not hungry."

"I don't give a fuck if you're hungry or not, you're coming with me. You think I'm gonna leave you alone? You're running around like a lunatic—breaking into buildings, digging up shit, skulls in boxes. How can I even know if you're telling the truth?"

"I'm not lying!"

"This sounds seriously delusional, Cass. Look at yourself—"

He dragged me into the bathroom and held me in front of the mirror. "If someone saw you inside that shed, they'd shoot on sight. I would have."

I stared at the gaunt creature in front of me, black leather jacket hanging from it like a shroud. Nearly as tall as Quinn, the pale gray eyes now gas blue, fired by blood behind the iris; a corona of blond hair and one skeletal hand lifted as in greeting. *I am the one who will make a serious woman of you; come, let us embrace.*

"Cassie, please." Quinn touched my face and flinched: I knew that he no longer saw me, only the thing in the mirror. "Come with me. We'll go to Norderby, there's a good restaurant there, I think it's open in winter."

"I'm not hungry."

I stalked into the bedroom and paced between the window and

the desk. Quinn followed, his fingers laced behind his neck, and watched me without speaking.

At last I stopped and picked up the copy of *Skalltrolleri* from the nightstand, opening it with enough force that the spine cracked and pages flew everywhere. I snatched up a color photograph of a goat's skull with spiraling horns, perched atop a triangular rock that formed the prow of one of the stone ships. Wildflowers surrounded the stones—hawkweed, black-eyed Susans, some sort of flowering ivy—so that the stone boat floated in a sea of blossoms and green. I stared at the image, feeling my eyes burn through the cheap paper, and thrust the page at Quinn.

"I'm not delusional. Someone took these photos. Someone on this island." I scrabbled through loose pages until I found the book's cover photo, a man's torso as intricately encoded with symbols as any page in *The Book of Lamps and Banners:* swastikas, lightning bolts, skulls, flaming wheels. "This person! Whoever he is, he has Tindra. And the book."

Quinn's tone grew almost pitying. "Cass, you don't know that. You *can't* know that."

"Why not? Because it's too crazy? Because I'm crazy? Crazier than this place?" I pointed out the window to the black heap that gave the hotel its name. "Crazier than refugee kids living in a fucking ship container? Crazier than someone shooting people in the eye with a tranquilizer dart?"

"Baby, listen to me." Quinn tried to grasp my shoulders and I pushed him away. "Even if you're right about what you saw back there, and this guy has her, there's a good chance she's dead now."

"What if she's not?"

I squeezed my eyes shut, willing myself back into the place Tindra had shown me, the place where I'd died and never left.

Cass, Cass.

A car drove slowly down the dark alley, a man's hand extended from the window. He had a knife. I wanted to run, but I couldn't move, couldn't breathe, couldn't stop what had happened once and never stopped happening since.

Cass, Cass...

Someone pounded my breast. "Cass! Cassie, can you hear me?"

I opened my eyes and looked into Quinn's. I was slumped on the floor. Quinn knelt in front of me, holding my chin. He lifted his other hand, pointed at the ceiling, and moved his finger back and forth. "Can you see that?"

I tracked the finger, nodded. He lowered his hand. His face had grown so pale that the lines tattooed there appeared to glow.

"You were gone," he said. "You stopped breathing, it was like a candle blew out. I was right in your face and you couldn't see me."

"I see you now." My voice came out in a hoarse whisper. It hurt to talk, and my chest ached. "What're you doing?"

"You blacked out. I was scared maybe your heart stopped. I punched you." I winced when he pressed his hand gently against my left breast. "It's all I could think of, I don't have any Narcan."

"Shit." I stared at him, dazed.

"We should find a doctor, or—"

"It was just another blackout. I'm okay, I'll be okay."

"Jesus Christ, Cass! 'Just another blackout'?" He took my hand and placed it on my chest, so I could feel my heart pounding like a mallet. "Know what that is? That's you, dead, if you don't get straight. Here..."

He sat me on the bed, got a glass of water from the bathroom. "Drink this. Then we're going out. I don't care if you're not hungry. I am."

"Isn't it late for lunch?"

"So it'll be early dinner. You wanted a vacation." He pulled me to my feet, holding me up as he kissed me. "Let's go."

CHAPTER 52

Norderby felt like a medieval-themed LARP where all the players had gone home. The walled city would have fit inside a football stadium. Timbered buildings with stone foundations, cobble-stoned streets, a warren of arched passageways that led to shops selling tea, coffee, souvenirs, upscale housewares, designer clothing, blown glass, woolens. Lots and lots of woolens, all from Kalkö sheep, a heritage breed supposedly dating back to the island's first settlers and known for producing wool that had a remarkable ability to resist water and cold. Their wool had its own advertising campaign. Nearly every shopwindow featured a beautifully composed photo of some-one facing blizzard conditions—atop a cliff, on an empty beach, in the shadow of a pine forest—their only protection from the ele-ments a bulky, neutral-tone knit sweater and knit cap.

I moved unsteadily, grateful for Quinn's arm around my shoulders. The fact that I might have died barely registered. I felt detached from the notion, as though it was a pink thought bubble floating away from me. My body felt pretty much the same, something tethered to me that I could do without if the thread snapped.

Still, maybe Quinn was right; maybe I needed to eat. Most of the shops were shuttered until spring, so I was surprised by how many people were in the streets. If the island had only a few hundred year-round residents, most of them seemed to be in Norderby this afternoon. Couples walking dogs; young women carrying children; cyclists with baskets full of shopping bags. We passed a small grocery crowded with people filling net bags with bunches of turnips and carrots, bottles of coconut water and Fruktsoda. In the window of the police station, a marmalade cat watched passersby with impassive yellow eyes. Despite the cold and an occasional urgent flurry of snowflakes, nearly everyone eschewed anoraks or overcoats for cable-knit pullovers or cardigans. Most people ignored us. The few who didn't stared with suspicion bordering on hostility.

"It's *The Stepford Wives,* with sweaters," I said as Quinn steered me down an alley too narrow for any vehicle larger than a bicycle.

"Those sweaters cost more than our airfare. The restaurant's over here, I hope it's open."

It was: a small half-timbered building with diamond-paned windows and an immense oak door with iron hardware that wouldn't have been out of place in Helm's Deep. Inside, it smelled like a bakery. Fragrant steam billowed from an open kitchen; a few dozen people sat at trestle tables, hunched over plates or laptops. Geraniums filled the windows. The temperature differential between here and outside must have been fifty degrees. I immediately started to sweat.

We found a table in back with a view of the kitchen stove, a huge cast-iron antique surrounded by tattooed young cooks wearing yellow aprons. A waitress brought us a basket of flatbread and handed us menus in English. I didn't look at mine. The smell of food made me sick.

"The kitchen is slow," she said, apologizing. "One of the cooks is on vacation."

"This place is famous for its saffron pancakes," Quinn remarked as she walked off. "Good sausage, too."

"I'm—"

"Stop." He pushed the basket of flatbread toward me. "Eat."

I picked up a piece of flatbread and began to break it into smaller and smaller pieces. Quinn ordered the lunch special for both of us. The place didn't serve anything but beer or cider. Quinn got a beer. I got a pint of local cider that tasted more like ouzo than apples.

We sat without talking. In the pretty room around us, people chattered and took pictures of their food when it arrived. I set my camera on the table and stared at it, thinking of those cardboard boxes in the shed, skeins of blowflies circling the ceiling. Quinn finished his beer and ordered a second. The waitress returned, apologizing again for the slow kitchen before she hurried to another table.

Quinn took a swallow from his glass and set it down. "I'll be back in a few."

"Where you going?"

"Just sit. What's that girl's name again?"

"Tindra. Tindra Bergstrand."

"Tindra Bergstrand," he repeated. "Right back."

He shrugged on his leather jacket and left. I finished my cider and ordered another, watched one of the cooks pour brilliant orange batter into a skillet. The stove's gas flames leaped in their ring burner, a fiery blue eye. After a while, Quinn returned. I picked up a fragment of flatbread and pretended to eat it.

"Okay." He sat and leaned across the table toward me, his voice dropping. "So I went by the grocery store—the post office is inside. Said I was looking for a guy named Bergstrand. I told the woman I did some carpentry for him ten years ago, I was back in the area for a while and wanted to find out if he needed any more work. Turns out he's dead."

"Dead?" I stared at him, confused. "What do you mean?"

"What I said. Four years ago. Dropped dead in the middle of that big supermarket just out of town, she thinks it was a cerebral hemorrhage. Nobody was upset, she said. Turns out he wasn't very popular."

"Because he was a neo-Nazi?"

"She didn't say. Just that he 'was not a nice man whatsoever.' Whatsoever that means."

He sipped his beer. I crumbled a bit of flatbread between my fingers. "But then what about his Herla podcast?"

"What about it?"

"Their site said he does a podcast every week—they had a picture of him, he looks just like Tindra."

"They could be running old programs, or someone else could be doing it now."

"Then why didn't they change the photo?"

"Who knows? Maybe he has a big following and they want to capitalize on that. The show doesn't use his name—it's *Valî's Hour*. Maybe it's a rotating thing. Maybe there's always a new Valî, like there's always a new Doctor Who. Or maybe they just never bothered to take the photo down. Do we even know the show still exists?"

"It does. Those guys Erik was talking to, they listen to it. One of them asked him about a book that was mentioned on it last week."

"So maybe Erik's the new Valî."

"But then why wouldn't he have his own photo on the website?"

"Maybe he doesn't want his employer to find out he's a white supremacist. It could be anything. The deal is, the guy you're looking for ain't here."

I glanced up as the waitress set a steaming plate in front of each of us. She smiled and left, and I turned back to Quinn. "So now what?"

"Now we eat." He picked up his fork and pointed it at me. *"Mangia."*

I managed a few bites of pancake, rearranging what was left so it looked like I'd eaten more. Quinn glared at me, but when he'd finished his own food he finally sighed, defeated, and reached across the table for my plate. As he scarfed down my lunch, I asked, "Did you find out anything about the other guy? Erik?"

"Like what?"

"Like his relationship to Tindra. Like whether he was the guy who raped her."

Quinn chewed a mouthful of pancake and swallowed it. "No, Cass. I didn't ask the postmistress if she knew anything about the local rapist."

"It's not funny."

"Who's laughing?" Quinn dropped his fork onto his plate. "This is a wild-goose chase, Cass."

"I told you, I don't care. I'm going back there. If there's a farm and outbuildings, there has to be a house, too."

"And what? You're going to ask them if they've kidnapped someone?"

"I'm going to get inside and see what I can find."

Quinn laughed. "Really? How?"

"I don't know. Cause a diversion. You lure them outside and I'll go in. You could garrote one of their sheep."

"Now you're being an idiot."

"Well, something to distract them."

"Forget it." He wiped a line of sweat from his forehead. "Let's call it a day."

"No. I'm going back."

"I'm not driving you."

"Then I'll walk."

I got up, pulled on my leather jacket, and headed outside.

Overhead the sky had deepened to violet, turning the cobblestoned alley into a shadowy passage lit by glowing windows. I started back toward the main street, my head down. Several people passed me, talking eagerly in Swedish. A young woman laughed and I looked up quickly. She had dark hair, a wide mouth, sly intelligent eyes.

But of course it wasn't Tindra. Would I have even known if it had been? I'd never heard her laugh. I'd spent barely a quarter hour with her in a dimly lit garage, listening to her ravings about a smart-phone app and the rare book that had been stolen from her, a book I knew I'd never track down, a book I was finding it increasingly hard to believe even existed. Maybe I really had imagined it, strung out on basement crank. Maybe Quinn hadn't pounded my heart hard enough. If Tindra was dead, maybe I was, too.

And even if she wasn't dead, even if I wasn't dead, I'd still never find her. And why should that matter so much? I swiped the hair from my eyes and thought of her hunched on the floor of the garage, hugging her dog, her desolation so powerful that even now I could taste it, bitter as the residue on my lips and tongue.

What must it have been like, to be a child assaulted by a family friend, to be betrayed by your own father, to strike out on your own when you were only fourteen? How did someone come back from that? Because, damaged as she was, and young as she'd been, Tindra had come back. I stared at the ground, my steel-tipped boots clacking against the cobblestones, and kept walking.

CHAPTER 53

Hey, wait up."

Someone tapped my shoulder and I spun around, foot poised to kick. It was Quinn.

"Jesus!" He did a little dance step back, hands raised in surrender. "Why'd you run off? I had to pay the check."

I didn't reply, just walked on fast. Quinn followed. When we reached the street, we headed to the car, got in, and joined the line of vehicles creeping toward the stone gate that opened onto the real world. I shoved the camera into my satchel and threw the bag onto the floor.

Neither of us spoke. Quinn seemed subdued. I waited for him to say something, to rail at me for an entire laundry list of failings: drinking, drugs, my refusal to face what I'd done to him, done to myself and my art.

You're like heroin to him.

But he only stared at the vehicles ahead of us as our car made its way through a roundabout. We drove past the sign pointing toward Slythamn, circled round a second, then a third time. I looked at Quinn.

"What are you doing?"

He didn't reply. We drove by the big-box stores we'd stopped at the day before, past a strip mall and a cul-de-sac of red-and-white modular houses, until the island's compressed sprawl gave way to farmland. After a few minutes, a large low-slung structure loomed up alongside the road. In front of it, a plastic sign flapped in the wind, some of its letters missing.

JÄRNH DEL

JO DBRUK

TRÄ Å D

Brand-new farm machinery shone beneath floodlights, excavators and tractors. A garage bay held pallets piled with oversize poly-wrapped sacks containing grain and fertilizer and gravel. We pulled alongside the few cars and pickups in the parking lot.

The building was old, its metal siding buckled and rusted. Beside the door, a constellation of bullet holes circled a faded ad for a riding lawn mower. When Quinn turned off the ignition, I opened my door. He leaned over and pulled it closed before I could get out.

"No. You stay here."

I opened my mouth to argue, but his expression shut me up. I watched as he went inside, giving a nod to two men who stood talking by the entrance. Once he was gone, the men glanced over to where I sat in the car, staring at me with open curiosity. I stared back, and they turned to resume their conversation.

It grew cold. Quinn had taken the car keys with him, so I couldn't turn on the heat. The sun had long disappeared. After a few more minutes, Quinn returned. He hopped into the car, tossing a plastic bag into my lap, backed up into the road, and drove toward Norderby. I looked inside the bag. It contained a pair of deerskin work gloves.

"What's this?"

"Your hands are freezing."

I rubbed them together, my fingers like icy twigs. He was right.

"Thanks," I said. I set the bag between us and leaned against him. "Do you ever miss New York?"

"That's like missing being young."

We returned to Slagghögen. It was close to full dark now. In the sky, a few stars glowed like holes punched in worn fabric. Quinn parked out back, left the car, and headed across the lot and into the hotel without looking at me.

I turned to stare at the annex. No lights shone in any of its porthole windows. I opened the car door and listened for voices, a computer game, television, but heard nothing. The rusted Saab was gone. Apart from our rental, the parking lot was deserted. Bleak as the place had appeared the night before, this felt different. It felt utterly empty, the desolation not of human misery but abandonment.

I sat in the car, studying the annex windows for any sign of life. Finally I gave up and went inside. The girl at the desk gave me a curt nod. I nodded back, opened the door to head upstairs, then stopped.

"The people who were staying in that other building. Did they leave?"

The girl shrugged. "I don't know. We don't handle it."

"Who does?"

"Refugee services from Stockholm. They let us know when some-one's coming in, but not when they leave." The girl frowned. "Was there a problem?"

"No," I said, and continued upstairs. Quinn was lying on the bed, laptop on his chest.

"Any news?" I asked.

"Freiburg won, two–zero."

"I mean about the rest. Tommy or Harold."

"I don't know. I don't care." He closed the laptop and set it on the nightstand. "I changed our flight."

"What?"

"To tomorrow morning. We leave at ten-thirty for Arlanda. The flight to Reykjavík's at two."

"You said we have till tomorrow night!"

"I changed my mind." He stared at me, green eyes clouded with despair. "I can't do this, Cass. I can't watch you do this. You're killing yourself."

"I'm not——"

He raised a hand wearily. "I'm not listening. The only reason I got you that crank was I was afraid of what would happen if you got it yourself—you'd get arrested, or OD, and I wouldn't be there. I thought it'd be better this way. I fucked up, I know I fucked up . . ."

His voice broke, and I felt as I had years before, when I learned he'd taken off with a girl he'd met in Harlem one night. A spike in my heart, love and desire bleeding out with nothing but grief and fury to replace them.

"Don't." I tried to touch him, but he pushed me away. "Quinn, don't . . ."

"I'm going back to Iceland. You can come or not. But if you don't get clean, I'm done."

"I'm not——"

"Shut up!" His despair twisted into rage. He stumbled to his feet, and I saw that the bottle of rum on the nightstand was empty. "I thought it might be different this time, but it's not. *You're* not. I went to prison—I *had* to change, Cass. You never did. I'm too old for this. So are you. You're out of control and deluding yourself."

He walked to the window, pressed his palms and forehead against the glass. "We need to drop off the car and get to the airport by nine. If you don't want to come to Reykjavík, you can go back to New York. Actually, I think that's what you should do. I can't deal with your shit anymore, Cass. Get clean, then we can talk."

I went to his side and started to argue. He whirled around and again pushed me away, hard enough that I fell against the bed, and stormed out of the room.

I listened to his footsteps as he hurried downstairs, dug my fingers into my thighs as I waited for him to return. A minute later I heard the sound of a car engine. I went to the window and looked down in time to see the Jetta peel off, spewing gravel and mud in its wake. I listened as the engine's roar grew fainter, then died away entirely. I remained by the window, willing him to return. But he didn't.

CHAPTER 54

That might have been a good time to quit drinking. There was no booze left in the room, and I wasn't going to go out looking for more, not yet, anyway. It might have been a good time to flush my tiny stash of crank down the toilet—enough remained for only a few more hits.

But I didn't. Instead I paced the room, from window to bed to bathroom, then back again, slapping my hand against the walls as though testing to see if they'd give.

Quinn was wrong. I wasn't deluding myself. I knew what I was doing, knew that I was sustaining a decades-long process of metabolizing grief and fear and fury. Calibrating my tolerance for alcohol and speed and whatever else I could pump into my bloodstream, so that I'd be able to stumble out of bed and do the bare minimum of whatever was necessary to keep myself alive.

I knew that if I lost Quinn again, it would be for good, and I would die. Not immediately, maybe, but soon. My life had closed like a camera's aperture: the only light that found its way in was Quinn. It wasn't enough. Nothing was enough.

I gathered the loose pages from *Skalltrolleri* and piled them onto the desk beside the laptop, picked up my satchel and pulled out the stolen Nikon, removed the lens cap, and stared at the circle of black glass.

A skull stared back at me. I gazed at it until my eyes ached, until the distorted reflection of my own face shrank to a white dot and disappeared.

I replaced the camera and sorted through my drugs. The Vyvanse was gone. The only speed I had left was the cheap crank Quinn had given me. As for the rest, I had one Percocet, some ibuprofen, a single Vicodin, three Xanax. Enough to get me onto a plane back to New York in a semiconscious state. Once there, I'd contact Phil and spend what remained of my money on one last bash.

I dumped everything back into my bag, took a shower, and once more began to pace.

Hours passed. I knew Quinn would return, probably when the local bar closed, unless he got so wasted that he went home with someone else. I took another shower, hoping the cold water would extinguish the fire burning up my nerve ends, got out, and dressed and lay down on the bed. My thoughts pinwheeled from Quinn to Tindra to Harold to Tommy to the app to *The Book of Lamps and Banners* to Gryffin to a dying dog to Quinn. A photo of a tattooed man holding a ram's skull. Darts and a human eye that was also a target. Boxes crawling with maggots. An alley at 3:00 a.m., broken glass and blood on my hands. Tindra. Quinn. Me.

Somehow I zoned out, the twitching, twisted half sleep that comes when your speed-fueled body is too depleted to function but the amphetamines still claw at your brain. I didn't know what time it was when Quinn returned. He made no effort to be quiet. I heard the door close, the clink of keys tossed on the desk, footsteps crossing to the bed. A thud as he dropped one boot onto the floor, followed by the other. He collapsed beside me without removing his clothes, reeking of cigarettes and alcohol.

I waited and, when his breathing didn't slow, rolled over to put my arms around him. He covered my hand with his, drew it to his face, and kissed it. I counted our heartbeats as we lay like that for a long time, both of us awake. I stared at his broken face, just a shadow now, until I couldn't bear the silence.

"I can't," I whispered.

"I know," he said, and turned away from me.

CHAPTER 55

Quinn's breathing slowed. He began to snore. Tomorrow he'd have a murderous hangover. I sat up and watched him, at last leaned over to retrieve my camera. Low light would make it difficult if not impossible to capture anything but a range of shadows stretching across the bed; no details of face or hands, no trace of the tattoos and scarifications that mapped his life without me.

But that seemed right. In many ways, for decades, Quinn had been a projection of myself, the shadow of a memory of someone I'd lost when I was young. Perhaps that was why all the photos I'd taken of him as a teenager had disappeared: they'd never truly existed in the first place. Quinn had become indistinguishable from my longing for him.

My eyes burned; I was too dehydrated to cry. I'd crossed over to a place beyond grief or fear. I'd lost everything, even, for the moment, the need for a drink or speed. I'd outlived the world I had evolved to inhabit; not a dinosaur but a rodent, scrabbling for shelter in the cracks of the twenty-first century. I groaned and roused myself, and went into the bathroom to take another shower.

When I was done, I dressed quietly, went into the other room, and sat at the small desk. The Svarlight CDs were where I'd tossed them, alongside Quinn's cigarettes and laptop. I picked up *Stone Ships*, cracked open the laptop to let a sliver of light fall across the jewel box. I almost wished I had some way to play it. Not that the track list was all that inspiring, though "Within the Petrified Darkness We All Disappear" held some promise.

I squinted at the final production credit at the bottom of the back cover—*Album produced, engineered, and mixed by Gwilym Birdsong at Svarlight Studio.*

I felt my breath catch. I searched to find the artwork credit:

Front and back cover photographs by Big Delusory Whim

BDW: Big Delusory Whim.

I read and reread those two credits. I started to breathe way too fast, my thoughts falling like dominoes: a stream of words, letters, names, forming and re-forming in my consciousness the way that the symbols from Ludus Mentis swirled into a pattern just beyond my comprehension.

It's all code.

I breathed deeply and closed my eyes, trying to force my heart to slow, fighting to grasp and hold on to the solution to a puzzle I hadn't even known I was attempting to solve. I found the pen and paper I'd nabbed earlier and made my way to the bathroom. I closed the door and turned on the light, perched at the edge of the tub, and scribbled on the paper:

BIG DELUSORY WHIM

GWILYM BIRDHOUSE

I cross-checked each letter, drawing a line through every single one, stared at the piece of paper. The letters matched out. "Big Delusory Whim" was an anagram for "Gwilym Birdhouse."

CHAPTER 56

Nathan Ballingstead had told me Birdhouse raised sheep on a re-mote island, the Faeroes or Hebrides or Orkney. He'd been right: he just had the wrong island. I tried to imagine how a middle-aged one-hit wonder could become the person who'd shot the photos in *Skalltrolleri*.

But just like the rest of the planet, the music world has no lack of white nationalists and white supremacists, especially these days. Hard-core rock and rollers and fingerpickers in the American heart-land, Scandinavian metalheads and folk singers, and, apparently, an English folk-rock balladeer. At some point, Birdhouse's nostalgia for an England that never was had tipped over into hatred for those he believed had destroyed it.

Was it enough to turn him into a killer?

I had no proof that he'd done anything except contribute to the planet's vast landfill of forgotten vinyl, cassettes, and CDs. Bird-house's songs had always shown a love for puns and clever wordplay; any die-hard fan might have decoded the anagram before I did, but how many of them would know about *Skalltrolleri*? The book had such a limited print run that only a few members of his extremist cohort might ever have seen it. Same with fans of bands like Jötunn's Egg. If they were in on the joke, they might have been reluctant to blow his cover. If word ever got out beyond his Nazi fan club, his mainstream career would be over. But that had pretty much deep-sixed a long time ago.

Yet could Birdhouse have known about *The Book of Lamps and*

Banners? Nathan had recalled talking to someone at a book signing, someone who'd gotten wind that Harold Vertigan had a line on an extremely rare volume. Had that person been Birdhouse? Had he then killed Harold and stolen the book?

I'd found darts and that eerie eye-shaped target in the woods, etorphine and a Svarlight poster in a nearby shed. How hard would it be for a sheep farmer to get his hands on a half gallon of animal tranquilizer?

Probably not very. I'd seen a documentary where a biologist nailed a charging grizzly between the eyes with a single tranquilizer dart. At close enough range—in a small room, or somehow hidden in a crowd, or at point-blank range if you were shooting a dog—someone who'd spent hours at target practice might do pretty much the same thing.

That could explain Harold's death and the theft of *The Book of Lamps and Banners*. What about Tindra's disappearance?

I sank onto the bathroom floor, staring at the piece of paper. I'd believed that Tindra had returned to Kalkö to confront her father and the man who'd abused her.

But her father was dead.

I'd assumed the other man must be Erik—but what if he wasn't? What if he was the same man who'd taken the photos in *Skalltrolleri*—Gwilym Birdhouse?

CHAPTER 57

I shut off the bathroom light and returned to the bed, where Quinn lay snoring. Even if I managed to wake him, he'd be too groggy to hold a conversation; also, royally pissed off. Almost certainly he was still drunk. It would be difficult, probably impossible, to make him understand what I was saying, let alone process the information, until he sobered up. This didn't bode well for him catching that morning flight to Stockholm, though I knew from experience that Quinn's powers of recovery could be impressive.

Would he believe me if I told him about Birdhouse? Probably not, and if he did, I still doubted he'd change his mind.

I can't deal with your shit anymore, Cass. A recovering junkie can be as pitiless as one who's still using.

If I could find the book, he might feel differently. We'd have enough money to start over. No one would miss me if I disappeared and started a new life. Greece would be cheap; if not Greece, someplace else.

And if I found Tindra here on the island, too, all the better. If she was dead, or had fled, I might still be able to track down Birdhouse. Tindra intended to make him disappear. With enough crank in me, and a blunt instrument, I could do the same, to both Birdhouse and the mobile that held Ludus Mentis.

I did a quick search for anything that might be useful and came up empty-handed. I had the two darts I'd found in the woods, and my camera. That was it. I didn't bother checking online for any additional news about Tommy or Harold Vertigan. They were someone else's problem now. I put on an extra pair of wool socks inside my cowboy boots, then pulled on every sweater I had in my bag, shrugged into my leather jacket, and slung the bag over my shoulder.

I stepped to the bed and gazed down at Quinn. If he was right, I'd already died once in the last twenty-four hours. I'd survived all those years without him by daring to hope he was still alive. Now I could scarcely believe that I was. I touched his scarred cheek, bent to brush my lips against his eyelids. I opened my bag and took out the copy of *Dead Girls,* found my pen, turned to the book's frontispiece, and wrote:

For Quinn, then and always. Love, C.

I removed the page from *The Book of Lamps and Banners* and ran my fingers across the papyrus, feeling those thousands of tiny brushstrokes. I wished I could read them, like braille; wished I understood whatever secret language was encoded in those strange and frightening images.

What would it be like to experience the world like that, every object and face and shade of light imbued with meaning and portent? Crank made me feel that way, and alcohol, even though I knew they were killing me. Maybe if you truly understood *The Book of Lamps and Banners,* it would destroy you, too.

Carefully as I could, I slid the page into my bag, and set *Dead Girls* on Quinn's laptop. If he woke in time to catch his flight, he'd be furious to find the Jetta gone, but he'd manage. A taxi to the airport, a call to the rental agency with some lie about where to locate the car. Or he'd just cut and run.

I took the car keys and went downstairs. The receptionist was long gone. I peered into the tiny office, then tried the door. It was open. I slipped inside and rifled through every drawer I saw. I nicked a small flashlight, a cigarette lighter, and a pair of scissors and hurried outside.

The cold hit me like a body blow. I strode to the car and got inside, switched on the ignition, and cranked the heat. I sat and stared up at the window of our room, dark as those in the annex. I was waiting for Quinn to come outside and find me and drag me back upstairs, back into whatever life we'd cobble for ourselves out of the wreckage of the last few decades.

I knew that wouldn't happen. I dug my pinkie nail into the crank and snorted enough to feel the familiar explosion behind my streaming eyes. I dropped the baggie on the seat, pulled on the deerskin gloves Quinn had bought for me, and drove out of town.

CHAPTER 58

I headed toward the sheep farm, wishing the radio worked so I could blast it. I held little hope that Tindra was still alive. Boxes full of flesh-eating larvae and animal skulls, an amber earring tangled with a few strands of dyed blue hair. A drug that killed you in a few heartbeats. I'd focus on the book: search the shed, then see if I could enter the house without being caught. I knew how crazy this was but didn't care.

A quarter moon glowed through clouds in the western sky, just enough light for me to find my way back to the narrow dirt road I'd already traversed twice. I didn't pass a single vehicle. I slowed the car to a crawl, straining to see the trail. When I knew I'd driven too far, I turned back.

This time, I found it. In the distance, somewhere past the shed, a solitary light gleamed through the trees. A house, maybe. I pulled off the highway and parked beneath a thick stand of spruce, sat for a while to make sure I hadn't been followed.

At last I put the keys under the floor mat. First place someone would look, but with luck that would be Quinn. I grabbed my bag and got out, ran across the pavement, and headed down the winding dirt road.

A fine sifting of snow covered the ground. I tried to determine where I'd come upon the dead fox and the birch with its carved eye-shaped target. After a few minutes I quit trying. Moonlight glimmered through the evergreen branches overhead, the fractured light making it more difficult to see. I couldn't tell whether a patch of white in the distance was snow or birchbark or a house.

Once the moonlight disappeared abruptly, as though someone or something had blotted it out. I halted and held my breath. I could smell my own sweat, fear and methamphetamine and booze. A branch creaked. Dry needles fell like rain. I began to walk again, pausing often to listen for any hint I was being followed.

I heard only the scratching of pine boughs stirred by the wind, the occasional chitter of a small bird or mouse disturbed by my passing. I'd lost sight of the light I'd glimpsed earlier. Cold surrounded me like a second skin. I could no longer feel my toes inside my cowboy boots. The deerskin gloves helped, but soon my fingers started to tingle. I clutched my bag to my chest for warmth.

The shed couldn't be much farther. Unless I'd missed it. I fumbled for the flashlight in my pocket. I'd been reluctant to use it, but now I switched it on, swept the pencil-thin wand of light through the darkness in front of me. A metallic thread shone to my right—barbed-wire fence. I stepped toward it and aimed the beam across the field. The sheep were gone. Another minute and I saw the shed, its windows aglow. I crouched, then realized it was my flashlight's beam reflected in the glass.

I clicked off the flashlight and walked around back, my boots crunching on dead leaves, and stopped at the door. I turned the knob and stepped inside. I recognized the shadows of the corner table, the surfboard suspended across the beams, the pegboard holding tools. I stood with my back to the door, finally switched on the flashlight.

Everything appeared as I'd left it. Withered pelts strewn across the table, the dead raven lying on its side with outspread wings, one unseeing eye fixed on me. On the floor, a maze of cardboard boxes.

I dropped my bag beside the door, stepped to the cardboard box where I'd found Tindra's earring, and knelt beside it. I scanned the dirt with my flashlight, looking for anything I might have missed earlier. Hair, a fingernail, a shred of clothing. There was nothing.

I hesitated, then took a deep breath, removed one of the deerskin gloves, and plunged my hand into the soil.

Tiny things wriggled through my fingers, moist and unmistakably alive. I tried not to gag and dug deeper into the earth, until I touched the bottom of the box. Black beetles emerged frantically from the soil and raced to the sides of the box, where they struggled to climb. I gritted my teeth and continued to sift through the box's contents: damp soil and seething larvae, nothing else.

Relief overcame revulsion as I withdrew my hand. Something caught beneath one fingernail, something small and rigid. Pinching it between forefinger and thumb, I carefully pulled it out, shaking dirt and maggots from it.

I fixed the flashlight's beam on a piece of plastic, once translucent pink, now dulled to a smeared gray. An orthodontic retainer. As I brought the flashlight closer, I spotted two brownish objects snared in the twisted wire that dangled from the plastic. Teeth.

I took a moment to calm myself, then quickly smoothed the soil so it would appear undisturbed. Maggots coiled and uncoiled in the dirt before disappearing beneath the surface. I stood and searched for a piece of paper, settled on a crumpled paper bag in a wastebasket. I wrapped it around the retainer and placed it in my bag.

I wiped my hand, pulled on the deerskin glove, and did a final circuit of the room. I stopped when my gaze fell on the miniature refrigerator, and crouched in front of it.

This time I didn't bother looking inside. Instead, I removed one of the photos taped to the door.

Why do people hold on to photographs of lost loved ones? A person you haven't seen in years, decades even; someone who died, or ravaged you with their infidelity and left you for another; someone who fled you like a burning car wreck; someone who would kill you if they had the chance? I'd kept every photo I ever took of Quinn O'Boyle as a teenager, only to lose them all; I never knew how or where. He had retained a single one, the only proof that the two of us had a life before the one we now inhabited.

When I looked at that photo, I didn't see Quinn but my own obsession with him. I never knew what he saw. We cling to these images not because we love the person they portray, but because they're markers on the highway to death, showing how far we've come, how few miles are left before the road ends.

The photo I looked at now showed a girl of thirteen or fourteen, sitting on the hood of a white car. She wore rolled-up jeans that exposed long skinny legs, a short-sleeved plaid shirt loosely slung over a pink camisole, one strap falling off her shoulder. Long dark hair, tousled by the wind that lifted the hem of her shirt. Her head was partly turned, her brow furrowed and mouth open as she looked at the man who stood a few feet away, as though asking him a question.

It was the same man whose photo I'd seen on the Herla website, the host of *Valî's Hour*—Tindra's father. He appeared several years younger than the man in his thumbnail picture online. Both he and the girl seemed unaware that their picture was being taken. The photo was printed on Kodacolor stock, dating to the early aughts, before digital photography was cheap and inescapable. Matte finish, unfaded, good resolution.

I removed one of the other photos on the fridge door. It was printed on cheap white card stock, not photographic paper, using an inkjet printer. The print head needed cleaning, which gave the picture the out-of-focus look of one of those 3D comic books from the 1960s, the kind that made your eyes hurt if you tried to look at them without the flimsy 3D spectacles included with your purchase.

I didn't want to focus too long on this photo. A night shot with the same girl—Tindra—sitting hunched on a picnic bench, illuminated by a bonfire, a sullen orange cloud in the lower-right corner of the frame. The girl was topless, her hair drooping in a single long coil over one shoulder. I couldn't tell if she wore anything else—the lower half of her torso eroded into shadow and flame.

But there was no doubt she knew she was being photographed. She stared directly into the camera, her expression complex. Petulance and irritation; a challenge that I recognized as bravado. Triumph, perhaps, evidenced by a barely suppressed smirk.

The remaining photo was worse quality and shot indoors under harsh light. I could see enough to wish I hadn't.

I stared at all three photos, then slid them into my back pocket. I opened the fridge, the flap door to its tiny freezer. A plastic ziplock bag was inside. Not one bag but four, one inside the other. It was how you stored drugs, or unused film, though it wasn't the best way to keep film safe. Moisture and the temperature differential when you removed it from the fridge could damage it. Drugs were more forgiving.

The innermost bag held neither film nor drugs but a plastic jewel case with a photo CD inside. Another outdated technology, introduced around 1990 by Kodak and long surpassed by scanners and more sophisticated digital processes.

This wasn't a Kodak disc, and someone had written *2004 Farm Stats* on it in Magic Marker. I was willing to bet a commercial photo lab would never have processed whatever images this disc contained, and that they had nothing to do with farm statistics from 2004. Whoever shot those photos of the thirteen-year-old Tindra had taken a whole lot more of them, but he'd been savvy enough not to store them on his computer. I replaced the ziplock bags in the freezer, pocketed the CD in my jacket, and returned outside.

CHAPTER 59

I ran through the woods until I tripped and, with a sickening lurch, fell, taking the weight on my knee. I sprawled on the cold ground as I caught my breath, finally stumbled to my feet. I limped out of the evergreen cover, crossed the road, and walked, following the fence. Adrenaline and pain momentarily canceled out the cold. I tried to guess how much time had passed. Not more than an hour. That left a little more than two hours until dawn.

The moon had vanished behind the black wall of conifers. The road felt increasingly claustrophobic, tunneling into a darkness that seemed solid. I kept moving, dragging one foot, then the other, as though I walked toward an unseen cliff edge.

Phantom lights appeared in the darkness, random dots and lines that merged into symbols. An eye, an arrow; horned circles, spidery swastikas, and fiery grids. Threads of poisonous yellow light streaked the sky overhead, forming a map of fragmented insignia.

I struggled to make sense of them, the way I used to read acid trails as messages from the future, even though I knew what this really signified: the early phases of amphetamine psychosis. Even when I closed my eyes, the symbols remained, branded on my eyelids.

A voice whispered my name. I knuckled my eyes until the symbols disintegrated into blobs of red and muddy orange, blinked rapidly as I tried to focus. I saw no one.

But in front of me shone a single light. I stared at it till my eyes watered, wondering if this was another hallucination. It didn't move.

I broke into a shambling run and halted where the road divided. To the right, it dwindled to a snow-patched, grassy track through the woods. In front of me, the road continued for a hundred yards, ending in a broad sweep of well-tended land illuminated by a powerful floodlight atop a barn. The wind carried the scent of woodsmoke.

Scattered across the clearing were a half-dozen boxy structures resembling giant plastic Monopoly houses, all tidily kept. A two-story building, red with a green roof and a line of decorative stick figures stenciled along its white trim, half a dozen large propane tanks propped at one back corner. Two pickups were parked in front of a separate garage, along with the same blue Volvo I'd seen earlier. Near the garage stood a blue playhouse emblazoned with a cartoon bear. Two crossed axes were nailed above the door of a shed like the one where I'd found the dirt-filled cartons. There was also a single telephone or electrical pole with no lines running to it.

The harsh floodlight made everything look garish and staged, a movie set waiting for the principals to show up. The impenetrable wall of black trees surrounding the homestead intensified the unsettling effect: the floodlight seemed like a futile effort to keep back the encroaching forest.

I eased back into the shadows and stared at the house. Above the front door hung a disk painted with a black sun, an Aryan Nations hex sign. The decorative stencils that ran under the eaves weren't stick figures but runes. The pole was a totem carved from a single tree, stripped of its bark and topped with an elongated man's face—long mustache, beard, Viking cap, and a single deep-set eye, all chiseled meticulously from the tree trunk. Odin.

Someone had swept neat paths in the snow between house and vehicles, barn and shed and playhouse. The large propane tanks were lined up as precisely as tenpins in a bowling alley. Despite the black sun and crossed axes, Odin totem and runes, the homestead seemed utterly mundane. It was easier to imagine its inhabitants as law-abiding Swedes whose taste ran to folkloric remnants of their country's culture than as white supremacists. I had a vision of myself as Quinn—as anyone—would see me, a gaunt figure staggering to the edge of someone's yard at 4:00 a.m., peering out from the trees like a demented scarecrow. I'd be lucky if they didn't do what Quinn had warned: shoot me on sight. I turned and began the trek back to the main road.

CHAPTER 60

Within minutes, all signs of the homestead disappeared. My despair was indistinguishable from exhaustion and grief—grief for losing Quinn, and also Tindra. I'd had no plan as to how to find her, only crazed intent. Now even that was gone.

When I reached the fork in the road, I stopped. The snow was deeper here, drifted against tree trunks. It covered the dead grass and tangled undergrowth that choked a trail narrower and, I suspected, older than the one I'd just left. A disused footpath, not meant for vehicles.

I could lose myself here. Quinn wouldn't bother looking for me. He'd assume I'd gone off on a bender. Which, I suppose, I had. I'd heard of people bottoming out, and knew plenty whose floor was the grave. I always imagined the process would be more dramatic: flames, screams, broken bones, blood; the orgasmic rush as the drug kicks in and the needle falls from your arm and you never feel your head hit the ground.

This was more like the endless magnification of a photographic print, the image losing definition as it disintegrates into grains of light and shadow, until any distinction between darkness and light is erased. All that remains is negative space.

Threads of light wriggled behind my eyes, through my skull. I opened my bag and dug around until I found one of the darts. I felt at the side of my neck until I detected the pulse of my carotid artery. With my other hand I pressed the dart against the skin, feeling the needle press against my skin without breaking it. I counted to a hundred, trying to summon the strength to take that final step, and fall without stopping. At last I lowered my hand and dropped the dart into my bag.

I trudged on, with no sense of time or where I was. The air sparked with ghostly symbols, eyes and arrows and wheels. I heard a constant low thunder in my ears. Eventually I had to pause to rest. I braced myself against a tree, scraped up a handful of snow, and pressed it against my injured kneecap as I stared at the trees on the other side of the path. Birches, not evergreens, and larger trees with smooth gray bark: a grove of ancient beeches that encircled an area thick with gorse, the remnant of a farm or other homestead.

I crossed the path, underbrush scraping my knees. The leafless canopy allowed the sky to show through, the color of charcoal ash. Wind parted the branches, the air no longer resin scented and evocative of Christmas but of something far more ancient: leaf mold and desiccated feathers, bones beneath the frozen earth. A shadow hulked in the center of the clearing, a pile of boards or an abandoned dinghy. I pushed through the thicket to see what it was.

Gravestones thrust up from the snow, each one the point of a spearhead the size of a boogie board, arranged in the shape of an arrow. When I reached the stone that formed the arrow's tip, I saw it wasn't a tombstone but a slab of rock hewn into a ragged point. I stood at the prow of a stone boat—the same one on the cover of *Stone Ships,* a vessel picked out with dragon's teeth.

I stooped to touch a large rock encrusted with lichen like peeling gray paint. Slowly I walked around the perimeter of the ship, my hand resting for a moment on the tip of each stone until I returned to where I'd started. I counted sixty-seven. Shivering, I counted the stones again as I tried to distract myself from the freezing wind.

This time I came up with sixty. I tried a third time—fifty-three—then a fourth. Fifty-one.

My numb despair loosened into wonder. In the darkness, surrounded by snow and ferns and stalks of dead grass stirred by the wind, the stone boat really did look as though it moved upon the sea, the rustling of vegetation indistinguishable from the susurrus of waves.

It was an optical illusion that couldn't be captured by any camera—there wasn't enough natural light, and any artificial illumination would dispel it. Thousands of years ago, someone had designed this monument, a trompe l'oeil that had outlasted any folk memory as to its meaning or purpose. I tried one more time to count the stones—sixty-two—and walked away.

CHAPTER 61

I returned to the path and continued walking, clapping my gloved hands in an attempt to warm them. Even with two pairs of socks, my feet prickled with pins and needles. I'd gone too far now to turn back.

To steady myself, I counted my breaths. After nearly a thousand, I saw a metal sign nailed to a tree. Freckled with rust, it looked like it dated to the early 1960s—a picture of two primitive log cabins surrounded by pine trees. A hint of blue in the background suggested water. I swiped snow from the metal to read the faded printing.

SOLSTRÅLENS STUGBY

I saw no sign of buildings, not even ruins. I kept walking, curious. The wind grew stronger, flattening my hair across my scalp. Colder, too, carrying a brackish smell—I must be very near the sea. The trees grew more sparsely, their limbs twisted into corkscrews. The persistent low thunder in my ears became the sound of waves.

Before me stretched a vast darkness, white fringed with spray. Waves crashed over onto a pebble beach as I walked to the water's edge. Miles and miles away, fairy lights glimmered, diamond bright: the running lights of container ships and ferries that plied the Baltic between Sweden and Estonia and Finland. Huge clumps of bladder wrack littered the beach, like bodies washed onshore. Plastic bags and bottles were everywhere, lengths of yellow nylon cords snagged on driftwood. Heaps of dirty snow turned out to be chunks of broken Styrofoam. A dead seagull lay atop a sheet of metal, its foot trapped in a refrigerator grating. I smelled rotting fish, a whiff of diesel fuel.

I hugged myself, my leather jacket little protection from the unrelenting wind. Icy water oozed through the soles of my cowboy boots. I took out my camera, turning sideways to shield it from the spray, popped the lens cap, and shot a few pictures of the ruined beach. There wasn't enough light, but that didn't matter. The process of focusing, of framing the world as I wanted to see it, was enough. I replaced the lens cap and walked farther along the shore, searching for the cabins pictured on the metal sign.

I nearly missed them, hidden within a dense stand of cedars a hundred yards from the beach. The trees and cabins occupied a miniature peninsula, separated from me by a twenty-foot-wide channel. During high tide or severe weather, it would have been impassable without a boat.

Now the water was only an inch or two deep. Patches of ribbed sand rose above the surface to provide solid footing. I saw no lights in any of the cabins, just a wash of pale gray that stood out in stark contrast to the black cedar. I gave a cursory glance over my shoulder, then splashed across the channel.

The frigid water flowed more swiftly than I'd anticipated, sucking hungrily at my boots. I found purchase on a small sandbar and stood for a moment, buffeted by the wind, before making my way to the other bank. I scrambled onshore and hurried up the beach, my knee ablaze from the icy water and the Baltic wind. I slipped and skidded on wet rocks before I reached hard-packed sand, then a wild hedge of dwarf rugosa roses and bayberry, and finally sandy soil feathered with pine needles.

The sky was noticeably lighter now, the silhouettes of evergreens faintly green against indigo. A memory of summers past still clung to the lonely spit of land, the smells of balsam fir and bracken. Fist-sized stones marked out a path now thick with moss and pine needles.

The point had been scoured of snow by the steady wind, but my boots squelched as I ran the last few steps to the closest cabin, nearly invisible behind the cedars. I slowed, looking for the door. Tree limbs had overgrown the roof and walls, as though seeking to protect the structure from the wind, leaving only a glint of windows.

I limped to the side of the cabin. An immense cedar had fallen during a storm, a mass of crushed branches and dead greenery the size of a bus, exposing the cabin's side wall. This was what I had glimpsed from the beach—weathered siding that had originally been rust colored, now gray. It appeared older than the log cabins depicted on the sign, more like a prefab cottage from the 1940s with board-and-batten siding. The torn tar-paper roof revealed uninsulated rafters and crossbeams.

I rubbed at the only window, frosted with grit, and peered inside. A single unfurnished room, open to the rafters. Its stained plank floors were spattered with the husks of insects. I could see the sky softening to violet through holes in the ceiling.

I turned and walked to the back of the cottage. Four other cottages stood within view, all as overgrown as this one, each with its own weather-beaten privy. They'd been sited to allow a discreet distance between them, screened by spruce and pine and the ubiquitous cedar. Beyond the four cottages was another channel, easily twice as wide as the one I'd crossed. The narrow peninsula was practically an island, connected to the mainland by a slender spit of land. In heavy weather, it actually would become an island.

Whoever used to vacation here valued privacy. On the far side of the channel was the forest. A mile or so through those trees was the homestead, guarded by a one-eyed god whose ancient worshippers might have built the stone ship I'd seen.

The cabins appeared neither nostalgic nor threatening. Like the homestead, the scene was disconcertingly mundane. Gazing at them, I felt the prick of damage, like a single hair plucked from my skin, and when I ran my tongue across my parched lips, I tasted something more acrid than salt or meth: the chemical afterburn of trauma. If Tindra Bergstrand was still alive, she was here.

CHAPTER 62

If I'd brought the burner, I might have tried to call Quinn. But there was no time to return to the car. Before long it would be sunrise. I chewed a few ibuprofen, hoping to quell the fire in my knee.

I pushed through the cedars, until a gap between the trees revealed a screen door. The door buckled when I yanked its handle, but I pried it open and reached for the knob on the inside door. It was locked. I rattled the knob, then set my shoulder to the door and pushed until the cheap wood gave way.

Like the first one, this cabin consisted of a single empty room, reeking of mouse urine and mildew. When I switched on the flash-light, an animal skittered across the rafters, sending down flakes of clotted dust. The roof had caved in, boards and tar paper dangling above the room's center. I crossed the space cautiously, looking for loose floorboards, ran my fingers across the dank walls to feel for a hidden panel or door. I came up cold.

The next cabin seemed pretty much the same, barricaded by dense cedars and utterly neglected. But its screen door opened easily, and so did the door that led inside. I stepped through and clapped a hand to my face.

The stench of damage poured into my nostrils like fetid water as I swept the flashlight's beam across the room. It was no larger than the others, but the roof was intact. Green carpeting covered the floor, like the artificial turf used around swimming pools, peppered with mouse droppings and shredded pine cones. The eye-watering odor of mouse urine was compounded by an earthier scent, just as foul. The cottage must have been downwind of one of the outhouses.

I dropped my bag, knelt painfully, and rolled back a corner of the green carpeting. The softwood floor beneath was riddled with holes from wood-boring insects. I dropped the carpet back into place, stood, and looked around.

The carpet didn't extend to the back wall. I walked over and saw a metal vent installed in the floor. I aimed my flashlight through the vent but couldn't see anything. When I crouched to hold my hand above it, I felt a slight warmth. No one would heat an abandoned cabin in February.

I yanked the edge of the carpet and began to roll it up. Halfway across the room, it exposed a plywood trapdoor, about three feet square, with a small brass handle. The carpentry was careless, or maybe it had just succumbed to the cold. The plywood had split and the adjoining hardwood splintered. Screws protruded from the hinges. I set down my flashlight, grasped the trapdoor's handle, took a deep breath, and yanked.

A wave of noxious air enveloped me, much warmer than the room. I sank to my haunches, grabbed the flashlight, and shone it down into the hole.

"Hey," I called softly. "Hey, who's down there?"

No one answered. Squinting, I made out the top of an aluminum stepladder about two feet below me. I couldn't tell how far it extended to the floor beneath it.

I slung my bag over my shoulder, grasped the flashlight between my teeth, and maintaining a precarious hold on the floor's edge lowered myself until my boot touched the top step. The ladder wobbled, but I kept going, until I could grasp the ladder's side rails. When my boots hit the floor, I grabbed the flashlight to look around.

I stood in a room half the size of the one above, with poured concrete walls and floors. On an Ikea coffee table sat a gallon water jug, half full, and a battery-operated lantern that wasn't switched on. The only other furniture was a futon mattress pushed against one wall, covered with soiled sheets printed with cartoon animals. Above the mattress a wall vent exhaled a breath of hot stale air. A white enameled bucket with a lid served as a chamber pot. The place reeked of shit and piss, and also of something dead.

I switched on the lantern and stepped to the futon, breathing through my mouth so I wouldn't have that ghastly smell in my nostrils. It made no difference. Fear seeped into me as my hand grabbed a sheet. I hesitated, and pulled it back.

CHAPTER 63

She lay there motionless, curled on her side, arms crossed over her breasts. She wore the clothes I'd last seen her in—black cargo pants and white T-shirt, both now filthy, and a black pleather motocross jacket. Dirty white socks but no shoes. Her matted dreadlock was crushed beneath one shoulder. Loose sequins winked from the blankets like spiders' eyes.

"Tindra," I whispered, afraid to touch her. "Tindra, can you hear me?"

I couldn't see her breathing. Her pale face looked bruised, lavender deepening to gray. I sank onto the mattress beside her, slipped my hand beneath her T-shirt. Her flesh was cool.

But I felt a flutter beneath my palm, so faint it might have been my own pulse. I moved my hand slightly, pressing until I was sure. She was alive.

I picked up one limp arm and shone my flashlight at the crook of her elbow, looking for the telltale sign of a hypodermic needle. I found none. The other arm was the same. I turned the flashlight onto her neck, and there it was: a tiny hematoma, marking where the needle had entered her neck. It might not have hit her carotid artery, just a vein, but that would be enough. I pushed up one of her eyelids. Only a pale corona of iris showed around the dilated pupil.

I shook her gently, then harder, to no avail. Whoever did this had done it before. He knew to give her enough etorphine so that she'd appear comatose, even dead, but not enough to actually kill her. I wondered if this was what had happened when she was thirteen, or if it was a pattern that developed later.

Kneeling on the futon, I dug my hands under Tindra's shoulders and tried to lift her. I could barely get her to move. I cursed, sweat pooling between my breasts, and staggered to my feet, trying to shake off rising panic. An hour or two ago I wanted to kill myself. Now I wanted to get the hell out of here.

That grayish tinge could mean she was already gone—that she'd suffered brain damage, or was suspended somewhere between a fatal overdose and unconsciousness. I could leave her here. I could clamber up that ladder and race back outside and . . . what?

"Fuck," I whispered.

I dumped my bag's contents onto the futon, sorting through them frantically. The Nikon was useless; my wallet was useless; the scissors and cigarette lighter were useless. I had barely enough drugs to get me high, except what remained of my crank.

That left a couple of ballpoint pens, a retainer wrapped in tissue, a photo CD, a few black T-shirts and underwear, my toothbrush, and two tranquilizer darts, one empty.

I stared at the motionless form on the mattress. After a minute I swept everything back into the bag except for the empty dart, the scissors and lighter, a ballpoint pen, and the baggie containing the crank. I picked up the spent cannula and scrutinized it.

I couldn't fuck this up. I only had one empty dart. I needed pliers to do the job right, but I might be able to make it work with scissors.

I placed the dart's needle tip near the crux of the scissor blades, held my breath as I closed the blades as gently as I could. I needed them to grasp the needle firmly enough to pull it free, but not slice through it. I exerted as much pressure as I dared, and very slowly pulled. It took several attempts, each more difficult than the one before. My hands were sweating, and I shook from cold and nerves and the beginnings of withdrawal.

On the fourth try the needle emerged. I dropped it onto the table, wiped my palms on my jeans, and used the tip of the scissors to disassemble the dart, prying out its various parts. Plastic chamber, black plastic plunger, plastic stop, a minute wad of control felt, the red nonreturn valve. When the cannula was empty, I filled it with water from the plastic jug. I swished it around and dumped the water onto the concrete floor, repeating the process several times.

I picked up the needle again, avoiding the tip, and managed to force it back into its nearly invisible socket. I flicked the lighter and held the needle in the flame till it glowed orange, then set the dart on the table's edge.

While the needle cooled, I cut a long strip from one of the cartoon sheets. I examined Tindra's T-shirt until I found a spot where the fabric seemed relatively clean, and snipped off a tiny piece. Then I wrapped the long strip I'd cut from the sheet around Tindra's biceps, just above her elbow.

I filled the cap of the water jug with water, about a quarter teaspoon. I opened the tiny ziplock bag of crank and poured the water inside it, added the bit of cotton I'd snipped from Tindra's T-shirt. I closed the bag, made sure the seal was tight, and shook it vigorously. You don't cook meth the way you do heroin, but you have to ensure that the crystals are fully dissolved in water before you inject it, otherwise they clog the needle.

I let it sit for a minute or two—I couldn't wait any longer. I opened the tiny baggie and tipped the meth-soaked cotton into the hollow cannula, shaking it until the fabric settled at the bottom. Using the scissors, I poked in the nubbin of felt, no bigger than a pencil eraser, and the black plastic plunger. Last of all I slid the ballpoint pen into the chamber, point up, to serve as a charger.

I sat beside Tindra and grasped her forearm, just below the crux of her elbow. It had turned white as soap from the tourniquet's constriction. In contrast, the veins beneath her skin looked as though they'd been drawn in azure ink. Holding the jury-rigged hypo in my right hand, I pressed the needle against a vein, the ball of my thumb on the pen charger. If the needle broke or slipped, she was done. Same if I missed the vein. I counted to three, steadying my hand, and jammed the charger as hard as I could.

The barrel of the pen shot through the chamber. The needle held, puncturing her skin. I exerted more pressure, trying to squeeze as much of the drug into her system as I could. I counted to thirty and withdrew the needle, a bloody filament dangling from its tip, undid the tourniquet, and threw it onto the floor along with the spent dart.

"Come on, baby," I whispered, pulling her into a sitting position. I grabbed the jug and sloshed water onto her face. Her head lolled, mouth sagging open. I slapped her cheek, shook her violently. "Tindra! Goddamn it, wake up!"

She gasped. Her eyes flew open and she stared at me, her expression gormless as a doll's. I slapped her again, dragging her to her feet. She punched me and began to scream, babbling in Swedish as she lashed out, knocking down the stepladder. I pushed her against the wall, covering her mouth with my hand.

"Shut up!" I grasped her chin and turned her head. "Look at me—can you see me? Do you remember who I am?"

Her gazed fixed on me, then the cell around us. The tawny eyes filled with tears. I took that for a yes.

"Do you remember me?" I repeated. "In London, I was at your place in Brixton. Do you remember that?"

She nodded.

"Tell me what happened."

"Han tog mig! Han—"

"English! I don't know Swedish."

She drew a shuddering breath, her chest heaving. The crank had kicked in, her pupils already shrunk to pinholes. Her fingers tightened around the dreadlock as though it were a lifeline. "Where am I?"

"On Kalkö. Do you remember coming here?" Again she nodded. "Those empty cottages on the eastern side of the island, that's where we are. This room is beneath one of them. Someone is holding you prisoner. They drugged you and brought you down here. Do you know who that is?"

Her face contorted; I thought she might throw up.

"Ville," she croaked.

"Do you mean Gwilym? Gwilym Birdhouse?"

"Yes. Ville, that's his name in Swedish."

"Okay." I backed away from her, picked up the stepladder, and placed it where it had been. "You need to listen to me. I want you to climb up that ladder. I'll be right behind you. We need to get out of here right now."

She grabbed me, surprisingly strong for someone who'd just had her body jump-started. "Do you have it?"

"What?"

"The book? He took it—did you find it?"

"Are you out of your fucking mind? No, I don't have it."

I pushed her toward the ladder. She twisted away and stared at me, wild-eyed.

"We have to get it. He has the book and my mobile. We need to go back and get them."

"We need to get the fuck out of here before he comes back and kills us."

She was younger than me, fired up from crank and etorphine, the speedball from hell, but I was bigger and stronger. "If I have to knock you out again and drag you up there, I swear to god I will. Or I'll leave you here for when he comes back."

She began to sob, then pointed at her feet.

"My shoes . . ."

I ripped the covers off the futon, lifted it, and found her white Vans wedged beneath. I tossed them at her. She started to pull them on, stopped abruptly, and looked at me. "There's somebody else."

I'd already grabbed my bag and stood beside the ladder. "What?"

"Another girl. There was another girl here. Girls."

"What are you talking about?"

"At the farm, I heard them—Freya and Erik, they were whispering. A refugee girl, more than one. I don't think they're alive now."

"Jesus Christ. What the hell are you saying?"

"I don't know! Only that's what I heard."

Her eyes went in and out of focus. There was more etorphine in her system than crank. I had to keep her moving. "Okay, you can tell me while we're walking."

"Where are we going?"

"I don't know. Come on."

CHAPTER 64

After Tindra climbed out, I shut off the battery lantern and followed her up the ladder, lowered the trapdoor, and rolled the carpet back across the floor. Everything looked as it had before. For a while, terror and adrenaline had canceled out the pain in my knee. Now that I had a moment to breathe, the ache returned.

I walked gingerly to each window and peered out. The trees tossed, branches raking the cabin's roof and walls. The wind had come up considerably. The sky had brightened, sunrise still a little ways off, but not for long. I saw no footprints or any sign that someone had followed me.

I turned to Tindra. "Do you know where we are?"

"Solstrålens Stugby—the Sunbeam Cottages. It's an old holiday camp, he owns it now."

"Who owns it?"

"Ville." Her voice caught. "It was—I grew up there. Here. It belonged to my parents. When my mother died, my father stopped the business. He got weird, and it got like this..."

She kicked at a wall black with mildew. "Ruined. He fucked up everything."

"We need to get out of here." I limped to her side. "Here, let me lean on you..."

"What's wrong?"

"Nothing. My knee, I banged it, that's all."

Once outside, I started toward the shoreline. Tindra stopped me.

"Not that way. There's no tide in the Baltic, but this is a gale."

She wrapped her arms around herself and tilted her head toward the water. "That stream there, it will be too big now to cross—the wind pushes the water up from the beach." She turned and pointed at the woods. "That way is safer."

I stared into the trees. If we continued straight through the forest, we'd eventually reach the homestead, only from the opposite direction I'd taken earlier. "It's too close to the house."

"Are you afraid?" I looked over to see her bouncing on her heels. The crank had kicked in; she was wired. "Are you afraid?" she repeated.

If Quinn had asked me the same thing, I would have lied. Instead I nodded.

"You don't need to be." Her eyes glinted in the faint light. "I'm going back there."

"That's crazy."

"He has the book and my mobile. I know where they are. Do you know what he'll do with them?"

"I have a pretty good idea. But isn't the app encrypted?"

"Yes, but it doesn't really need to be. What's stored on the mobile is a binary, compiled from the source code. Which is stashed in the cloud. The mobile is the least important thing in the long term. But I couldn't bear to lose it—it's a..." She gave me an odd smile, wistful and also desperate. "It's a talisman for me. Like a camera might be for you."

"Yeah, but none of that's going to do you any good if you're dead. Or me."

"We won't die. The house is never locked. They'll still be asleep. But we need to go now. Come on, this way..."

I avoided her gaze—going with her really would be crazy. But there was no doubt that the wind was now a gale. It would be impossible to cross the channel behind us.

And despite everything that had happened, the memory of *The Book of Lamps and Banners* still worked in me like a drug. If Tindra was telling the truth, I could accompany her to the house and nab the book, then figure out some way to get back to the car, and Quinn. I didn't care about the app—just thinking about it made my skin go cold—but if Tindra was given an ultimatum, I suspected she'd choose Ludus Mentis over *The Book of Lamps and Banners.*

"All right," I said.

CHAPTER 65

When we reached the shelter of the trees, I asked, "You sure you know the way from here?"

"Yes. There's a path. I used to run back and forth between the cottages and the house all day long."

She walked on ahead of me, holding back branches so they wouldn't smack me in the face. Once my eyes adjusted, I could see the path, bordered by the stumps of trees felled decades ago. In summer, the ground would be thick with ferns and wildflowers and tall grass, difficult to navigate. Now thin snow covered everything. The dense firs provided some protection from the wind.

I was running on fumes. It had been hours since I had a drink. My skin itched, my eyes swam with random blots of light, eyes and arrows and indecipherable letters.

"Your app," I said. "I think it imprinted on my brain."

"It's supposed to do that."

"Why? It's horrible. Like an acid flashback forty years after the fact." She remained silent, so I tried another tack. "Back there—what were you saying about someone else, a girl?"

"In the kitchen. Freya said, 'We can't have another one,' and they argued about it."

"Who argued?"

"Her and Erik."

"Shit." I struggled to process this information. "So this guy Birdhouse, he assaulted you when you were a kid, and you're telling me he kidnapped someone else and murdered them?"

"I don't know. I think so."

"Do you know who it was?"

"That's all I heard. They stopped talking when Ville came in. I think that's when he drugged me."

"Freya and Erik—I saw them at the rally in London. Who are they?"

"Erik worked the farm when he was younger, for my father. They were very close, like brothers. This was before my father met Ville. I think Erik, maybe he was my mother's boyfriend—I think they had an affair, but I didn't understand. I was too young. Maybe I'm wrong. But I always thought that was why Erik seemed to hate his own wife. And when my father died, he left the farm to Ville, not Erik."

"Why?"

"Ville had enough money to keep the farm alive. It never earned much—the holiday cottages, that was how we made money when I was little. Then my mother died, and Solstrålens Stugby closed. And my father met Ville and gave him the farm. Erik was upset, but he got over it. Now he and Freya run the farm for Ville."

"She's his wife?"

"Yes. But he treats her like a slave. Like an animal. He beats her."

"How do you know?"

"I saw it."

I recalled how Erik had spoken to Freya in Victoria Park; how the sleeve of her sweater rode up to expose a valknut tattoo and a band of raw skin above her wrist. I started when Tindra touched my arm.

"Are you okay?"

"I'm fine." I scooped up more snow and pressed it against my knee. "Tell me what happened, whatever you remember."

"First, tell me how you found me."

I gave her an abbreviated version. When I stopped, Tindra frowned.

"Meth? I can't believe you gave me meth. Is there more?"

"No. How much further?"

"A while—it's over two miles to the house. When I was a girl,

I could get there in twenty minutes." She glanced at my leg. "Maybe you need a doctor."

"Why didn't you tell me your father was dead? And a white supremacist?"

"My father? Why would I even think of telling you that?"

"How did he know Birdhouse? Was he a fan?"

"I don't know. Probably. I was too young to know about his music then. My father met him at a dog breeder's in Scotland. They were both raising Kalkö sheep—they're quite popular in Scotland. There was a woman who bred border collies, she had a litter, and my father and Ville were looking at the puppies on the same day. They both wanted the same dog. They ended up going to the pub to decide who should have her. By the end of the night they were friends."

"Who got the dog?"

"My father. But he said Ville could have breeding rights when she was old enough. Ville started coming to the island to visit. He and my father had some kind of business arrangement—Ville gave him money. Ville kept sheep, too, but he was more of an amateur—what do you call that?"

"A gentleman farmer?"

"Yes. It was a hobby for him. But Ville's sheep did really well, better than ours, because someone else actually ran the farm for him. When I was eleven, he started spending his summers here on Kalkö. He was at our house all the time. He always paid a lot of attention to me, and I crushed on him—he was good-looking and still kind of famous, right?"

She ripped a curl of birchbark from a tree, tearing it into ribbons as we trudged through the snow. She spoke quickly, but her tone remained detached. I wondered how many times, if any, she'd told this story; if Ludus Mentis had truly made it possible for her to overcome the traumas she'd experienced, or simply deadened her, the neurochemical equivalent of smack.

"What about the Nazi stuff?" I asked. "Did Ville turn your father on to that?"

"My father believed in a fairy-tale Sweden, the way white Americans believe in a dream. After my mother died, he got very angry about everything. The holiday cottages failed. The sheep died. He worked for a while at the cement plant, but then that failed, too. After Ville came, things got easier, but that was when my father began to talk more about Swedish identity. Vikings, the stone ships, folk music. He was too old for the skinheads—Odium, bands like that. He thought they were immature, too violent. He liked Viking rock."

"Is that black metal?"

"Of course not. It celebrates our heritage—myths and the sea, how fate rules us all, whether we like it or not. Some of it's very good. Also very loud. But my father mostly liked folk music. Swedish folk music, and Bob Dylan. Ville would bring CDs for us to listen to, and sometimes he'd play tapes of his own songs. He talked about how it was important that we Swedes treasure our own ways and beliefs, otherwise they would be lost, the way traditions were being lost in England. My father and Erik, they agreed with that—they didn't need to be convinced."

Her voice grew more thoughtful. "I don't know if my father was always racist. I never heard him or my mother say anything about it. In school we were taught that all people are equal, but that was easy to say. There were no black people on the island then. I never saw a person with brown skin till I went to Stockholm. And when the cement plant brought in migrant workers from Bulgaria who would work very cheaply, my father wasn't happy about that. But I was gone before the refugees started arriving."

"Did you know he had a podcast on the Herla Network?"

"One of my cousins in Stockholm told me—she was horrified. I was, too, but I wasn't surprised."

We walked in silence. An owl called, and something small chittered in the underbrush.

"How did it start?" I asked. "With you and Gwilym?"

"We would have a bonfire on the beach at night, and he would sing to me. I loved that, though some of the songs were frightening.

Ravens picking out dead people's eyes, ghost women. He said that folk songs were supposed to be scary. There was one about two dead sisters and a bone harp that used to give me nightmares."

She twisted her dreadlock around a finger. "I was really smart, but no one ever thought I was pretty. But Ville always told me I was beautiful. He'd bring me presents, clothes he bought in London. CDs. He took pictures of me, he said I could be a model if I wanted to."

"He was grooming you."

"Yes."

Her voice was controlled, her face composed. She seemed untouched by the cold, or any of the events of the last thirty-six hours. Except for her pallor and the lack of an artisanal sweater, she might have stepped from one of those ads for Kalkö wool. I sensed that same chilling absence as when I first spoke to her in the garage: the void left when someone has ceded emotion to something even more powerful and destructive.

She cocked her head at me. "You really don't look good."

"I'm fine," I said. I knew I wasn't.

CHAPTER 66

We walked, the only sounds our feet crunching on the thin snow and the hiss of wind through evergreen needles. My jaw ached from clenching my teeth against the crank and the cold. My entire leg had started to feel numb.

"What happened to your boyfriend?" Tindra asked.

"Huh?"

"The guy with the glasses, the bookseller. What happened to him?"

"You mean Gryffin? He wasn't my boyfriend."

"Why not? He seemed nice."

"He's a geek."

"I'm a geek."

"You're an entirely different level of geek—you've invented some kind of mind control app."

"It's not mind control. It's a symbolic language."

"It's fucked up, is what it is. The day after I left your place, your friend Lyla tracked me down. She said you'd gone missing, you and your dog. Her brother went to find you, he got some text that showed your dog had been killed. What happened?"

Her composure broke. She began to cry. "Bunny—someone poisoned Bunny. I don't know how, but they did. In the park, we were going to the demonstration, and suddenly he fell over and then he was dead."

"And you recorded it on your phone?"

"I thought he was having a seizure, I wanted to show the veterinarian so she could help him. But he, he just died so quickly, I never had time..."

306

"It was the same drug that killed Harold. The same thing he used on you. Etorphine hydrochloride, an animal tranquilizer. This——"

I reached into my bag for the remaining dart. "There's enough here to knock us both out. Have you ever seen one of these before?"

Wiping her eyes, she nodded. "I think so. Something like it—on the farm when I was still at home. There was a bad ram, with enormous horns. Me and a friend were playing in the field, the ram attacked us—it tried to gore her. We ran away and my father called a man he knew from Norderby. He came over with one of those guns and shot it and took it off in a trailer."

I put away the dart. "Why were you even at that demonstration? Did you meet him there? Ville?"

She began to walk, fast. I caught up with her and grabbed her arm. "Tell me—how did you know he was going to be there?" She said nothing, and I tightened my grip. "Tell me, damn it!"

"I keep track of him online," she finally admitted. "There's a Herla discussion board where he's active. I log in under a different name to see what he's doing."

"You're stalking him."

She pried my hand from her arm. "If you want to call it that. When I saw he was going to be in London, I texted him."

"When was this?"

"A few weeks ago. We started talking a few times after that. I told him what I'd been working on. That I was developing an app to help people recover from trauma, and forgiveness was part of that, but it wasn't something you could just program into an app. So I needed to see him."

"And he agreed?"

"Yes, a few days ago."

I shook my head. "So you arranged some kind of date at a Nazi rally?"

"I wanted him to trust me."

"Trust you?" I tried to get a suss on what was going on. Maybe she wasn't lying to me outright, but she was hiding something. If she'd really wanted to forgive him, her plan had backfired, big-time.

It seemed likely that Birdhouse had raped her while she was unconscious in that cell beneath the cottage.

"Back in London," I said. "When you told me about Ludus Mentis, you said you'd been abused as a kid, but you weren't afraid of him anymore. You said when your code was complete, you were going to make him disappear completely. What did you mean?"

"Nothing. I was wrong. I don't need the book for that—I can make him disappear now." She took a breath. "There's a flaw in the unfinished code. But it's not a bug. It's a feature."

"This bug—it's what happened to me, right? When you showed it to me—I had a flashback to when I was raped. It was horrible. It didn't help my PTSD. It triggered it."

"That was the first time I shared it with anyone. I didn't know what it would do."

"But now you do. It triggers a memory of the most terrifying thing that ever happened to someone. I mean, how the fuck do you make a feature out of that?"

"*I* do nothing. *It* finds where traumatic memories are stored and restores them. Once I have the book and finish the code, Ludus Mentis will be able to shuffle those same memories so that they no longer have the same emotional power over you. It's like shuffling a deck of cards to get a different outcome. But now—"

"But now it triggers a flashback. A violent flashback. Maybe you weren't sure what it would do when you showed it to me, but you figured it out pretty fast. I only looked at it for a few seconds. And if somebody else . . ."

I thought of Tommy. Did she even know he was dead? "If someone else was exposed to it for longer," I went on, "someone who had PTSD, or a history of violence—it could make them crazy."

She nodded. "Yes. Like a berserker. You know what they are? Viking fighters who became like animals in battle."

"So if that's a possible outcome, why would you take a chance on letting a bunch of neo-Nazis get hold of it?"

"It was a mistake. A big mistake, yes. But I can fix it." In the near darkness, her white skin, black hair, and black clothing made her seem like something conjured from the snow and icy wind. "Him, my father, Erik, those people in the park . . . how do we live with such evil?"

"Going to the police and telling them about those missing girls might be a start."

"The police here will do nothing. People on Kalkö disappear. Women, refugees. There was a fire, and the police did nothing."

"But you have proof—he put you in a cell and drugged you! And you said he killed someone else. I think you're right."

I drew the retainer from my bag. "I found this in his shed. He has boxes there where he puts animal skulls to decompose. Did you know that?"

"He showed me when I first got here. For his photographs, like in the book. He's very proud of his pictures."

"It's not just animals. You need to show this retainer to the cops."

"*Dra åt helvete.*" She pushed away my hand. "Did you go to the police when you were attacked?"

"Yes."

"Did they help you?"

"No. But—"

"'No. But.' Do you know how many times I've heard women say that? 'My husband, he hits me, I know I should leave, but.' 'I walked somewhere I'd never been before and was attacked and raped, but.' 'My father murdered my sister because she kissed a boy, but.' I am *not* going to the police. I'll be done before they get here."

I shoved the retainer into my pocket. "Did you tell Birdhouse about *The Book of Lamps and Banners*?"

"Of course not," she replied, too quickly.

"Listen to me." I pulled out the dart again and brandished it in her face. "Harold Vertigan was killed by a dart like this one. So was Bunny. It's the same drug Birdhouse used on you. He must have known about the book! Did you tell him when you met in London?"

"I don't know." She wouldn't meet my gaze. "Maybe I did say something. But it was an accident if I did."

"I'll say it was a fucking accident."

"What business is it of yours?"

"It's my business because I got dragged into *your* business."

"No one dragged you into it."

"Your friend Lyla did."

"Lyla?" Her eyes widened in alarm. "Did she send you? Is that why you're here? Did she send you to look for me?"

"No." I stared at her, confused. Why would she be afraid of Lyla? She and Tommy were Tindra's only friends—more than friends, Gryffin thought.

So why did she look terrified when I brought up Lyla's name? And why hadn't she once mentioned Tommy? I shut my eyes, suddenly dizzy.

"You did it," I said slowly. "No one else knows about the app, no one else knows what it does. Tommy's PTSD . . . when Bunny died, you sent him the video, and when he found you, you used the app on him. Witnesses saw him arguing with a woman. It was you. That's why he attacked those people without warning."

"I loved Tommy! I didn't kill him. The police did."

"The police didn't. Gwilym Birdhouse did, with another of his toy darts. They'll see that once they get the toxicology report." I began to shake. "You saw what it did to me. How could you do that to Tommy?"

"Because of Bunny. I wanted Tommy to find Ville and hurt him."

"But you knew what would happen—"

"I didn't know. I saw what happened with you, but that might have been a spurious effect. I needed to find out if it was replicable.

"When Bunny died, I knew it was Ville who killed him. Harold, then Bunny . . . I put it together. Ville stole the book, and he knew I had developed the app. The dart that killed Bunny was meant for me. Maybe not enough to kill me, just to sedate me. But enough to kill a dog. I texted Tommy that Ville was at the rally and told him to meet me there. When he did, I showed him Ludus Mentis—I hoped he would hunt down Ville."

"But you knew you couldn't control it."

"It doesn't matter now."

"Have you used it on yourself?"

"A few times."

She raised her head to stare at me, and I felt the way I had when I saw my reflection in the camera lens at Slagghögen: that I gazed into the empty eye sockets of a skull. Using the flawed version of Ludus Mentis on herself hadn't relieved Tindra's anguish. It had allowed her trauma to consume her, like the larvae in Gwilym Birdhouse's cardboard boxes.

Tindra's icy hand touched mine, and we halted.

"We're there," she said.

Through the trees I saw the back of the same house I'd observed earlier. There were no lights on other than the floodlight. The shadow from the Odinist totem stretched across the yard, a black path leading to the front door. Between us and the house, a mass of weedy-looking trees formed a thick natural hedgerow.

I looked at Tindra. "Do they have a dog?"

"Not anymore."

"How early do they wake up?"

"Early. Erik has to go check on the sheep." She glanced at the sky. "But this won't take long. We should have plenty of time."

She started toward the house. I pulled her back. "What the hell are you doing?"

"I told you, I'm not afraid of them."

"Well, I am. Do you have a plan? Tell me."

"Do you know the story of the Alder King?" she asked. "In English, I think people call it the Erlking."

"Like the poem by Goethe?"

"Goethe mistranslated it. It's a Scandinavian legend, not a German one. The alder is an evil tree that captures young girls and kills them so it will grow. It's a real tree, and it really is evil—see those?"

She pointed to the hedgerow. "Those are alders. They grow where the ground is boggy. They have a bacteria inside that allows their roots to grow underwater, and they grow so thickly they blot the light, so no other plant or tree can thrive around them. If you cut down an alder, a hundred new shoots will grow from its base."

"How do you get rid of it?"

"You can't. Erik said if you let goats eat the alders one year, and then pigs the next year, the alders will die. But you see that hasn't happened here. And you can't burn them, because their roots are underwater. They just keep coming back, no matter how many times you think you've killed them."

Without a backward glance at me, she darted off.

I took off after her, but as soon as I hit the hedgerow, I floundered. Too late I realized she must have known a way around the alders. My boots punched through a skin of ice, sinking into frigid water. I slogged through it, muck the consistency of wet cement sucking at my boots. When I tried to move, I couldn't. I'd heard of treacherous marshland and quickmud: Wasn't that what preserved all those sacrificial victims thrown into northern European bogs thousands of years ago?

My chest tightened. I reached for two branches in front of me, grasped them, and pulled myself forward. After a moment, the mud released my boots. I dragged myself a few more feet, until the mud gave way to dead grass, and I staggered into the yard.

I wiped my hands on my jeans and opened my bag to check that the Nikon was undamaged. My fingers brushed against the leaf from *The Book of Lamps and Banners.*

I stared at the page. *It's all there, not a line missing. I'll be able to complete writing a code that was begun thousands of years ago.*

It was too dark for me to make out the luminous figures, but I knew they were there: decapitated heads, green arrows and swastikas, a tree whose uncounted branches grew from a single trunk. On the reverse side, runes that I couldn't read, though maybe the people who lived here could.

Angar's work, beware, this is power . . .

I headed toward the house.

CHAPTER 67

Tindra had been right—the door was unlocked. I wondered if there was a single working lock on all of Kalkö. I stepped inside warily, armed with the scissors.

Boots and shoes were neatly lined up against the wall of a spotless mudroom. Anoraks, knit caps, and parkas hung from wooden pegs. I grabbed a cap and yanked it over my head. Turning, I spotted the tote holding Svarlight CDs and T-shirts on a bench beneath a window, three pairs of felted slippers beside it. A pink geranium in a white pot perched on the windowsill.

My boots leaked filthy water onto an immaculate striped rug as I set my bag down and removed the dart. Very carefully, I placed it in a pocket of my leather jacket, then walked unsteadily into the kitchen.

Three brightly striped rag rugs covered the floor, lined up with military precision. There was a brushed-steel stove and matching refrigerator, high white counter and matching stools for a breakfast bar. Wineglasses in a wooden wine rack. A white bowl of lemons. In a birchbark frame, a homemade painting of Thor's hammer flanked by S-shaped lightning bolts. More geraniums.

I went to the sink and gulped water from the faucet, then scanned the room for a weapon, grabbing a wooden mallet from a container of kitchen utensils. I stepped hesitantly to an open doorway and found myself looking into a well-equipped home studio: a table with two laptops and a desktop computer; microphones, speakers, audio interface for a DAW, and snarls of cable; a filing cabinet. Two glass-fronted barrister bookcases against one wall; windows covered with heavy black plastic to muffle outside sound.

In front of the filing cabinet crouched Tindra. She whipped around, relaxing when she saw me. She turned back, snaking her hand into the drawer, and withdrew a smartphone; stood and walked past me into the kitchen without speaking.

I didn't move. Tindra had said she knew where Gwilym had stashed the book and her mobile: here. I stepped quickly to the filing cabinet and yanked open its drawers. I found nothing but farm reports and business statements related to Svarlight Studios, each with the label's logo and the slogan MUSIC FOR A NEW DAWN.

I went to the desk and rifled its drawers, came up cold. I turned to stare at the bookshelves. They must have held hundreds of volumes. I crossed to one, lifting its glass front.

Inside was a miniature of Harold Vertigan's library. Elizabethan ephemera, plays, and broadsheets devoted to the rise and fall of Dr. Lambe, rumored to be a sorcerer. An early English translation of *The Hammer of the Witches*. I ran my fingers across their spines, pulling out books and pamphlets as I searched for *The Book of Lamps and Banners*. Nothing.

I turned to the other bookcase. A black-and-white poster had been taped to the front glass, obscuring whatever was behind it. Not a poster: a black-and-white digital negative image, scanned into a computer and painstakingly manipulated, the file printed on high-grade white transparency film. An intricate and time-consuming process, almost as much so as its analog equivalent; something that only artists with serious money can afford to do now.

It was a night shot of a human rib cage, on a shoreline that I recognized as the one by Solstrålens Stugby. The rib cage looked as though it had just washed up. The bone arches glistened as though they'd been dipped in silver, dark strands of kelp wrapped around them like hair. The photo had the texture and tonal range that you'd find in the best analog shot, a breathtaking array of gray tones, a black so deep you could fall into it and drown.

I drew closer, mesmerized, *The Book of Lamps and Banners* momentarily forgotten. How had Birdhouse gotten that shot? I knew it was his: I recognized the eye behind the viewfinder, the stance of the man who held the camera: the way he'd angled himself to capture a sea darker than that endless expanse of sky. No stars, no moon. Black ribbons of seaweed woven in and out of the rib cage.

It was only when I got closer that I saw that the black ribbons weren't seaweed. They really were hair, long and tangled, attached to what looked like a piece of black shoe leather.

A thump echoed from somewhere above me. I froze. When no one appeared, I stepped silently into the living room—another paean to Scandinavian modern, with a black leather sofa covered with gray and white sheepskins. There were more photographic prints on the walls, all of them framed, all of them Gwilym Birdhouse's work. Rams' skulls, cairns. A very young woman, long blond hair veiling her face but not the sun wheel tattooed on her exposed breast.

At the far end of the room, a set of stairs led to the second floor. It all smelled of beeswax and lemon polish, and, faintly, of gingerbread.

I walked to the foot of the steps and gazed up at a landing dark as an attic. I heard no voices or other signs of life. Clutching the mallet, I padded upstairs. I halted a few steps from the top, let my eyes adjust to the shadows, then took the last few steps onto the landing.

In front of me stretched an empty hallway, with a door on each side. Heavy black curtains obscured two windows, allowing slivers of light to escape. Several large frames hung on the walls, but it was too dark to see what they contained. The air smelled of unopened windows and spoiled fruit.

At the end of the hall, Tindra stood beside another closed door, face illuminated by her mobile as she tapped at its screen. As I walked toward her, she glanced up, shielding the mobile with her hand.

"You don't want to be here," she whispered, her voice calm. "Go."

A glance at her mobile proved she was right. Poisonous yellow light escaped from beneath her fingers like gas. Instantly, I was overcome by nausea.

"Don't," I gasped.

She slid the mobile into her pocket and slipped into the room.

A few days ago, I might have been capable of fighting off a berserker, or running, but not now. I closed my eyes and pictured Quinn: not the boy I'd obsessed over and lost long ago, but the man I'd found all these years later, wearing his grim history on his scarred skin; as damaged as I had been but somehow able to transcend that, content with the life he eked out from ancient vinyl. Content with me, broken as I was. *I'm sorry, baby,* I thought, and went after Tindra.

CHAPTER 68

nside the room, the scent of damage wasn't metaphorical but an animal stink of blood and sex and excrement and fear. The room was even darker than the corridor, heavily curtained windows visible only by seams of gray light. The blue eye of a computer monitor winked from a desk.

A large bed took up most of the room. I heard deep breathing, also a gargling snore. At least two people slept here. As I took a step forward, my boot fell on something soft. I kicked at it—a mound of clothing, not a body.

I stiffened as something moved beside me: Tindra, her face a rainbow mask where the light from Ludus Mentis leaked onto it. She crept to the side of the bed and stood there, holding the mobile as though it were a candle. Again I found myself entranced by that malevolent carnival light as I heard an echo of my name.

Cass, Cass . . .

I wrenched my gaze away, kept my eyes shut until the voice died away. When I opened my eyes, I saw Tindra leaning over the bed. She moved the mobile slowly back and forth, its glow illuminating one of the sleeping figures: Freya.

"*Freya*," murmured Tindra, her voice a sleepwalker's. "*Freya, vakna.*"

The shadow in the bed stirred, turning so that her arm flopped onto the mattress.

"*Freya. Freya, vakna. Titta pa mige.*"

Freya's eyes fluttered open. The light from Ludus Mentis took on a scarlet tinge. "*Vad är det?*" she asked thickly.

Tindra whispered something I couldn't hear. Freya bolted upright, flailing at the tangled bedclothes. Her hair hung loosely to her shoulders, and she wore a long shift, sleeveless. In the coruscating light I could clearly see the valknut tattoo and circle of abraded skin I realized must have come from a restraint. The bruises on her arms extended to the base of her throat. Tindra's implacable calm gave way to pity.

"Du också?" she asked.

Freya nodded, tears spilling down her cheeks. There was terror in her eyes, and pleading. Tindra met her gaze, then turned to me.

"I said you should go."

I didn't move. Tindra shrugged and raised her hand higher. The mobile's glowing screen began to pulse, releasing a cascade of light: crimson, toxic yellow, acid green. I heard a gasp as Freya gazed transfixed at the screen, trying to shade her eyes with one hand.

As though a prism had been shattered, the light exploded into a fountain of sun wheels and tridents, crosses and arrows, numerals and runes and crowns, horned circles and ideograms, hashtags and swastikas: a thousand lost alphabets flowing across Freya's face like rain over a darkened window. She stared uncomprehending at Tindra, as though she'd awakened from a bad dream to a worse one.

In the bed beside her, the other figure moved. I heard Erik's voice ask sleepily, "Freya?"

When she didn't respond, he pushed himself up, crying out in confusion, *"Freya, vad fan gör du!"*

Freya remained mesmerized as Ludus Mentis scattered symbols like an out-of-control projector. I could no more look away than I could stop breathing: I felt myself sucked into it, too, heard that sibilant voice hissing my name.

Cass. Cass. Cass.

At the edges of my vision flickered my younger self, like a phantom figure captured by CCTV. A car drove up slowly behind her, its headlights joining the galaxy spinning from Tindra's hand. My boots echoed down the deserted alley, I saw the girl squinting, dazzled by the headlights as a hand reached for her from the car window.

"Cass—look at me, Cass!" a voice urged.

My head snapped back. The hand was Tindra's, grasping my wrist. My fingers loosened and the mallet I'd been holding hit the floor. I scrambled away, saw Tindra gesture at the mallet, then at Freya.

Erik shouted, struggling to climb from the bed as his wife bent to pick up the mallet. She straightened and with nightmarish slowness turned to her husband. He fell, hitting the floor with a loud thud. I heard him scrabbling to crawl away as Freya stepped closer and one of her bare feet came down on his back, pinning him. She was a big woman, with muscular arms: as she grasped the mallet with both hands and lifted it, it seemed insubstantial as a broom. Erik screamed.

"*Sluta! Freya, sluta! Jag är ledsen, jag är ledsen...*"

Freya raised the mallet higher, iridescent letters and symbols flickering around her like moths. I watched, my horror building as I felt myself falling back into my own loop of terror and helplessness, the dark room now a dark street, Erik's cries my own as I tried to run. That spectral hand reached for me again, and I saw the knife it held, knew what happened next as it had happened a thousand times before, in dreams and night terrors and the moments before a blackout. The hand was within inches of my face, its blade engraved with letters and symbols that I couldn't read, that made no sense, that had never been there before.

Light blinded me, incandescent white. The world divided into before and after, with me posed between, seeing it all at once: the barefoot young woman dancing along the Bowery and the ravaged woman observing her from a lifetime away. My footsteps continued to echo through the deserted alley as the car drove up alongside me and a hand extended from its open window. But I no longer felt fear but rage, a pure cold fire that burned through me as I halted, turned toward the car, and, instead of running away, grabbed the hand with the knife.

My fingers closed around a wrist, the knife flashed and spun into the shadows. Someone screamed: not me but Tindra as her mobile flew from her hand. In the dark room Freya grunted, counterpoint to a rhythmic, muffled sound as she lifted and lowered the mallet repeatedly.

Erik's cries had ceased. The mobile struck the wall and dropped to the ground. Tindra stumbled toward it, but I still had hold of her. I yanked her so she faced me and saw in her eyes terror and fury, anguish and guilt, and the inexorable longing for annihilation and revenge that had consumed her.

"Don't," she whispered.

I pushed her away and strode to where the mobile lay screen up. With all my strength I brought my boot down on it, grinding with my heel until I felt the screen shatter. I ignored Tindra's shrieks, shoving her to the floor as she tried to stop me.

Tindra had said she didn't need the mobile except as a talisman—from her screams, a talisman she couldn't bear to lose—but I wasn't taking any chances. I stomped on the mobile until it went dark and kicked its fragments across the floor. Maybe someone with military-grade forensics at their disposal could trace the data from it, but that wouldn't be my problem. No one here would be able to use it. Tindra flung herself at me again, screaming in Swedish. I sent her careening against the wall. She dropped to her knees and crouched there as I yanked the door open and stalked into the hall.

CHAPTER 69

Only minutes had passed since I'd come upstairs. Rage had burned away my fear: I felt as though that pure white light ran through my veins. I pulled the scissors from my pocket, clutching them like a zip knife, checked to make sure the remaining dart was where I could easily grab it. I took a few steps down the hall and stopped.

To either side was a door. Neither betrayed any trace of light or sound. I looked from one to the other, chose the one on my left, and walked inside.

Immediately I was assaulted by a smell. Not the hot fetor of the bedroom but a strong chemical odor like that I'd detected in the shed. I ran a hand across the wall until I found a light switch. I gave my eyes a few seconds to adjust and tightened my hand around the scissors.

There was no one in the room. Black plastic sheeting had been nailed over the windows. Metal shelving held camera equipment and a digital printer, big enough to reproduce photos the size of the one in the studio downstairs. Work lights were clamped to the shelves, aimed toward the far wall.

But this wasn't a darkroom. There was no sink, no trays for chemical baths, no clothesline to hold drying negs or prints. The shelves were filled with large jars, and for a moment I thought I'd stumbled on a cold room designed to store pickles and jams put up by Freya. I edged closer to the shelves, pulled one of the jars toward me, and almost dropped it.

The jar was filled with human teeth, some still attached to a jawbone. They floated in a cloudy liquid, along with flakes of white particulate. I shoved the jar back onto the shelf, averting my eyes from the others, but not before I glimpsed what looked like a distorted, doll-sized face pressed against the glass.

I turned, the edge of the scissors biting into my palm. Beneath the blacked-out windows was a bed, covered with the same plastic sheeting. A delicate array of white objects was arranged across it—bones, small ones, disarticulated so I couldn't tell what kind of animal they'd come from. The image of the dead fox popped into my head, disappearing when I saw a human rib cage at the head of the bed, small enough that it could have encircled a basketball, with strands of dark hair woven between the ribs.

I backed away and stepped out into the hall, whirled, and found myself staring at Gwilym Birdhouse. He wore a bathrobe, his hair tousled and face creased from sleep, and held a gun with an almost cartoonishly long barrel, pointed at me. A tranquilizer gun. He raised it, the mouth inches from my right eye.

Before I could move, someone struck me from behind. I heard a pneumatic hiss as I fell, catching myself before I hit the floor.

I looked up and saw Tindra. She stared at Birdhouse with the same fathomless gaze as when she'd first recounted her abuse, her eyes dead-black. Birdhouse looked at her, stunned.

"Tindra?"

She didn't move. I saw the dart he'd fired embedded in the wall beside her. As Birdhouse took a step backward, I grabbed the dart from my pocket and lunged at him, burying the tip in his neck and squeezing it.

Birdhouse flailed at me, arms pinwheeling. His gaze fixed on Tindra as he gave a hoarse cry and sank to his knees. I watched, ready to kick if he made any move. But he slowly dropped to the floor, as though lowering himself into bed. His eyes never left Tindra. After a minute, his expression relaxed, and he grew still.

Tindra stared at him, walked over, and nudged his face with her foot. From the room at the end of the hall came the same rhythmic sound, like someone pounding a tom-tom. I ran toward the stairs. I didn't need to see what happened next.

CHAPTER 70

I raced into the small studio and tore the black-and-white photo of a human rib cage from the bookcase. I began to ransack its shelves, tossing aside self-published tracts on the Zionist conspiracy, eugenics, the occult roots of Nazism, the collected works of Savitri Devi and Julius Evola and Miguel Serrano, books about the Kali Yuga, Asatru, and the Wild Hunt, until the shelves were empty. *The Book of Lamps and Banners* wasn't there.

I surveyed the mess, trying desperately to think of where else the book might be. The kitchen? Upstairs? One of the sheds or outbuildings?

I rummaged through the desk again, crawled on the floor to look under the bookcases, tossed the rug aside to see if there was anything beneath. There wasn't.

I looked at the window. Gold tinged the sky. It was almost sunrise. The infernal drumming from upstairs had ceased. I couldn't hear Tindra or Birdhouse. I wondered if he was dead.

I returned to the living room, lifting up the striped rugs and Kalkö sheepskins, moving furniture, running my fingers over walls and floorboards in search of some secret panel. Still nothing. I went into the kitchen and flung open cabinets and drawers, the refrigerator, the stove. I had just stepped into the mudroom when I heard someone behind me.

"Don't bother."

It was Tindra. She held a clamshell, with a title stamped in gilt letters:

Youth: A Narrative, and Two Other Stories, by Joseph Conrad

She opened it and withdrew a book the size of a trade paperback, its fragile, half-bound covers crisscrossed with twine to keep the whole thing from falling apart. A book bound in human skin; a book that left a trail of bodies in its wake.

If it did *exist, it would be priceless, because it could change everything,* Gryffin had told me, just as Tindra had described her app. *Ludus Mentis is going to change everything.*

Now she tossed aside the clamshell and said, "I told you, I knew where he'd put it."

My shoulders slumped. "What will you do with it? Your mobile's dead."

"Mobile?" Her face twisted into a triumphant smile. "I don't need that mobile—it was just a good luck charm. Maybe you did me a favor, smashing it. Like I told you, the encrypted code's uploaded into the cloud. All I need is this."

Her hands tightened around the book as she lowered herself to sit cross-legged on the floor, raptly staring at the cover. I flashed to her on the garage floor back in Brixton, bent over her laptop with Bunny at her side. She looked as she had then, intently focused, yet also younger, a girl perusing a text before a big exam.

She opened the volume and stared at a page, tracing a finger across the lines of indecipherable writing and jewel-tinted images, nodding to herself. She didn't handle the volume carelessly, but her face held none of the reverence that Harold's had and displayed none of the wonder I had felt when I touched it. To her, the book wasn't an advanced philosophical artifact. She was reading it as code. I felt as though something sharp had lodged in my breast.

He that doth professe such dessire as to see the Devvill must seek Him yre and no further.

I went back into the mudroom and picked up my bag. Nestled alongside the photo CD was the missing papyrus leaf.

I found the cigarette lighter and held the page in front of me for one last time, not letting my gaze fall on the seductive images there. I turned it over to stare at the runes I couldn't read.

Beware, this is power . . .

I thumbed the lighter and drew a corner of the page to it. A bright thread crept across the papyrus, flickered into a blaze. The papyrus began to curl, sending flecks of black spiraling into the air. Greasy smoke filled the room, releasing a faint scent of incense and scorched hair. For an instant, a ghostly panorama hung before me: towers and trees with eyes, red-capped waves, a sky with two suns. The moon, its craters and dunes as clear as if I gazed at it through a powerful telescope. A world within our own, a world now lost forever.

Then the flames licked my fingers and I let go of it, watching as the page disintegrated into embers and gray ash that floated through the room like wingless insects.

"*Sluta! Vad fan gör du? What are you doing?*"

Tindra stood in the doorway. Her eyes widened; she dropped the book and grabbed a glowing wisp that turned to ash at her touch. I watched her dully, too exhausted to fight if she came at me.

Instead she turned to chase another burning fragment, then another, snatching at the air and watching in horror as it all turned to ash. Only when the last ember had winked from sight did she halt, panting, her hands smudged with black. A pall of smoke hung over the room as she looked at me.

"Why?"

"You said it would change everything. It's already changed enough."

She sank to the floor and stared at *The Book of Lamps and Banners*. "Did you at least scan that page? Screenshot, anything?"

"No."

She clutched at her face with her hands, her slender form shaking as she began to sob. I watched her but said nothing. After a minute she gasped and straightened, still trembling, and avoided my eyes.

Her expression twisted between rage and despair, and there was a red streak on one cheek where she'd clawed it. When she finally looked at me, she appeared utterly wasted, as bad as I imagined I'd looked on some of my worst days, this being one of them.

For a long moment we stared at each other. I felt as though I gazed at a broken reflection of myself when I was roughly her age. I wondered what she saw, staring back at me. Finally I tilted my head toward the stairs. "Is he dead?"

I thought she wouldn't reply. "No. I wish he was," she said at last, with that same cold composure I had first observed in London.

"What about Freya?"

"I don't know. She'll be in shock."

"You used her. Like you used Tommy, like you would've used me . . ."

"I didn't use her. I set her free, so she could do what she was longing to do."

"No. It was what *you* were longing to do."

"Maybe."

"What will you do now?"

"Call the police." She looked at the window, the first shafts of light slanting through the trees.

"The police?"

"You were right: I need to tell them, if there were other girls. Freya won't remember what happened up there. Her husband has a history of hurting her—maybe she called the police, maybe not. But someone will know. She had a psychotic break, and killed him. Who could blame her?"

She got to her feet, the book in her hand. "I will remind them about Ville, about what he did to me when I was a girl. That when I came here now to see him, he drugged me and locked me in that cellar, but I escaped. Anything I did was self-defense."

"You think they'll believe you?"

"They'll believe what they want to believe. That is how it is on Kalkö. But they have a record of what happened when I was thirteen. This time they'll have to do something."

She stared at me. The terrifying absence was gone from her eyes. She looked exhausted, and resigned.

"Thank you," she said. "You saved me."

"Likewise. Remember to tell the cops that when they arrest me." I dug into my pocket for the retainer and photo CD, handed them to her. "Here. I think the police will want this."

She nodded, and I went on. "Why did you kill him first? Erik? Why not Ville?"

"I wanted Ville to see it. To know what would happen to him. How it would feel."

I glanced at the back door, grateful I hadn't witnessed Freya clubbing to death her abusive husband. I was too beat to run. I hoped Quinn wouldn't sleep through his flight. When I looked back, I saw Tindra watching me closely. "How did you get here?" she asked.

"I drove. I left the car out on the road, then walked the rest of the way here."

She regarded me thoughtfully, then turned and walked into the studio, returning a minute later. "You made a mess in there. I almost couldn't find them."

She held up a set of keys and started for the back door. "Come on. I'll drive you to your car."

"What?"

"I would have died down there. And if you're here, it will only make things confusing for the police. There are too many things. Questions. Too many people. Erik. Tommy . . . It will just be easier."

She looked me up and down. "I think you need a doctor. Where are you staying?"

"That place by the slag heap."

"Slagghögen?" She laughed, the first time I'd ever heard her laugh. "That's such a dump."

She held the door for me, and we stepped outside, blinking in the late-winter light.

CHAPTER 71

Tindra commandeered the old blue Volvo and drove, turning when I pointed at the end of the dirt road. I sank down into the seat, my bag in my lap, trying to stay out of sight.

"No one will see you," Tindra said. She'd set *The Book of Lamps and Banners* on the seat between us, now safely tucked back into its clamshell. "Even if they did, it wouldn't matter. On Kalkö, they see what they want to see. The cops are all asleep. Whoever's on duty, he'll just be thinking about his coffee. Because, as everyone knows, there is no crime on Kalkö."

When we reached the Jetta, she pulled over. "Can you drive okay?"

"I'll manage." I reached to open the door. "Thanks."

"Wait." She picked up *The Book of Lamps and Banners.* "Your geek friend—this is his, right?"

"It was, till you bought it."

She shook her head. "I canceled the transaction as soon as I knew it was stolen, back in my flat." She held out the clamshell. "Give it to him. He should have sold it to a university. Make sure he does that now."

"But—why?"

"I have no use for it. The code is broken."

"What about your app?"

"What about my app." Something dark flickered in her eyes, and she shrugged. "We will see about that."

I took the clamshell, slipped it into my bag, and stepped out of the car. Tindra leaned across the seat. "You should leave quickly. I'll wait to call, but..."

"I have an early flight. Thanks," I said, and closed the door.

I managed to make it back to the hotel, my hands barely able to clutch the steering wheel. When I reached Slagghögen, I parked and staggered inside. Lightning played across my vision: not Ludus Mentis, but withdrawal. The girl with the Mohawk glanced up as I walked by, then turned back to her mobile.

Quinn was still asleep. I dropped my bag, peeled off my jacket and boots, and sat on the bed beside him. I knew if I lay down, I'd pass out. I was afraid to close my eyes for the same reason.

"Hey." I grasped his shoulder. "Quinn, wake up, wake up..."

I shook him until he blinked awake. "Hey," he murmured. The smell of smoke and alcohol on his skin made me flinch. His eyes widened. "Cass? You okay?"

I shook my head. He put his arms around me and held me close as I began to shudder uncontrollably. When I could finally speak, my throat was raw. "We need to go now. To the airport."

"To the airport? You're coming?"

"I want to go to Reykjavík," I whispered. "But we have to go now."

"You better shower first." He sat up, wincing. "Me too."

He helped me undress and climb into the shower. I held myself upright, hands braced against the plastic cubicle as I shivered helplessly despite the scalding water. It had been at least twelve hours since I'd last had a drink, the longest I'd gone without alcohol in decades. I doubled over, convulsing with dry heaves as I slid to the floor and collapsed.

I don't know how long I lay there, the tremors of withdrawal causing me to jerk back and forth, my head smacking against the wall. Probably just a few minutes. People die from withdrawal, but I wasn't going to check out in the shower stall of the Slag Heap Hotel. I finally dragged myself up and turned off the water. The room tilted around me as I stumbled back into the bedroom.

"Jesus, Cassie." Quinn got me to the bed. When he started to open my bag to look for clean clothes, I stopped him. "No—be careful."

I gestured at the clamshell. He picked it up and frowned. "Joseph Conrad?"

"No."

He opened it, stared at what was inside, and clapped the slipcase closed again. "Holy shit. You found it."

"I told you I would."

He leaned over to kiss me, then set the book on the bed stand. He handed me a pair of clean black jeans, socks, a worn black sweater. "See if you can do that by yourself while I jump in the shower."

When he came out, he dressed quickly. He replaced the clamshell at the bottom of my bag with the Nikon, rolled up my filthy clothes, and set them on top. "You have any crank left?"

"No. Just a few pills. Xanax, mostly."

"Good."

He finished gathering his things, checked the room one last time, handed me my bag and my leather jacket. "Let's go."

He hugged me to him and we walked downstairs, Quinn nodding at the girl at the desk. *"Tack,"* he said.

"Tack," she replied without looking up.

CHAPTER 72

W e made our flight, barely. There were only three other passengers. Just as well—I might have drawn attention to myself,
shivering in the waiting room as if I'd just been pulled from an icy
lake. As it was, no one looked at me. I swallowed a Xanax that kicked
in just before we landed in Arlanda. We had another short layover,
then boarded another nearly empty flight, to Reykjavík, without incident. I took another Xanax, and passed out.

I don't remember much after that. It was like a walking blackout, only without the benefit of having had a drink. But somehow
I got through border control in Keflavík. Fears over the novel virus
had yet to hit Iceland, and airport officials there are used to drunks,
which must have helped.

The next time I awoke and was fully compos mentis, it was two
days later. I was in Quinn's place, lying on his futon. The overheated
room reeked of cigarettes and weed, but there was no sign of any
booze. Quinn bent over me, stroking my forehead, and helped me
to sit upright.

"Here, baby. Drink this." He held up a bottle of electrolyte solution
and slipped a straw through my cracked lips. "I've been getting some
into you whenever I can. Do you remember?" I shook my head. "I
didn't think so."

I sipped the blue liquid. "This is disgusting," I said.

"I'll tell you what's disgusting." He took the bottle and gently
cupped my chin. "Watching you convulse for the last two days. I
thought I lost you."

I shuddered, my muscles contracting uncontrollably. "You still might."

Quinn lay down on the futon and put his arms around me. "I know what it's like. It's gonna take a while, baby. I looked to see if I could check you into someplace here, but it's tough. Long waiting list. And you're American. They don't like American junkies mooching off their health care. And this whole virus scare—things are starting to get weird."

I spent the next few days writhing on Quinn's mattress, begging for a drink, a bump; begging him to kill me. Gradually the tremors eased, and the gut-wrenching nausea. The craving for alcohol and speed did not.

When I was strong enough to get up and sit with Quinn at the table and eat a few bites of a proper meal, I finally told him everything that had transpired since the night I'd left him and found Tindra. I was stone-cold sober by then: a mutilated marionette, every string cut and every sticklike limb twisted into an unnatural shape. I didn't care that another drink would kill me. But losing Quinn would mean another kind of withdrawal, one I couldn't survive.

Another week passed. Quinn began to leave me for a few hours while he went to man the Eskimo Vinyl table at Kolaportið, the flea market where he did most of his face-to-face business. While he was gone, I searched every inch of his place, looking for a bottle, a pill, anything that might get me off. Other than a few cannabis seeds and stems, I came up cold. I chewed them, washing them down with water that smelled like rotten eggs.

I was getting better, but I was still in no condition to go out looking for a liquor store on foot. Plus, I knew Quinn would kill me if I did.

Instead, I started taking my Nikon and wandering around the wasteland of black lava that surrounded the warehouses and cell towers by Quinn's place. I had to ration the number of photos I took—until I found another source of Tri-X film, I couldn't squander the few rolls I had left. And I had no way of processing the film.

That would change. During those days outside, with Reykjavík's cold wind buffeting me like a wounded bird in flight, I began to come up with a plan. I brooded on it as I lay beside Quinn each night, listening to him breathe after we'd fucked, not like teenagers but like people who'd washed ashore after a plane crash, amazed and a little frightened to find ourselves still alive. One morning as I cradled a chipped coffee mug and Quinn sat smoking a cigarette, I said, "I have an idea."

"So shoot."

I told him. He listened, and I saw his expression change, from dubious to suspicious to obdurate to pissed off until, finally, he sighed and shook his head.

"Christ. Hurricane Cass. You're fucking crazy, you know that?"

I leaned forward to lock my arm around his neck, pulling him to me. "And you fucking love it."

"You think it'll work?"

"It'll work." I kissed him, tasting cigarettes and black coffee, that lingering trace of something bitter I'd known since we were seventeen. I drew away from him, took his hand in mine, and kissed one knuckle.

"I need to get straight," I added. "Do whatever the fuck it is people do to stay sober."

"You need to go into AA."

"Or something. I'll figure it out."

"How long do you think all this will take?"

"I have no idea."

"Will you come back?"

I looked at him, his green eyes and scarred face, clean shaven after the days in London and Sweden; the close-cropped graying hair that did little to hide the cross that had been carved into his scalp decades ago, in some ritual I never wanted to have explained to me.

"Like a bad penny," I said, and kissed him again.

CHAPTER 73

T he next day, I booked my flight back to New York. News of the novel virus was everywhere now. Quinn was edgy. I did my best to reassure him, without much luck. He had a lot to be edgy about—that I'd fall off the wagon, that I'd never come back, that my plan would fail.

"Look, we'll work something out," I said. Outside, the early-March rain hammered at the Quonset hut's metal roof. It sounded like a bomber had dropped a million ball bearings onto the structure. "But I'm not staying here. It's too damn cold. And dark."

"Whatever. Greece, I can handle Greece." He paced to the window. "And you need to take off for a little while so I can have a drink without having to hide the bottle."

"Very funny."

"I'm not joking."

When it was midmorning Pacific Standard Time, I used Quinn's mobile to call Gryffin Haselton. He answered after the first ring. When he heard my voice, he disconnected. I called back: same thing. At last I texted him.

I have the book.

Seconds later, Quinn's mobile chimed.

"What do you mean?" demanded Gryffin.

"I have it. *The Book of Lamps and Banners.* Where are you?"

"What? Wait—"

"Shut up and listen to me. Are you still in London?"

"No, home. San Francisco. Where—"

"I'm flying back to New York tomorrow. You need to meet me there. I'll text you when and where."

I took a breath, then gave him the figure I'd decided on. A shit ton of money, but a lot less than what Tindra Bergstrand had intended to pay him. Gryffin laughed.

"I'm not kidding," I said. "I'll give you my account number, you can transfer the money as soon as you get it."

"But that's *my book*!"

"Possession is nine-tenths of the law. When you're dealing with the black market, I think it's ten-tenths. Trust me, my father's an attorney."

"But I don't have that much money!"

"You will once you sell the book. Start working on it, let me know when you're ready. See you."

I handed the mobile to Quinn and flopped onto the bed beside him. "Nice," he said. "What *are* we going to do with all that money?"

"Me? Rehab. Somewhere warm. California, maybe, one of those places where rock stars go. Then back here. Then Greece, when this virus thing blows over. With you."

I ran a finger down one of the vertical incisions beside his mouth, leaned in to kiss him. He tasted of Myer's rum, the closest I was going to get to it for a while. But then he pulled me on top of him, and I almost didn't care.

CHAPTER 74

Quinn drove me to the airport in the morning. We walked to the security gate, arms wrapped around each other, so it was hard to tell where his leather jacket ended and mine began. When we reached the gate, he pulled away, holding me at arm's length. "We keep doing this," he said.

"Doing what?"

"Airports. Leaving."

"At least we're doing it together. And coming back."

We kissed one last time, my face buried in his neck. As I drew away, I whispered in his ear.

"I know," he murmured, stroking my cheek. "Me too."

I headed toward the security gate, glanced back to see him standing where I'd left him, arms crossed. As I turned the corner, he raised his hand. Then he was gone.

A week later, days before the lockdown was declared, I met Gryffin for lunch at the Gramercy Tavern. He'd arranged a sale with another private buyer, including a codicil stating that, after sixteen months, *The Book of Lamps and Banners* would be made available to researchers through a deal with the Getty Library. I didn't ask how much money he'd gotten. The fact that the Getty was involved suggested he wouldn't have much to complain about.

He sank into the banquette across from me, his messenger bag beside him. It was raining outside, that heartless rain you get in New York in early March. At the bar, people sat watching the latest dispatches from the West Coast. Based on the numbers scrolling across the bottom of the screen, the news wasn't good.

Gryffin took off his wet raincoat, folded it, and set it on the banquette. "Where is it?"

I patted my bag. "Relax. It's right here."

A waiter appeared and gestured at the raincoat. "Do you want to check that?"

Gryffin shook his head. "I won't be staying long," he said, and gave me the stink eye.

I ordered a bottle of Dom Pérignon. When the waiter left, I opened my bag, removed a new clamshell slipcase, and handed it to Gryffin. He looked at the title embossed on the front:

Please Kill Me: The Uncensored Oral History of Punk

"Very funny," he said.

He set the clamshell on the table, opened it, and tenderly picked up the volume inside. He stroked the cover as though it were a woman's face, opened the book, and gazed at a page, entranced. Only when the waiter reappeared with our champagne did he replace the volume in its slipcase. With great care, he placed it in his messenger bag, zipping the compartment.

"Well, that's that," he said.

We watched as the waiter opened the bottle and filled our glasses. Gryffin picked up his flute. I did the same. We clinked glasses. He drank from his. I set mine down, and Gryffin looked at me as though I'd started to brush my teeth at the table.

"You're not drinking?"

"I quit."

"You *what?*"

"I quit." I pushed my glass toward him. "The champagne's for you. Congratulations."

"You quit?" He took another sip, eyeing me warily. "What about that guy Quinn? What's he think?"

"His idea."

For a few minutes, neither of us spoke. I watched the light slide across Gryffin's eyeglasses, the way that strange green pigmentation in one iris glowed like an emerald flame. He stared at me thoughtfully, refilled his flute. Finally he said, "Well. Good for you. For getting sober."

I made a face but said nothing. Gryffin sipped his champagne.

"What're you going to do with the money? If you're not drinking. And, you know, shooting up or whatever you do. Did."

I leaned back against the banquette and glanced out the window at people dodging the rain. A large black bird flew down to perch atop a parked Tesla. It cocked its head, staring at me with one beady eye, then flapped off. "I'm looking to buy a place. Not here—New York, it's the fucking suburbs now. Nothing but rich assholes."

"Yeah, but now *we're* rich assholes."

"Speak for yourself. I'm taking a month or two to get clean. Then I'm going to Greece with Quinn. Find a house and build a darkroom. Maybe I'll rent a place out west. Or, I dunno, Maine."

I rested my hand on top of my bag, feeling the camera's familiar weight inside. "Now that I can afford to work with film again. We'll see what happens."

I stared at the table, feeling that black line of static crackling between me and the bottle just a few inches away. I turned, grabbed my leather jacket, picked up my bag, and slid out of the booth. "Look, I gotta go. Enjoy that champagne."

Gryffin watched me as I stood, his expression almost wistful. He raised his glass to me and nodded. "Stay out of trouble."

"I wouldn't count on that," I said, and headed for the door.

AUTHOR'S NOTE

Some years ago, while researching an earlier novel, I came across a single mention of *The Book of Lamps and Banners* in the ancient Arabic magical text *Picatrix*. Immediately I decided to use it in a future story of my own. To my knowledge, no copy of the actual *Book of Lamps and Banners* has ever been found, and while I consulted various incunabula and existing works of magic, astrology, alchemy, and the like, the mysterious volume described in this novel is fictional and of my own devising. Any errors of fact or fancy are mine.

ACKNOWLEDGMENTS

As ever, numerous people helped me in the writing of this book: if I have inadvertently forgotten anyone, I apologize profusely and will rectify that in any future edition.

Huge thanks to my agent, Nell Pierce, of Sterling Lord Literistic.

Thanks as well to my editorial team at Mulholland Books: Josh Kendall, Emily Giglierano, Helen O'Hare; my publicist, Alyssa Persons, and marketing director Pamela Brown. I am incredibly fortunate to have worked twice now with an amazing copyeditor, Susan Bradanini Betz, as well as Betsy Uhrig.

To Martha Millard, with love and gratitude for her continued support and guidance.

Dr. Elma Brenner, specialist in Medieval and Early Modern Medicine at London's Wellcome Library, generously shared her expertise and permitted me to examine a number of incunabula as well as the Wellcome's sole example of a book with anthropodermic binding.

I have a number of dear friends who are serious book collectors. Over the decades, they've shared their passion, knowledge, and secret lore with me, at used bookshops, antique stores, flea markets, conventions, yard sales, and in dark back alleys in the United States and abroad. Here's to Joe Berlant, John Clute, Paul Di Filippo, Mike Dirda, Peter Halasz, Pamela Lifton-Zoline, the late Bob Morales, Brad Morrow, Peter Straub, David Streitfeld, Henry Wessells, and

Jack Womack. I promise never to fold down the corner of a dust jacket again.

Many people read various versions of this book in manuscript and offered suggestions to improve it, including Jim Kelly, Jeff Ford, Ellen Datlow, Robert Levy, Cara Hoffman, Kirsten Holt, Nightwing Whitehead, Bill Sheehan, and Jeff Ford. Special thanks to my punk brothers in arms David Baillie and John Auber Armstrong, and a shout-out to Anthony Vincent Dominello, who caught a number of errors that no one else did, including me. Kristabelle Munson offered moral support by way of the Criterion Collection. Judith Clute again showed me parts of London I had never seen, including a peculiar boat in Rotherhithe.

Huge thanks to all my Swedish friends, who helped and encouraged me in more ways than I can name: Jan and Isabella Smedh and everyone at the English Bookshop in Uppsala; Sarah Bergmark Elfgren, Johan Theorin, Linda Skugge, Johan Anglemark, and of course Mats Strandberg and Johan Ehn, with whom I had a revelatory late-night conversation about how "It's all code."

Most of all, I want to thank Lotta Ekwall-Erickson and her husband, Per, who so kindly allowed me to stay with them on Gotland, the inspiration for Kalkö. Lotta read several drafts of this book, offered suggestions for place names, corrected my Swedish, and served as a guide to not just the real islands of Gotland and Fårö but their fictional counterpart.

Finally, all my love to my partner, John Clute, who has shared his life and library with me for the past twenty-six years and never tires of my questions about books.

ABOUT THE AUTHOR

ELIZABETH HAND is the bestselling author of fifteen genre-spanning novels, most recently *Curious Toys,* and five collections of short fiction and essays. Her work has received multiple Shirley Jackson, World Fantasy, and Nebula Awards, among other honors, and several of her books have been *New York Times* and *Washington Post* Notable Books. Her critically acclaimed novels featuring Cass Neary, "one of literature's great noir anti-heroes" (Katherine Dunn)—*Generation Loss, Available Dark, Hard Light,* and now *The Book of Lamps and Banners*— have been compared to those of Patricia Highsmith and have been optioned for television. Much of her fiction focuses on artists, particularly those outside the mainstream, as well as on the world-altering effects of climate change. She is a longtime reviewer, critic, and essayist for the *Washington Post* and *Los Angeles Times,* among many outlets, and for twenty years has written a book review column for the *Magazine of Fantasy & Science Fiction.* She is on the faculty of the Stonecoast MFA Program in Creative Writing and divides her time between the coast of Maine and North London.

MULHOLLAND BOOKS

You won't be able to put down these Mulholland books.